W9-CCC-436

CHEOPS

A Cupboard for the Sun

Also by Paul West

FICTION

A Fifth of November*
O.K.
The Dry Danube*
Life with Swan
Terrestrials
Sporting with Amaryllis
The Tent of Orange Mist
Love's Mansion
The Women of Whitechapel and Jack the Ripper
Lord Byron's Doctor
The Place in Flowers Where Pollen Rests
The Universe, and Other Fictions
Rat Man of Paris
The Very Rich Hours of Count von Stauffenberg
Gala
Colonel Mint
Caliban's Filibuster
Bela Lugosi's White Christmas
I'm Expecting to Live Quite Soon
Alley Jaggers
Tenement of Clay

NONFICTION

Master Class
My Mother's Music
A Stroke of Genius
Sheer Fiction—Volumes I, II, III
Portable People
Out of My Depths: A Swimmer in the Universe
Words for a Deaf Daughter
I, Said the Sparrow
The Wine of Absurdity
The Snow Leopard
The Modern Novel
Byron and the Spoiler's Art
James Ensor

**available from New Directions*

CHEOPS

A Cupboard for the Sun

BY PAUL WEST

A NEW DIRECTIONS BOOK

Parts of this work appeared in different form, in the following: *Conjunctions, First Intensity*, and *War, Literature, and the Arts*. Thanks to the editors of these journals.

Images on pp. 32 and 261, from George A. Reisner, *A History of the Giza Necropolis* (Cambridge: Harvard Univ. Press, 1942–55); courtesy of the Asia and Middle Eastern Division, The New York Public Library, Astor Lenox and Tilden Foundations

Image of Osiris on p. 188, from Oskar Seyffert, *A Dictionary of Classical Antiquities* (New York: The Meridian Library, 1957)

Book design by Sylvia Frezzolini Severance
Manufactured in the United States of America
First published clothbound by New Directions in 2002
Published simultaneously in Canada by Penguin Books Canada Limited
New Directions Books are printed on acid-free paper.

Library of Congress Cataloging-in-Publication Data
West, Paul
Cheops : a cupboard for the sun / Paul West
p. cm.
ISBN 0-8112-1519-9 (alk. paper)
1. Cheops, King of Egypt—Fiction. 2. Egypt—History—To 332 B.C.—Fiction
3. Kings and rulers—Fiction. 4. Time travel—Fiction. 5. Historians—Fiction.
6. Herodotus—Fiction. I. Title
PS3573.E8247 C48 2002
813′.54—dc21 2002010474

New Directions Books are published for James Laughlin
by New Directions Publishing Corporation,
80 Eighth Avenue, New York 10011

IN MEMORIAM

Agha Shahid Ali
John Hawkes
Alan Jolis
Charles W. Mann
Carl Sagan
Philip Young

CONTENTS

Many of the most heartfelt outpourings in what follows are intended to be declaimed; the named personages come forward and perform vocally. *Sprechstimme* perhaps. Whichever music is seemly, if any, is up to the reader. Weill or Berg?

CHEOPS

A Cupboard for the Sun

. . . the immensity of the here and now . . .

—Hermann Broch, *The Death of Virgil*

And so evil a man was Cheops that for the lack of money he made his own daughter sit in a chamber and exact payment for services rendered.

—Herodotus

Famous for building the biggest pyramid, of Giza, his tomb. Herodotus recounts that he was indifferent to human dignity, and used forced labor for his huge enterprise. But he had great knowledge and a lively interest in the religious sciences of his day. In 1954, two solar barks were excavated at the foot of his pyramid.—Robert Boulanger, *Egyptian and Near Eastern Painting*

The great pyramid seems no more than a vulgar little building. I even regretted that I had gone near it.—Jean-François Champollion, *Travel Journal,* 1909

ONE

Afterbirth

1 ▲

Osiris loves to have an amaryllis by his greasy plate, even when, as now, he does not eat. With a curt smile, he rises from the table, pauses halfway down the stairs and drops his cigar-butt into the fire-bucket on the landing. A swift faint fizz follows, then he descends the rest of the way, songfully wondering why so few of his tenants have turned out to greet the arriving guest, a "reporter" from 500 B.C., making his second visit, by camel, donkey, and sloop.

Osiris does not know, but he is sure the king will be ready for this visitor, who's hot and bothered, especially when on tedious royal assignments such as this; and after all the fuss and protocol of visas and permits. The visitor, a German-sounding Herr Rodotus, actually a Greek, tends to arrive with one main idea carefully saved up. And here he comes, shaggy from river travel. Already he has noticed something that recalls his first visit. What was missing then is missing now. They have not advanced, he decides, they're still in the pitchblende era, with manure always lurking. Just look. Nothing has changed.

"Mr. Osiris, sir, how good to meet."

"Drop it, do. Please drop the sir."

Osiris is hardly listening, having tuned in to some of his favorite music, which plays from deep within his brain. Once heard, never forgotten, it is certainly not the music of Egypt, this no doubt adding to its appeal. Herr O'Dotus (Osiris can always spot a pen name) bows, providing another view of his tousled dusty locks. Clearly this Osiris is unaccustomed to receiving guests from far and foreign parts. Not unmannerly, Osiris seems much wrapped up in the trance of the yarn-spinner, unreachable by the short sharp bark of a neglected guest.

"Boiled alive, then diced up," Osiris tells him. "This is why, essentially, I dress as a mummy."

Herr O'Dotus shudders. This is the afterlife already?

"Mere biography," Osiris says. "I reminisce for strangers, just to warm them up for the king. 'Twas a fleeting memory of early subjugation. Remember, this is *our* time: 2600 B.C., not yours, not yet 500 B.C."

"Got it," Herr O'Dotus says, lying. He is deeply bewildered.

"Of horrors," Osiris is telling him, "watch out for those who would put you under, do you in. This place is crawling with assassins and thieves."

It always was, Herr O'Dotus thinks. They use sleds and boats, pack animals and sedan chairs, but no wheel. Their world does not go round.

Osiris, out in the broiling sun that powders a landscape void of wild flowers, yearns for his upstairs chambers, the peace and ivory quiet of them, chambers such as another civilization might have put together far in the future: gold with the blurting radiance of the naked sun, and white with underground plastered alabaster. Polished gold against white matt. He does not want visitors today, which he has set aside for internal music. Despite his holistic, chronic grasp of tongues, he doesn't want to talk, certainly not about whatever this O'Dotus is yapping about. The sumptuous chords of his Delius music are one thing, but the impetuous bark of O'Dotus is another, and he resents it, as he resents many of his duties. Most of all, he longs for his chambers when the Mildew Maids have taken over, waxing and polishing with lackadaisical vigor: plump Katrina and svelte Marlise, who at the primpy climax of their double act set the spigot exactly between the two parallel basins, and fold the lip of the toilet roll into an envelope's point. Oh to have such mildly interrupted, anachronistic serenity, he thinks, instead of having to oversee this and a thousand other places and other times as well. In the old days, when he had less to do, when so-called civilization was fairly new, he would sit at the provided clavier to make music of his own, but, thanks to a defective left eye (not put together quite right after he was dismembered), he could never read the left-hand music on the stand. With experience has come tedium; with augmented power a surly reluctance, and a partially suppressed desire to do appalling things. Don't tempt me, Osiris is thinking, as O'Dotus blathers on. I have unnatural powers at my disposal, and I am not bound by the constraints of time and space. I am the ideal. I am the only one to greet you, and I am not a man at all. "What may I do for you? What do you think I'll do for you? Need you be here at all?"

"Point the way to His Majesty, sire," O'Dotus tells him. "I've come a far piece. I never did meet him, though I did write him up according to legend. Lead the way if you will."

Off they go by the boats, the huge diaphanous shape of Osiris going first. Through him, O'Dotus can still see the land- and riverscape: a mirage maybe through another mirage. Perhaps what lies in store will be riot and confusion, mayhem in a blink. Osiris seems to glide above ground, above sand, while O'Dotus limps along behind, legs still cramped from his journey through the Nile Delta southward, against the current as far as Memphis. At one point, a change of boats had been needed for the Nile's tawny embrace, and imprinted on his brain, something emblematic: a marsh cattleman was lifting a huge rat aloft by the tip of its well-planted tail as if in triumph, the whole animal as long as his arm. O'Dotus noted the scene on papyrus, hoping for more. He has come to observe. His vocation is looking. *Aisesthai,* he murmured to the heaving river, I look, I see; I am a Grecian aesthete. Seeing this, as he sees all things, Osiris scoffed and rocked the boat in his mind's eye, roughening the ride, promising himself the Greek would receive an aesthetic kick in the rear sooner or later.

Meanwhile, the king sits waiting, fondling his daughter in an absent way, pondering his first and last pyramid. Better late than never, he thinks. I have really done it this time. They even come from Greece to admire what we do. I could tease him by offering to build him one of his own.

2 ▲
CHEOPS

I learn Greek from his lies (his rosy-fingered dawn and all such semi-military bombast). He tells me how a certain queen had her coffin set above a city gate, crammed with gold: a treasury for paupers, and how the Massagetae ate the corpses of their aged relatives. When I wake, after dreaming of birds of prey that cruise in vain over the ocher desert, wadi upon wadi, I never get back to sleep—the middle-aged lack of which in its profoundest form makes for love-handles and paunch, or so the Greek has told me. Now, I tremble too much that, in the offing, the same pirate awaits me. This fellow's lips are a-bubble with lies about Egypt, and I wonder how any one man can know so much unless lying about it.

To acquaint him with some kind of truth, I have one small working group diverted from the pyramid proper (to reward them, I'll pamper their families, fatten them with fish and beef cut up on open-air slabs). The group will demonstrate to him how we plan a pyramid from the first, clearing a small area as if it were a plateau, and then assembling upon it a dozen or so smaller and smaller square boards, so that the resulting structure resembles an untidy step-pyramid. "That's how," I tell him. "A miniature in the mind's eye, more for me than for them. Lifting big blocks they get injured, but my, how they soldier through out of homage, just to work."

We have the same old argument each day, at the start of our so-called interview. "Tell me again," I say.

"I write so that the deeds of men not be effaced by time."

"Why should they not? Have you never heard of life-weariness, when someone gets sick of everything and wants to lay down his tools, not be remembered for *anything,* but sink into the dust, sand and lime, be forgotten?"

"Surely," he answers, "you don't have yourself in mind. If I've ever seen a case of grand megalomania, it's you, your majesty, if I may."

"Hogwash, Erodo. I could have your tripes cut out and fried in front of you for that. One Greek more or less would hardly matter."

"Just my point, sire. That's what I'm talking about."

"Oh, you are talking about *important* men?"

"Men important by their circumstances, no matter who they are. That would include me." I lip-synch his Greek with wry finitude.

This self-styled democrat is a blusterer, really, ever mauled and mangled by interpreters, but clear enough to be recognized for what he is and would like to be. We don't get that many Greeks coming our way, although they've been overrun time and time again by Persians. Perhaps that has put him on the defensive. Like certain women, tempted but ready to flee, he has a special way of loitering, easily plucked back, but light-footed in case of panic.

How he stares at me, wolf-like, seeing (no doubt) how I tend to cock my head to one side, also a dog-like posture; but in my case a quizzical indulgence half-suggesting leniency. My eyes are blue to him (they are really green), their pupils sunk low toward the ground as if to simulate some rising horror, even as my tipped head suggests I might welcome its arrival. What affronts him, I think, is the expanse of white above the iris, which leaves half my eyes buried behind the lower lids. He thinks I am hiding something, refusing to look at something, recoiling from some unmentionable gorgon, some gross beast of the dunes. What a hanger-on he can be, everyone saying to me why don't you deknacker him and ram his severed head into a bag of blood? He's no good to us, he's a bloody Greek who's bound to get it all wrong, slander us to a man, and certainly misreport your own valiant magnificence. I never do, nor do I set him to work building or even sweeping sewage. There is something fiercely intact about him, as if he had been educated almost beyond the resources of his personality, but not quite. A good-humored jester, yes. An imaginer rather than a wise historian. No doubt what I like about him is that he seems to embody licentious guesswork, demonstrating spunk rather than accuracy. So: suffer him another week, then; suck the old coot dry.

Now, what was it he said about being unable to learn our language? It was as if it was a language unspoken, he said, a silent dumb-show, written with loving care for goats—with clouds (rare), embers and skiffs; but requiring work for the undercover mind.

"Like a code?" I asked, but he seemed to ignore me.

"More like a sign language," he said. "Requiring an instrument more resonant than the human voice to get it across. The race of Egyptians should have been born deaf-mutes so as to best keep their language to themselves."

A Greek joke? I could not tell. I told him Greek if anything was too public, sounding too much used by orators. "You have loudmouths," I said, "you are a loudmouth people. We have heard. You all gather and yell. Our language is a magic lantern show; it flits past you like a daydream. And you wonder if you've been dozing at the public baths, subject to some idyll of plentiful water and soft billowing muslin. You may be right about its evanescent qualities, it being closer to the gods than Greek ever will be, and with all those mathematicians messing about with it; but also I think you have to credit it with its lists. It is a wonderful tongue in which to amass lists of provender. If it is eerie, it is also severely practical. In Egyptian you know where everything is, and whom it belongs to. In Greek? Well, I won't ask you. Different horses . . ." He wrote it down. He is learning fast, although he still has trouble adjusting to our chairs with their short legs, an easy sit for crouching Egyptians, but for him a bitterly disguised torment. I tell him to wait until fashions change and there he will be with his legs dangling. (A man on a throne, though, knows how to tuck his feet under as if they might be chopped off by some envious rebel.) *He* does not like to sleep sloping downward, he explains, his feet touching the bottom rail. Such a posture amounts to slithering, he says, and he always wakes (he's lucky he does wake!) feeling he has lost weight during the night.

I would not indulge him but for his brains, which are agile and constructive, sometimes too much so, as when he equips us with a history we have never known. I ask him why. "Why fake it," I ask, "when you can document everything that is around you?"

"For the sake of pageantry," he says, intent upon his prowess as a writer—not merely a recorder, or a witness. It is not how things are that impresses him, but how they affect his mind and heart, what he makes of them; and this leads him into wild conjectures, voluptuous garblings of the details our lives are made of. I do believe he is an old heroic poet looking in life for what may not ever be there. Tell him a bogus legend and he at once believes it, eager to know how some willing hearer would regard it; and this is how he compiles his "tapestry of facts," as he calls them. In this way, he dotes on curiosities, which he is very quick to discover—as when, peering at my eyes, he finds the minor twist in my left from constant blinking, which enables me to see better with the other one. He says the Greeks have several words for this, but such words, I tell him, apply to Greek eyes only. My own have gazed on wonders that no Greek ever dreamed of, and so be it. Cosmopolitan, he says.

No, only of this region, I tell him, for once playing him at his own game.

He scoffs, but writes it down, as he always does, fattening his load of legend with the story and its author, forever attributing, and thus getting himself off the hook. If a million dead men would write a lifetime's books for him, he would let them. His head is a vast bureau. He is a snapper-up, a diagnostician of morsels. And, on this day, he seems to have an endless fund of beguiling samples (a capital entertainer he seems, needing only a thin rug and a pot of sup). I am glad to humor him, but he will never by my keeper of antiquities.

Oh well, better to have an Erodo on the premises in the springtime of his career than endlessly debate mediocre politics and the captious behavior of the Nile with my juniors, I who have long pondered the chances of an unprecedented exit from this planet, much as Erodo plotted his swoop and dive into Egypt. *I always wanted somewhere else to go,* much as I loved the people I was born to rule, I wanted a different dimension not mine alone, but as willing to house me as a quite silent pyramid. Not Greece, oh no, where your tenure would be always uncertain, or the Moon, too lonely even for an Egyptian pharaoh.

Perhaps I resented Erodo's prophetic side, the times (too many) when he said he would become a confidant of Pericles and the poet Sophocles, whoever they were, and actually receive from the public treasury of Athens a purse worth the cost of a lavish mansion for exquisite public delivery of his geographical meanderings. This knack for shooting the mind forward was something I envied, although he made no effort to instruct me in it, or even encouraged me to take an interest. He could be severely self-contained, the jailer of his flab. How could he know that the poet Sophocles would compose a poem in his honor? Will the star known as Betelgeuse welcome Egypt with open arms when it decides to loosen itself from Africa and cruise gently skyward, with the Nile affably spilling behind it?

3 ▲
ERODO

No peering in this despot's ear to find flea or noise of the sea. He smells disease or invaders that way. Need I formulate all in coherent sentences he cannot in any case understand? Never mind what he blathers about in his knowing Greek, not enough language to choke a frog. Amazing he has survived without a Fool or retainer to guide him, shifting from one to another, as with his wives, without apparent system. All are fodder to his hubris. He thinks he controls the weather in its gross and minor mutations. Claims to find the job boring but never for one minute abandons it, omnipotent as a river. Says he *is* a river to his people; a gutter is more like it. But I must scout him, and watch for dementia, sniff around for lies. Who in this country is going to tell me the truth anyway? Better to pile up impressions until I have the whole country, garbled but complete. Get him to open up for me the treasury, the library, the graves, the carrion pyramids themselves, guarded by whom I cannot tell it must be no one at all; perhaps by some ghost army of the mind, its imagination rotten with wasted memories. He seems eagerly bored.

4 ▲ CHEOPS

He is watching me in that strange hunched posture developed from sitting in our chairs, a critical gaze by any means, but one full of juridical empathy.

Who he, I wondered.

Who he, I'm sure he counters, sly fox of the duet.

"Dost thou," I begin, then shed such obsolete folderol. "Do you realize, Erodo, that the whole thrill of being a king vanishes when I think of all my forebears, stretching from those unknown distant periods?"

"All of it bullshit," says this renegade and radical.

"Only for Greek shitlickers," I answer. "It makes me weary just to think of it, and, anyway, I fix on the arbitrariness of the entire succession, more willing to tolerate the inroads of some assassin than the slow-motion hand-me-down of the departed great. Why, people have tried to frame me, saddle me, if you follow. (I don't know the Greek for it, but I'm sure you have words for such things.) And you have the whole dubious 'family tree' to kick as well."

"That," he sighs, "is why we every now and then get booted out by some despotic landlord who can't read."

"Yes," I say, "and we install a polished blue hippopotamus in tombs to placate real monsters. Now, *there*'s a Greek word!"

"Yes," he murmurs modestly, "I helped to bring it into being. You have to have certain words, after travelers and expeditions and indeed rumors have . . . Well, you know the rest. River-horse, for instance."

"Indeed I do," I say sardonically, "just as *we* needed what I will draw for you, but say as *nak,* for when our sperm comes spiraling out of us to land . . . well, wherever it lands. Look." I draw it roughly in the grease on a plate and he looks at me inquiringly as if I have been pulling his leg. Can this be true, his eyes say. Are these people really the same as us? He looks again and still sees

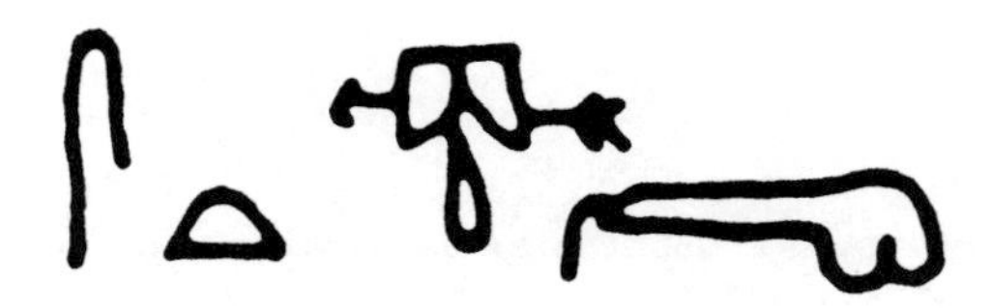

"Oh," I add, "and for women crying out at the moment of climax. It cuts both ways."

I can see that his book of Egyptiana will soon fill up, even if only with queens moaning, and spurting men. "In fact," I reassure him, glad to add fuel to his flame, or make things more explicit, "we also have *nek,* which as you will see forms the latter part of *nak.*" I show him the two side by side, the diagrammatic penis on the right longing for syrupy completion. "Look, they are calling out for each other."

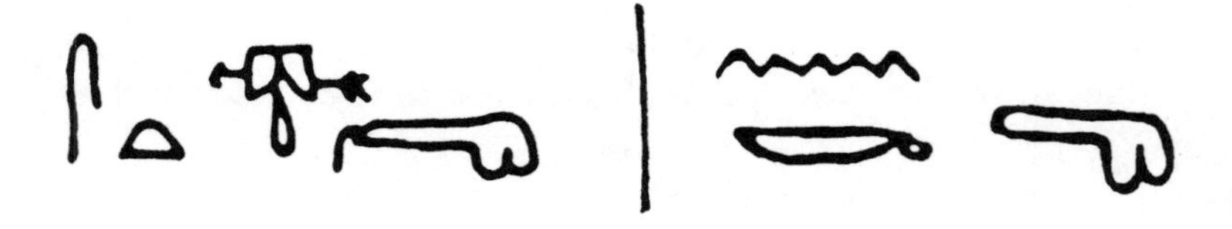

"Notice too," I inform him, "how on the right you have what may seem to you water rippling and a pouch or a pair of lips, that vanish, of course, when your barrel squirts, clearly from the pair of balls, leading to—well, you figure it out—a half-disc and a hook or crook."

"I see it now," he says, sighing as if remembering some ravishing intimate encounter before he became a scribbler.

"*Nek* leads to *nak,*" I explain, quite redundantly. He is gasping for air in our fuggy quarters, so I suggest the terrace with its incessant view of the Nile. He slumps down onto cushions, fatigued by his short excursion into local erotica.

"You could draw a box around each pictogram," I say, "but we don't bother to. The trained eye can swiftly separate what from what. But you can see how close our written language is to actual phenomena whereas Greek is at some remove, with lots of twiddly bits, like iota subscript and so forth. *Our* language stays close to bodily and other processes, and the creatures acting them out. Don't you think we're a little move advanced than you fellows, for all your sciences and math, your republics and your 'hoi polloi' as you call them?"

He falls quiet, as any Greek would when confronted with a prodigy of a superior civilization (having shed the attitude that before merely saw little twinkling waters, and baby toys describing a complex event). Egypt has him conquered quite, as I prefer.

He appears transfixed, as if he has never seen a "dirty" drawing in his life. "It's the mouth," he says, "I do like the way it's sideways, not as in life, unless—Well, never mind that, and I see the little twig or teat at one side, or the top, properly seen. Most pornography is rather general and exaggerated, but this is pleasingly literal."

"I am glad you like our filth," I tell him. "In theory I am in control of all this stuff, although not of what precedes it. I have a theoretical veto I never enforce. I am all for candor and bluntness in affairs of the loins. After all, as others see us anyway, we spend most of our lives wandering around half-naked. Not only that, I find something soothing and sustaining in the very length of time it takes to draw *nek,* say, though *nak* is more perfunctory. I can just imagine a most urgent male, eager to write down his intentions, visually slurring the ripple or the lips, say, and then, afterwards, being too tired to accomplish the crook and the half-disc."

"Do you mean," he inquires, "that your people write it down even as they do it? I mean, is there a kind of calligraphy by hand accompanying the event, one that worsens in caliber as the thumping and shaking increases? What a ripping idea. It's a sort of graphic obbligato."

Such conversations established us on an almost schoolboy basis. We were fellow conspirators on the front lines of lower language. He had no wives, not on the premises anyway, and I had too many.

The old primal urges gave us a colloquial log to burn and helped us on our way to issues more complex. I often remarked on his willingness to wear our linen, quite the thing in hot dusty Egypt, laundered in the Nile or some canal. Perhaps he took to it because it evoked the river, some portion of which lodged forever in its mesh, trapped and tinily green. He was *wearing the Nile,* I thought, and this gave him a vegetal aura, undoubtedly made him feel one of us, more at home with people he thought lived among a catalog of commonplace things. In days to come he would quiz me about the divine rights of monarchy, and why anyone had the right to inherit power over others, a notion that stuck in his throat and made him prickly. Nor could he understand why we had no coins, but instead used ounces of silver, fleshed out not as that metal at all but in pots and pans, linen, grain, necklaces, and cows. What a cumbersome system, he said time and again, leading to involved bookkeeping and complex lawsuits. I agreed, but pointed out to him the closeness to us of the physical world, close as no abstract system of money would have been. Did he follow? I doubt it; I think he saw us as deliberately leaning backward, as if we were brewers forcing the mash through a mesh into a vat. Old geezers all.

Into certain ways he settled with aplomb, not as if to stay for ever, but in the manner of one who follows the local lead, with reverence and charm: bronze razors he was drawn to, for instance, tweezers, and hair curlers made of gritstone. These he took to and wrote about with carefree attention, as well as kerchiefs and the braids we kept in baskets of sweet-smelling wood. Our mirrors were of polished bronze, unless you were very wealthy, in which case they were of silver. Clearly he felt in the presence of a solid, suave civilization, for all its lack of dressing tables and desks. The Greeks, he said, were more bookish and had been so for a long time, but he rejoiced in what he liked to call our down-to-earthness, mitigated increasingly (as he said) by a tendency to get fancy, to overdecorate, in which he saw the seeds of decay.

"Wool," he said, coming from a land of sheep.

I offered him a cloak for the cooler of our two seasons, and he draped it around him, chuckling at its sudden warmth.

"Wool," I told him. "Never in a tomb."

"So as not to create the illusion of the dead being cold."

I agreed with him, offering him shirts, kilts, skirts, all of which he salted away for his eventual departure, to brandish before the audiences of Athens who would applaud his travels.

Some visitors resemble bats by coming out only at night. Some are like leeches that suck you dry of food, friendship, proverbs. Others, like Erodo, seem to fit in but keep to themselves facets of self that do not belong, and these you discover layer by layer, bit by bit. It took him only a week to discover in a pyramid an unfinished gap, amounting to a geometrical hovel in which he soon set up camp (or housekeeping, if you will). To my own mind this was an above-ground dungeon, big enough for a man to sleep in, but merciless as rock. He swathed the interior with fresh linen and fudged up a bed of sorts, leaving the mouth of his cave wide open, at least until he developed the idea of rigging a curtain along a straight-grown twig. All this sufficed, or rather it was as little as met his needs since he went there only to sleep (the stone kept it medium cool). His main endeavor was social, of course. When he came out, he appeared no more cramped than everyone else. What creatures of the night kept him company, I do not know, and I mean animals, knowing also that certain loose women, unable to resist a Greek, attended him for special services (even certain women who up to then had not been loose at all). Over all such, I preside, less with power of life and death, than with right of scorn and envy. He had come to stay or, since he chose an abode so slight, not long at all.

His cave he picked for benign reasons. It faced north, and thus remained tolerable even during the heat of the day. It was almost unnerving to sail by and see a human face situated in the vacancy, almost as if a corpse of some workman were jutting out, thankful for so illustrious a resting-place. He could have had a tent, even a pavilion, a cool apartment to himself, with water splashing nearby, but this was his choice, not so much a yearning to go slumming as a cleaving to cool rock. The heat of Athens was one thing, but that of Egypt a living terror, to him at least. Also likely, I think he had a longing for deserted places, an odd thing for so gregarious a traveler. Every now and then, he just had the desire to get away from us all, our twisted mores and bare bronze chests.

One day, parading around with my retinue, as I sometimes did, I caught a glimpse of him naked just outside his cave. Erodo was no nudist, not in public anyway. I shooed my followers away and hid behind a rock to watch him kneel, bow, pirouette, run in place, and lift imaginary weights. He was keeping fit, of course, no doubt for some future war with the Persians. I wondered, though, that so bookish a man should devote himself to quite another pursuit, as if he expected trouble from us, or from some faction, in spite of his well-known attachment to myself. Perhaps he just wanted to be strong.

It is well-known that strangers from another country display exaggerated interest in the oddities of their hosts: the six-fingered hand, the face with the triplet of eyes, or four nostrils, the habit of talking through one's navel, the musicality of certain toes, square kneecaps. Even if you have not yet encountered such creatures, a piece of you half-expects to; and, more amazing, you will one day encounter some entity who finds the conventional arrangement of *your* face a stunner, not to mention your commonplace habit of speech. The difference, for Erodo and me, between our spoken and written language is a mild example; but extremer ones come easily to mind, suggesting that the range of human antics, serious and trivial, is much wider than ever thought. I have to be careful, I tell myself, not to think him that normal just because, in so many ways, he looks it. And when he goes back, having acquired some patina or mannerism from us, he will seem strange to his compatriots, and we, in our turn—*I* certainly—will have gained something from him: something rubbed off, and thenceforth offered up on the altar of sacrilege, for punishment or ridicule. When in Egypt . . . When in Athens . . . No one has yet completed that aphorism, but one can see it coming. Perhaps Erodesque will invade our vocabulary as a tribute to an infectious interloper long since gone.

My spies have already seen him punching a bag full of sand, at some risk to his knuckles and wrists—perhaps as some desert trick to take home with him and pass off among the unsuspecting Athenians as "desert" behavior. Whom should he wish to pound in this fashion? Does his fury boil or is he a colossal bluff? The more I see of him, and the more he explains himself and his seafaring, squabbling, abstract-minded people, the less I understand him: the receiver of goods and ways, the scribe of habits, the annotator of bizarre maneuvers, and epic poet *manqué*. Perhaps he is just a *manqué manqué*. I am not the one to know, having been provided to him for his entertainment value in this dull place. I wonder if he will ever be able to tug my inmost secrets out of me: my recklessness in family affairs, my otherworldly yearnings, my lust for honor, all of which keep me in the job I have, entitling me to all kinds of privilege, merely inherited—a fact that sometimes, not always, troubles me. Come into the fold, I tell him, to dancing girls with filmy gauze over ill-concealed limbs, minty syrups, and food to make your liver weep. He declines with a polite tremor of the lips, then invites me into *his* ridiculously small hovel that already reeks of sperm and oestrus, dung and sweat. If only he had lived on a river, he would have been a clean invader.

Following him around, I can only marvel at what he must have heard during our somewhat gaudy palace events, he in his well-wrapped linen swath, peering greedily at the heavy makeup of our women, as if black mascara and red rouge were unknown elsewhere. They all make themselves up in the same way, the well-to-do ones with nothing better to do than play the lute while punting along through a papyrus thicket. He saw monkeys toying with the lap belts of women slouched in angular, provocative repose on huge cushions, their very pose that of the courtesan, borrowed from her for much the same purpose down to the tattoo of her calling on the thigh, plus an unguent cone and a lotus flower affixed to her ponderous wig. So much for correct behavior. Lutes and lyres lull him, composing an actual orchestra rather than a minor sideshow. Stirred by votive gifts being passed from hand to hand—phalluses of limestone and wood, symbolic spoons being appraised and exchanged—and agitated coiled and uncoiling dancers doing their best to outwriggle each other to the swooning music, he must have been surprised by how Greek this all was, wondering if we were putting on a show, a series of such shows, just for him, the man from Never-Never. I can only hope he took the same pleasure as I did, in the rattling sounds made by the dancing girls, at each and every banquet he frequented. The girls wore nothing save a G-string, undulating in such a way as to make the tiny stones in their hollow beads shake and hold steady. I have many times surrendered mentally to such a click-click overture, at the same time wondering where it would end, and how. Erodo made no attempt to accost these accosting, ready girls, keeping his straight Greek nose clean for his hosts' sake, I suppose, but he must have rejoiced at the talk, roughly translated by his interpreters or, if I was near, by myself, full of royal panache and carpentered disdain—I had heard it all before, yet lingered on its buoyant ordinariness.

His face amazes me, not compact like my own and sprinkled with little facets of self-torture, but wide as it is long. His huge jaw actually widens the lower it gets, his eyes close together betokening (I have always been taught) a sneaky, devious nature, certainly he's not to be trusted; and jug ears, so that, if you're not on your guard, you might think you confront an enormous chalice or sackbut you have to lift by the ears before imbibing from the resolute, leaking mouth. He looks like a death mask of a misanthropic jester, say, or a monster of the mangrove swamps, huge, distended, blundering, yet of course with an agile, interfering brain behind it all. Here is a face that has already seen too much: too many nations in torment, too many invaders slopping beachward, too many captives being dragged to extinction while pelted with rotten fruit. He must sometimes have been observed skulking in a street corner, festooned with sackcloth and papyrus, a huge sun hat on his head, the foul rag dangling down all the way to his feet. In other words, he appears a grotesque apparition of rags and calico, a massive bib in front of him, all the way up to his nostrils (then what looks like an executioner's mask obscuring his eyes and cheeks)—in a word, nothing of him left, a remnant of a human draped in the remains of his tent. What a telling abstraction he seems, so much so that, at times, when he disappears it is as if nothing of him has been lost; a mere dragon of unavailability for such devious minds as mine to torment themselves with.

A living corpse.

5 ▲
CHEOPS

Watching him as I do, with almost rabid fascination, I note the natural athlete in him; yet having dallied here long enough, he is fat despite the privations of his journeys. I wonder if he intends to participate in certain religious ceremonies, if allowed, for it is in them that our dancers and athletes put their limber bodies to the test, not so much to enact their piety as to bring about a pious feeling in the watchers. Disporting themselves thus, they embody the vigor of the sun (though also, I'd have said, its lethargy too); whereas dancing at an intimate party or a slap-up dinner is more an affair of elegance and suave motion, performed of course also by professionals. I used to wonder why we Egyptians, creatures of the sun, hardly ever engaged in spontaneous dancing in our own right, to get a little giddy or to surrender ourselves to a catchy rhythm on the harp, shoulder harp, oboe, or lute. It was as if this had been squeezed out of us, monopolized by professionals. Yet in other affairs of daily life, we conducted ourselves quite personably and candidly; it must be the enormous hold upon us of superstition and religion. There we dare not trespass. So Erodo has no chance of infiltrating the solemn dances, only of being an onlooker. I have heard of Greek dancing that goes to frantic excess, with savage improvisation, and occasionally, victims torn to shreds by drunken maenads and helots sworn to violent calisthenics; and I sometimes wish I could accompany Erodo when he at last leaves and returns to these demonic tribes, basking in our more prosaic glow of decorum. Alas, my mission in life is not to go anywhere at all, except to maraud, or to enter my pyramid, where honorable workers, kissing and fawning on the dead, contract horrible diseases. So it is said. I am the man who goes nowhere, the one man who *is* none. But I have had my fill of dainty gatherings and solemn athletic rituals. I too want to hunt the frail chamois somewhere. Perhaps it was worse in the old Kingdom, with instrumentalists facing each other in pairs, each accompanying a different vocalist with their sedate, quiet lyrics. Later, under foreign influence, music was bound to get wilder. Why, there were even orchestras of naked girls, just the thing for Erodo, not that music was ever regarded as a proper profession (whereas dancing, because devout, was).

The problem, as Erodo pointed out (as if we were stupid), is that our music continues to be improvised; it has no scheme of notation and therefore remains permanently losable, even though the words survive. Does this mean that music is so ethereal, it dare not show its woof or texture, whereas dance by sheer repute shows a stronger, more lasting face?

I recall seeing Erodo, for once accepted into a group of my citizens—Chancellor Meketre's retinue if I remember aright—sitting comfortably in a riverboat under a discreet awning, while the household staff speared fish and captured birds, all for dinner on board the boat. This was an overnight sortie, which pleased Erodo no end with the prospect of coolness and delicate breezes. Overcrowded, the boat might have sunk with all hands, but six oarsmen kept it stable (and a watchman of the night, and the oarsmen lolling about half-asleep, trailing their fingers through the tepid Nile). There Erodo sat, a neat, compact figure in a perfect little chair, facing inwards while the chancellor faced aft from a much ampler chair approximating a throne. I am always having to watch these aspirants to office, who, having climbed, desire to climb farther, giving such as me an excellent chance to snip their dangling balls off. Was this, Erodo asked himself, not twice as good as hunting or fowling from a chariot in the desert? Here in a skiff on the waters of the Nile there was no clapnet to fill with birds, but there were fish aplenty. Being the guest of honor, and curtseying or touching his forelock to indicate his delight at the role, Erodo is treated as if he himself were chancellor or the prince, not quite knowing which is which; I see him hiding behind the reed blind fitted with peepholes, awaiting the signal from one of the crew, saying close the trap. It is for such events that Erodo was born, with his expansive nature coming to the fore, his Greek actually receding and his few words of pathetic Egyptian making themselves heard. A new hedonism arises in him, less crude than anything Greek; he has begun to desire something local to advertise himself with, something like the rawhide shield affixed to the matting covering the skiff's cabin (although he does not want the chancellor's or the prince's semi-abstract heraldry of fishes, but what he discerns *en passant*: a mimosa tree, perched at the water's edge, with a hoopoe, two shrikes, and a redstart warming themselves in the sun's dying rays. Or he would like an ivory hound constructed to open its mouth wide when the rod within its lower jaw is pressed). His vision of himself tootling upriver with musicians serenading him mellowly from the banks is almost enough to make it worth the long journey home to Greece; but of course he does not go, advancing from spell to spell like a child enthralled by a magician, half-inclined to ask me for some royal favor enabling him to stay by the river inhaling his own farts. Rather that than heading back home for the long, awful chore of writing down all he has discovered here and lied about: a pastel, naked, erotic civilization addicted to the boat song, and vast stone cenotaphs empty but for one, and that day soon.

I began to envy him his luscious daydreams, his freedom to go his own way, picking a country almost at random, managing to overlook the countries in between, as if he had a preconceived bias against Libya or the Sudan. He was not to know, not from me anyway, how a certain of my wives, highly educated in some foreign land and arriving here almost by accident, had gone to unthinkable lengths to keep me well, ordering me to eat fish only, to eschew honey and bread, to restrict my helpings of wine and drink two pitchers of water daily. Shulamith, she. It is when you encounter such women that you realize even you have something miraculous within you, to give and to revere. She kept me alive and hale, brought out the gentle side of me that dallied with small animals and spared dozens of the condemned. All for what? She drowned in our beloved river, saving an unknown child. And that was that. That was a that. Cheops became a ghost of his old self, no longer lethal, but tentative, willing to let others run the country, build, destroy, appoint, discharge, hunt, even eat. I arrived at a total point of not caring, although maintaining some dignity in the purple folds of pomp. In a sense, then, although this happened much earlier, I became the ideal target for such as Erodo, vulnerable and dependent, eager to listen and happy to die.

I once told him—one octave below laryngitis as they say—that, in my view, all in this world was corrupt. I knew he would ask me if this dictum applied to me, and I told him yes, it was the very reason I allowed myself certain odious liberties. Or I used to, my later view being that, after a certain point, you do not have to labor to be vile, or even good. These things come about whether one tries or not. I endured for 119 years, having a great deal of scope for good and ill, but I was never able to shed that more or less mechanical view—akin, I suppose, to the mechanical dog that opened its mouth.

He babbled when I told him this. Please, simple and slow Greek, I told him. Or Egyptian of any speed. Why wouldn't he learn our language? The images at least, even if he couldn't speak it (the easier course).

Oaf, I told him. It was like having a doctor who asked you for a papyrus containing love poems and your own wild interpretations of dreams. He read it because he was treating you for something or other, but didn't like it either; although he was reluctant to give it back. Up his rear end with it then: such was my proposal, horrifying our Greek once again. He was always hoping I would be better than I was.

"Why that huge lumbering building?" he asked. "All for you, to yourself?"

"Obsession with volume and space," I said.

"But what about everybody else?"

"They're not pharaoh," I told him. "Simple."

"Just think of the money," he sighed.

"I do, all the time," I told him. "I am quite fanatical about it. I never get enough."

"Your own daughter sat in a chamber and took money for services rendered. *Your own daughter.*"

"Now there's a story," I told him.

"They say, those who tell me things," (he called out as if speaking to me over a distance) "that from each client she demanded a stone, and with those thousands she could have built a pyramid of her own."

"Without asking her father for a sou."

He snorted unamiably at this.

"What kind of a story is that, Erodo? Doesn't it stink of fabrication? A canard put about to discredit me?"

"You have a bad name, sire."

"I am truly a ghost. The truth is ugly, and this is why some put our prophets in prison." When I told him this I felt a chill invade my being, a benign waft perhaps, but distantly glacial, from a cold mineshaft among the stars. Was it time to be going? Was I 119 already? No, this was merely time for the rehearsal.

He sees me now as I am. The veil or web has fallen away. In the baking sunlight my boils and ulcers come into full view: a dozen runny noses amalgamated, no doubt as punishment for living so long (*abiding* I call it); but also perhaps an incentive to hasten me out of sight, toward some other dimension where such as I find solace.

"Oh, you look so awful," he says comfortably, "your face in the light seeming all fragments, little islands each run by a tin-pot dictator. Honest."

To gratify him, I make my squint worse, not informing him that, since who knows when, I have not seen too well with either eye. Two formations have taken over the front of my vision: in each, a huge bedraggled spider within a silver, shunting web, this the result of blood that has dripped from somewhere in my head, swelling severely. I am going blind, surely, but I try to dislodge the floating membranes by winking, looking left and right, up and down; but as the jelly shifts so does the obstacle floating within it. Now and then either a piece of the spider breaks off and slides downward, or the web breaks and becomes a doily. Then I see opportune, gorgeous flashes of my surroundings, sometimes Erodo's face, sometimes my own face in a shiny metal. Mostly, though I get a shimmer, a whirling circling ingot I cannot dismiss without closing my eyes completely, which is blessed relief. I have finally figured out, compliant phantom that I have become, how the blazing morning light is bright enough to burn through both the spider and the veil. The dark does nothing to either, whereas the light of day manages to hit both impediments, scattering itself in a nonstop series of whirling haloes. It is the day I cannot abide, all other times being bliss.

"Boils, blindness, you pestering me," I say, "it's all sent to try me, to get me ready for the last journey."

"Into your blessed pyramid," he chides. "You just wait till I get back to Greece and tell them all about you. They'll come and *put* your eyes out for you, just you see."

I am not concerned. Most of the bad has come my way already, and those who will seat me in the pyramid will know they have me already, that this isn't so much practice as it is the real thing. Perhaps, they say, he'll take that accursed Greek with him. Perhaps he will eat him in the pyramid. The dead will eat the dead.

After I'm laid to rest, how can I be any good: 119 plus some two thousand, not so much a vampire, oh no, as a worn-out sun-squirt, milling around to wait my turn in the huge triangle I built. It takes that long, but I am certain I have been sent for.

"Come on," I tell him, "the procession is ready to process. I am going to test the chair."

6 ▲
CHEOPS

It is a procession of punishable length, drawn almost entirely from my own family (something Erodo asks about, as he would). He shuffles along expectantly, not so keen on the event as he is on the off-chance of stepping into some dead man's shoes. Perhaps at this "do," somebody will be killed off. The colors are blinding, to me most of all, who cannot abide the medium caress of daylight. This is afternoon. Wherever you look, whatever else you are looking at as you keep your place in the snake, you see that extraordinary Egyptian red, in which the smooth flat sides of the pyramids have been soaked. From whatever point you approach, you can read the message—the obeisance to stars, to kings, emblazoned there by superior workmen, little guessing how wind and sun will erode their efforts made with breath-held fervor. Was there ever a red like this Egyptian? I doubt it, though of course somewhere there must be a star of roughly that hue, Betelgeuse perhaps, our huge red eye in Orion.

It takes an hour at our dogged pace, I riding of course. During this rite, my feet are not supposed to touch the ground I am soon to leave. All I hear is gasping from the older retainers who resent the merest slope (Egypt is not that flat a land) and a mutinous whispering I have grown accustomed to, as I have also to Erodo. How many more times for this? Is this how the pyramid workers felt year after year, marching in—as regular as the seasons of the inundations of the Nile—from their elementary quarters through the big stone gate? Is it time for a farewell? I think not, nor even for a greeting, as we draw in sight of those low gaps in the walls that resemble ventilation holes, but which, after a short distance looking horizontal, tip up and take aim at something sublimer than mere air. The angle they climb at is predetermined, like everything else; I have spent my life getting these things right. Do you wonder I have never had time for anything else? Getting it wrong would be a tragedy, for me at least, maybe for everyone under my rule, to whose greater and commonplace glory I have devoted myself lifelong.

Erodo is peering, pretending to measure. At his unvoiced suggestion that we are looking at a ventilator, a mere outlet-inlet, I shake my head in its ornate cap. It is much more than that, but he cannot see what; and that is his role of course, bringing himself here in order to look stupid while libeling us. Thank Thoth he seems to say, I thought you might suffocate in there, but he is not allowing for the colossal cooling power of all that masonry, one block every four minutes. I will need my thickest robes. Indeed, I have them on posing, settling on the throne consecrated to the memory of my cosmic father Osiris. Now Erodo looks truly baffled. What have we come to see, to do? What could this be, a slaughterhouse for lions?

In we go, and I am ministered to with lamps. There are tapestries, sacred texts, and votive couches, none of which I can see clearly in that gloom, but they're identifiable by traditional placement, as before. They do not sense how dead I already am, indeed, how little my mind lingers on the ritual; I am already out there, star-struck, as required, wondering not about these holy matters, but the kind of propulsion needed. Faith? Poetry? Music? A special suction from the god himself? Odd how in the popular imagination, we deal only in abstractions, treating personalities as ciphers, complex maneuvers as mere outlines. Not so. All is detail, everything is different, nothing repeats. But, if you believe that much in uniqueness, you're bound to stand at some distance from it, just to keep your balance. Who wants a pyramid in his grape arbor? It is important to have to parade out here, all the way trying to think holy thoughts, and so arrive in a state of moderate piety. I do go through the motions, but hardly ever thinking what I am supposed to think, my mind not remembering *The Book of the Dead* at all; but perusing the length and width of a corridor upon whose walls whoever was here last inscribed a series of mystical formulae, intended for no eyes but mine, poor as they are. (Erodo will soon report on my eyes when he catches up with the gossip. Almost anything will serve his purpose.)

Not for the first time, but with greater accuracy, I notice that worldly-wise look come upon him, as if he has not only twigged what is going on, but has suddenly (he a Greek accustomed to Attis and Osiris, and now *this*) come into his own as a sage, a prophet, a seer. He and I are epochs and civilizations apart. I am a murmur come to life, fleshed out to make his livelihood for him—a creaking gate from the dark ages he now oils and makes fun of, deplores and puts to the oral test. Having hauled me out of the long-lost world, he now has the face himself of one who travels into the future by the same number of years: 2600—500—2000. It must be some kind of distant viewing; he infects me with it, so we both look far beyond ourselves, who we were, and all the rest of it. There was Cheops before Erodo. Then there was Cheops now, with Erodo. No doubt there will be Erodo afterwards. But there is also what Erodo's successors some two thousand years after that will think of Cheops. Something live courses through us; he knows it has come to stay, even if it won't make us eternal.

The odd thing is that, if he is engaged in some kind of retrospective recovery—retrieval by allusion and libel—is that much different from the bizarre transit I myself propose for my ending, pooh-poohed by pragmatists and believers alike, mathematicians and fuel suppliers? Erodo and I are up to the same game: the pressure of mind on time. Not without its willful aspect, a kind of holy chicanery that, once accepted, delivers you from all temptations. Not that he wishes to lie beside me and keep me company; he is the permanent spectator, ever ready to say I saw Cheops do this or that, at least through his contemporaries' eyes I did. And then, after flourishing in the white heat of composition, he comes to believe his own account, dropping *they said he said* down to *he said,* and all is permitted beyond that point.

By what magical combination do we meet at all? Is it revenge that drives me Erodo-ward? Was it his own tabula rasa that sent him to Egypt in the first place, his mind twisted by the way old Homer called my country *Aigyptos,* but the Nile *Aigyptē*? Or was it some rumor that our landscape was littered with flakes of limestone on which workmen sketched bits of pornography (the naked lady riding her lute), or shopping lists of ointments, spoons, and mandrake fruits?

"I thought you were dead," he began.

"I get a lot of that," I told him.

It was so long ago, but all he is doing is dreaming of me and his own future renown; he springs toward me and his future. Verily, I belong back in *The Book of the Dead* and should leave magic to harlots.

7 ▲ CHEOPS

After sundry further conversations with him, none of them on such momentous topics as before, I admit to having plunged us both into deep thought when I remarked to him, "Does it work? Of course it works. Look at me. I'm here, am I not, after two thousand years!" On a more trivial note, I garner from him, and copy out in Egyptian red, some pictograms from among his papers; the gist of these he declined to explain, leaving me in the learner's lurch. Seeing ✈ I at once thought I had seen something similar, not a bird, in my distant childhood, of even hovering near my pyramid; but [ear] baffled me quite. [wheelchair] was perhaps a bird of some kind at ease on its nest. [racquet] I identified as a spoon, to us an erotic thing always; and I managed to discern a mere difference of stroke between [swimmer] and [wave]. [figure] reminded me of Erodo at his outdoor exercises or our best religious dancers. It was an entirely new world, and my interpretive skills came to life again, especially seeing [camera], which I thought showed two people with only three legs hiding behind a horizontal bottle not pouring. Or was it a two-headed monster with full complement of legs carrying a flask of hellfire for the day when we would be tried, put in balance with a feather? (How could we lose?)

When I addressed him, he was trying to finger-massage a tooth that was bothering him. In language I thought befitting what I had drawn, I described the images I'd shuffled around until they made some kind of sense; he had no idea what I was talking about. "Hovering over Giza," I began, "it must be some divine bird, diving in a curly motion, and you too become a bird on its nest watching the adults swim in the Nile in various styles, after which they are brought to judgment bearing a sexual spoon in their hands. What else have I forgotten? Oh, the three-legged monster, which eats you up if you are found wanting." Erodo was not impressed by this little flurry of nonsense based on a code he found opaque, but I followed up with the actual signs, hoping he would relent. His tooth was what occupied him, so my little ribbon of combinations went by the board. I was seated there, in the presence of my artifacts, wondering why we Egyptians lived so short a life: thirty-five was about the limit. Perhaps I had devised an image of that so-short life, applicable not to me, alas, hooray, but poignant:

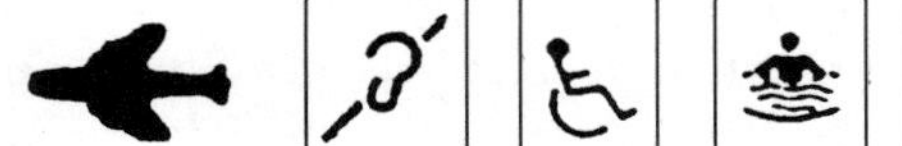

What was I doing? Just making the best of things. Here he was, confronting me with signs from somewhere on his travels, some place where he felt a real foreigner, and I was trying to fudge up some kind of translation for him, little as he appreciated it.

"Can't you help?" He shook his head.

"These are just mementos, then?" I persisted, but he just shrugged. "Whatever," he said eventually.

"Not Egyptian," I told him, "of any period. We do have swimming and fishing and birds, spoons and nests, but I can imagine they, whoever they are, have many more things than we do in this relatively pastoral civilization, known mostly for its attitude to death."

"Don't say that word," he said. "It gives me the jitters."

"Us too," I told him. Don't be a chump, Erodo. Help me decipher."

Well, in a fashion, he did, but my mind was on bigger things, of which he knew nothing, not having encountered such problems as being a revisiting soul, courtesy of Osiris and the Belt Stars. He had no conception of what happens to a resurrecting king when he owes allegiance to a line of stars: when he is actually a baby star himself, subject to star-law and star-ways. How did your lungs respond to the lack of oxygen up there, or the smoke from all that divine fire? Did the others accept you as one of the club, one of the resident ghosts? I had heard rumors about the demands of Belt-living, requiring you to have a guide and friend just to show you the ropes for the first thousand years. And then, of course, there was—would be—the whole business of getting back to Earth, a new apparition, all your old slanders draped like earthworms around you, you pissing and shitting without warning, thanks to the change in air pressure, the lack of starry heat. Was there no etiquette to transmigration?

All this I sounded him about, asking if he knew anything about how the other stars in the Belt, say, helped you on your return, you being a newborn star? It was a matter of age, I told him, but he knew nothing and admitted as much. Did he not realize, I asked him, that if you extend the line of the Belt Stars it leads you right to the dog star Sirius, by which we all, ghosts, birds, and gods, navigate. He had no idea, and in the end I decided against pestering him further. Erodo and I went for a swim instead, all thoughts of our conflicting languages forgotten, and an ecstasy of well-swum fluid made us friends again for a sunrise or two.

Then sleep, after which I awoke to a gallery of chattering female voices, some of them long gone, but as present as an earwig that has crawled into an ear to use its pincers.

Ah, the long-lost melody of some of them, an enclosing wall of vocal signatures, never as blurred as they were going to be when I ascended, as was my birthright. Ah voice, inextinguishable and chirpy.

Merytyetes: Burly, bouncy, with muscle behind it, this is the voice of someone young and confident—perhaps a little middle-aged-sounding, but clearly enunciating and ripe with energy. You heard this voice when she wanted you up and out into the baking sunlight; it was as if she had inhaled the sun and breathed it out with never a syllable slurred. An overbearing woman? Her voice is insolent and brawny.

Henutsen: Silky, insinuative, deferential and, until you see her up close, the voice of an elfin, elegant wisp, but never so, actually she's a blockish, rather hirsute creature with straggly hair, who might have developed these tones so as to deflect hearers from her appearance. Ever responsive to what anyone else says, she answers in a manner soft and almost lisping. Wearing an iron mask, she could have fooled anyone. The next voice is that of a stepmother.

Nefert-kau's voice always had a smile behind it, as if some utterly competent, well-versed woman were interviewing you. Quite deep and resonant it was, a column of air never failing to repose on a velvet pedestal. She had learned somewhere how to speak in an authoritative manner, yet the very sound of her suggested deep clefts, pleats, in her body, as if she were some fabulous musical instrument from far away in the stars. I could listen to her for hours without speaking. A spellbinder she was, who was not a magician.

Enhetteres: Tinny, hoarse, shrill, best heard at a distance down a long tunnel, not just scolding but presumptuous, conceited. She had a trick of disappearing and returning hoarse from her absences. The forgotten one.

Why *voices,* you ask. Well, it's a different thing from breasts, buttocks, and so forth; and I confess I always responded more to voice than to anything else, always remembering the sounds from above when I was in my mother's womb: delicate, thunderstruck, pensive, august, fur-soft, or like the purr of the young lion at the tent flap. If only I had been able to put them together and listen blindfolded; it would have been a symphony to take into my pyramid. That would be going from a world of hieratic writing, with all the signs attenuated, shrunken for the sake of speed, back into the old hieroglyphs, time-consuming and imposingly suave, at only a short distance from the realm of the senses, where a feather was a feather and remained so, and a snail was a snail, and remained so.

Merytyetes

8 ▲
CHEOPS

Does this old boy have a trace of sentiment, grace, harmony in him? Does he miss anybody held dear? Or is he the pure type of episodic traveler, "making do" with whatever emotions he finds on the way? Does he care, or does he skim over us all, eagerly searching for mores, indifferent to commotions of the heart? I ask.

"Oh," he answers, "I am always running into this or that infatuation, and then running from it. It's the modern way, sir." So he *is* one. I had suspected as much, and I guess he has no more intimate fondness for kings than for doxies. Surely he has had some kind of bond, other than the one he bleakly reports with his uncle. No, he will not divulge it, but his face is far from the blind cipher of the man of the world; something in there has creased with suffering, misgiving, the yearning never to be severed from someone pure in heart, someone almost too dear to be beheld. No, it will not come out of his darkness, but I can see that something, someone, has cut deeply into him, some black-eyed Greek goddess. We Egyptians are prone to be "burned by the sun," too sentimental to last long, and too committed to the other life to care much for this one. He finds us, I think, churlish and crude, patrons of a river, yet after browsing in our poetry, a bit prim and proper. "Did you never," I ask him, "feel that sickening turbulence in your being when you found you were not complete and never would be? Calling out for that other?"

He shrugged without a smile, made a self-deprecating grimace that told me he was remembering something passionate, and firmly clasped my hand, not one of his usual greetings. He was here to observe, not to tell.

At this point, after my lugubrious meanderings about death and immortality, I thought I needed a lift, not only to get me out of that mood but to distract myself with a story that was tender but ended less well. "Once upon a time," I began, but he winced the wince of a scribe. I began again, explaining that one of my sons, a big strapping fellow with a covetous air, had taken a fancy to his sister. No names, no punishment, I thought. "Sometimes this happens in a family and you dismiss it as puppy love, easily replaced by riper distractions. But no, their overtures, mutual it seemed, grew more and more obvious as rival suitors fell away, and I decided that, the next time we sent a deputation to another king's court, she should go along to further her skills as a scribe—a career whose nature I loathe but which I hoped would give her something profitable and mindful to do. So the moment came, she was already eighteen, and we all wept, but she clearly enjoyed the whole idea of escaping from the rigid palaver, the otherworldly preoccupations of her father, he of the slightly puffy Mongolian face. Why, down to Abydos she could have been sent to check on the several solar boats kept there, or even deliver into safer keeping than Memphis that tiny replica of my Mongolian face. Off they went, she determined, as I found out, to make more of the trip than a mere secretarial opportunity. While she was away, I often tried to imagine what her life was like in that distant palace, among strangers, bargaining with men of the world, and trying to get on with other girls. All I ended up with, however, was a set of scenes, in which she perched or lay, doing nothing much, clearly awaiting a call that never came, except the one to duty—what some of our scribes call "the drawing board."

"You should have hung on to her, old man." Erodo is overfamiliar today, no doubt inflamed by the potential of my story. "You never know what these young bitches will get up to once they're out on their own. Athens is crawling with them, and we have a special name for them."

I was hurt and shocked, although mostly because I had been hurt and shocked by Heduanna's behavior. Certainly she did her secretarial work, but she allowed her imagination to roam in unusual fashion, no doubt responding to the spirit of the place, farther south and even warmer. There had been no way to reach her, none that was convenient, and rumors began—the old rumors—that I had sentenced her to a house of prostitution, begging only a pebble for each service. That is how an innocent-seeming scheme can get you a bad odor, even among your own people. I did nothing of the kind, being rather an absent-minded recluse, ever a little weary of kingship except as it concerned me (and in this I practice a cult of the infinite I am). Such word from her as I received was conventional, remote, disingenuous, although what she was concealing I never knew. My daughter was on leave, her brother had the perpetual sulks, and I vowed to make the journey to bring her back, once I could get away.

"Sounds to me," Erodo said, "as if she'd gone to the dogs. Rape-bait if you ask me. Some of these southern tribes have wild and uncouth practices, the farther south the more savage. So my informants say."

He's just a scribe, I thought, and he's talking down to *me*.

Yet clearly he was hooked, he wanted more, trapped as ever by his lust for a yarn, a vignette, a scene; he would turn it into something full of crescendo and climax, gentled with his customary affable chat, the manner that convinced everybody he was on the level.

"What a bloody fool, my lord," Erodo joshes. "You had better put it right pronto." Surely he knows what happened, being now here, anachronistically. Does he not get it that we are like flies lolling on membranes, waiting to be swatted?

9 ▲ CHEOPS

I hear that female voice once again, unsure which of the full-bodied lower ones. All I know is that, first, it offers a statement, burly and joyous, from the depths, and you think she's finished and that will be all; but then she follows up with an even burlier utterance, as if the first has given her a lift, and you are dealing now with extra relish. It's as if this voice had suddenly adapted itself to the sensuousness of the world and is stating it. Some men yearn for such conversing, whether or not they, as I, have a harem of some two hundred with whom to stud when the mood takes you; but not I, who prefer tones altogether more yielding and submissive.

"Your missing daughter's voice?" asks Erodo, but I am not addressing him any more; I am fingering through a complex past in search of something benign I turned my back on. The only way to cope with it seems to be to bog down in the preliminaries, sideways gestures, so as not to advance into the painful stages of the event. This means of course lingering, imagining, in part enacting her role myself, as I no doubt always should have. Heduanna attributes her eminence to secretarial flair. That is hardly my fault. Young as she is, or might seem to a different civilization, she *is* well-tried; if not the belle of the religious dancers, at least the queen apparent, in Giza, a lovely high-class spot to bathe and laze in if you have not happened to be copying out masses of important civic and foreign papers. Why, she dreams, any one of a thousand aspiring scribes could have been chosen, combed from all over the city—girls of undisputed family loyalty and flawless linen compressing their hips, each with an eye to advancement or, failing that, discreet intimacy with some high ranker, preferably one of military disposition (a protector, and not one of those death squad members leaned on by the hierarchy). She has made it at last, thanks to her father's intervention. She will never have to look back on herself as a failure, just a smart high-born girl who almost went nowhere. She will listen and take notes on the proceedings of the third conference. She has just the right kind of fawning, obedient face, and, who knows, after her revels with her brother, the right *âme noire* to egg them on.

I did not shelve her, but gave her a chance to do what she is best qualified to do. Not exactly an arriviste, she does happen to be a climber, soon to gain rung blisters on her palms. She used to live here, hectoring her women to pound and pummel all those linens marked with her cartouche, insisting they dry and fold everything with the exquisite finicking care of someone who traps and marshals butterflies. She loves a romp, of course, whether tactless or not, and assumes the approval of those highly placed folk who watch her and wonder. She does not notice the plotters and the spies, the liberals and foreigners, but sees an audience for her, a wave of affable admiration, which is not what I see at all. One day (this is the farthest from her thoughts), they will clean them all out, and the frolicking crowd, sons and daughters of the Nile, will be homogeneous all over again. Even birds and pets will have to explain who they are in that commonwealth of night. The father can safely install stone images of himself, and his kin, all over the desert.

She's been instructed: Just bring your skills, she has been told, and you will be made welcome. Promotion through ovation, dear child, whatever else you propose to do with your life. By all means, when you get there (having first sampled our stately river at length, and enjoyed the company of the gentlemen aboard, whose names you will be told beforehand, and of course yours to them), once you've arrived, you will encounter a carefully selected corps of men. They will be bonded to secrecy on pain of death, so the field will be open for your undisguised wiles, even as you show them how a first-class lady scribe performs her allotted tasks. Just do not ask *too many* questions about whom they intend to punish and evict. Please leave the technicalities to those who best understand them. They will make their mark as required and that will be the end of your labors. With this honor may come an increased allowance; an extra parrot may squawk your way. You are also to understand, dear child, that nothing will be stinted on your behalf. You will be appreciated and fêted, as befits your rank, whether or not you blink at the military gentlemen got up in savage finery, makeup, wild bloodcurdling emblems. These conferees, as they will be known, asked for a feminine touch among them to relieve the martial monotony, and this you will provide with whatever finesse occurs to you. Be confident, dearest princess. Such an opportunity may never come your way again. The conferees have rather prosaic, ordinary wives, who will not have been invited to the deliberations; so do not hesitate to grace the occasion with a flash of wile or smile, the obsequious smirk that implies nothing more than a woman of the world in the making. Neither slut nor homemaker, you will charm them to death as you scribe away, roughening your hands on papyrus, even as they ponder the overdue weighty matters they have been summoned to settle. The future of our regime, any regime, need not concern you. You may hear talk of reprisal, something about "the Libyan line," but pay it no regard. You need not even supply snacks as there will be serving men to do that. Just get the proceedings written down in perfect order, and dream of luxury caravans to come, well-furnished boats on the Nile, yearning for your return. With cartloads of flowers commissioned by a grateful father. You will be a real Egyptian princess, chosen for brains and looks, rising to the top of elegant society, unlike those other ladies who never quite make it, in their faces the unappeased look of those who are poorly prepared. You will of course manage to keep all proceedings to yourself, even if you overhear something drastic, while transcribing something else. Some of our allies can be most obliging when pressed.

Habituated to the prose style of master officials, she recognized the hand, hands, behind all this, quite wishing they would cut the cackle: elegantly vivid in places, but too much for her to stomach, having already become familiar with—what would she call it—the cosmic glamour attempted by her father. (Does she know or care about his failing eyes, full of murky tendrils, or filaments, yield of exploded capillaries in the retina? She does, but she has grown familiar with his idiosyncrasies, almost depending on them for conversation with him.) At last allowed to go, she knows she has to be careful, rising from the eggs on her nest like the mythical osprey, yet dispatched like a parcel, to foreign parts full of foreign parts. Let loose, she tells herself, as never before, but only because I have taken too many liberties.

Who is heaviest-handed, then? My father, or his aides? They have a solemn, steely grip on geography, about which I am supposed to know nothing. Just head southward and keep my milky nose clean.

10 ▲
OSIRIS

She almost faints, then all of a sudden recovers, nervously rearranging the many intimate possessions she has beside her on board the Nile boat. She wonders: might she be exposed as a daydreamer; one who entertains impossible, reckless notions about of all people a brother? Might she be considered some kind of plotter? Is there a scheme afoot she has no knowledge of? Well, just so long as her father remains safe, which is almost the same as saying he remains enigmatic, inscrutable; while she lives it up as a scribe, writing faultlessly, yearning as she always has to remain where she is going—a showpiece, an exotic marvel. Oh to be a high official's mistress! Such dreams she keeps to herself, as almost always. She worries that, should she end up not sleeping alone, she will blab something in her sleep and imperil her whole family. This terror is real, nurtured by contact with her father and his assorted wives. She is supposed to feel royal, but she doesn't quite believe it. A virgin should know better, but she does not; she has held her brother at bay with the perfect trance, not only resisting his every overture but thoughtfully embalming him in adoration. On the loose now, as she sees it, she becomes impatient for life as an adult, but is afraid to squander her welcome on the wrong person, not sage enough, not even shrewd, not solicitous enough, bearing a girl's freshness.

New to all this, she retires to the little converted steerhouse where her smaller bags are, and tries to write, not for practice, but somehow to make sense of everything. She is delighted, she thinks, I alone am chosen, unless there will be more just like me when I arrive. I have been considered for months, behind my back, and have come out on top. Glory be. She does not dare to write this down, but she pretends to, idly maneuvering her forefinger this way and that; doing nothing final. She raises the peppermint-smelling mat over the doorway and scatters scraps of invisible writing into the Nile, past them fast, wondering which of the gods is watching her, wondering at her introverted tact, her devious honesty.

She has to be careful; her father has always told her that, warning her against zealous eavesdroppers. The thought of him and those tutorial moments long ago, when he actually took time out to brief her on being a princess, tempts her to want to go home again, but she has come too far (or at least in his probing reverie about her she has, his decision not to let her go too far having faded). The conferees would perhaps be there already, *men alone,* almost in holiday mood, Abydos being more or less a resort town, a haven of myth, where the whole world might like to come and play. Can she, she wonders, think and dream in code, lest her thoughts be lethal? Almost giggling, she thinks I am the bride of Abydos, my face and gestures, even my leg-crossing ways, construable but not definitively corrupt, oh no. She curls up, swathed in new, fresh obligations, when she had assumed she would only have to play her entire life, envisioning the various things men do but not taking them seriously.

She is even ready for the so-called heroes, soldiers maimed in tribal battle who stump around on wooden legs they have smoothed out with knives, then polished with sand, aiming for a daylight glow. Ah, she says, so as not to offend in bed, like having long toenails. How coarse my untrained thoughts can be, she murmurs. It would be easy now, she decides, to become a midstream hoverer, one who having edged one foot fractionally forward brings the other up to join it, thereafter maintaining the stance on a secure basis, but never going farther and persuading herself she hasn't made any substantial change, nothing that commits her anyway.

Far from her now, but attuned to the mellow wraith of her departing form, Cheops accuses himself of holding her back, of mentally tugging at her lest she get into trouble; even now he doesn't quite fathom why he has sent her away—not incest, no, not for education social or otherwise. Perhaps to make himself suffer for once. He misses the lissome apparition of her, bouncing in when Erodo shuffles out with scarcely a glance at her. Do I desire *her*? Did she desire *me*? Whose image is she? Is that what we say? She's the image of her mother, her father, *that's* what we say, ignoring all evidence to the contrary.

Resuming—no she never even paused for him: she torments herself with what she is going to hear, overhear, resisting even while inscribing it. Cruising the Nile in what she still considers a speedboat, she racks her command of language in order to escape the havens of her sometimes sheltered life. You cannot advance, she thinks, without overbalancing, nor can you go back without some river mud stuck in between your toes. Just think: I am a royal princess on her way to do her duty, for which nobody in the world would think I was in the least prepared. If I get it wrong, they will ask me to denounce myself in my own words . . . She tries to steady herself, with a random image of some wellborn woman unearthed from her widow's tomb, sheathed like a spear, that rigid and slender. Death must have surprised her in the midst of health; she reads in the rictus of the mouth a touch of innocent shock. She must have been felled by—felled by what? How do I not know? Am I that new to life? By her head, bay leaves reposing on a few threads of some fabric, and juniper berries indicating what? Her funeral robes have long ago rotted into the silt.

Heduanna finds this image just far enough away, a counter to her dreams of modern grandiosity (at least in her father's court). She is not going to arrive at all, the boat is going to turn around and take her home, all being forgiven. She does not have to go whoring among strangers as a scribe after all. Her inbuilt vulgarity-warning dismisses what fails to fit. Her serene, oblivious view—a sort of retrospective vizor of taste—bypasses all that she finds uncongenial. She continues in aloof delicacy, one eye (half an eye) on the main chance, the other on some emaciated lady she has no name for but for company calls Tabubu. To herself, fastidiously mouthing it, she attempts a song she has learned by heart:

> I turned my face toward the door,
> for I was waiting for my brother to come to me.
> My eyes were in the street, my ears listening . . .
> I was waiting for Pamehy.

But she has not, as the rest of the song says, found another; she has found the smudged image of the future, in which all is thwarted beginnings, nothing comes to fruition. All she has, to hold on to, is a certain skill with hieroglyph and hieratic. The impenetrable-looking bow wave swirls past her in a furtive curl, a maid brings her a sweetmeat, and the sky closes in with a thin rind of cloud.

Her mind's eye feeds her more than it should, saddling her with a ruddy-complexioned, rather pointy face, huge brown eyes and dismayed mouth, as if death had just enough time to discomfit her at an early age. She would like to rise above this face, but for some reason she feels bound by it, as if destiny, espousing her, had made of her a compulsory martyr. She would relish a sea change in the heart, but more than that, a metamorphosis unthinkably far from the slight ballet of sending her underwear to the launderers hourly. Above all, she thinks she has the diplomatic gift for being led, for divining a man's direction, and she has read enough in her superficial way to learn how forward a reticent girl can be. When her magic day arrives, as it surely will, it will amount to instant recognition: a green light, as they say in the modern age, which will follow the sun's last tweak, and a new life will begin. All she has to do among the bustling men at the conference is be hospitable, ceremonious, cordial, and the world will be hers, never mind from whose hands. After all, look who her father is.

Heduanna finds this reclaimed image just far enough away, a match to her dreams of rescue by politico, chamberlain, an official of the royal cemetery. If she seems an arriviste, she is also an impetuous dreamer who casts upon all who appear before her, to tell tales or beg a diaphanous scarf, an eye not so much avaricious as well-versed in quality. The disparity between her dreams and the coarse gruffness of all her intendeds does not occur to her; her vulgarity-warning dismisses with blithe finitude whatever fails to fit. In this she reminds herself of her father, who claims to regard all landscapes, city plans, tracts of geography, in terms of the structures that are no longer there and have been replaced, thus proving himself forty or fifty years out of date for the sake of continuing to live among things familiar. From all this, of course, he excepts the pyramid, for obvious reasons. He is merely making his case. The modern world of his own time does not exist; it has replaced nothing he cares about. So they share this gift for looking away, past, and through, he as pharaoh, she as scribe, continuing to thrive in aloof delicacy—one eye she has on the main chance, the other on someone she named Tabubu.

Trembling a little before main chance envelops her, she tidies up her already tidied possessions, as if preparing for sudden departure to some exalted rank. It *will* all be very sudden, she decides, as in the romantic poetry lovingly inscribed on a stucco-coated papyrus:

> "Look, I am yours," I shall say to him,
> and he will boast of me,
> and allot me to the best harem
> of someone among his followers.

No, she knows nothing that harsh will happen. Eyes will meet. They will "click," as the old saying goes, and that will be that: durable infatuation, with her cuppable, sweet bottom twitching madly for a third of a century after. From than on, she will be like a groomed paragon, no longer taking dictation or improvising verse, but much gifted at the gold-splashy reception among elegant armoires—the inveterate folder of ribbons, the inscriber of gratuitous greeting cards entrusted to obscure letter carriers who speed across the desert, or merely down the street.

On her father goes, tracing her every mental motion with almost fetishistic envy. Oh to be young again, "setting out." Now more than ever, she feels obliged to take stock of her being, not in the old casual way that didn't count for more than an afternoon spent on sherbet and prattle; but final, remorseless, what you have behind you before really setting out your stall. She hears a levitating flute, seeking an even higher note, its sound eerie yet technical, and she knows what it means. She sees what some Sudanese have brought from the south—where she is headed—the cloven hoof of an amaryllis just before it bursts into bloom, finally free of the leathern basket in which it traveled so far, its root in its own dung, its power slowly muscling up the empty-looking stem. Whatever her conclusions about herself, she still feels empty, not delivered up in full glory, no doubt because she was born so high to begin with. She tries to content herself with a prophetic modicum, wondering hard about that invisible next step among cogent strangers, away from familiar cabinets and fabrics. She is going to witness the arrant display of bravado in the presence of severe loneliness, and she does not relish the thought, all the while her far-seeing father thinks of the eternal isolation confronting *him* when he becomes a star.

Old proverbs assigned only to dust arrive and haunt her, especially the one saying I love you too late, possibly addressed to the sun-god or to any potentially forgiving deity. A monster of punctuality her girlfriends call her, but she is that only for parties and dances, or with work assignments. In all else she is late, professionally so, having learned it from her father, that great sucker-up of wandering Greeks. Incongruously, she predicts her own lateness, knowing it is inattention to timetables rather than a snoot cocked at life. Yes, she feels, she will die of the sunburn disease long before she commits herself to anything ephemeral. She notes that you can never measure a live snake. She is agile and unpredictable.

Against rainy days, she has hoarded in a cupboard some exquisitely surfaced papyrus boards, ready to be written on when, as she tells herself, she has something to say. Their margins are feathery and snowlike, crinkly to the touch. She will use them to report her doings (and undoings) to her father. He is glad to imagine—to intercept, overhear, however he must do it. She will eye the soft hue of the board and open her soul to him, hinting at a promotion based on startlingly good work at the first few conferences. It is not as if she can tear the papyrus up after writing something tactless, but she could, if she wished, smash it against some piece of furniture, then replace the fragments in their pretty box again—the gesture made, the sentiment canceled. She looks forward to being in the presence of men of heft and rank, for whom (she hopes) she will have a special metallic radiance. She is inching from one life to another; unaccustomed to exotic thoughts, she feels the need to sit, trailing her hand in the race of water; she suddenly remembers the world she has left behind: in the pool with her sisters, feeling the first cool of evening, telling one another to make water for its warming effect as their pee sits next to the blood. They rarely did it, but the idea enlivened them.

She should not have leaned backward to that pool memory; it has brought her even farther into her temporarily lost world. It is a rickety stool, held together by wooden pins, mark of the scrupulous craftsperson no doubt, no resin used; but the whole thing is slotted together like an idea kept in the mind. Here she sits, before getting up, urging her body this way and that, always toward some calculated future, knowing from her mother's knee that in order to move forward you need not remember anything or the enterprise will founder. The chair does not creak, not in a major way, until she has left it and half-bounced away, reluctant to be caught rising from it. Then it does creak, retaining the memory of her, rendering a last salute in the midst of a thousand minutely registered settlings: the slack way her body used it, sat and slumped, eased itself forward or backward, waiting to be born. The loud bray of a small orchestra may stir her from it, as they get to work on some innocent theme; and other women, flushed by now, reveal the lines painted red over the veins in their breasts as the party gets under way.

Of late, her feet have begun to preoccupy her: being wide, they demand some freedom, which is possible in a country where the bare foot is de rigueur. But a wide shoe, as befits, is too long as well, so she has to endure the constant disparity between the one and the other, and she ends up cursing cobblers and slipper-makers. She tries pads, but there merely hinder her step. Seated, making a fine dust, she uses pumice against her calluses, sliding her heels about in the palms of her hands. She does not have to file her thighs, of course, though she has heard rumors of bewhiskered veterans wearing them away to smoothe a non-existent callus. She knows full well that, at even the seemliest parties, both men and women sport artificial beards, and the women, sometimes, beehives of melting wax on their heads, all to add raffishness and stern ornateness to their appearance. She has seen the world already, she tells herself, so there cannot be much to come. She is from the metropolis, en route to the provinces.

11 ▲
CHEOPS

Erodo is slicing through my reverie, his quizzical eyes peering through my glaze and, perhaps, rebuking it.

"How long have we been friends?"

"Aren't you presuming, Greek?"

The Greek thinks not and adds, "She'll be all right."

So, the Greek has been reading my mind, plumbing my distant viewing, my anxiety coupled with relief.

"I think it would take years, Erodo. Look how far I have had to come to sit next to you, an image afloat on a membrane. Since, long ago, I made it to Orion, I am allowed back now and then."

"Please yourself, boss. I count myself lucky to run into you. The real king."

"Then we are friends, of mutilated time and muddled privilege. To be frank, I am torn. I now think sending her halfway would have worked as well. In a way she's enjoying it too much. I can tell. But who am I anyway? A creaking gate."

"A rotting portcullis."

If his acid jocularity were not that of an educated man, I would call in some of my secret police and put him to the test, racking him and twisting him. I don't because, let's face it, we are birds of a feather; in Greece I would probably behave just as badly, out of my element, without a fitting handy slang.

"I was once," he babbles, "a heavy-armored infantryman. I loved nothing better than getting away, ever in a dark mood when I had to come back. My grave shall be in the market of Thurii, in Southern Italy. I shall probably die of plague."

I can see him as he was, winging his way toward me over the ages like a diving seabird, even as I flap toward him out of puff. Somebody set us up. I refuse to ask him about *his* daughters, his books, his public, his lies, his affable pretentiousness. What does an epic hero say to a regional reporter after all? Need I explain my thoughts, that I was traveling the Nile with her, to lovely Abydos, her missing guardian, while maintaining my hands-off/hands-on policy? She has to be weaned, which means she has to be blooded too. This is an old predicament, especially for old kings. There is the *ka,* which occupies the living body and gets celebrated in the rites and offerings in the funerary chapel. But someone such as I has also the *ba,* the part of a king that soars to Orion and becomes a star. Gods feed it and goddesses give it suck. Well, she has her *ka,* but no *ba*. Why my *ba* should worry about her *ka,* I am unsure; we are beings of a different stamp, intended to go our separate ways.

12 ▲ OSIRIS

She has still not figured it out: the way her father, either back in his own time, or in the extra time allotted him, views landscape. His pyramid soars and points—to the uninitiated, alone and blank, but for him, the center of a massive graveyard full of those who built the pyramid. For as far as the eye can see—Cheops's, that is—the desert is crowded with graves, and from this vision he takes enormous pleasure, thinking of the bones and beads, the linen rags, and the emptied carcasses—entire generations laid to rest, almost on top of one another, creating a desert topography, mottled and uneven. It's as if a million sleeping forms hugged the land, awaiting the call to further labor; he himself, when feeling low, feels he is looking down at some packed audience, as if waiting for a political speech. The effect is oddly dignified, though evoking a glorified slum, in which as a centerpiece he presides though without anyone being there. Clouds of magnanimous glory are behind him. Where he learned such a way of disposing the landscape, apart from learning from his ancestors, his father especially, he has no idea. He is sure he has not picked it up from some cruising star; rather, from those rumored places where many stars cluster together. That must be it, although he has been unable to see such places, whose repute has come to him from the clever Arabs. He constantly entertains a mapmaker's view of this region, delighting in the fact that he has caused everything in sight, revamping and excavating the sand, furnishing entire generations with a permanent resting-place; one day perhaps this will all be dug up by pensive Germans and astute Britishers, or by Osiris himself in an agricultural frenzy. Cheops as Erodo used to see him—the mythical man alongside the real one—enjoys the sense that he has "given rise" to all these souls, fitting them into a shell century after century. He has carefully imposed himself upon history, as if no other pharaoh existed and all the workpeople were his own, lying still and used up in this graveyard adjoining all the other countries the fabled Erodo has visited.

That such a pre- and post-potent king should have descendants at all awes him, as if he did not have enough—two and a half thousand years B.C. times—oh, how many families and tribes, long thousands upon long thousands? Thinking this way, he decides he may even have caused a shift in human history—made massive inroads upon the private lives of all those devout masons and lifters, committed to him only, and his omnipotent take on the starry afterlife.

Erodo, certain he has caught the monarch in the depths of some huge dark dream, says something withering intended to cut him down to size; but Cheops is aswill in his own grandeur now, his imagination full of the countless spare busts of himself (heads mainly) strewn hither and yon over the burial fields and in the graves of the hoi polloi, and in the noblest tombs of all, just to remind the dead of who he was, and now by certain magic *will be* again. How many copper copies of eating implements do those graves, these tombs contain? He cannot bear to think how many, nor of the lost livers, hearts, kidneys, private parts, bowels, lips and brains, all of which—at least in his colossal fantasy—merge into one vast slop of fermentation, a manure heap, in which the ultimate anonymity of loss serves a dynamic overlord. He does not think these thoughts fully, but they hover against his brain as if someone of gentle sentiment has edged close and keeps nudging him to be less arrogant, less blatantly divine.

Does it matter, then, who the pharaoh has been, or is now? Are they not all as bad as one another, consecrated to magnificent adornment and vaulting egos, manufacturing for tourists of the future a landscape that, though tattered, still reeks of their ancient, incessant majesty? Their esthetics was one of death, that is all, and their obsession was with things. This, Erodo already knows, having kept his eyes open en route, determined to acquire as much gossip as he can, yet knowing no deluge of it will ever exceed the colossal masonry of the vacant desert. This is why he teases the uprooted, reborn Cheops, who thinks himself a star.

13 ▲
OSIRIS

This, then, dear reader, is a study in swank, but of that notion raised to unthinkable heights, entailing no doubt the glad extinction of millions, but, more importantly, the gigantic self-promotion of the human brain—as if to prove that, if only you push your obsession hard enough, you will have your way. Brain will turn into star. Now, this is not a matter of intense wishing, such as we find in the intenser Romantic poets and the most harebrained dictators; but rather of reckless escalation, with all thought of the human slipping out of sight, replaced by an athleticism of sheer will. Imagination lags behind in all this; a nice toy for sophisticated imaginers, but only (for these monsters of self-boosting) a preliminary shift, never turning chalk into cheese, or gray matter into churning star. Who is to know what Cheops made of himself; but doing so required him to exclude from his thinking all thoughts of failure. He was a monomaniac of prowess, stripped of all paternal or filial thoughts, all concern with charity or benign kingship. That much is clear, and it may be exactly thus that someone, in another sphere, becomes the best orator or samurai. There is nothing else in life, and this is how, and why; an outlandish idea can home in on itself until something magical happens, and the human yearning to be Osiris makes it possible to become Osiris the star.

Time and again his daughter resorts to the fond little circlet of girl swimmers that adorns her bedroom wall, the girls appearing to swim right into her bedchamber, urged forward by solid water, neutrally advanced, so to speak, as if they know who is at the other end of their motion. What Heduanna does not glimpse is that these girls, this scene, may well have come from one of the shafts in her father's pyramid, somehow copied and let out into the world again to receive in full dignity the serious members of the conference she is going to attend. So it is a lyrical, morbid scene, there to accompany someone into another world: scanty, perhaps, candid, and irresponsible, their complexions blotchy or blowsy. Perhaps it is a monument to bad Egyptian taste, like a dare to deathmongers, a quiet voice making itself heard amid the churnings of the second-rate, yet appallingly moving, a glimpse of all that can and cannot be. A bunch of young female scribes coming in for prey? Something like that, but she cannot recall her father's having brought it into the house and installed it. Could these erudite young women be swimming backwards then, through some divine contortion of limbs? No, they have forward-coming, or merely forward, faces whereas the etching might be stronger, although taboo, if it surveyed a group of pink young bottoms mooning away. The impersonality of that concept, wafted toward whoever might be looking, afloat on hypnotically overflowing water too, would improve the art and enrich the cult of death. She cares not, having spent hours peering into what if anything rests behind the girls depicted. It is as far as she goes in quest of surrender, willing to abandon logic for rapture, but only so far, and wishing her father had left it where it was, uncopied, aimed outward from the planet toward some paradise of unruined girls.

Finally in Abydos. Obliged to be present in good time, but persuaded to wait in a small anteroom crammed with papyrus and pens; she hears an eventual commotion, the brisk, bustling sound of bigwigs in motion, being bowed to, stroked, and ushered in. She glimpses the fuss of ancient protocol through a crack in the door and inhales a big waft of male aroma (the day is inhumanly warm), from pomade to something that smells like seawater or early-morning flatulence. She sees the exaggerated bravado of those exalted enough to be summoned but not high enough to have developed a free way with their rivals. This is the world of men, she instructs herself: not to be trifled with, no matter how clever you are. Her role, as the only woman there, is to appear at the last moment; to be hastily introduced so they can get down to business on time, which means, she concludes, no time allowed for courteous presentations. It is as if she has to appear, pretending to be the hostess with compliments and drinks, then suddenly change into superscribe, leaving them in the lurch, except of course they will have been in on the "surprise" from the first. She will be seated and that will be that, unless she makes her own pauses and deflects attention to herself, as is her presumed right as a woman.

Yed Chirh will arrive last with his usual banter and impatient bray; he's a man who has almost no time for anything, who had subordinated all to some as yet undivulged purpose. As the preludium advances toward his appointed time, she inhales the gathering fug, certain it echoes another from somewhere she dare not think about, not male, not an offshoot from the barber's shop. Finally there comes the shuffle of important feet, the suck and slam of a door. In walks the one in whose honor this meeting is held. He must be in a withdrawn mood, she notes, a man with so much to think about that his mind has buckled. Since the papyrus she holds has thumb marks from being held so hard, she wipes its surface with saliva and prepares to start again, not so much nervous as eager. They may be going to talk, but she has to write, of schedules, timetables, roundups and (as they love to recite) selections, exemptions, and exceptions. "You will be mainly concerned with numbers," she has been told. "Get it all correct and you will be the heroine."

His bow is minimal, not quite low enough to befit a princess; but he gives her the once-over, allowing himself, even as he busies someone with his trappings, a kind of bemused approval, aiming into the middle distance a private bouquet to himself announcing that he might, he just might. Nose too big, she decides, and I know what they say about that. Eyes of the unsnubbable know-it-all, his manner nervously imperious as if he has no patience even with his own fame. It is notoriety anyway. Clearly a man of infinite memory, mechanical bravura. She is glad to sit down, for a brief truant moment a young matron who has swum her way toward them through a brimming pool, and who therefore need not be diffident about anything. Now she is one of them, shunted to the side of course, which also this morning happens to be the center of attraction.

Everyone begins to mutter at once, but this is merely nervousness making its hangdog way into the meeting. Now rises above the noise the impatient, exasperated whine of Al Hasid, the censor of home affairs. They all cease. A crow has died above them. The numbers begin, recited without more ado, as if a grocery order long postponed at last claimed the field. She is so amazed by the banality of it all that she fails to get it all down. They forgive her, the princess, then she gets it right, and they go on. The dialogue starts: mainly functionaries from remote areas who have a grievance or some crass tale of disobedience to spell out. He is not interested, much, but he lets them blunder about, guffawing at him and yet doing the seated equivalent of an obsequious flounce. All these men are jockeying for position, for some reward, looking for extra duty, and boastful as schoolboys. They need to impress him, and to make him wonder how, stuck out there in some godforsaken desert town, they can have lived their lives without him. "If only you'd come and see us, sir." They have come home to roost, their nails newly trimmed, their faces shaved against the grain for an early morning gleam. She wonders how it can be so obvious, these men whose main duty so far has been to seize and kill. She soon identifies the limp-mannered junior who keeps volunteering and seems, to them at least, a dab hand with numbers, at one point leaning over her and offering to correct her. It is all beneath her pen, yet above her: boys' play, a puzzle of conformity and greed, a straight route to new medal ribbons and congested-sounding titles, far from whatever mattered in the world of Heduanna.

After a short while, Yed Chirh allows his gaze to settle on her again, full length, from headcloth to heels, conceding, allowing, that she might just pass muster. What is that pawnbroking look? It says he just might take an interest; and he offers her a secret, barely visible smile of complicity. Now she knows that he knows all about her, from her wide feet to her calloused heels, and can take it in his stride. Abydos meets Thebes, over the equations and formulas that manhandle the intricate details of so many other lives. Something slight appears to go on between them, a scintilla of a glimmer of an overture? No, rather a code unspoken, blinked in an arched brow, the little finger allowed to dangle over a newly inscribed word. She can feel it beginning in her bones, although she knows nothing will happen at table, not among the uniformed retainers, from vizier to constable, but "off," as stage managers say; when he is standing up and the problems of the day have been fixed to his satisfaction and he can, however briefly, relax like a human being. He has that pending look, with some kind of proposal in reserve, and it slowly swells during the bureaucratic palaver as the room heats up.

Then he seems to have won his way with them, certainly with the hothead clique, one of them a commanding figure for a man so negligible in physique.

"You know Abydos?" She was still wondering about the hotheads and the shrimpy look of one among them, but this is rigor unbending, almost debonair in an icy way.

She says not, not really, but she has heard the old capital is romantic and fabled.

"It will be better," he answers. "We are thinning things out everywhere. Some of us."

"I wouldn't doubt it," she says automatically, wondering if he will be able to sustain this conversation for longer than a few moments.

"How about Memphis?"

"I know it too well," she says. "My friends, who know it better, praise it all the time, but it could also do with a little trim here and there. *You* know."

A taut silence follows.

"And everywhere else?" She is being deferential, inquisitive.

"Ah," he laughs, "we're at work all over Egypt, with a new plan of course. Such is zeal." His face is a crag against disappointment, and she asks herself what on earth happened to him once upon a time.

"You should come here more often," he says. "We need good help."

She flirts a bit. "You never know. Do you think I could be spared?"

"Say the word," he tells her. "and the right one will be in someone's ear. We will citify you all over again."

"And I'm here all alone."

"Invite your father if you wish. We are eager to convert everyone to our sweeping ways."

"Well, sir."

Back he moves, to business, his cohorts, having clinched things. Has he really, she wonders, said something definite? Am I that easy, *a royal daughter*? *That* eager?

"After such a high point as this," she daringly whispers to his back.

Without moving, he answers her under his breath: "But *this* is every day, dear lady. This is high politics! It has nothing to do with the palace and the summer house. We are going to stir things up, are we not? Can't you tell whom we are going to throw out and whom we will lock away for ever?"

His cronies begin to agree with him, slackly, obviously, puffing their assent past him to her. She finds herself in a claque intended for disgruntled leaders, maybe even higher. She wonders how it would be to become increasingly familiar with men who need nothing any more, but to be witnessed. It cannot be easy, she decides. One day she would become just another of those witnesses, followed at best by abrupt restoration to her father's court—at worst, the huge mahogany door that clicks open under the hand of the headsman within, the one with the crumpled smile, telling her it's time to take the plunge, in private, milady. Just you come through the door, thank you, and we'll do the rest. It'll be all right, honest. We'll do it, four hands lifting you up as if you are flying. Quick, like.

She shudders. Worse things could happen, but this would be enough. Does she really want to mingle with such men, as distinct from writing down their most secret thoughts? Surely this kind of meeting he proposes—the clandestine within the surreptitious—is exceptional, and not the kind of social life she's meant to have in Abydos. It should all be less heinous. Deep water, she murmurs. Watch out, Heduanna, you have been sent here to broaden a mind already misbehaved.

Not a man given to musing, Chirh is wondering which of these bumptious buffoons told him that in the last war military tactics had exploited knowledge of the "trapdoor spider," with its deadly web. Ridiculous, he thinks. They take me for a military fool, and anyway I have juicier fish to fry. (I abandoned my career as a cocksman on the Nile.) Correctly siting his lips the correct distance from Princess Heduanna's upraised hand, he has noticed in her face something tantalizing: what he calls a Carpathian flatness, especially beneath the eyes, which denotes lack of ebullience, something he prizes in women: something more than obedient, even if not at first visible. She washes her hair, he tells himself. All of it. Then she feels young again. One of *those,* not exactly in the first flush of it, yet not quite peeling. Some rouge in that pasty complexion. Now, is that Hittite, gipsy, or Semitic? It's certainly not gipsy. She might be persuaded to come to heel, before the mellow drift into indifference. I have heard that the father is aloof, self-absorbed, much more concerned with the dead than with the living, and with the line of succession, keeping the Libyan line at bay. Would he even notice? No one is going to think twice when I import another scribe from the capital. Why, if I imported a troupe of loin-rich dancing girls from Arabia or Athens, I'd get away with it, provided I allowed certain of my colleagues sucking rights. It remains entirely up to me, whether my manners are curt, abrasive, riotous, sleek, or those of an overpromoted peasant.

Heduanna is far from being a climber. She starts from the top, anyway, so there is only down to come. Wrong sex, she thinks, for everything. With her penchant for misbehavior, would she be willing to pour all her energy and will into an affair, just to be among those selected from the forecourt of erotomania? Would they say, oh Chirh has fallen for a princess, but really no more than a simple scribe? Whores his way through every conference and takes the refuse home to savor? Treats every gathering as if it were an assignation in a desert tent. Don't you know, he has a trick most high-ranking men might envy, amalgamating all that his life lacks, and then shoving his life into the mess, like a lightning bolt making sulfur. This is to say, he rams his all into what he has not, setting the world ablaze. In some, this might be called commonsense ambition, but in him it's hellfire, trying to make the rump of the world obey his unappeased lusts. Can't you see this in that lean wooden bobbin of a face, that introvert's outward peer—with the eyes so weak, their energy seems to have been left back in the knees, and the oiled uncurly hairdo, parody of a swimmer's? His lips beg for rouge, his ears for the further hand of the waxworker. He is the idol as ogre, the debonair death's-head.

She spends much of the morning in a dutiful trance, at first impressed by the huge bridgework erected over the entrance, anonymous address of the state security office; then by the stodgy, heavyweight arrivals, hearty men barking with laughter. "No blabbermouths here," she hears on top of some crack about ghettoes bursting at the seams. There is an oaf from far upriver, with a badly behaved mongrel dog called Geb. Other names register more faintly. One fellow is neat and dapper, suaver, more to her taste, she thinks. Are they, any of them, she wonders, aware of her spotless linen, her indecisive gestures, her face that trembles between smile and smirk? She has never dreamed there could be such a thing as the stark white security suit with its golden buttons, but several aides are wearing it—with a gleaming dagger stuck in the belt and a black silk cravat knotted tiny. Is there really, in so innocent a civilization, any need for a secret police? They remind her, these conferees, of erotic cartoons she and her brothers shared and giggled over, depicting various sexual positions; but, because they were on fragments of pot, the blissful faces of the participants had twisted into a savage rictus, a ravenous leer gone sour, so that the presumably pleasurable congress became something of an ordeal. One hand yanks the woman's pigtail. Another grasps her wig. A prolonged phallus, too long to enter, wastes its sweetness on the desert air. Is this what life in Abydos would be like? Organs as long as arms? Phew.

The committee or synod gets on with its work, while Geb the unruly dog romps outside. Gnats, which Erodo complained about, have invaded the chamber and evade all attempts to swat them. She tries to concentrate on numbers, times, other cities, departures and arrivals. These, the real phenomena of plotting, she swiftly transcribes, wondering if someone else of higher rank than she (higher even than a princess?) will translate them into ciphers. There is incredulous guffawing talk about corpses burned to a crisp, hilarity as a voluptuous young girl enters and delivers a set of tablets Yed Chirh has asked for. Gasps of astonishment follow her out. Her face was painted bright red. Now Geb the dog is throwing up. Asphyxiation, someone drawls, and it is unclear if he is talking about the dog or some victim to be. "It is dishonorable." someone pronounces, "not to carry out what our future demands." "Just as long as we leave a few of them for manicure training," someone obscurely drawls. They guffaw anyway, in a mood more primitive than the one they arrived in. Deftly, she gets most of it down, amazed at the transition from fact to rumor to abstract notes, as if none of what they are planning ever existed.

"Shall we move down then?" No one budges because Chirh has not given the signal. Slumping sideways, the oaf seems asleep, heedless of his dog. "Virtue," she hears, then "hot and cold," attributed to no one she has heard of, followed by "Don't deport them whatever else you do." "Come work with me," the trim leader is saying to her, and no doubt has been for some time under the cacophony of talk. She demurs with a bashful pout and works extra hard at her pen. Now they flirt a little, as she strives to get down certain numbers that he charitably repeats for her. "Banter," he tells her, "it's all banter, really, but we do get some urgent things done from time to time. We are louts, I admit it." He sips his beer, wafts its bouquet toward her, proffering, enticing. "You're pleasing to the eye, *and* you're a princess." Help herself she cannot, every inch a scribe. Those stone statues outside once belonged to someone superbly royal, now dispossessed or dead; but what can she do about that? She has to live in the present and seize her chances. It is the same with those who go wandering by the river and get taken by crocodiles or drowned. Their bodies are handled by the priests, placed in a sacred coffin, and regarded as more than human by the people of the place where the death occurred. I am here with crocodiles, she decides, and if they carry me off, I will be dealt with gently by those who find me afterward. It is not all bad, is it?

The noise of a small informal buffet confuses her even more. "A historic day, and we were here." She hears them almost break into song. "Don't let go yet," Chirh tells them, "we have a lot of work before us." Sneezes. Swigging sounds. Eructation at the sound of which no one flinches. Who concocted this party? Someone already deep in his cups asserts, "A vagina defiled by foreign sperm will always be a cesspool. And no Egyptian broom can keep it clean." She is horrified. Is this even brothel talk? A high bird-like voice says, "Consider the matter closed." A deeper one retorts, "And close that bloody vagina too." Roars of assent. Chirh is watching them, not critical but aloof as stone, as an ambitious Egyptian should be. He is waiting for them to finish, to acknowledge his silent glare, and get back to business.

Now three of them are sitting on the rug in riotous good humor, singing and toasting: the ringleaders, she assumes. They stagger up and climb onto the ornate chairs and toast again—to some Movement she knows not of—and thence ascend the table, traipsing around and around. It is as if they have relieved themselves of some appalling burden, fulfilled a promise long shirked. Heduanna knows that something dreadful had been channeled through her hands, ready to be passed by word of mouth to all and sundry. How on earth, her brain asks later, could she associate with such duffers, such thugs? What was her father thinking of? Yet it is as if she hadn't attended the black ritual she witnessed, couched as it was in roundabout, vague terms; was it not a civil ceremony gone rancid, or warriors with their visors down? She feels she has missed something deadly. To be sure, she is flattered by Chirh's attentions, but, she reasons, a compliment from him under any circumstances must be like a spritz of birdlime from an overflying mob of ducks. She shudders with a delicious tremor of having survived, the flame having singed her box of sweetmeats.

The bright part is that, having been exposed to their gaze and sanctified, she now has enough standing to go on to something else—not *with* Chirh of course, but in some remote hinterland of his domain, buried once more but in an elaborate winding-cloth. I have been tampered with, she whispers between chews, but I have survived. I have come through with colors flying, just like a worthy matron flowing clear and three-dimensional through the liquid barrier. I had to do it only once, thank God, and now I am free to move on. I have been seen.

This is all very well, a luscious pipe dream, but she has not reckoned with the loutish bravado blatantly on show in that fuggy conference chamber. Odd, she recollects, how, in spite of their elevated ranks, they all greeted one another in the usual way by tapping their fingers against their kneecaps on entering. So what had that chamber been beside a testing ground for greenhorn scribes? A place where the sadistic sport of bluff commanders took on an aspect of wedding confectionery while Chirh rapped his pointer at a series of charts (numbers and phrases mainly). She looks the other way; they look away from her and then look back: she is the only woman in the room and, although similar in function to the tight-mouthed waiters in their shark-white tunics trimmed with gold, their collars flashing with ponderous symbolism—she is more connected through her flying pen with the sordid gravamen of the talk. They just float in and out with trays and asbestos napkins while she gets it all down for later scrutiny: a scheme for rebellion, innocent as an alchemy experiment done by a famous wizard, or the long-awaited result of some vexed excursion into the calculus, worked out in detail with curves and sweats rather than cheated into being out of the answers in the back of the text.

All that happens now remains in her sobered mind, except that its culmination happened in the real world with soldiery, bandits, and knives. Oh, she credits herself, I have come close to the foul midden of some ferocious beast of the desert. She knows she has not gone with him to wherever, the next stop; to his headquarters or his villa; has not embarked back down the Nile with her major kitbag, and minor purse, which contains her potion for seasickness (or river-vapors) just in case. Of course not. But what is she doing, then, idly scooping gossip, and noting postures from a glossy conversation she's overheard? Because she has not gone along, metaphorically or in actual fact, she feels free to flirt with a scenario, taking all precautions, then awaiting whatever riverboat will collect and deliver her to where he is (he does not travel with his doxies, but rather *sends* for them, reeling them in to his presence). In a daze she hears fingers snap, heels shuffle, and someone escorts her to whoever escorts her next. Her memories are of a pillow, a blanket, for what seemed like a hundred years. She journeys forward, while her muscles drag her back. Oh, never to arrive at where is it? She wants the trip, the voyage, the pilgrimage out to last a *thousand* years, just in case, after all her misgivings, hesitations, demurrals, and refusals, she is making the most colossal mistake of her life. There are so many words for saying no. Yet she is doing it for the sake of excitement, danger, thrill, never mind her temporizing and stalling. She is bound to get there, utterly handed over to others, who will get her there for consumption, no matter what. Now she sees where all that scribing has taken her. Just for the sake of novelty, she wishes she were moving through a landscape of snow, smeared, crammed with it, which she has never seen; or even, better, the artificial landscape of a child's model farm so small that its tininess ties her down and keeps her from going far at all. Where is she going? For now, under stress, she cannot remember, but knows it is new to her; her father has not exactly toured her around, at first keeping her close to her brother, then at length keeping her from himself. She floats onward to a destiny in which the imagined has greater force than the real. She feels rendered up to the devil, hapless in his deep-sea grip. There is A and there is B, she says. I have only to allow B into A in some token way, some vestigial form of it, and I will begin to grow, to be twice the woman I am. I will only go so far, doing nothing disgraceful, daintily floating on the fringes of what men love to do: no more than that. I will be the princess charming on the outskirts. But she knows she has already wandered into the killing maze, where hunters abound and the gentlest orphans are defenseless.

Where she ends up, though, after horse and camel, is a place of blinding light, a street corner with a few splendid villas at odd angles set back from the track. Wait here, they tell her before galloping off. No one waits with her and, for a moment, she feels like a stranded prostitute, though she knows nothing of the trade and soon dismisses the thought as a romantic abstraction. She cannot believe she has been dumped thus, foodless, helpless, perhaps in Arabia. Shakily, for something to do, she stacks her bags on the sand, her purse and three douches in oilskin on top, presuming she has to be ready to move at a moment's notice; she has already become initiated to the urgency of the whole foray. They have instructed her in this. *Be quick*. It must be morning. She has been traveling by night. A few passersby swathed in white linen look her up and down and pass out of view. (What happened to her empty bed? Has she been buried in sand, in a coffin? She had always thought such terminal tasks her father's work.) Two men seem to be loitering, sheaf of flowers in hand. To greet whom?, she wonders. They do not exactly look like any beaux, or professional greeters. Perhaps they are mourners, then, Greek like Erodo, a bit lost and quite without colloquial Egyptian. As the sun moves, she moves backwards into its easeful shadow, fidgeting in the shade like a schoolgirl after a long day's penmanship.

She calms herself only when riders appear at the far end of the rather palatial street, at least until the mirage swallows them up and makes their figures roil and swerve. Deliverance is at hand, she concludes, with a bath and clean sheets, a bed low where the feet repose. One of the riders may be her dapper, austere man of war, but she still cannot be sure, even as the two loiterers move out into the road and stab the horses, which throw their riders, who in turn are stabbed repeatedly for several minutes. The radiant flowers have been thrown aside, bloodless. One man races away east, the other scurries into a garden and vanishes. The only person frozen is Heduanna, whose life has spun upside down and not yet righted itself. The silence followed by screams has made her balk, then shrivel, in a heap on the ground. An idyllic reunion has gone by the board, but, also, she may have been saved. Her *kat* is pure. She is no *tahut*.

She makes no attempt to run to the bloody mess in the middle of the roadway, but remains pinioned on a thought: Had I left with the others to sail downriver, I would have missed all this. I was at a weak moment, after the scurry and hurly-burly of the conference, and being uninvited to join the remaining few for a drink or a laugh, I was casting around for something of equal excitement—a reason not to go home. That was all. Chirh must be dead, his blood all over the road, and therefore hated. He was plotting, planning, something abominable, but I cheerfully wrote things down for him. So what is wrong with me? Am I too desirable, so much so that I no longer know how to resist anyone? I should be banned to the desert with one fire and a torn tent to end my days in. I am not fit to go home to brother or father.

Against her better will, she steps toward the heap on the ground, then halts. People are coming, in slow-motion from the houses, weapons in hand, all men. She steps back, realizing she may have been a witness, but she pretends to be utterly uninvolved. She could have been looking the other way. With tears in her eyes, trying to decide where to go next, she plays the role of uneducated ignoramus—rather cleverly in fact, weeping at the outrage, the blood, the screaming, but gesturing at her bags and waving toward the empty roadway.

Even as she is urged away by dispassionate witnesses, Heduanna thinks only of adjectives: ungreeted, unwanted, uncollected, uninjured, knowing that all such things are dreams and she will awaken with a book beside her as she untangles herself from sleep, Chirh still snoring. But which dream can it be? Was there a bed near this street corner in Thebes? Did assassins actually enter the bedroom? Or is the entire event hospital-induced? If only she could enter the "next-door dream," in which Chirh survives, still whispering to his bizarre, stunted deputy oddly named Syrup; he, who kept his mocking, jaundiced eye upon her thourghout the clandestine meeting in Abydos, home of Osiris, king of the underworld, the West and the East.

Much of her life has gone up in smoke, but only if she takes the assassination seriously. It is a situation from which she can withdraw without taint, or so she thinks, and just begin again, making her way back down the Nile after a thorough secretarial sojourn. She little suspects her father in his bemused way has had a hand in this killing. Everything he does he defends against someone, denying the people the use of temples and press-ganging them to set up enormous pyramids. This fowler or hunter downs all rivals without for a moment taking his mind off what interests him most: his so-called solar boat, an inaccurate term for his "Orion boat," but vivid in its local way. Is he sure the Sun isn't a star of some kind?

Now she is hoping not to be demoted to the ridiculous technical disinfection service. Her father, in his oblivious way, takes care of business, but devotes much of his mental activity to purges, to onions fed to the pyramid laborers, to boats made from acacia wood, sarcophaguses made from red granite, underground niches created in a traditional four-cavity burial chamber; to stucco wigs and gilded uraei, and sandstone ceilings that collapse. It is strange, she thinks, how much of the stuff that fills the world should come to occupy him more than people's lives. She would not put it past him to cover his tracks by having the two assassins beheaded and the severed heads sent home to mother, except that this would only expose tracks of some kind. Tongues and eyeballs removed of course. She has no idea what he might have in store for her, but she trembles at the very thought and realizes that, without someone like Chirh to guide her away, she has no means of escaping, say, into Greece or Arabia. Erodo, she thinks, is too much of a hanger-on to be of use, and, in any event, he would arrange something only to make flagrant capital out of it in his chatty, companionable prose. What is it she dreads most? Not his defective eyes gleaming with something approaching pain, but the contraction of his almost Chinese face into a mask as he gives his Buddha-like nod of approval, and the tiny glazed eyes light up with a sparkle stolen from the basilisk Erodo speaks about. She knows that, already, somehow, enough has happened to her to last her for life, yet with so many years ahead to be soldiered through. How many catastrophes will she need? All she has to do is scribe on with her mind completely shut off. Something gross has rubbed its pelt against her sleek thigh and will no doubt go on doing the same until the Nile dries up.

Very well, then, she will settle back quietly into penmanship, never aiming too high; knowing that the ever-present Erodo is yet another spy bound to bleat the truth sooner or later, in some contorted form, but plain enough for her father to act upon. She sees heads floating in fish ponds, heads of mothers and sons. Was there ever a Chirh's wife? Is she too already finished off? Heduanna of late has found herself able to suck from the recesses of her soft palate a small leathern tongue-like thing that has lain there covering the uvula for weeks, obtruding and infecting, prelude perhaps to diphtheria. It is no more than a flap or flaplet, but just possibly the first step towards suffocation, for those doomed to eternal life. This flap or disc would surely be enough to produce, if ever she tried to speak and tell the truth of her journey to see Chirh, the authentic sounds of quinsy: strangulation from within—as if some dreadful gibbering, arcane scream were to soar forth from one of the canopic jars containing the removed innards of someone mummified. She moves on. In the bizarre world of Egyptian balances, there is the famous one—dead heart in one pan, the apocalyptic feather in the other—against the commonplace one from the poulterer's yard, when a live chicken stands in one pan against dead weights in the other, and all is settled that way. With mummifying priests wearing jackal masks at their labors, you never quite know whom you are dealing with, she thinks; always a mask behind the mask, always, even in an anthropoid coffin, a painted stucco mask over the withered mask of the occupant.

When she gets back, the worse for wear and in a constant state of tears, she has a conversation with her aloof father, who consoles her about the tedious life of the scribe, quite overlooking the Chirh affair; he then explains the absence of Ka-wab as diplomatic. The senior prince next in line is attempting his first mission to another court, just for practice's sake. Indeed, this was true: Ka-wab should have been sent on this kind of mission before, but perhaps his being more than a little portly had interfered (indeed, he had promised to lose weight before leaving); or had his attempted liaison with Heduanna kept him back? Well-rounded men, by the way, unless of unusually vigorous intellect, striking looks, or wealth, do not always find themselves prepossessing in the eyes of younger women, and Ka-wab was not in the first flush of youth, having too much lazed by the river, consumed too many sweet drinks, eaten well at his father's table.

His father had no evil intentions on the crown prince, although those who came after him could have done just as well. It would not have been hard for this thirty-year-old to be beguiled into bad company of anonymous variety. Nor would it have been difficult for those who wanted to block the line of descent from an auburn, strawberry, or red-haired Libyan mother to get Ka-wab drinking a bit more than usual; marooned in a strange court, he would be lost, prey to any seemingly charitable well-wisher. At any rate, he did not return, and no news of him was had. Was he afloat in the river somewhere or, unmummified, buried in a pauper's grave out beneath billions of grains of sand? His father grieved, and so did Heduanna, she lamenting opportunity lost, high rank wasted.

"Is he far away?" she asked, her bottom lip trembling against her will.

No, he told her. It was something to do with the semiannual cattle count. When he returned, he would have had valuable experience in discussing routine affairs, with which he did not usually concern himself. "A little like me."

She winced at this, as ever finding it incongruous that, apart from the main household, he kept several mistresses, in whom he took a decreasing interest, so much so that he had even spoken of letting them go free. This was a thought for which Merytyetes despised him. It indicated his gradual weakening, he who had forced the people to haul stones from quarries in the Arabian mountains, then ferry them across the Nile. Gangs of some hundred thousand at a time. His daughter could never work out whether or not he was a hard, exacting man or someone committed to the finer, more ethereal things.

It was he who had come up with the idea that his people should build a road along which the stones would be dragged. This work occupied ten years. After three months, a gang needed rest, so he had his overseers stagger timetables so that the work never ceased. Perhaps Ka-wab had had his tongue cut out before being assigned to one of the work gangs, where he would spend the rest of his days, all his protestations ignored, as befitted workmen who had little time for even their own lives.

"You briefed him, then?"

"Oh yes, not that I needed to. He briefed himself before going; I just added a few touches."

With whom, she asked: and was given a long recital of viziers (three grades of them), master masons, and gang leaders, none of whom she knew because her father kept his administrative chores separate from household routine.

He invites her to take wine with him, quizzes her about the meetings, never mentioning Chirh or his death, but cajoling her, soothing her out of her swivet; he murmurs names she might have registered and expresses amazement she has not. Thus do many Tohfas, Shafias, Aimans, Mohammeds, Nasrys, Azzas, and Moustafas go down the drain. He begins to believe she never went to Abydos at all and questions her closely, now bringing up the name of Chirh, the meetings' president. She pretends to go blank again and speaks in generalities: a severe, learned man with a fierce gaze, a little impatient with his underlings, someone not to jest with unless you wanted to risk being dismissed. It all sounds normal, the kind of blarney she has used many times to shield her crushes from him and his basilisk gaze.

"A womanizer?"

"Not so's you notice. No."

"No sign of slack behavior?"

"Too busy, father, to get into that kind of thing."

"I should promote him then."

"To what?"

"A Vizier in the making."

"Do as you please."

"We cannot afford to waste good men. How would you like to invite him to court for some good news?"

All she does is shrug. Her father's games weary her, especially when he starts squinting the one eye to save the other from light or half-light. Then he starts rubbing them, dabbing them with a water-soaked silken scarf. The local doctors are no more than mountebanks and have not helped him in the least. She wonders if Erodo has provided some relief with ideas from another culture. She feels balked, with two men missing and her part in their lives reduced to naught. She is back, but to what, to whom? With Merytyetes relegated to the role of dead cipher, not even planning meals or outings, she has resolved never to become a copy of her—whose role hovers somewhere between poised passivity and a haughty growl, little ever said, as if she has come out of a cloud. Merytyetes, who has been the wife also of Cheops's father Sneferu, and was destined to go on being a reverend lady of the court, long after father and son were dead. As the wife of the heir apparent (Cheops), she had already enjoyed considerable réclame, and had the demeanor, the wit, and persistence to make her way through the intrigues of court, giving herself all through the title of *wrt hts*. Certainly she thrived better than the one known locally as "the unknown queen," suspected of having lived, but certainly dead and buried, lost like a playing card in the recesses of Giza I-b, as it would be known. Perhaps at some point she was deprived of her queenly title.

Heduanna marvels at the way she herself has negotiated the maze of court intrigues; but she attributes her success to her somewhat naive suspicion that she is of only average intelligence, a nice girl no one would want to kill, friend to Kha-merer-nebty, daughter of the disgraced vizier Kanofer (drowned rats sinking together). The only person she feels close to in this retinue of the ambitious, the corrupted, the rejected, is Hemiunu, another shrewder vizier who, like all viziers, bears the title "Overseer of the King's Works." He is main architect of the Great Pyramid, "The Sun's Boat," a man of imperious, sage face and mordant impetus, an unlikely friend for Heduanna; but of no side, without snobbery, as good to animals as to daughters, and fond of the word lapidary.

TWO

Underworld

14 ▲
ERODO

Stuck in his preferred kennel, Erodo—no part of the court's comings and goings—revels in compiling lurid fiction about the king, magically introduced across time, to the blaze of his gift. Marveling at the papyruses and bits of broken pottery that reveal over-long erect penises, all with retracted foreskin, Erodo makes a mental note to ask about circumcision, wondering if lubricant has merely done its work well, or if the foreskin has been amputated. Why are they always erect for business? He wonders, having a Greek chuckle at this unnecessary question. He knows, having already made his way into (and out of) Cheops's harem, which he has come to, magic-carpeted through time (or so he thinks, certain now that his auspices are magical). His destiny anyway is to write more fiction. And so, having heard about a missing prince (confusing Chirh here with Ka-wab, of course), he devises for Cheops—this master of the difficult—a scene in which the young prince's foreskin, still attached, is tugged, stretched, then lubricated, until it begins to fan out like a thin cap, and so on, until it measures the same size as the prince's head, over which it is carefully adjusted to suffocate him, with the end tied, indeed sewn up, and that is how Chir-wab as he calls him is borne into the bowels of the pyramid, with a sheeny growth starting at his loins reaching as far as his head and enveloping it.

Or they had holy women stretch it, roll on it, rubbing their saliva into it, until it had thinned out and become almost transparent, enabling watchers to see one another, and, eventually, if they waited long enough, his very head sheathed in it, rigged hard at the neck with a cord. This was not to kill him of course, though many young princes had gone that way, judged superfluous and expendable.

I am told many stories, he lazily thinks, about the "deciduous" quality of the Egyptian aristocracy, which enabled them to be self-judging in the sense that, looking at one another, they could tell which person needed to be written off next and how. It was amazing to me how suddenly this took place, and had, ever since the first dynasty, with always enough survivors left to run the country. To be sure, there was a surplus of princes in this land, a state brought about by marriage and the production of children through other means such as the harem. And there were certain highborn ladies who, in order to climb even higher, took the name of some famous beauty, or harridan, which means that you find many names with II or III after them. Safety in numbers. Other highborn ladies, such as Merytyetes, the wife of my friend Cheops, kept themselves in the family picture by marrying again (she, after Sneferu's death marrying his son Cheops and then, after Cheops had died, getting herself appointed administrator of the harem). Clearly, it took a good deal of fortitude and imagination to keep one's head above water during these long dynasties, what with drowning, execution, and torture so prevalent; although by and large the palace populace withstood palpably well the ravages of murder. Only a nation so drawn to the afterlife, to its paraphernalia in the present, could prosper in so forceful and stoical a way, perhaps regarding survival as an almost artistic skill. I have often thought that only the lip service paid against incest prevented the Egyptian nobility from restricting itself to a single family, thus gradually thinning out, the line enfeebled until all that was left was a small congeries of babbling idiots, easily overcome by even minor armies from outside. There is something wily and potent in such fanciful titles as *Great One of the Five of the House of Thoth* or *Chancellor of Lower Egypt,* or *Queen of Upper and Lower Egypt,* which survive all mutations, the vacant titles continuing while the heads that bear them fall by the wayside. Famous, notorious ladies bore the line royal from one dynasty to another, more properly though, not bearers of territorial or social titles, but infatuates of the *kat*. Cheops's mother, for example, lived when the power of the royal house achieved an absolute of domination, perhaps never equaled again, with the society beneath them utterly organized for state purposes (pyramids, death, purges, onions, and garlic). I mean the working, laboring, slaving classes. I have heard the name for them: the *latefundia,* which I believe to be the class responsible for procreation and breast-feeding. After Cheops and a few more, things began to deteriorate, although a lasting memorial could be found in the Giza pyramids and the two Dahshur pyramids of Sneferu.

Many old priests speak of the death of Hetep-heres, mother of Cheops; and how he scrambled to a niche partway down the shaft of her tomb to deposit for her use in the next life an offering of food: a true vision of the ungainly, it is said, for was he that young and agile? The ironic thing about this entombment is that her grave was broken into not long after she died, in spite of rigorous guarding procedures and the general mastery of all affairs by Cheops, whose control of just about everything was total. Her alabaster sarcophagus was found empty, though much of the magnificent furniture otherwise provided her for housekeeping in the afterlife, remained untouched. Of course, even stricter supervision followed at the Dahshur cemetery, but the horse had gone. This lady, gifted with a great gold bed canopy, who had outlived her husband. The objects in the tomb had been sealed by the mortuary establishment of Cheops, her son.

Imagine, then, the rage and distress that ensued. Imagine the tact and reassurance required by Hemiunu the vizier, whose job it was to persuade the grief-stricken Cheops, mourning her in the next world, to shift her burial site, sans queen, from Dahshur to Giza—and then to carry out this adventurous plan. Having already witnessed the downfall of Kanofer, one of the other viziers, he conducted himself with exemplary politic sagacity throughout his task, one eye on the intemperate king, the other on the space once occupied by the missing queen. His own mastaba at Giza is huge, as no doubt befits one who has rendered perfect service. In his tomb lay, as one report stated, the bones of an old portly man whose massive skull indicated exceptional mental capacity. Viewing his two canopic jars, sealed, and some ox bones left as a food offering, my witness confessed to feeling an air of "undisturbed emptiness," perhaps the consummate peace and quiet so able a gentleman had longed for after long dealings with the irascible Cheops, who now is talking to me, in ostensible disregard of my supposed slanders in an earlier time. I notice the falter in his manner, the look of pique masked by a spurt of gentle good humor. This is a man to be watched, and parsed. See how he sets it up.

"In the first place," he says, "there is the overall feeling of being metallic, a special sense of metallurgical radiance that does not come from sucking fruit, my boy." I am not his boy, nor his ally. "A horse has taken a running jump and slithered up my back, my poor aching back, then settled, suddenly fleshless, its exposed rib cage taking the place of mine. I feel no flesh but just the rigidity. I know I am being groomed for something special, but then I am used to that, having schooled myself in abstruse otherworldliness for years. It is then that I feel the hardness of copper plates sitting where my shoulder blades should be, my own rib cage, my kneecaps. Where this hard stuff has come from, I have no idea, but I sense many parts of me denatured for some unknown special purpose. Possibly, a tiny *shaduf* has taken up residence in my thigh and can be seen from the outside, peered at by those who expect the worst. Parts have an icy carapace, others a sheath of intensified bone. I slow up. I breathe a monstrous cold steam. My feet seem encased in horn. Am I saying enough? I have been taken over by some force that reveres only flint and stone. This is not being human at all or even kingly. To kneel takes hours. To stand back up is onerous. To speak requires a devilish crescendo of slow-motion mutters. Whatever change is taking me over is none of my own devising, of course not; but I can tell it has something to do with the solar boat and my subsequent transition to the Belt—the Orion thing. Perhaps this is what it means to be case-hardened, to feel granite wings impeding; or to be a *wedjat* eye scrutinizing all earthly remnants; or the little clay horse of childhood transformed into a rock-steady steed a dozen times my normal size. Am I to go in water, towed by some hard-breathing gazelle, as of old? No, my destiny includes no such fripperies; but it does force into me entire artifacts of our civilization. I can feel them embossing my skin, my flesh, then ramming a way into my structure so as to be steady. What?"

I ask him if these intrusions into his being deform him and if there is pain. "Imprison that soft hand," I say, "and let him rave." He is not listening; a grave delight has begun to daunt him in the presence of mere humans.

"You don't get it, do you, you flirty old Greek, you stubborn old accuser; you don't know your lies from your truths, your fibs from those of others. Let me tell you the pain is sometimes indescribable, mostly in the joints and the liver, the heart, the lungs, as if I were cracking open to discharge something like molasses. You would never know, the creak and rage of it. This is Cheops yielding, but only in order to live among a different race of beings. See those cold-looking things up there? They are full of fire, and to live among them calls for what I call negative ability—a huge putting-up with suffering as if being scorched alive. *You* will never achieve it, only having to put up with some scalding commentary on one of your mendacities. The worst part is having to calm one's emotions, no longer mourning or yearning. I left food for my mother in her tomb, but I tried not to get upset when thieves broke in and stole her body, never found. I "reburied" her, with fastidious calm, in Giza. I dote on my grandson, my eldest, I am not sure how old, but am I downhearted? Yes, but it is not going to stunt my willpower or my zeal. The more appropriate I feel my mission, the less human, of course; my eye trouble is only the first of a spectrum of maladies I have to endure in order to exempt myself from the human race."

He raised his hand in a lax, fumbling gesture. His face looked blocked with fervor, as if he was listening to a distant summons only he could pick up. He was, as they say, gone out; but I caught a quick glimpse of him before I turned away to shield my eyes from his preposterous radiance. Pieces (excerpts) from the map of Egypt had replaced his skin, and bled profusely from the graft. His teeth had turned mahogany brown, with maggots curling animatedly between them. The eyes, about which he complained so much, looked fairly normal; which I found strange, assuming they would be the first to go in this grotesque transformation (though of course I could not see the seething blur within). No doubt about it, he was changing—not subtly as women change in middle age, but with a roar, as if voluptuously poisoned. My seeming friend of (by now) weeks was a self-willed giant, willing to adapt but not to cease complaining. He looked bigger, more uncouth, somebody's idea of a goofy baby boy, born a monster, growing up worse. But this, dear readers, was only how he looked. Within, he must have remained much the same old man, older than time itself, buzzed and man-hauled back to life; what I would call a pertinent monster of rectitude: he knew where he was going, he knew all the changes involved (as if crossing from the Sudan to Arabia), and he was willing to go. The thing that killed him was his having no control over the succession.

It had taken me almost a month, without going to any great lengths to fathom him, to realize that all he looked out on and savored were his pyramids, possibly his own pyramid alone. Something more massive than himself or his kind occupied him to the end, and it had to be so, or he would arrive like an emigrant and be turned away for lack of stature. This was why he commandeered people by the thousand, restricted their rations, closed their chapels (to keep them working), and generally broke their spirit with mindless heavy work. The only concession he was willing to make was their final resting-place in the shade of the pyramid, so as to ready them too, for an ultimate journey equipped with a few pots and pans. He was grandiosity personified, a porer over master plans that lay inert on the floor of his throne room, but in the maelstrom of his mind unfurled like sails, making of him not even a monarch, a king of kings, but a force that told the Nile how to behave. When a man thinks along those lines, he either goes mad or proves his point to the very end. Dictators I had seen, but never anybody so—how shall I put it?—brazenly grand, so afflicted with *dimension* that he could no longer think on the human scale. It was only a matter of seeing him through to the end, like the observer I was, and remaining in his good graces: something like wooing a dune.

15 ▲
PRINCESS HEDUANNA

Poisonous old toad, arriving here out of nowhere uninvited and unwanted, he wears me down. My father sees something in him, to be sure, maybe a visiting spirit from somewhere. This Greek, he goes nowhere without an interpreter, which makes him seem almost unnecessary. Quizzes me about my trip to Abydos. What was I really doing there? (He has heard something, so who told? My father?) Whenever he talks to you, he has his interpreter there, and that makes me feel sickeningly ill at ease. He believes that any royal court needs its interpreters. They give the place a certain worldly tone, or so he says. I think they give the place an air of bribery, a way into deceit, but who asks me? How come he knows why I went to Abydos and what I did there? Old lecher feigns to lay his hand on me, his tool stuffed up his backside like all the Greeks. I've heard about them. Maybe my father told him I was easy meat: Just grab a fistful and she'll be all over you, like foam. Well, my father has another think coming.

"Was it interesting, my dear?" He writes everything down.

"Oh it was more than that," I tell him, "it was memorable. I learned a lot. All kinds of people, some of them well-known."

"I should have come with you. If I'd only known—"

Startled, my response to this halts his speech as if I have actually said something. Maybe he reads minds.

"I don't think so," I tell him. "No Greeks."

"Ah," he sniffs, "a closed meeting."

"No," I tell him, "an Egyptian one."

That calms him but somehow saps his alertness. He is staring at me, appraising the meat, I suppose, but makes no further move. It is not that I think myself the most beautiful of princesses, but I do seem to attract a certain type: bumptious, clever, hypocritical. I can just see touring the mile-wide Nile with Erodo, listening to his incessant theories about the river and why it floods in summer, or why Egyptian women urinate standing up, or why foreign men spill black semen. *No breeze flows from that river*—he is always saying this through his interpreter, which has become, around here, almost his badge of office. My father laughs at him, who takes all pictographic script for Egyptian. He thinks Hittite is Egyptian! Egyptian women, he claims, sound to him like blackbirds. He should think again, for a politer bird. *Aiguptioisi,* he calls us: *I-gup-ti-oisey.* He even thinks Dionysus is the Greek version of Osiris, what a blasphemy! He beats about the bush, pretending he dare not say the name Osiris, but he ends up saying it anyway. Then he says, in his fluent Greek to a stumbling interpreter, which is like choking a donkey with cream: "Whoever Osiris may be, if this name be pleasing to him, then by this name I address him, measuring all things against him." But he is rarely that wise. He does not always seem to know that a name, and its pronunciation, have a certain power best not neglected.

My father's mouth is wide and bulbous, and Erodo's is cramped and almost rectangular, as if he is unaccustomed to speaking, being a born listener, with eyes that always look higher than you, searching the distance for something even as he grills you; the big forehead, with its few matted scrolls of hair, almost butts you while he squinnies into the far-off; and his pupils are so small as to be almost invisible, giving him a needly, sardonic look. Perhaps this Greek is a defiler of boys. He has been everywhere, or so he claims, and so must be a kind of worldly tourist, having soaked up the ways and wiles of a million men; sometimes it's as if he's at a loss for what to do or say next, so big is his store of manners. He yaks away about cinnamon, gold, amber, and all kinds of delights, and we listen, but to me he's a poseur, a blabbermouth, a fraud. We don't know who he is, but *he* does, insisting he's a magician.

16 ▲ CHEOPS

It came to me in sleep and woke me. Perhaps how wonderful, to have by me some scribe from elsewhere to put my case aright, in *their* writing, after I am gone, though I will be far from that. He will know how static I sometimes get, waiting it out, and how strange it feels to be always speculating about the changes in my body, wondering how it will feel to be transformed (like a lightning bolt striking a disemboweled ox). What a unique opportunity I have, reintroduced into the swarm of history having met, and been able to correct, one of my ancient chroniclers.

"Hold hard there, old man. That's wrong."

"In a pig's ear it is. I'm going on."

"Don't you care to get things right?"

"I have to make them vivid," he announces, "or those frantically searching for the facts will not attend. It is as mercenary as that."

So I let him have his way with facts, knowing that, upon all events and deeds, he will impose his gorgeous web, his rich-woven skein of color and music, chattering and gabbing, lurching and leaning, until the reader gets quite hypnotized, just like a snake. Who am I to dissuade him from his acknowledged destiny, pulling words from all over the flat land we inhabit through the warped mouths of his interpreters. It's as if some of those interpreters must already be dead, and he keeps them functioning with magic Greek arts: except some of the words they vouchsafe him were dead to start with, out of date two thousand-odd years ago; yet somehow they've been uprooted for a certain majesty's pleasure, to limn a forgotten folkway, to bring back a long-vanished god, a dried-up river.

Oh, Erodo, I want to cry to him, tell it all to me, now, as you will tell it to the nations of the Earth, as it will be spoken and read. Give me what you Greeks call a preview, please, so that I can savor my departure before I go, even if I go to something grander.

"Feu, feu," he says, meaning the Greek for *alas,* "I am worrying myself sick how to do it; not merely updating all the old lies (which must seem vague chromatic illustrations to you), but trying to poke a transition into Osiris—or Osiriana, as I sometimes call it, and will in the future too. I would like to follow you every step of the way, missing not a trick, a shift, a change, but keeping even pace with you, as an old king gives up the ghost to a younger king, but secretly turns into something prepossessingly grander."

"*Feu* to you too," I exclaim. "There you cannot go, or they would send me back. I spend my time looking at maps of pyramids, but my true course is forbidden, even to you."

17 ▲
OSIRIS

You would think that, when he comes to pray to me, as he often does in—forgive me—a way I would call fraternal, presumptuous, he would do it on his sloping bedstead, or even in a chair like his mother's, saying polite, reverential things; or in the company of Hemiunu, Vizier and Overseer of All the King's Works. He might whisper the words to himself while visiting his mortuary workshop near the Valley Temple, in the pyramid town at Giza. But no, he has to journey, almost alone, in darkness, to his own tomb, deserted for the night by his artisans, laborers, and construction gangs, but supervised by a sage guard or two. He begins with some strange noble babble about inlaid butterflies in silver bracelets, mat patterns in gold or faience overlay, flower patterns in headbands and crowns, gold-cased chair legs, feather patterns on the bodies of Horus hawks; it's as if he's getting himself in the mood, but in fact specifying the ordinary things of life on Earth, which he adores (contrasted with the smashed furniture from the First Dynasty at Abydos). You'd think his mind might be lingering on such events as the death of Chirh, something on which to speculate for ages, or the disappearance of Prince Ka-wab; but what seizes and torments him is the difference between his orderly life, and the chaos brought on by what happened in his mother's tomb—first when thieves marauded into it, scattering things right and left; then when his attendants bundled her stuff into a box with an inlaid lid, for transportation on the inundated Nile to Giza. He worries that in the next world, things might arrive higgledy-piggledy, not in the right order, so he might not have his favorite gold razor to hand, or that little spouted gold cup on its small gold saucer, or those other razors (round-ended, rectangular); or the little golden nail implement, or the copper needle, the ointment spoon. It is clear that he despises turbulence, and that the plundering of his mother's tomb disturbs him constantly (as well as the transportation of the leftovers by Hemiunu to Giza, an event not watched by him, he having gone through the whole business once already, when he witnessed her embalmment in the mortuary workshop at Giza, then sailed in the funeral to Dahshur, accompanying her up the causeway to the pyramid itself, after use of a purification tent on the terrace). After all this, Dahshur no doubt became a silent place again, sharing in the kind of silence (and orderliness) he craved, compared with the bustle and commotion going on at Giza, the new funeral site. What went into his mother's second resting-place with all expeditiousness, was landed at the foot of the very causeway up which stones were being dragged for the Great Pyramid, and lugged to the mouth of the newly finished shaft.

It was here—some workers' crude wasteland—that he chose to stroll and commune, worrying no doubt that he had installed the wrong food offering to his mother's spirit in the niche partway down the shaft, agitated that there is no alimentary offering eloquent enough to apologize to a mother for shifting her bones, or rather for shifting her possessions to settle around an empty coffin. Other matters preyed on his mind, of course, such as visits of state and foreign excursions; but this was one of the severest ordeals of his life, minifying others that, to almost anyone else, would seem of greater import and potential for grief.

What cheers him is the tidiness of his life, even to the extent of huge plans for his pyramids, done in elegant detail—this, compared with what might follow, when the user of all these items would have passed on, leaving them to his successors. (We know all about the behavior of successors.) So then, his prayer will often begin with an incantation that recalls a boating scene with attendants leading animals, and weathered blocks with his face thereon in profile; pottery jars with black paint marks; bed canopies; beetle-headed bolts, copper casings, curtain boxes, chairs with papyrus arms, carrying-chairs; bone tools, besides chisels, punches, knives; ewers, basins. Headrests and mud sealings, wine jars, bag-shaped pots, flat-bottomed tubs, bowls with spouts, and flaring flat-bottomed ones, concave-sided pans, ovoid jars, collar jars, squat-shoulder, neckless-shoulder, high-necked and barrel jars, foreign jugs; shallow bowls with external rims, bent-sided bowls, bowls with recurved rims, molded and roll rims, bowls with contracted mouths; and so on, endlessly it seems, the whole point being that this was all his stuff that he loved and knew exactly where it belonged. The moving of it all to his burial chamber gave him the fits because he was a creature of habit to begin with, and voluminously possessive. He wanted to take it all with him, in the correct order, with everything tabulated according to its own resting-place in life, and then refigured so that he might find it in the dark of that pyramid. Was it merely the dark that frightened him: not the dark of the interstellar spaces, but that of the pyramid abandoned nightly by its workers, even the jackal-headed priests who remove bowels?

So every prayer begins with a recital of his earthly goods, most of them anyway, and occupies hours, as if he can say nothing else, being devoutly materialistic. Truth told, he finds all this stuff (as I think of it) reassuring in a world where everything else is on the move. Worse, surely, to find it as it is in a world where everything is traveling at speed but looks static from an Earthly distance. Resolved as he is to journey beyond the stars; he wants these things to cocoon him, to protect him from meteors and the sun. He would love to go, but he won't. He'd like to go, but he doesn't. This is no doubt why he responds poorly, as Erodo claims, to the liveliness of events on Earth: births and deaths, murders and suicides, outbursts and pleas. He stays aloof from much of this uproar, saving himself for something vastly superior. I question if he knows every object by heart, its texture and shape, its history and purposes. He tries to afford himself the time to peer at everything in his compass in order to know it better. Odd that such a stick-in-the-mud should address himself to gigantic earth movements, the cutting and dragging and lifting of enormous blocks. Constant commotion in the landscape seems his nectar; but alone in his chambers he kneels in the presence of razors, jars, nail picks, like a supplicant, asking their trust and attention in the next world, and in the right order.

Unanswered, he begins to try and justify his prayers, reckoning that the lack of a response from above actually made a man clearer to himself than ever. The first thought, of course, was one of indignation, having gone to so much trouble only to produce a soliloquy; but this is soon followed by a caustic chastening that allows the human voice an echo, a definitive one, and encourages even further prayer. It had to be so, for him at least; grandiosity such as his demanded an answer, yet was seen to be so massive as soon not to need one. To the vital question of *What will happen to me, if not nothing,* he could be vouchsafed no answer at all, but his self-assurance helped him to envision the things he wanted. Who would deny so important a man, who, like some future national leader looking out on a battlefield littered with dead, sees a population of graves and mastabas, noting how neat it all is. To a man who regarded a woman as a farm, this was a proportionate, lapidary paradise, all his own devising; he little realized that he and his grand dreams had botched the humble dreams of thousands, turned into pack animals until they collapsed or died. Of all this he had some inkling, yet never enough. The old death-bargain of the departed's heart weighed against a feather meant less to him than it should have. He never gave a thought to what he had imposed on millions, entirely for his own sake, and how much that offense outweighed any feather.

Yet the universe does not go by featherweight at all, it simply moves onward, and vast amounts that people vow to remember get forgotten, overgrown, converted into amiable copses and dells of unselfconscious green trees and luxuriant, chromatic flowers. The planet has only a botanical, biological memory. So, what he has not been aware of won't thwart in any way his ambition to become a star. It will not matter that he has not invented the candle-clock or the wheel, the radio or anesthesia. He rests content with his titanic lot, and with the way his pyramids will last and last, a little battered and much explored, having carved his scar for him.

So his prayers in those echoing shafts and temples become a

means of clarifying himself to himself, clean and sharp as flint, amid the morass of superstition to which he pays lip service. That his mother could be snatched from her tomb in the dead of night by insensate plunderers grieves him no end, more than the misery of his daughter or the disappearance of his eldest son, Ka-wab. He meant well in all this, more or less, getting the daughter out of the house, off the premises, the son in much the same kind of endeavor; but now he's convinced not that blood is thicker than water, but that vainglory is thicker than blood, which, at any moment, may rebound to the vainglorious one's detriment.

One thing, however, puzzles and upsets him, and this is the matter of reserve heads, to be found scattered about in many burial chambers; these function, for a not altogether forgetful nation, as a compound biological relic to remember by. Where a head goes missing, one lying nearby will do. What makes better sense? The battlefield analogy prevails here too. The difference is that, in death chamber, shaft, or niche, the bodies look alike, the heads do not, so you make sure by dispersing a dozen copies of Princess Merytyetes's head and her husband's too, she having a consistent look of blithe adjustment, and well-tempered good cheer, she is gifted with a chubby prognathous face, a jaunty cast of the jubilant eye, a tender pliant mouth, small humble nose—in short a woman bustling with keen friendliness. Her husband seems more ordinary, lacking the high-class regality of his wife, yet gifted with a calm ruefulness that might yet enjoy a fit of anger. Thus might a reserve head or two bring about that magical feat unpromised in the tomb, except under unusual auspices imposed with a more or less loving hand, of bringing the mummy back to life.

To Cheops, however, the chance of an error's being made in the mass production of reserve heads, or even errors, means that his capita flung around the desert, and scattered underground may represent him ill; nor does he want to be saddled with a vague face on admittedly broad shoulders, which is not the way he wants to be remembered. Of course, however, he is reckoning on his one head's surviving such a grave robbery as lost him his mother (though in her case the entire body was taken). He does not want to be anonymously beheaded. They could leave the head and take the torso. That would suit him. As it is, he has a mortifying vision of heads being detached by his own workmen in his funerary workshop. The head, he reasons, must be allowed to go hurtling on and out to Orion even if the rest remains behind. Would perhaps a severance at the neck help the process? He does not know, but remains tormented by the simple, mundane presence in funerary equipment—handled by even unpromoted folk—of something such as a pair of scissors, poor rival to a head, or a reserve head, but then perhaps it's likelier to remain intact and unstolen.

He has his reasons for pondering this, a king surrounded by mayhem and robbery, his mind on ethereal things. His second-best yearning is to scatter thousands of reserve heads over the landscape—just to remind people of his reign.

18 ▲
PRINCESS HEDUANNA

Would I have if he had asked me to, not doing much but just enough to spur him? I might have, with my eyes on the ceiling and my breath held. It would not have taken long, would it? Not one of those droning episodes, but just a sort of scattering, then over, time to think of the past. Nothing daring to it: oh no, I don't know enough for that; but with either Chirh or Ka-wab, one like a bird of prey, the other a pillow, I wouldn't have known what to do. We all have our moments, of course; but Chirh was looking for something more than a moment, he wanted a long-term commitment to his own idea of an orgy. I should not have gone. If I'd not, perhaps Ka-wab would have been here when I got back. Is that why he was sent away? Did my father send him so that something bad could happen to him; or was it an innocent mission innocently invented? When there is almost nobody left, you yourself end up a nobody, whatever you have between your legs, your ears. My father is odd, unable to estimate things on the scale of time. It all happens at once. Effect precedes cause. He worries most about his mother's body being stolen. All else is trivial.

19 ▲ CHEOPS

Not praying now, I hear a kind of click or snap as the prayer ends, and I know I have been restored to the plane of everyday, in which, nonetheless, dreadful things happen. I become a goblin, say, a djinn; and go creeping along those sealed passageways, descending or climbing with almost mechanical power, feeling my way along as unknown, rough surfaces tug at me. I *slink* along noting the utter absence of rats. I have my own ways in and out, I am the king. So I come to this niche, and worm my way in until I can feel the canopic chest we brought here. Now my bearer holds his flame downward to increase it and I see how the niche, reachable with both arms, is an irregular place. There is a sound of the sea, impossible but what? A distinct smell of aromatherapy comes from somewhere other than the niche. By torchlight I see a hulking bull ready to charge, but this is only a hulk of black light. The niche is swarming with loneliness; and my insides droop with the chill. I have come to do the unpermitted thing. My mind fills with *lest*s until I can bear it no more and lumber at the canopic chest resting against the wall. Stunning thunder in that place as I open the tight-fitting lid. I feel I am delving into Nile mud, which at once dries on my skin and begins to squeeze. Suddenly, I would give anything not to be here. Bizarre facts come to mind, such as the temerity of the grave-robbers. My mother was buried a Nile's width from Memphis, by night, which means they could work uninterrupted, and with indiscriminate noise. As the story goes, I did not myself place the food offering in its niche, but I did. I believe the taint of beef, controlled putrefaction, hangs in the air of the pyramid. Here it is, lift the lid; almost reeling. My bearer retreats in terror to the facing wall.

He comes closer, firmly commanded. There are four identical compartments, at least two of which are liquid by torchlight, suppuration from some floating organ or other at which I dare not look, let alone touch in the feeble light. My mother has become a fluid, is still moist, segregated off, and what is wet is no doubt seeping from one of the four compartments, under the dividers, into the others. Disassembled, Hetep-heres is becoming one again, in readiness, yes, for her sublimest journey. And I am revolted not to be in there with her, except the four compartments remind me of a carpenter's box—prosaic, portable. I cannot distinguish the red from the yellow from the imaginable green, but I *know*. Who can imagine them stealing *this?*

Where she was first buried, in the small pyramid to the south of the Bent Pyramid at Dahshur, the gap was too small for any but the tiniest dwarf. (Neither did the tomb have any superstructure, such as an offering chapel. The mouth of the shaft was crammed with stones of all shapes, plastered together. A layer of limestone followed, gravel debris for the most part.) This is no doubt why they left behind the contents of the canopic chest, why the furniture remained, and her alabaster sarcophagus. Perhaps she was buried elsewhere, and I don't remember. Has the new blotted out the old to that extent? My memory departed with her body, that must be it.

The torch gutters. We process outside: upward, down, then upward again. Thank the gods for night air. If I were a wiser man, I would have my bearer strangled on the spot and dipped into the Nile, but repeated visits would create too many bodies. Who would believe it of me anyway? Those who think ill of me would nod. Those who don't would exclaim in fear. All that reassures me, by daylight, is the Egyptian red of my pyramid, the exact color of the sun. This cheers and steadies me during my guilt-ridden wait. I should have done better for one of the great ladies of the old kingdom, imagining her once again carried forth in her ebony and gold carrying-chair to visit Imhotep's temple complex, a marvel for the eyes; or scrutinizing the bare, rocky plateau where I myself was just beginning to build.

How had that heart-mauling conversation gone? It had been the one he dreaded most, he, Hemiunu, as well as one I did not want at all. To hear this terrible thing was to want not to exist any more.

Hence the vizier's shifty approach. "It may sometimes, your majesty, be better not to have one's body confined to any one place, but rather to become dispersed, giving a little of oneself to all; so that, when people ask, you point in a certain direction, at the tomb, say, which is enough, while mentally you envision a shower of physical particularities that has blown away and descended." This was his stock-in-trade, palatable only if you knew what he was up to, unacceptable otherwise; but he persisted in this mode of meticulous obfuscation, in vain hope of converting you to some gritty creed.

"It is holier in the long run, matching all of one's particulate being with the full extent of the world." He was preaching res extensa without knowing it, long before it became any kind of doctrine. ""It is better," he went on, "not always to be at home when they come knocking for you, if you see my drift. Such is the ethic of dispersal, my lord, enabling the defunct human to cover more ground and, in fact, absorb more new energy within its tiny place. One should perhaps beware of being too local, too concentrated, such that any passing, neglectful eye would overlook the body in one word, and move on to other ventures. I am preaching, I suppose, the doctrine of scatter, as with seed."

"The point, the matter, my dear man?"

"Shall I to it?" His lips quiver.

"What else? What disaster are you busily preparing me for? Do you have the unneglected tradition of severed heads in mind? Live long around here, and you soon realize the danger."

Deep breath, a slow blink in that scholarly, tumid face. Then: "Your mother's body has gone. It has been stolen. The grave has been plundered."

I do not respond for ages; all my seepage has stopped. There are bad things with which I cope, then there is anything to do with Hetep-heres, doubly my mother, at the mere mention of which I become insensate, out of control. He must be lying, suicidally so. "Tell me again." He does, but I cannot take it in. This is in the realm of the does-not-happen.

"It has," he sighs, "but all else remains."

"Empty sarcophagus?"

"Empty, my lord."

"And where *is* she?" His gesture, helpless and forlorn, says nowhere, and I know we have lost the dearness of life.

Who else would have had the courage to tell me, or indeed the wiliness, next to the education? Erodo would have made an ungainly meal of it, word man that he is; and not a living wife would have dared. This, then, is how you promote people, although they recognize how close they are, being promoted, to having their heads removed. They take chances and try not to have too many dependents, just in case. Other kings would have had him tell, then beheaded him in secret for the offense given. Such is not my way, not recently, and I cherish Hemiunu for a certain heroic quality I wish my sons had more of. When I add up his pallor, his trembling lips, the dry breath suffocating his mouth, the audible rumble from his stomach, and the stench of fear coming off his face, I can only applaud, in my miserable, motherless way. The wound is permanent. Guilt moves in like an inundation from the Nile. I should have set more guards. I should have kept a lonely vigil myself for the first few months. I should have buried her nearby, or nearer-by. I should have kept her in the palace, in gorgeous sublimity, ready for when we take off together. Now the question becomes where to find her. Who on earth would want her in the condition she is in? No one save Osiris. For aid in this, I call in the magicians, exempting them from all taxes and exactions, and my own suspicion.

20 ▲
HEMIUNU

His mother's gone, her box empty, and if I do not handle this right an ax will fall. Goodbye to indolent sunsets on my porch. Keep him calm, then, put him off the scent with heretical theories. Reassure him how easy it will be to transfer what's left to Giza, ever the preferable venue. Stroke his almighty hand like a mother. Help him to envision her in flight. Use the name Osiris plentifully before he collapses with rage. Tell yourself this is the job you chose, so don't run away from it now. Let him infer from other sources that your mastaba is going to be huger than anybody's, unless that enrages him too much. We all know what happened to Kanofer. Strange how Cheops obsesses about his mother, *grande dame* to be sure, but not that giving a troll. He must be in love with the woman he thought his mother was, but she is going to be famous in history as the corpse who flew away. Don't tell him that.

21 ▲
ERODO

Sooner or later the ribald stranger ceases to grate on his host, or he gets himself thrown out, to pester those in another country. Here, thank Zeus, I seem to be on the way to being taken for granted, a madcap historian, a lurid commentator, a willful sage. Whatever; I am beginning to feel the first shreds of sympathy for the Cheopses, all of them, especially the daughter Heduanna, and the pharaoh himself, who seems a man of palpable density without getting fuzzy. Good, I say; the more he comes into view, the more I want him to. Cruising around with his bearers in one of those carrying-chairs, sometimes hidden behind a canopy, he looks more than regal, although I have some idea of what plagues his mind. He is not quite the monarch, being carried to a plateau to feel the sun's heat on his tired, unresisting eyes. He is more the visionary—scoping the joint, ready for takeoff, but held back by convention—by daughter, son, sons, the painful memory of things not done with kingly finesse. At some point, a career that has gone bad cannot be retrieved, it can only be confessed to, at a party for aristocrats, say, or in an intimate chat with such as me. I listen, make notes, curse the interpreters, and politely ask him if I have overstayed my welcome.

"When you consider the number of years you've traveled," he answers, "you might consider asking for an extension. I don't get to visit with wandering Greeks every day; and you are certain to be my last. Have you contemplated moving into shinier quarters? In any case, you haven't even explored that much around my pyramid, not even yonder big rock."

I could never, I explain, work up much feeling for that big crude thing. "It leaves me cold, the rock does."

"So would any pyramid. We don't design them to be hothouses. A certain dankness is necessary, the chill in the bone a needed qualification, Erodo. But you are welcome to wrap yourself in the finest linen, or drape yourself in a blanket when you go inspecting. If you know how to get in. There are always ways."

Am I wrong in detecting in him an access of amiability? Why has he warmed up? Things I know nothing of seem to have cheered him like a snake. Perhaps the impending end about which he talks incessantly. Perhaps the faint hope that royal life was a picnic has faded; and he's now reconciled to the rough-and-tumble of it, killings, maneuvers, and all—the dire politics of Being Someone. Or did he get a better view of Orion the other night, encouraging and crystalline? I don't usually advise kings, talkin' and chillin' as we put it in our Athenian slang, in the correct conduct of their remaining days. By way of answer, he tells me his most recent dream, in which he wakes, realizing he is sheathed in his own sarcophagus, put together from slabs or sheets of green stone: the stone that eats flesh! He has become the cannibal of himself, he says. I am almost on the point of saying "Correct, that's not half bad," when I halt, look away at the heaving color gamut on his walls. I change my mind, saying, with the prestigious calm I can sometimes put on, "Steady now, your majesty, it's only a dream. Nobody is the cannibal of himself." I had met them, though, on my travels, and watched them sink to their own doom, aghast at the disasters they could bring upon themselves—Turks and Hittites and Scythians. Dissimulation is not my strong point, but candor ranks high. I have discovered that a certain rude, peasant strain in Cheops responds well to blunt honesty.

"Well," I tell him, "I wouldn't ignore my own bliss."

"*You*'re not a pharaoh."

"Well, I've traveled," I say, "when I might have spent the time staying put. Amazing how cross some people get with you just for moving about—in Greece, doctors and philosophers. Tax collectors. These people are a plague."

I am a Greek, from the civilization of sweetness and light; I have to help him, at least make the offer. "How can I help?"

For a while he says nothing, dumbfounded no doubt by the sudden change in his Greek tormentor, who should surely be roughing him up, by royal agreement.

"Oh, to be rid of all this," he says, gesturing at Egypt, Memphis, the river and the sand. "I have serious things to concentrate on, and I weary of looking after so many, even of setting them to work. Do you understand?"

Not altogether, I am thinking: you despots always baffle me. I end up wondering what beauty you get out of it all; then I see the pyramids and get the point, even as I brood on the arthritis in the joints of his laborers, all from too much lifting and squatting. Leprosy too, and abscesses. I would not be an Egyptian for anything. Just imagine, Erodo, what they do to young girls to keep them chaste.

"I understand," I tell him, "but isn't the twilight of life supposed to be the phase of reconciliation, in which all manner of things comes together for adjustment and stoical resolve? A man can't back away from all his lifetime has entailed, can he? You don't quit just before the end."

"I should," he says abruptly, as if confessing something he's already well into, "have given my mother a better send-off the second time. It was all right, of course, but I could have laid it on thick, with more swank, more music, say; to apologize to her, wherever she is, for installing an empty coffin. What did I say to Vizier Hemiunu? *Put the lid back on and don't ever mention it again.* What a hoax. I should have been able to manage things better—in a more subjective, filial style—but I left it all to him, the epitome of discretion; and thus became even more obligated. Some viziers you throttle, there's nothing for it, but as for him, I only added to his renown. The word got out that Cheops couldn't muster the right degree of grandeur, for a mother yet; he was too interested in his own building site, the first ground-breaking ceremony for which she had actually observed." I could see how this failure gnawed at him, threatened to ruin his ascent to godhead, his good-byes corrupted by guilt.

"You know what, Erodo," he begins again, "I sometimes feel like a man cut out of stone and brought, just a tiny bit, to life. I have wide shoulders, huge ears, a fuzzy false beard, and the top of my head is missing, smashed by some grave-robber no doubt. I am thus depicted, in a smaller design, revealed pulling an animal pelt over my head, using all the right muscles; in another watching bunches of hair grow out of my knees and thighs. Thus they draw me while I'm alive, sneering, saying he will be gone soon, he is going."

22 ▲
OSIRIS

Among the things now besieging him was his mind's tendency to reproduce scenes of court life—with courtiers and others in fancy raiment, all scrambled together heedless of time, or clique, or invitation, and mostly women, for whom he always had an appetizing eye. Disjointed scenes from last year or ten years ago would mingle in his mind, he said, quite unfitting for him in the present (not much entertainment at all, these days, and all of it staged by his wife Merytyetes, as grande a dame as had ever haunted anyone's halls). He could never quite sever the faint menstrual whiff that came off Meresankh I from the fruit juice and onion aroma of Khentet-n-ka, the bouquet seeming to come from her very pores. Nekaw, on the other hand, was always murmuring to herself some line of poetry, which, if you heard it clearly, was full of obscene words that did not make her smile; while Nebty-tp-itf-s seemed always to have the hiccups, and other guests tried to help her, startling her with a sudden grimace or proffering some sweetmeat on a spoon. Meresankh III, prey always to scoliosis, a disease Egyptians did not recognize, strained her body to rise from stomach level, yearning to look people in the eye, but grunting and groaning as she tried. All these surrounded him as if a female maze had come to life, enclosing him, with Atet, ever ready with a scent of sulfur, and Neferma'at, correcting her stammer with a series of sharp inhalations.

"How in hell," says Erodo, who has been listening to all this, grateful for a not altogether misspent youth, "can you put up with all this in one skull? Don't they ever go away, recede? Are they permanent residents of your nostalgia?"

"Some," Cheops sighs, "would call me henpecked. I prefer to think of it as lust gone wrong. You desire them, bring them into the harem, and then they turn on you after the first clinch or two." Erodo's interpreter asks leave to quit the room, and leaves them together, now effectively silenced but for the crudest, most basic exchanges.

"Damn," says Cheops.

"Hell," Erodo answers.

"Only one life to live," says Erodo, making his knuckles crack while wringing his hands.

"One too many," Cheops tells him, his mind ablaze now with all kinds of social frippery—the very things women ask him about, especially Merytyetes that punctilious force of nature, possibly the one eternal woman in their world. Besides that, questions of etiquette and rank flood his mind, preoccupied as it is with matters of astronomy, trajectory, and soul travel.

"Ah," says Erodo the Greek, sensing the man's displeasure, "what you're talking and complaining about is called *metempsychosis*. We Greeks have a word for it. You mean travel of the soul outward."

"Ah, there was one, someone's daughter of course. I'm getting forgetful in my dotage as we all do, don't we?" Cheops is speaking with hurried improvization as if his mind were too slow for his mouth, and Erodo recognizes this.

"Slow up, old man, they'll be after you all over again."

"Yes, they bloody will, and then . . ."

Erodo waits, but nothing comes of it. Cheops has lapsed into a royal silence, with an admission fee charged. It was always a habit of pharaohs.

"Anyway," Cheops resumes, "there was one, Kha-merer-nebty, luscious young female I must say, and she had all of us at court gasping for breath. For once, a woman had come out right, and you know all about the incest. She was perfect, and she had a habit of walking among us as if a lion was strolling in front of her on a long leash. You never saw the lion, but you knew it was there, full of a low virile growl. A male lion. Daughter of a certain Grand Vizier she was."

"What became of her?"

"Married some perfectly routine courtier whose name I forget. Was he a vizier? No, just a scribe-type."

Merytyetes the scarce has sidled up to them, making an offering of either resplendent cheekbone, as it were, airing herself festively. "Oh, it's all real," Cheops exclaims. "I wasn't dreaming after all." Merytyetes's wonky eye, it was rumored, came from eating rancid fish and washing it down with beer, a habit she persisted in for reasons unknown (revenge, perhaps, simply to annoy her husband with her unpresentable face). Different generations of women pestered his desire for them, all of them at different times in the past; yet all of them were too highborn and too inbred to seem altogether different from one another apart from their physical and behavioral oddities.

Meresankh II had a man's burly hands, Hetep-heres II had a high equine whinny, with which to greet even the shoddiest of jokes. Nefer-hetep-s, drink in hand, stabbed her fingers into the soft region above the hip while addressing people from behind. The uproar in his head would never be complete, or endurable for that matter, without these ladies *of his* and their rattle; but within it all there was another level, a plateau of appetite, on which existed his wives as they were in private: Henutsen berating him for slouching about; the one whose name eluded him screaming when he leaned over her sleeping form and tried something inventive; Nefert-kaw constantly interrupting him to air her gash; but, most of all, the proud, bold, high-cheeked Merytyetes, her gaze one of exalted indifference, her big eyes voracious, her height an emblem of contempt. Haughty and overly competent, she should have been married to several kings, devouring them weekly.

"Yes," he says, "we all go to the same weddings. I tell you, I know everybody's conversation backwards. It doesn't pay to argue, or to complain. Why, even the biennial cattle count is something of a relief. If I had my time over, and were not pharaoh, preposterous thought, I would like to be some kind of scribe. Not like you, Erodo, but one who comes up with nicknames for the women, just to introduce a bit of levity into social assemblies." Erodo laughs, imagining Nebty, Neffie, and Hennie, but he finds the chore of limited amusement, and Cheops says not a word further.

Merytyetes, who has been listening with imperious eyes, looks them over as also-rans. Her snub nose gives her an oddly contained, concise look, all of her sardonics pent up within her face.

"You gentlemen," she says lazily, with a special pawnbroker's look at Erodo, "don't have enough to do, just talking among yourselves. There have been murders in the kingdom. My son Ka-wab is missing, not to be found at his destination. And *you* hold a seminar. What do you think this is, a university? Then we could train people in the building of pyramids. On the contrary, gentlemen, people are already leaving. I have a nose for such things and can always sniff out the coming end of a civilization. The sun is going down on us already."

23 ▲
CHEOPS

I have a sneaking feeling that I am trying to teach myself what I should have known all along. Why do we find these elementary lessons so difficult? We last all these years only to discover that the only thing left is a launch of the soul up to Orion, if you believe that much. The day comes, as it did for Mother, when there is going to be utterly nothing else for you ever. You can't escape, you are doomed. Why then do we have so much trouble with day-to-day living, always complaining and whining about it; instead of telling ourselves to make the most of every second, whatever that might be, because it will not come again? The number of seconds is finite. Why can we not dwell on the instant and, with passionate attention, turn it into itself into forever? Life is so good, say all these dead in the pyramids and the mastabas, even at its worst, that we would never trade anything for it. Erodo has gleaned this from Greek philosophers. He pops his favorite phrase at me, hoping to convert; and although I understand it, he having schooled me relentlessly, I can make only half-gestures toward it. Why are we so stubborn? *Ē monochronos ēdonē,* he chimes at me, intending *the sweetest single instant,* or something such; and at once I think of something to complain about: fever, rain, murder, marital strife, and lose the magic of the instant instantly.

24 ▲
MERYTYETES

Malleable clay, we, culled from Nile mud and its crocodiles, with tiny fish forms skulking within it. Woman must ever expect to marry her father, sleep with her brother, be the constant target of uncles and nephews—as if, as he says, we were farms. Amazing that we survive it all and contrive to look cheerful. As an old lady I will enter the harem of Chefren, it is destined to be so; I who have called herself *wrt hts* will refer to myself as being in an honored position therein. (If only he were less of a mamma's boy, I think.) It has nothing to do with evil and brutality; women, as the saying has it, do come into their own sooner or later. Not that I do not have other sons, Baw-f-ra and Dedef-ra, brothers to Meresankh II, a queen to be. There is constant gossip about a queen with red hair, an exile from Libya, whom no one has ever seen; but the gossip is based on artwork showing red lines across the yellow hue of her headdress. These were merely standard drawing-lesson lines, found elsewhere in art. A similar misconception refers to a dress's pointed shoulder, all very pretty, but in truth a wig-like thing akin to the headcloth of a pharaoh. There was never any red-haired queen, though several red-blooded ones. Young Hetep-heres II, for instance, miserable wife of Ka-wab, intended to be buried in the first twin mastaba in front of my own pyramid. Why all the mystification, I never knew. Oh that my man did not spend his time on heavy masonry, forever adding to mastabas; then erected chapels of rubble and brick, changing his mind about interior chapels, quite bewildering his working gangs. While the huge pyramids go up, we sleep in terror of having our throats cut. This is why, when one walks about the echoing halls and the chromatic chambers decorated by painters for whom there is no money, one must have an erect head and a dry pleat.

25 ▲
ERODO, TENTH BOOK

I was just thinking how the Egyptians make a model of their earthly life to accompany them on their journey into the afterlife, inevitably reducing the scale of certain things, but taking with them (as it were) life-size pots and pans, tools and toys. They also make model gardens to beguile themselves with, starting with a copper-lined box, in which sycamore fig trees (made from wood with singly attached leaves) hem in a copper-lined fount supposed to hold water. At one end of the box a verandah awaits miniature guests, supported by gaudy columns painted in a design based on bundles of papyrus and lotus flowers. There are usually three small drain spouts atop the verandah's roof. These lovely boxes can often be found positioned in a tomb among the elaborate wall decorations painted there to remind the dead of what daily life is like—from granaries to slaughterhouses, villas to libraries. This is their theory of the model, sometimes extended as far as model boats with cloth sails and carefully woven baby nets enclosing tiny carved fishes. Only the people are missing, but there they are in the coffin alongside. Though in many cases, if they're woodworkers, they are allowed into the box proper to give the model its tiny plausibility.

From such boxes (not the coffins), it is not far to what they call the Persian garden, rectangular with high walls and subdivided into four equal sections by canals meeting in a central pool (not unlike the division into four compartments of the canopic chest in which Cheops's mother's viscera were put). The Persian name for these gardens was *pairi-daeza* (meaning "wall surrounded"), rendered into Greek as *paradeisos,* far from a far cry to *paradise* itself. Is it not wonderful how the human being, unable to muster the rest of the world into a generalization, contrives to limn it in what we sometimes call a symbol; which, without actually spelling something out, gestures at it, hints and points? The receptive mind absorbs its import, and goes gladly about its business thinking it has dealt with the whole world when in fact it has only noticed a splinter. There is what we have, and then there is what we do not have (or cannot control, anyway). To get the second to invade the first, like drops of blood dispersing in a cup of water, is the way to go: not dissimilar to what happens in some tombs when a reserve head, a *wrong* head, gets in among the bones and is called *intruded.*

At their banquets, the Egyptians wear garlands of flowers with little birds perched on them to peck their heads and brows, so as to keep them awake as the evening wears on; a formal dinner in any country is a tedious affair, and I have seen my share. It is entertaining to hear these tiny birds chirping away as they depart their stations to snap up a morsel of food, then return to the exact place to resume their proctorial duties. With Cheops and his court as with all others, this is the way to go, unlikely to change in the next hundred years.

There, I ramble on again. No time like the present for a further recital of foreign doings, foreign faces. Erodo writes again, even if only to remind Greek readers that in Egypt only the dead are truly respected. I say this because, at a recent garden party of Cheops's, out in his luxurious Nile-fed garden (many canals), Cheops is reclining on an inlaid couch, one elbow on a cushion. He lifts his goblet to Merytyetes while attendants fan the royal couple, bring them trays of refreshments, and keep the music going apparently without plan: winds, strings, and faint drum. It would all seem splendorous, of uncommon delicacy, but for the head of Chirh, which, upside down so as not to drip, hangs from a ring attached to a palm tree, its foul animal smell masked, but only somewhat, by a pair of incense burners stationed nearby without intruding, and jasmine bouquets in the hands of the regal couple. One can be nauseated, if observant, which I contrive to be while reconnoitering the court. These people are wilder than anyone would think, and bottle up their feelings in a peculiar way: the more pain they feel, the more they inflict it on others; so in a way the severed head helps alleviate the loss of Ka-wab, their son, the eldest and the next in line. (They obtain no news. In a country of little communication, news is almost a mythical construct, always late and, over its long journey from event to ear, mostly garbled; so the news has this constancy: it may never be true, but the artifact of some overheated imagination far away, and the overheated imaginations in between.) Chirh's head merely goes along with the array of flowers arranged for the latest garden party, and he will stay there until he stinks worse than any midden. Meanwhile, Heduanna, whose story I have managed to pluck out of her for later consumption and embellishment, sits with her back to the head, and tries to forget her friendship—or whatever it was—with Ka-wab. In her is a very strange mixture of grief and languor, not to be mimicked anywhere else on Earth. Now, was Chirh killed for being incompetent or was he the villain of the piece? Such affairs remain ambiguous here, and you need to watch your neck.

Later, in a secluded corner of the garden, Merytyetes the heart-broken mother who puts on a good front, is telling me how fed up she gets with the way artists depict her, her right side being the good one. "Always seated with long, long feet that must be symbolic of something, my right arm afloat, my left crooked to help me inhale a lotus blossom. Just look at those feet, as if I were wearing slippers as long as my calves!" The interpreters wince at this, but the king is on the other side in his room, listening to poetry. The face of Merytyetes in profile is convex, and her nose looks quite flattened into line with it, giving her a look demure and uninvolved, which cannot be true. She has, though, learned how to live at court and knows the ropes: do not grieve openly, she tells herself, even if your precious eldest son has vanished, perhaps been murdered. Cheops in his bluff way says he'll be back soon, not that anyone has had any communication with him; it was Cheops, after all, who sent him away on an expedition of diplomatic urgency. I believe him, I too expect the portly prince to return. Merytyetes is holding her breath, watching a painter execute what I would call an elegiac portrait of their last few days together, she facing him with her hand over her right breast; he erect, drawn at the walk; hosts of household things around them (spoons, razors, flints, scissors); and then snakes, owl, feathers, water birds, and a hippopotamus head. The lotus she sniffs is bigger than her face. What a proud bearing she has, queenly and genial in one, always looking at you with an expression of subdued amusement. Her taint of proud officiousness is made milder by her look of the female athlete: her neck almost burly, her head tilted back somewhat as if she is breasting the winner's tape, ears small, her lips thin enough but stretched by a smile. Visitors fall for this lady, who sweeps them off their feet, such is her propulsive grace; but less so when she is worried, as now. She is not going to break down, but some of her extrovert buoyancy has gone. She is little seen except at public functions. People, if invited (otherwise they wangle it), come to see how she dresses, she being a leader in fashion and gifted at both makeup and the style of the pointed shoulder. Accustomed to her own way, she challenges no one, and prospers unduly. Her interest in clothing does not, however, extend to fabric and decoration; she has been heard, when among her closest clique, actually making fun of the elegant designs and creations put about by Queen Hetep-heres, such as "faience inlays of Neith emblems in gold sheet lying face down beside the easternmost of two palm capitals of carrying-chair poles." Just the sort of thing the queen-mother insisted upon, in her way adopting the terminology of future scribes and scholars. Commenting on a young giraffe encrypted with tiny quatrefoils: "Nubian no longer," she scoffs. "Egypt forever!"

Mooching around the court with my rotten, stunted Egyptian and my nosey mind, I pick up certain currents, not all of them favorable to the best-looking women. Merytyetes mentioned her feet being depicted as long, possibly symbols of something or other; but the symbol they most closely link with her is the lotus, quite openly claiming that she is, as they say, a carpet-biter or addicted to women. She is portrayed in full view by a painter or sculptor, holding the big lotus blossom to her waiting mouth as if she has never seen a thing so beautiful before. One sees, but I do not believe it. Lovelier goblet-shaped flowers have been brought down the Nile from distant Africa. I can imagine this lotus bloom taking a female's fancy, but it all depends on what you think a *nek* looks like, wide open like a rotting flower or cuplike for the gods. Any slander, Merytyetes puts behind her, arguing that the body is the body, and what it does, with whom, is one's own business. In this, she is not only ahead of her time, but a warrior queen, of the right dimension. These people, these Egyptians, relieve themselves indoors, shave their bodies every two days, constantly bathe in cold water. They thrive on pornographic cartoons and lascivious hyperbole, and they do not live much beyond thirty-five. They are entitled to their cravings, I suggest, whatever they are. Surrounded by gods and death, they tup like baboons.

26 ▲ CHEOPS

The cobwebs are back, they never went away. They dangle like bedraggled spiders behind my pupils, screens to cover a world mostly not worth seeing. Now and then I walk into chairs and people, although with both eyes affected in the same way I should be able to walk in a straight line and not veer either way. In the old days, before my condition became severe, I would squint the one eye so as to see clearly with the other; but with them both blurred, I just blunder about, never rebuked for colliding of course because, after all, a so-called pharaoh is a king. The cure, they tell me, on poor authority, is to open up the eyeball and empty out the blood that has swollen it; but what then? Somehow squirt Nile water back into it to keep it rotund? I do not respond kindly to this idea, but I can detect in my courtiers a shamefaced yearning to see the first monarch in history undergo it. They would not mind watching and mustering a cheap thrill, much as in earlier dynasties they watched the pharaoh porking his whores or emptying his bowels. None of that, these days, Osiris be thanked, but the court is aflame with talk of magicians doubling as doctors, much of it based on the tradition inspired by a certain Zaza-m-ankh, who performed for King Sneferu, my father. His mantle has now descended on a magician named Dedi, who claims to have all creation's mystery at his fingertips, and I am expected to submit to his inglorious skills just to save them from a pharaoh who is seeing less and less of hands that grope for his throat in the bedchamber, snatch one of his sons from ambassadorial chores, and pat the ass of his favorite daughter. That I need to see better is certain, but I need also to survive whatever procedure the mountebank comes up with.

How does that conversation go?

"The merest nick, your majesty, will serve."

"And then?"

"The eyeball, sire, closes in upon itself at once, thanks to a certain sponginess. It has been seen in Arabia."

"What then of the refilling operation? How would you do

that?" He answers that, with a thin, thin reed, but I know enough to tell myself that nothing comes along a thin, thin reed unless, well, blown along it. A straw would be too wide, would it not?

He chooses to explain the happy outcome rather than the technique, and I leave him be, agreeing that we will work on only the one eye, to see how it heals.

Erodo, who seems to have formed an affection for the old ogre that I have become, says no, do nothing of the kind. Just be careful how you walk about and, if troubled by a blot, turn your eye sideways or up and down until it clears enough for you to see faces.

Merytyetes urges me on, with her well-known passion for health and the forward look (she has little idea of my stellar ambitions). She does not know Greek, so she has to guess at Erodo's face to know how he feels about it.

Osiris I have not heard from, and I suspect it will be only afterward that he comes through, aiding and abetting or proclaiming a belated flat no. Urged on, I wish I had half an eye to play with, but that is dismal thinking for a king, and I mean to go ahead, come what may, in the interests of my own safety. A man going to Orion does not even need an eyepatch, lest he arrive at the wrong star.

With eyelids pulled back and restrained by copper clips, I feel the narrow straw go in and Dedi the surgical magician begin to suck. The amount of blood withdrawn must be quite small, but he spits it out with grandiose splutters into a shallow basin held by an assistant. Now he squirts water through the same hole, pausing to refill his straw, and soon the empty eye fills up, perhaps fuller than before, and I am in serious, kingly pain. The clips come off, and the eye is red and sensitive. They show me my reflection, normal apart from some tearing and swelling. The astonishing thing, provided I don't die overnight from an infection spawned in his magical mouth, is that I can see again, not without a blotchy blur here and there. The eye has mostly cleared, and at once the magician volunteers to do the other eye, no doubt scenting a double fee, but I resist, asking him about the straw-holes, which he says will seal themselves after a day or two, such is the resilient thickness of eyeball pulp. I can hardly believe him, yet his show is over and a success. With one eye I can just about see my way again, and now I can squint the other eye to purify the improved one's view. If you have one defective eye, opening it will blur the other's vision somewhat. All along I have been rehearsing the situation to myself: clammy light as of an Egyptian morning strikes through the blot, yielding almost perfect vision, whereas poorer light stops at the blot and creates a foiling, boiling motion akin to vertigo, while darkness affords total relief, dark meeting the dark. I mention all this to Dedi, this newly vindicated charlatan, but he laughs it off as the rationale of a mere king. And I am left to console myself with Merytyetes staring at me hard, willing herself to read my mind through the newly opened window in my eye, and Erodo shaking his head like a man with the horizontal ague. Perhaps, I reason, my visit to Orion depended on this test, and now I am free to go. If only ritual life among us were as simple as that, as taking an oar-boat upriver. I have merely submitted to someone professing what little gift we have in these matters; as if knowing that one day we shall do better and the local quacks will have to get on with conjuring alone, having quit surgery as an inferior form of juggling.

Now I see it, I, who have missed it hitherto. The all-seeing, omnipotent, unsparing eye that looks upon all of us has paid me an honorary visit, reminding me that I should not shirk the privilege of turning my gaze inward. I might even be persuaded to let Dedi fill my eyeball with blood all over again, cow's or sow's, but I don't, content to dub myself the wobble-eyed pharaoh who sees clearly with one eye, the left (more or less), and fuzzily with the other: the good and the bad. Leave them alone now, I say. If I were writing, I would draw a giraffe at the end of this sentence to denote something to come, seen from afar by him because he is so tall.

27 ▲
CHEOPS

Thinking, as often, of my stolen mother, I take my stance on the plateau to which she liked the bearers of her chair to take her, and marvel at the mastabas below, some of them quite humble, at least one of them huge (someone not satisfied with the standard size); I think of the mass of men and women, lost if you choose to look at them the wrong way—used up, spent, exhausted, never again to open an eye, and I find myself failing to adopt the traditional blithe view of death. I even feel sickened, as I stare at so many, just thinking of the human variety all laid low. It doesn't seem right to be reduced to such a low ebb, then annulled for ever, made into some kind of human paste. I know this is heresy, but what would a king's reign be without a little heresy? This is not a matter of so many reserve heads; most of the people out there assigned to death in the vast tracts of desert had no such extras. It is a matter of names, for the name abides when all else has faded, and I mentally picture some future scribe, a bit lost by the remains and offerings, managing to list the occupants and trying to guess what complex humanity they stood for. After years of toil and sweat, he stands there with his writing-board and checks off the list of occupants, awed by the orthography, and the disappearance of pomp into dust:

Prince Ka-m-sekhem
Prince Du-wa-ne-hor
Prince Min-dedef
Nofer and wife
Merytyetes

On the wall in there, two men are cutting open the carcass of a bull, extracting the heart for one of the men to hold up, not in triumph but in tribute. Will this be the funerary offering, together with—or in—a jug of blood? After a brief wince, I spread my mental net wider, covering more geography, and assemble a list of more vivid and inscrutable names:

Yasen
Pen-meruw

Ptahmerankh-Pepy
Ian
Nesuwt-nefert
Shepseskaf-ankh
Shad
Iy-zefa
Youwnuw
Qar
Iti
Weneshet
Ra-bauwf
Thenty
Queen Khent-kauwa.

Does it bear thinking about? Will these names in the future mean much to anyone? Murmur them, and the answer is a tune of nouns, no more than that.

I choke at the spectacle of all these thousands, writ large or small depending on their roles in life; some of them in rock-cut tombs not far from the royal rest house; many given a last-minute miniature to secure the burial of a child, a tiny slot really; and I think suddenly of the level of ordinariness to which death brings us all—rank notwithstanding. Stewards and viziers, laborers and kings. Yet I derive nothing at all from the thought: true but utterly unproductive, providing neither incentive nor reward. An isness. To what purpose, I wonder, all these shafts and chambers, chapels and offering-rooms, the cruciform's nuclei and doorjamb: the pillared halls, vestibules, serdabs, embrasure porticoes, and re-entrant angles; palace façades, and painted reliefs of people, with women weaving, ships sailing, rowers rowing, birds being trussed on a skewer, a young animal cradled in someone's arms. All ends with the funerary meal: even the dancers, clapping their hands and singing as they shake linen from boxes.

Who, I ask, shot like an arrow from above and landing in the mastaba of just about anyone, taking stock of the person and the contents. Quite a full complement here, if a king may say so: a portrait of the owner seated facing right in short wig, dry-looking goatee, long robe; and then, an under-table, with ointment, linen, bread; beer, two birds' heads, two visible lists, and stone vessels; also chairs and a bed, more garments, five granaries. No ships here, no tools, no walking canes. I wonder if they all divined from the sky what to include, to give a person a good send-off; or whether they received it from priests, so consistent, even in their use of holy formulas: "May the king give an offering, Anubis foremost of the beautiful land" (this, as if the prospect of death has reduced the deviser to some kind of babble). I wonder too if the stumbling prose style of the holy formulas is not intended to mimic the staccato quinsy of a dying man. They all get their titles and ranks in, never mind how humble, reminding me of job applications I have seen from up on high. Few of them bother to quote from holy formula, no doubt suspecting there is safety in names and ranks and titles (though not in opinions, conclusions, or pleas). As the buried dwindle in rank on the outskirts, their mastabas get smaller and the avenues between them become narrower, and you have to scooch between.

Lifelong I have been on the watch for insufficient response to life's preposterous abundance, though there must surely be other countries, and other worlds, more luxurious than ours. I have in mind those creaky souls for whom the minimum is ideal, who never take chances and go about with sealed lips, closed minds, and stitched-up rear ends. True, I make use of these people—usurers, tax collectors, number-mad scribes, bottle-counters and dream interpreters, but always I favor those with abundant soul, who return the potent gift of life with a plenty of their own, both saluting and honoring life the inexplicable. I prefer those who respond to the Nile in a Nilish way. They can be found in my court and retinue, vivid and daring people who think that, if a thing has been done before, it should not be done again; whereas if not done hitherto then eminently doable. These are my fire-eaters, not timid, not orthodox; which is no doubt why I have been assailed over the years with onslaughts on my caution, my tact. I am not here to be tiny or insignificant. They all know this; and, after all, how many pyramid-builders can a state treasury fund? So, as I survey the hosts cut down by death and sent off with blessings, I study life to be writ large by those with big pens, among whom there is one.

Strange as it sounds, as I look out from my pyramid upon the western graveyard, I develop an uncanny sense of looking at a community of living *ka*s: I am only doing on a massive scale what happens in poky little towns in the provinces, the whole point being that, by sheer insistence against the absurdity of death, we Egyptians regard the afterlife as a zone of the living, not some terminal useless dump. And what I begin, others will finish, as at Abydos and Dahshur. Thus, when some artist draws me on stone with paint, I am seen to be a creator, not kneeling with a beer-jar, holding a live goose or a haunch of beef, a lump of cake or a loaf, dangling a fly whisk or a fife, but dragging statues into this or that tomb so as to embellish the world, *my* world; I am depicted sitting at the south jamb of the entrance with eggs in cups above me. It is my pitiful will to have organized so vast a cemetery, as if life itself held no charm for me, but only the beauty at the end of the world; almost like bricklaying on a superhuman scale, though impossible with the occasional gigantic tomb (I am not thinking of my own); such as that of vizier Hemiunu. He is a mortal bank of his pelf, with standing as a man of conscience, brilliance, and tact. If you have a Hemiunu on your staff, foster him in the afterlife, so he will not cause you postmortem fidget for cutting so poor a figure among the tombs of the "little people." All the same, if you appraise his power according to the size of his mastaba, you will perhaps have overprized him; surely some quadrant of his massif must be written off to vainglory, never mind how much good he did me; the master of intercession, and so on, ever the virtuoso of the quizzical, skeptical smile as if he were dealing with an inferior intellect. Certainly he knows. He is one who witnessed the comeuppance of Kanofer, his predecessor: Kanofer's tomb in the old Sneferu cemetery at Dahshur has only one decoration, inscribed by his son (another Kawab, named prudently after *my* eldest son).

Ah, the postures and poisons of office! We agree to serve, which must always appear a disservice to others, who ironically would give their lives to serve instead. I have always made a point of not allowing any vizier to quit the office except for illness or extreme old age. No retirement, I always tell them; be careful before you accept this duty, for it will take you to the grave. You will assuredly not be building a huge tomb after you contrive to lay aside the office. Usually, only an elder statesman has the right qualifications; chopping and changing personnel is a waste of time, not worth doing, and those who venture it pay for it. I have pyramids to build, cemeteries to plan.

Bare, time-traveling old stick that I sound, conniver and hypocrite, I am the architect of the doomed; I take my stand on that, designer of long causeways, and huge insults to desert vacancy. Chirh was one of my own men; I thought they would tolerate him rather than kill him. My son Ka-wab needed what they call field experience, so off he went. Whatever I do gets me a bad name, a shuffle of whispers in the hallways: *Here he comes, he's done it again.* Only Erodo, that gossip and eavesdropper, seems to fathom my doings, and for long enough he understood me not at all. Perhaps, given enough time, enough papyrus, this old Hellene will set my story right, and wring new tears from Greek eyes at the slanders I submit to. He gives the impression of having traveled far in his estimation of my reign and temper, beginning with contempt, moving into semi-benevolence, and so into granting a warm penance. Glory be, we have won him over, although I don't think he has quite grasped my concern with settling people into their eternal places; finally we know where most of them are, which is better than their hurry-scurry while alive. A garden of corpses resembles a mouthful of teeth. A slow walk between the mastabas, along the streets and avenues of the western cemetery nourishes the hope that, one day, the whole of Egypt will lie as inert and still as this; courtesy of a ruler who sees beyond, and cherishes his little map of all those undone and settled in.

28 ▲
OSIRIS

Again and again—perhaps because the burial of his mother was the most important event in his life, together with her being stolen and "reburied"—he relives that day, his mind agog with lax, impertinent thoughts he blocks out, as if they provided the workmen with notches in the pit sides enabling them to climb up and down. The dead are supposed to stay down there, not come climbing back out after the ceremony is over. Strictly, there is to be no backsliding in this. There is no reprieve; there should be no way out, not even along the grooves cut for beams that helped the burial party lower the sarcophagus to its final resting place. Yet, if the body is stolen, do the rules no longer count? With his mother gone, is he not free now to do as he wishes with the meticulous rituals of Egyptian burial? Indeed, could he himself have removed the body, a second-rate thief, before others conceived of the idea? He half-dreams he is the culprit, having secreted her where she will never be found again: which is to say, no inscription on the electron metal of the lid, declaring Ḥtp-/ḥrś/ for Hetep-heres, along with all the other titles she bears as mother of the King of Upper and Lower Egypt. Has he put her somewhere in the palace, sealed up in a wall? Would he do such a thing, either before she was taken or afterwards; walling up the empty sarcophagus, or merely some vital possession of hers, such as the tall leather case with the caplike lid, the lid sheathed in thin gold, and emblazoned with an image of the god Min running around the cap's side? Often, he is several men: the grieving son, the mortuary attendant, the thief, the secreter of the empty coffin. He does not feel obliged to plump for any one of these roles, thus converted into compound king, free to do as he wishes provided the same mystery attend his mother's final resting-place. It's almost as if Hemiunu's transfer were an echo of the theft; when a certain stairway was cut into the quarry scarp south of the Cheops causeway. This stairway tomb would have been built exactly as things had been done in the previous dynasty (number III). Suddenly the site was moved, and an air of secrecy came over the planned event, for reasons unknown—no doubt Cheops's own sleight of hand, distracting the thieves from A to B, but enabling them to find B in any case. One open secret gave way to yet another, and Queen Hetep-heres disappeared into an obscurity comparable to the one Cheops himself felt on seeing his image drawn in his own funerary temple on a stone slab; in the image, he's looking upward at a slice of something reposing on a shelf. Of what? Something hitherto unknown, and reserved for just such an occasion as this, the burial of a great man. What was it a slice of? He never knew. How could he feel so appetitive about something unknown? It must, he concludes, refer to the sheer, brain-sapping hunger of a dead man in a tomb, equipped for the afterlife but unfed for ever after.

His mind gnaws now on the image of that niche, cut some twenty feet down in the west wall of the shaft, which is sealed with plastered white masonry. For all its five-foot height and four-foot depth, a potent slot, its own dimensions smaller. A miniature larder, he thinks. Into this, with uncertain breath and a savage headache, he repeatedly does his duty, shoving the horned skull of a bull to the far wall, the three leg bones after it, these wrapped in a mat of reeds. With a sigh, he sets two wine jars in position and unbends, not using the limestone boulder he has brought with him; he would have smashed the skull, to release his mother's spirit, but he doesn't, putting the boulder aside, fiddling instead with bits of charcoal, an eloquence of fragrant Egyptian wood.

The smell that meets him now, though, is one of decomposing beef or rancid oestrus, hardly the aroma of his perfumed mother. He inhales it (like a man, as he has been taught to do long ago), and assigns it to some other form of beings: beer that has "gone off," or the strict sulfur of the inundating Nile. He would rather sense no smell at all, convinced that pyramids and mastabas have a concrete odor, not so much of stone as of an acrid, dank powder, even in the driest places. Where the moisture comes from, he is not sure, but he thinks the air itself seems full of it; the chests and coffins are never quite sealed (witness his mother's canopic chest, planed so as to fit tight and not slip about). The very idea of enclosing bodies and their component parts gives him pause anyway, especially when he thinks of other ways—fire and weathering among them. He has not, of course, witnessed how a chair's legs rot over four thousand-odd years, as some of us have; it is a paralyzing sight, yet in its way a joyful reminder. The legs do not fall far, what they support lands on top of them, the chair dwindles into gloomy ash, recognizable all the same, falling into the shadow of its own blueprint.

We, who unprejudicially preside, envy humans their inability to see the long run of things, not as themselves at least, although of course other humans witness the end of processes and compose dubious, rueful elegies. They have free rein, and then they don't, and it is no doubt this irony that irks Cheops the revenant. Perhaps what irks him most is being unable to witness his own end, the body final after much turmoil and protestation. The mineral calm that descends is something he would like to have invented. What disturbs him is that he has not witnessed everything, which means someone at some point just chucked some of his mother's treasures higgledy-piggledy into the chamber, creating an instant untidiness. Who knows what was stolen by thieves, or lost by careless sextons? Some of his mother's things, he knows, must even have been hurled down the shaft by irritable workers, weary of royal pretension, and deathly fetishism. Some things, he knows, get lowered down with almost finicking delicacy, while others just get dumped, including such objects as the large basins that hold fresh-mixed plaster and, instead of being taken away for further use, are left behind by workmen either as part of the burial or as expendable. It is clear to him, as he ranges up and down the calendar of days, that the things *rescued* from Dahshur, where Hetep-heres was originally entombed, in some cases were just slung down the shaft into the pit, in a fit of weary indifference; the workers not knowing he would be looking on as the stuff was transferred to the second resting-place, courtesy of Hemiunu's finesse and grace with her empty casket.

29 ▲
PRINCESS HEDUANNA

Miserable today, mainly thanks to Father, who makes a habit of fouling things up, even when he is trying to do some good. Chirh, he tells me, was really one of his own men, clearly a man in danger. Have the same people seized Ka-wab as killed Chirh? I will never know the ins and outs of politics, and I am not sure Father will either; he neglects all kinds of things in favor of gigantic building, and other things slip his mind for weeks on end. Now he visits my bedroom, mainly to sit and talk, sometimes with Merytyetes in tow, such a regal, knowing woman with unspoken grievances of her own. They urge me to acquire more friends, to go out more, to give myself over to dance and music, but these urgings come from people with other matters on their minds. They do not care that much about art, which surrounds them; they care more about who's in favor or out, the relative size of individual mastabas, or for Cheops, the building blocks that arrive from the quarries daily. Making a big name for themselves, I say, at the cost of how many? He especially, tends to think of artists, if he thinks of them at all, as his fetish-makers, doing nothing private or emotional, but populating death with the correct figures. A conformist, he, estimating even mastaba art by its mere usefulness. I wish he'd loosen up, but his vocabulary excludes that, and anyway he leaves such things to me, his correspondent from the world of the painter. His view of art recalls the statues to be found in *serdabs,* those recesses in the south wall of the funerary chapel—just in case. The future I see as a bombardment by reserve heads.

So I am not at my best, moaning, whining, whimpering, having had too much happen, just when I thought I was at last getting into form. Someone said how *disheveled* I looked, and I answered, thinking of the grave-digging that typifies our culture, "dishoveled, you mean." Did not go down well. They like the obscene, but not the witty. Puns abolish time, do they not? I have few to test them on; I mean, I have many, but they aren't worthwhile test material, and all I get in return is looks of glum forbearance. Visibly, my father prefers his people dead and all laid out by the thousand in slots from which they never move, except when Osiris calls them in. Worst, though, is his view of illness and disease, which he regards not as bad luck but as nature's art, its slicing away at us as a means of self-expression. Nature wants us to suffer, so we assent, and the pain is tremendous. Why should he think thus? Must this king, who wants the dead lined up like soldiers, also use nature as an excuse? Would this be nature's only way of expressing itself? Hacking us down, infecting from below, we the raw material on which nature as artist works, mutilating us by the thousand? There is joy to nature as well, isn't there? Or must it all be funereal? Perhaps his view, so bleak, is that life cheats people so excruciatingly that they are better off dead. If so, what do we make of the pharaoh who harnesses an entire population to haul huge blocks from the quarries? It is he, not nature, who does harshly by us. He constantly makes loose analogies between himself and nature. He *is* nature, he says, but he is a star, he is Osiris already.

So I talk when I can to Erodo, the scribbling Greek, who at least retains a sense of sarcasm, believing only in words and turns of phrase, willing to lie and tease; the child springs eternal in him, knowing how to play. Too many of my so-called friends are intent on making a good death, swayed into it by solemn parents already close to the thirty-five barrier. We have no time to joke, they say; but my own feeling is that, no matter how little time you have, you have to muster a laugh. It's odd, I have seen the paintings in the funerary chapels, and there seems to be a current of lively opportunism running through, a joyous intervention in the serious affairs of daily life and death. The dancers curl in delight, the musicians without actually smiling celebrate something delightful.

Cheops's eyes, yes what about his eyes? He looks the same as usual to me, heavily made up of course. In the gaze there is nothing unusual, the whites not bloodshot, the stare good and clear. He does not talk about what's wrong, but he says it's serious; suggesting that one day he might have something done to put things right. I doubt it. Things would have to be much worse before he did that. But I can tell his depth perception is off. He wobbles somewhat when he walks, veering; and he sometimes blinks both eyes, squeezes one, then the other, but nothing comes out, no moisture, no blood. He talks about the strain of just ordinary seeing, but that is a private matter. I cannot enter his head. I think he means he has the usual headache that comes from too many puzzles on his mind—from murder to body-snatching, gross removal from the scene of a brother. Something is going on, though, with Merytyetes talking about moving into the harem, in a merely administrative capacity, as if I'd believe anything *she* planned. Is he perhaps leaving us to get on with his monster buildings? He was never the man he was supposed to be, forever falling short and making huge irrelevant gestures as a result. Merytyetes tells it all, that throaty, insolent growl of hers signifying something gone physically wrong with life.

I ask about Ka-wab but get no answer. If he has gone, it must be known how. Someone cannot just disappear, without someone's knowing the how. The most evil part of my mind, spurred by the Chirh incident, tells me that, to make their point plain, those who seized him en route to Meidun would no doubt have sent his head to us. So there is hope yet. Perhaps a day will come when people will be able to communicate more readily with one another than now, when the desert and sky are no longer a vast blank out of which no message ever comes. I count myself fortunate: the only one who has come back. Why should they spare a princess if they snatch a prince?

I'm a scribe. Almost. I have a solid, glittering career ahead of me, reluctant as I am to indulge in things of the flesh. Child of a dead mother, I'm an energetic, bright girl, who does not always concentrate or work hard; that's me, an addict of pool or pond, or an evening's float through the marshes in someone's punt. I should have been married long ago, able to take someone's majestic name, with only ten years to go before, as my father calls it, the sunboat comes for me. Oh that we might all go together, unscathed by jackal-headed priests. Into the shimmering delta of the gods. I am too young to grow up, yet I am too old to woo.

30 ▲
PRINCE KA-WAB

Would be better off dead in here no light no warmth left to die in my own time unfed uncared-for alone among the masonry that stinks of brazen damp fine phrase for outside use held captive here since I do not know I get weaker poorer all the time imagine they on the other hand arrive already dead and then a thousand years later they lie among the rubble or so I believe not anonymous like me a skeleton to be in this pungent grave with not even an ox bone to gnaw upon at first you shout and scream then you relax and get used to it it isn't going to go away and neither are you oh they could come at intervals and feed you but they don't see it that way I am here for some other purpose such as hide the next in line in some unidentified mastaba until he's shriveled down and by then it will all have been taken care of and happened the sooner that happens the better not that I care even an heir apparent would do that and I am no longer anything much a morsel a mite a leftover where no one can find me they really know how to do it just roll the big blocking stone into place and leave you to the underground air

31 ▲
PRINCESS HEDUANNA

I am yearning for his warm freckled hand wherever it happens to be. He will come in his own time. Is this my own time? Do they have him or does he have them, much popular support detaining him? If he were of the Libyan line like me, with an unknown, unremembered mother, things would be different. No one alive knows my mother's name or where she is buried, *if*. Perhaps the Nile took her to its bosom, sea snakes and all.

I save for him those zones he likes to fondle, they are no one else's. How could they be? His stamp is on them. I have been through it, but I returned, whereas most people don't: my mother, Chirh, and Ka-wab. This is a country of disappearances, understandable no doubt with so many crossbreeds mingling in the palaces, where they nowadays ask not are you related to so-and-so, but are you unrelated to anybody? Whom I'm related to is no longer there. We might be better off marooned in twin towers fifty miles apart, vainly calling out to one another. There are always forces ready to cart you off, ship you away, "un-relating" you as you go. I am past weeping. My father seems past even seeing. We are petering out, are we not? Time will tell, but too late for the likes of me. There is no one else I particularly fancy either. Damn them all: with their titles and bloodlines, my father's infatuation with his mother, and his penitentiary brothels. I have become a cipher. Now, that's a shame: a scribe with no sense of vocation, not any more, expected to wait and wait until the dead rise up. I cannot believe they, whoever they are, did not assassinate me as well, making a clean sweep of the line and its fringes. Does it bother him? Only fractionally, his mind being off in some private, distant place, his time now spent with his Greek hanger-on, the sly Erodo, a man of wealth with words.

I make a long sigh in the hallway and they all pause in their meaningless stroll to construe it.

I sigh again, just to keep them busy.

It is expected of me, but I see faces both jubilant and vain. It couldn't have happened to a better girl. So what was he doing? Getting experience of the wide world, no more than that. And what was Chirh doing? No doubt plotting to overthrow certain overthrowers. I pay homage to the god Pallor, who does not exist; he of anemia. Once upon a time there was a princess with a pinkish mole they all admired, right on her cheekbones near her eyes, and it set the fashion for long enough. Then it was over and done with, a fad faded.

32 ▲
OSIRIS

There she stands, beaker in fist, innocence destroyed: short wig, broad collar, panther skin over her short skirt. She has realized a good deal, but not yet wrapped her mind around the way their outdoor scenes painted in the mastabas and pyramids have an oddly indoor flavor; as if the additional enclosure of a tomb brought out the inwardness. These scenes are doubly sealed, seem hemmed in, punished, in spite of their bright contrasts. My own work, ultimately, I suppose, though you never know who or what is guiding the hand that paints. Out there in the heat, it is a world in which candles bend, and a curt, intimate miasma forms before the eyes. No wonder Cheops cannot see fully; he should not, it is all too much, merely sent to try him to the finish. This young Heduanna has a face younger than many children, an accident of nature, but also a sign of a gentle spirit; she shines out through her outer layer, and men look away half-blinded.

I see how thoroughly I can suppress conversation, that fleeting garbage of the race, the makeweight, the fungus, the thing that keeps the horrors at bay, whereas down in the dungeons Ka-wab is free to converse with himself and, in so doing, to convert himself to an untreated mummy. It is the grandeur of isolation they all aspire to, even as I keep my best attention on them, watching each and every fate unfurl itself. The mastabas fill up with the most sublime, intrinsic silence, against which I can smooth myself out again after too much hectic involvement with affairs. You would think that an infinite or infinite-feeling mind such as mine would have ample room for entire civilizations, say the history of Egypt's kings from beginning to end (pharaoh by the way a word they rarely use). Not so. For some reason, there is less room than you would think, even when I am at my most expansive, rocking with spleen as their tales unfold. I am bound to lose one or two of them sooner or later, lose track of them, suddenly finding one person huddled headless against a powdery underground wall, or another, wincing at a wine and beer reception in the king's palace.

How many other gods I have merged with, I do not remember; of course I don't. Why should I? Obliged to do my best for a certain few, I am not necessarily the most virtuous of the crew; I try to look out for them, but not as Atum, he of the sun, creating other beings by simply spitting. I *do,* however, remember the arm gesture of a man killing a hippopotamus.

33 ▲
CHIRH

Calling them up calling them out only the dead answer me and that in blurred gutturals I who did not deserve so cheap a fate cut down cut off in my prime I am a lion in a leaky boat and my spine is whispering

34 ▲
DJEDI THE BLUE HERON CATCHER

Oh, they are lofty all right. I had heard Cheops himself called rich in years, great in victory, the victorious bull beloved of Mast, he who protects Egypt and subdues foreign countries (a little prosaic, no?); King of Upper and Lower Egypt (ditto); he who belongs to the bulrushes and the bee (good), and son of his own belly. All the same, I being a virtual nobody, a buttercup among the bones, managed to take him on once in front of the Memphis palace. He said "I'm king," and I managed to stand up to him, saying "Don't presume with me." He bowed his head in agreement and walked on, being fanned. Great Cheops himself, whom I loved forevermore on the strength of that encounter. Let's hear it for the little people and their tiny graves.

35 ▲
ERODO

They're all around me, chirping and sniffling like bats, sipping ox-blood, or some kind of cream. More voices than ever before besiege me, no doubt talking about me, the outsider who isn't going to have a mastaba unless Cheops gets mighty careless. Or they're chuntering about him, what with his eye operation (scandalous magic if you ask me) and his chronic grandiosity (his apparent indifference to certain bloody or mysterious events). The deaths of others reassure him, I think; then he knows what to do with them, but what he really prefers is to have it all worked out beforehand, the place and the angles, the shaft, the pit, the tomb room, the offering room, all that funeral stuff. He likes afterward. He likes afterwards. I'll get it right soon.

This Memphis is the most populous city in Egypt. It has quite a cosmopolitan feel. So, when will it decline? Will I be invited to join in the rot? I'd be of some help, I think. We Greeks can always assist with that.

Words to bear in mind:

kinnamomom = cinnamon
deltos = writing tablet
bussos = fine textile
sindon = linen
kamelos = camel.

On I go, reinforced; it is never too late to learn, never mind who has used these words before.

Situations involving members of his inordinate family seem always to be coming to the boil, then going off it again, the cases of Chirh, the daughter, Heduanna, and the missing son in point. Proportionately speaking, these are minor losses, to him, because he at least has backups of all kinds. Sometimes he resembles a chess player, who loses pieces on a regular basis but always manages to replace them from a box between his knees, into which he dips without ever being called on it. He's the king and he controls the board. He is always promising better things to come; and his facility with Greek is amazing, even though we almost always have interpreters on hand for when communication gets difficult. If I am his shadow, he is my sun, it is as neat as that, and I marvel at the squabbles between us in the early days when he thought I was just a tourist, with no skills at all, far below the chaps he calls viziers—really prime ministers of a sort, the top dogs in the civil service. The correct word is *tjaty,* but *vizir* will also do. He chooses them from among his best scribes (including his daughter, I presume). Sometimes there are two of them, taking his orders and doing his bidding. Sometimes they put their necks on the block for major malefactions. On their chests they wear the emblem of Ma'at, the spirit of universal harmony; and the roster of great names in this regard includes Ptahhotep, Mera, Rekhmire, Ramose, and Paser, not forgetting Hemiunu of course. The size of their mastabas speaks for itself.

One thing continues to amaze me, and that is their belief that the afterlife matches their life of everyday. Some of the things provided seem symbolic, but many are just on hand for use, such as writing materials and various drinks. I find this uncanny, because so far as I can establish not a roll or drop has ever been consumed. So the whole enterprise continues on a guesswork basis sustained by massive trust. There is something childlike and naive about it. There is always a first time seems to be the pivot of their faith, and I am left admiring the way they duplicate the one world in the other, almost as if this world were not such a bad old place after all and it would be wise to replicate it elsewhere. Apart from being weighed in the balance at death, this must be reassuring to those who deep down question the absurdity of life. Or not. Perhaps those skeptics would prefer an afterlife of a wholly different stamp: I am left wondering about the priests who invent all this myth. Without them, things might be different and the mastabas would not be so crowded with the paraphernalia of the household gods so terminally in place. Not being a believer, I enjoy the spectacle of their trust.

Time to move on, I tell him; but he dissuades me saying there's more to come, he hasn't bungled everything yet, I'd better hold on, not that he promises an end to the disasters. Just go on being your chatty, informal self, he tells me in a Greek that's coming along in leaps and bounds, and of course that's what I'm known for, even if I get things wrong, as I surely did about him. What I need to do, he claims, is not look out for big events, which will take care of themselves (they always do), but get on with reporting the local facts of life, such as the fact that Egyptians live on meat, milk, and fats, with some bread on the side. The domestication of animals has come along empirically, one of the more absorbing sights being that oxen are often found alongside hyenas, neither animal, after a presumed initial burst of amazement, finding the arrangement odd. In fact, there are frescoes both below and above ground depicting shepherds marching their flocks of sheep on the banks of the Nile within reach of the crocodiles, an amazing and elegant sight that tells me something about the Egyptian character—only part civilized, with deep roots in the Africa of legend. It is not an easy life by any means, but it has its delights, as he tells me with an incongruously long face.

I am better at the empirical—word that to us Greeks means observant. I had rather put my trust in the things before me, and their magical presence, than in some clutter from the kitchen or backyard. I have seen superb painting on wood of the sun-god dazzling a well-endowed lady with five streams of closely packed rays. The individual lines seem arranged end to end with marvelous flowers. He "looks" the avalanche of them right into her face, from the huge red ball on his head, into her eyes, and her hands rise to shield her. Actually there are two suns in this painting, plus the usual birds and walking sticks, fly whisks and what seem to me decorative implements, ankh signs. (I initially took them to be their writing.) Or is she caressing petals of the various solar flowers, within reach, as she no doubt should? I find their sun worship the most convincing thing about them. It burns them to some degree (facial sores seem common beneath the makeup). It is hard to avoid the sun after a certain hour unless you make a fetish of avoiding it, which they don't; it is to be taken seriously and—unlike their omnipresent pots and pans, their linens and chairs—an object of impenetrable mystery.

36 ▲ CHEOPS

If they only knew what their king was now reduced to: wandering the night alone, going not as far as Giza, but scouting Memphis for an angle of stone, a niche in a wall, any space to force my body against the hardness of rock to gain some insight into what the dead feel. But they do not feel at all. To think so is a sentimental myth which I do not seem able to rid myself of. I have become a loiterer among outhouses, a cuddler of walls, looking for that paradox: the painless end. (For once I am interested in the responses of others.) Attracted by a huge block abandoned en route until tomorrow, I test its mineral cold against my overheated body, hoping somehow to penetrate it, lose myself in the cold obstruction at its center. But nothing happens; I feel only the night chill and make do with that, weeping for my mother wherever she is, perhaps not even buried; until a crew of scuttling homeless dogs comes over to nuzzle me where I lie. What use is this empire of the dead when your own mother is missing, a son as well? When the fates are against you and all you have to hold on to is what ordinary people do, at infinite cost, I have discovered the futility of being lionhearted. All my spies and investigators have come back empty-handed, waving at the vast expanse of sand out there, reminding me that Egypt is a land with almost no human population in most of its area: a ghoulish fluke, with a series of kings to torment. I always end up slinking back, face muffled, my robe dark gray (because I think that the true color of night, no doubt because my eyes no longer see truly). I mooch along, keeping to the shadows, half-expecting to run afoul of my own constables on their nocturnal patrols, but they, like sensible men, are no doubt sleeping too. A creak, a whirr, a hissing come and go in the breezeless night as the patron of mastabas hastens home to bad dreams, sidling in, as arranged, scarcely able to tolerate the whisper of his sandals as he flops along the hallways. Kings should not a-roving go unless they have ensured their welcome.

From now on, send someone else. Delegate everything. Send no dear person anywhere but hug them close to you as in a royal nursery. Bury no one. Allow no births. Permit no secret trysts. Lock doors, and especially lock up daughters. I can feel my world spilling out away from me, like a puddle of blood extending from my feet wherever I stand. Now in the bed I feel the mastaba cold come and seize me, immune to the frantic motions of my feet to warm things up. Can it be this cold on Orion? What do I know, mere imagist of the unknowable, owner of an incongruous cemetery?

37 ▲
OSIRIS

Perhaps because he couldn't solve it, he early on abandoned the problem about the smells. For some reason, to his nose anyway, as the Nile flowed northward it smelled of fish when it should surely have been the other way around. A brief conversation with Erodo had confirmed his belief that something odd was going on. (No wind blew off the river, Erodo reminded him.) It was not fish he smelled anyway, but something scorched, highly pungent, enough to make him sneeze repeatedly; and he had begun early on to associate this odor with crocodiles and their leavings. Just conceivably, sheep snatched at the riverside were the basis of what he smelled (he was sure it was not decaying crocodiles because they lived so long). Human flesh he discounted, though he shouldn't have, and then he laid the problem to rest, absentmindedly reminding himself to attend to it from time to time. Why he should sneeze at it, he had no idea, but he was willing to live with both the smell and the sneeze. He should have assigned the matter to a junior vizier for long-term investigation, but gigantic buildings caught his fancy more, though he would bring up the matter in conversation now and then, with only Erodo answering him. Erodo had much more time for the vagaries of the river, crediting the phenomenon of the smell to the "fact" that as the river flowed north the prevailing breeze blew its aromas southward. Surely, among the shepherds tending sheep by the bank there must be one with the answer, but Cheops never inquired, not even when slinking around in the dusk in mufti. It struck him then that asking such questions would attract suspicion. He could have brought the matter up in elegant chit-chat at court, but he never did, eager not to lose face by concerning himself with something so trivial, which nonetheless bothered him more than he cared to admit.

This streak of vanity in him did not apply to other matters, about which Cheops asked normally. Perhaps it was the suggestion of magic that deterred him. Besides, he was propounding a magic of his own at Giza, and it was clear now that, with so much else on his mind what with his mother gone, Ka-wab too, Chirh's head returned soon after Heduanna's arrival home, he was never even going to get to the point of asking. The smell could continue to make him sneeze, and he would put up with it. That the unusual phenomenon might have been the work of a mischievous Osiris did not occur to any of them, but divine mischief often goes unrecognized, even by savants, until many epochs later some avid researcher, some German geographer, say, planting barrels of oil in strategic sites across the map for a future war, catching a whiff at once asks how such a thing could be, not heaven-sent just to tantalize Germans. So does human history catch up with itself when the god concerned has moved on to something even more devious, leaving the fishy smell, the scorch, as a rune to be puzzled out by a Herr Doktor Professor from Munich. A more interesting question, to such as Erodo certainly, was this business of the river and the wind that never blew off it, which struck him as incongruous and would repay further study, in which he engaged, to Cheops's displeasure, Cheops adamant that things dismissed by him were nobody else's business, least of all touring outsiders such as Greeks. Cheops persisted in this attitude even after he and the Greek achieved some kind of rapprochement, after sparring and fighting for weeks. It goes to show how much the irrational governs human affairs, preventing the furtherance of perhaps worthwhile knowledge and the development of friendship. We have to manage these creatures nonetheless, second-guessing them year by year, until we weary of them. We make them sneeze, some of them anyway, trying to keep ourselves interested in other matters devoid of smell.

The question remains, I suppose, why, if we can go on interrupting such endeavors as novels, cannot we please ourselves in all matters? Which amounts to a broader question: If we are omnipotent—so many Egyptian gods vying not for attention but for elbowroom!—why are we sometimes powerless? A good question, only partly having to do with the electricity supply at high altitudes. It is a matter of tact, really, and also a tribute to whatever power (and there is one) dictates to *us*. The reasoning goes something like this: If we back off now and then, we can sometimes smuggle through an exploit otherwise impossible or subject to partial interference. So we cannot always be helpful, nor can we always get in the way, which accounts for those shining upland pastures in human thought and action when the human fancies he or she is free to pull off just about everything. The gods may not be crazy, but they are (a) selective; and (b) subject to interference from a still-fidgety first cause. Time will come, perhaps, when we achieve utter autonomy, and Egyptian *anagke* as the Greeks call it disappears. Not yet, dear reader, but I am at least here, opining and guiding, filling in the background that other speakers might neglect. We also like to exercise control, which means temper human rashness, as you may have already discerned in the career of Cheops, once woefully slandered by an Erodo who had never met him, of course.

When at last he falls upon Merytyetes's golden but sated body, it is indeed only to fall upon it. A man who has ploughed the palace and harem, scattering his seed hither and yonder, he is now in a quiescent phase, willing to take some of his sons back, especially those from whom he has withdrawn royal approval. Merytyetes plays a canny game with him, acknowledging his power, but indifferent to him physically; he has been used up. The remaining role for him now would be *paterfamilias,* except he is not much of a *pater* these days and never was much for *familias*. Cheops knows that truth and physical fulfillment lie in the mind, not the body, and he does quite well in this regard, attuned to music and poetry, with the complete fan of his people arrayed out there west of his pyramid, a huge null majority, many of them "moved out" in the sense that the things they kept by them lifelong remain beside them in the mastaba, but simply not getting much use. Instead of life, he now turns his gaze to reliefs of it, executed in various places near the tombs: scenes of fishing, cooking, eating, slaughtering, baking, all the usual rituals and routines made two-dimensional in the interests of death, not so much an end as a brief rite of passage.

38 ▲
OSIRIS

Mulling over the fate of Ka-wab, he visits Ka-wab's wife Hetepheres II, and his daughter, Meresankh III, wishing he didn't always have to take the family into account. He couldn't just send the fellow somewhere, as if he were autonomous. They come after him, blaming and caviling, as if he were not king. He envisions this rather portly prince—his son as well as their husband and father—with his craving for sweet confections, having an attack of faintness somewhere and being tended by a solicitous family who, knowing who he is, have sent a message by riverboat or express camel. It should surely be here by now, but no, the earth, the sands, have swallowed Ka-wab up, which makes him one of dozens missing.

"So life goes on," he tells Merytyetes.

"It ends for some," she says. "Do something, pray. Who went with him? I am entitled to know."

"Various retainers and bodyguards. He'll turn up, you'll see."

"Did you consult them?"

"Please do. They must have some idea, unless—"

"Trustworthy through and through," he tells her. "He's probably sowing a few wild oats. He's a big boy after all. He might actually be worrying about *us,* who are less sturdy than he."

She does one of her contained explosions and leaves him to

muse on court-bound women who never want anyone to leave home. After all, he is king of both upper and lower Egypt; he likes to spread the family name around.

More interesting than the doings of Ka-wab, which means he isn't much of a caring father (he believes in raw initiative if he can)—are certain conclusions about life and death, to which he has come over time without quite knowing it. He used to think of life as a superhuman feat, a vital project in which you asserted yourself to the maximum, each life having its own unique propulsive zest. He now believes it more important to achieve a rounded, complete life before death that leaves you untroubled and unharassed. Death is the only career, he tells himself, at which no one has failed; surely this is a more optimistic view of things, with no fretting about the corrosive impact of the Libyan line (who *was* that queen?), the weird social uniformity brought about by younger women naming themselves after older ones they admired, and born avengers bristling at the merest slight. It was something of a relief to stare out at the western cemetery next to his pyramid and think they have all accomplished it, the bad, the indifferent, even the laborers and master-masons, the gang bosses and the head painters, all lying in oblivious concert, tidier than they were when being born. This is not a point of view he shares with any but Erodo, whose cynicism has no bounds. Cheops certainly knows better than to spread the word about it among the women, either the respectable and respected (especially those self-dubbed I, II, and III); or the women in the harem, whom he sees in so static and wooden a way that he has commissioned bone-carvers to make life-size models of them, to be placed in a special hall with an obscenity stationed on its front. *Kat tahut,* it says: whore's cunt. All the same to him, stone, bone, or the flavored dead. Inert as distant stars, they all belong to him, his own, placed carefully in the otherwise undistinctive landscape. The only craftsmen he has not assigned to his statues of the courtesans he has committed to another chore, conducted at the foot of his pyramid, namely the design and construction of a solar boat some fifty cubits long; the boat is intended—well, he hasn't quite thought that out, but one idea that tempts him is to get up enough speed on the Nile to lift the boat into the air, at which point the rowers will leap out into the water. Some faith in aerial seduction keeps him firm and eggs him on, somehow combining slipway with boat.

39 ▲
CHEOPS

Ho, boyo, I exclaim to him, or something such, trying to seem exuberant and make him share the mood. I am at my old game with him, of putting his tiny fists into my mouth and sucking on them, a sensation he likes or he would fuss. First the left, then the right. One day, I whisper to him, when my mouth is as wide as my head, I will take on both, but you will be growing all the time. Not even his mother Merytyetes attempts this, and he won't always bend his fingers into a fist, limp as they are. I am dandling a prince, a crown prince to be, an immense relief from problems of tax and exaction my scribes and inspectors bring to me daylong, as if I had to know everything, persisting in delegating all. He chuckles, a sound between a volley of clucks and a tiny snort. Why does he like it? I run out of saliva sooner or later and must present an untidy image: the king at the dribble, the child with set fists. But we get on fine, his huge eyes close to mine, each of us looking at the other without the faintest sign of recognition, except we know each other's smell, that must be it. Did Hetep-heres my mother ever get up to such tricks with me, or my father Sneferu? Nothing has been recorded, nor will this be as it floats through my mind on the way to nowhere; I not having any literary facility, though an expert at negotiation. In some kind of primitive urge, I wet my finger and trace the tiny valley between his fingers, annointing him, I suppose, with royal spit. He prefers the whole hand or fist in my mouth, however, so I go back to that, remarking on the baby smell that comes off him: like milk going off, such as you might get, if you tend that way, from a cow's udder, together with a whiff of faintly malfunctioning digestion. He always has indigestion, and I wonder if that isn't something we should look out for, brace him for in later years.

Today's session (a literal sitting down) is over. He begins to squawk for his mother, who does different things with him. I am the fist-swallower. If he only knew that, I would be content. Perhaps he does know, able to sniff me at a distance like some piglet. If he grows up into a cleverdick, I will be delighted. He is my first, and he shall have all the titles I can bestow on him, not to mention the incidental, unofficial ones. I can call him *šr* (*sher*) for "small," if I want, or I will simply hug him to the end of his days; the eternal father until his fists become too big. Always I shove aside for him certain delicacies to the edge of my plate, chewing them for him, but not when he's older. As soon as he sees my initial motion, a mere wave of the implement, he warms to the game and leans toward my plate, eager to partake, a born bird. It is one way of keeping thin while nourishing the boy. Or I plunge into the Nile with him riding my back.

It is hard to look at him, but also consoling, to think he will one day take his place in some scribe's record of a certain mastaba, describable thus: Total, 9 shafts—2 queens, 3 real princes, 1 princess; 1 wife of a prince, 1 "prince," and 1 wife of a "prince." He the real thing, of course, enclosed in red granite. I treasure him for lying still, but I would treasure him more for moving about a lot, "going places" as they say, with an entourage befitting a real prince, his mind full of points to negotiate. I always wanted his hands out in the world, among his peers, and not to be sealed up. Of course they will send him back to us, his *ka* torn from his personality, and then we will know what to do; while the women weep for a life wasted, prematurely surrendered to the jackal-headed funerary priests. It is not as if he had ever aspired to power or intellectual command, without ever being a playboy. He just was too amiable to survive, I suppose, and I his corrupt liege lord.

So I tell Merytyetes my spies and informers are out all over the place, hunting for Ka-wab, whatever happened to him. He never arrived. He was not seen on the river or the land. (Nobody knew what he looked like anyway. He could not have been in disguise; he was not when we saw him off on that overheated day.) Crocodiles? Assassins? Ambush? Poison? None of it makes sense, but I am beginning to wonder if there is a connection between the death of Chirh—an act clearly aimed at my royal family—and what has happened to Crown Prince Ka-wab. The torture chambers of Memphis resound with cries of agony as traditional enemies are put to the question; but I believe the seizing of our son or whatever happened, came from a higher level than that of footpads or assigned killers. Within our own circle there must be someone who knows all about it, but who? You are not trying hard enough says Merytyetes, his mother, but I am, I just can't envision it. I saw the scene of his return, clear and vivid, but it never happened. Yet how could he have been king if he had never been out and about, as Chirh had, for instance? I ask her, but she is in no mood for reason, she wants her baby back; and so do I, that winning creature of the soft fists.

40 ▲
HEMIUNU

If I did anything right, it was this, bringing to bear on it all my politicist ingenuity, babying him through the long process of shock, rage, and desire for vengeance. I no longer feel safe, although I've discharged my duty. It could be any moment, strong-armed and buried in the sand among all the other displeasers. No flag, no stone, no word. Because of that, I daily go through the motions of farewell, and fully expect my mastaba to go to someone who has done him superior favors, but who? It is not that he is not grateful. Just that his gratitude wears out, like a sandal, and then you have to look behind you, wondering which smiling friend is his last thank-you letter. Hemiunu, vizier as was.

41 ▲
OSIRIS

Found next to the Nile with your throat cut, maltreated by those backing the Libyan line; o Prince Ka-wab, know that you are in mastaba 7110, with your widow Hetep-heres II in 7120. An image of you looking left appears in 7530. Your mother is elsewhere, but you will have run into her *ka* by now. Having been murdered, you were untimely moved, an unfinished double. Partly destroyed. Welcome to our number.

42 ▲
OSIRIS

Illustrious queen, Meresankh III, you will not know this, but you deserve to. You are in 7530, arranged for you beforehand. The presentation scene therein has no principal figure in its group, but both you and Hetep-heres II appear, pulling papyrus in a swamp, to the left of which activity stands Ka-wab, facing left. Four big inventories, thirteen estates. There's bird-netting and mat-making; men putting birds into a box and plucking plumage. Men are bringing cattle. And there are scenes of boatmen fighting ("coming forth from the swamp with lotus flowers from the Deltamen"). A sowing scene, and "tilling with sheep." You have a rock-cut chapel. You have a bl. gran. sarc. (blue granular sarcophagus).

Now to the great north-south hall. Enter from east, the doorway near south end of east wall: a shallow niche, pillared alcove; the burial shaft in the floor; in the north alcove, o illustrious lady, ten rock-cut statues of family women; in the south wall of the great hall, three recesses with figures of *ka*-priests.

Bleak reminder, if I may: you are the daughter of Ka-wab and Hetep-heres II. It will be good to have you with us.

Because the rock-cut tombs afford more space, there is much

more room for reliefs of many kinds; not only for rock-cut statues of Meresankh herself, Hetep-heres II, and the former's three daughters, etc., but also for wide-ranging scenes from Egyptian life. On the north side, the queen is standing, facing out, right hand dangling, the left on her breast; to the south her left hand is still dangling but the right holds a lotus blossom to her nose, and behind her on either side, two female attendants carrying personal effects. We see hyena and oryx being brought in, Anubis facing outward. We find also a boat-building scene, and, of great interest to Cheops, detailed depictions of craftsmen preparing funerary equipment: boats, statues, sarcophagi, canopic vessels, stelae, furniture, and personal adornments, plus, sometimes, as one of our German friends expresses it *"eine kleine verzierte Kugel"* (a small decorated ball). Some of these objects have been in use in daily life, whereas others are being crafted for the occasion of burial. Elsewhere, we see riverboats, rowed by six men, with Meresankh in her carrying-chair; a papyrus raft paddled by three men with the queen on her throne sniffing a lotus; a riverboat with its prow in the form of a recurved animal head, rowed by eleven men (Meresankh is invisible in a sheeted cabin). In another, the painter Rahay colors a statue, and sculptor Yenkaf is carving. In others: three men are hauling a statue into the chamber, one with censer in hand, one steadying the shrine; there are more men doing same with a seated statue, while others are polishing a granite sarcophagus. Another man is working on a wooden coffin, while one man is making a *ka*-door stela. Gold beaters melt gold with blowpipes, men cover a low stand and a round-topped chest with gold; two servants are making bed; a woman lays a fan on a chair. There's a woman with flap fan and bag; two women with monkey, two with a tray, a female dwarf carrying something on her head; five women almost obliterated by the ravages of time and chemistry, and again the painter Rahay painting a statue. A ploughing scene. Meresankh III and Hetep-heres II, daughter and mother, standing on a papyrus raft and pulling papyrus flowers.

Let me add (how copious Meresankh is):

Register of funerary priests

Pot of some kind on the open palm of man kneeling

Hand behind head, clenched, other hand making fist on breast
Man with live goose
Goose in arms now
Haunch of beef carried carefully
Water, ointment, incense, oils
Priest busy wiping out the footsteps of all
For this relief.

Their relegated splendor cannot fail to impress, of course, and their devotion to one another, more or less, in the context of so much royal-versus-Libyan feeling. The free movement of the *ka* from this world to the other is a notable happening, best revealed by Cheops's *ka,* which shall rove about across the centuries as if time were made of aether, just about freed of his personality and his idiosyncrasy, but also doomed to expiate in endless journeyings the undesirable portion of his being. The sad thing about him, and the well-to-do grandees of his mortuary nation, is that not one of them came forward and volunteered to be poor, to join in the fate of the masses, even to the extent of spending a workday with them, hauling and chiseling, even if only then to return to a palatial apartment with pond or pool and dancing girls in all their linen finery. It was a fate so useful to the high courtiers, all intent upon lavish burial, and nobody wanted to sample it, only, at a distance, to reap its benefits. Is this why so much dissatisfaction reigns at the final evaluation, when heart has to underweigh the feather in the other pan of the scale? Is this why the postmortem utopia envisioned by Cheops does not quite happen, and such as I enter into their lives with benevolent querulousness?

43 ▲
OSIRIS

For internal reasons, he has to go at least three times a day, perhaps even more when traveling by boat, with the vessel's motion making his innards lurch and wallow. Aboard, he has privacy and shelter in a simple wood-work deckhouse covered with linen sheets. For when he has to make a landfall, for private purposes he has the use of a similar structure, assembled in a trice and again wrapped in sheets of linen; but it is open at the top, whereas the little deckhouse shelters him from the sun. They pause, backpaddle, and land, the river being calm, the inundation not yet due. Off he trots, waving his attendants away, even the steward of the stool, and enters his little rectangular tent to perform on the drystool they have brought out and set central inside.

Ka-wab sighs luxuriously and settles to his chore, wishing he were home again and that his father would not send him off on senseless journeys somehow intended to groom him for a career as king. Crown princes usually make less fuss, eager to be on a quite different throne, but willing to soil themselves on either kind.

Back at the boat, the paddlers rest and doze, while the retinue resume their chatter and begin to exchange anecdotes of royal toilet behavior. Ka-wab knows he will not take long as, basically, he has been taken short. He sights the sky and loves its azure, unflawed and stark, well into the maneuvers of easing his overstocked body. A knife slits the linen from behind, and hands snake through with a cord that conveniently snags him around the Adam's apple and jerks him backward. It happens fast. He collapses sideways, neck broken, his robe in disarray, and the assassins withdraw, not dragging the body behind them as they go, as some might have done, but stealthily floating off, their day's labor done, their victim taken unawares. No one has noticed, and when they do, vaguely commenting on toilet training and toilet time (Ka-wab was no spring chicken), it is much too late. The landscape all sand is silent, a king-to-be has been annulled, and there is hell to pay when Cheops receives the news.

This is something he does not tell Merytyetes right away, but she soon gathers the gist from palace servants. A newspaper would have made a feebler job of disseminating the news. Cheops has the miserable sense of being severely alone, shorn of his heir, cheated of his line's continuity. Dedef-ra, the next son in line, is hardly one of his favorites. He now has to function with a cloud over him, ready to rain. Not that anyone can blame him; everyone knows about Dedef-ra's Libyan greed, his indifference to his father's needs, his zeal for autonomy and the rabid hue of his ego. He will eventually assert himself in scandalous ways, unknown to Cheops of course; but he is wretched enough to antagonize the remaining princes, genuine and imaginary, who will do their best to send him away on a military expedition he won't survive. Doomed to produce heirs, Cheops produced them from different wives that have trapped his fancy, having in his day also married both a stepmother and a sister. With so much inbreeding, the line risked a certain idiocy but also managed to produce people who looked much alike: stern, self-confident, somewhat overbearing, muscularly in charge of all smiles, large-nosed, thick-necked, and always with the head canted back to reveal the chin.

Ka-wab was hastily buried in an unready grave (7120) although later, in the reign of Chefren—perhaps to increase the quantity of funerary equipment—a sloping passage was cut into the burial chamber. A crown prince is a crown prince after all. This hasty burial meant of course that for Ka-wab, at first, nothing was ready; he was buried rough, without, say, scenes of hunting birds with throw-sticks and split spears, spearing hippopotami, journeying on the Nile with carrying-chair aboard and a private menagerie of dogs, monkeys, and baboons. No reliefs of him in his carrying-chair, being freighted out to the riverboat by a dozen men nipple-deep in water, bearing the chair shoulder-high while he slouches between the arms.

So Cheops, increasingly losing faith in himself, has now lost a mother by theft, a son by murder, and an envoy-provocateur by assassination, and is almost ready to assent to Erodo's view that he should let a Greek take over and run the polis as if that were the most efficient thing to do. Cheops's workgang goes to work to bring Ka-wab's mastaba up to scratch, providing sheer surfaces on which reliefs can appear: lions or lionesses with upright sticks emerging from their backs. At last the lining blocks go into place, toil of the Horus Mezeduw gang, proud of its work, sad about the occasion. Cheops the half-blind begins to hear music that is not Egyptian, from where he knows not, but he attributes it to his ears going wrong too, all part of his general disintegration as his women stare at him and cackle rebuke, wave at him imperiously and keep him waiting.

Hetep-heres II the sister-wife is like someone incinerated, a huge charcoal weeping; Meresankh III is blasted in her girlish springtime.

The question arises again and again: can the slovenly watch kept over Cheops's mother in her secret tomb at Dahshur, be compared with the feeble guard posted, if at all, on Ka-wab as he perched on the drystool in the desert? Heads fell. Guards and paddlers went into the toughest of Cheops's workgangs. No more river voyages from Buto to Heliopolis. Merytyetes loses her title of Queen Mother since the son is gone. Hetep-heres II, already acquainted with mastaba 7110–7120, in which a pair of favorite children were to be entombed in the first twin-mastaba ever built, lingers in front of Merytyetes's pyramid.

The figure of Ka-wab in the drawing of him and his mother will ultimately grace the façade south of 7120's entrance. It will show him thin, svelte even, quite the athlete he never was at forty; he is barefooted opposite Merytyetes, whose left hand rests on her left breast. A modern viewer would discern a tuning fork between them, but there was no such thing, and her snub nose has come unsnubbed in some obeisance to the laws of generalized visages.

44 ▲
PRINCESS HEDUANNA

Oh, the ugliness of it all. One descends from a serene enough discussion of Queen's Street, out there among the mastabas, and the exact width as specified by Cheops's department of public works—a discussion that almost seems to say we are not discussing the dead at all, but only one of the quainter suberbs of Memphis. Then the ugliness strikes you in the pit of your stomach. Killed by—well, nobody knows, although everyone has a theory. The amazing thing to me is how long it seemed to take for the bad news to reach us, even with small skiff-like boats racing back upriver, ahead of the riverboat carrying Ka-wab's remains. I try to console Hetep-heres II, his sister-wife, but there is little I can do, I one of those exported by the king who actually came back. He has a poor record of getting people back from the outside world, and Chirh was one of his emissaries too. Plots abound, of course, the day is never complete without a plot (and a dollop of enlightened incest). The result is this huge outpouring of royal dependents, all with expectations of some kind of favor, angling and maneuvering. I have no expectations myself beyond becoming a rather dusty, humbled scribe. Who will be next? When Cheops goes, Dedef-ra, the next son in line, will take over, and then anything can happen because, as they sometimes say, he has an agenda.

45 ▲
HETEP-HERES II

It is over then. No more need to hold his hand, persuade him to resist the taste of fruit, the second plate of something well-roasted. He ate as if, at the last interview, he himself were going to be weighed. What we thought could be done at leisure can't now, not, over the years, the quiet accumulation of tasteful decorative materials for the walls of his chamber, from fishing and birding, to bulls and carrying-chairs. All's tossed into the mouth of some demon, with whom we'd hoped to have no truck. We women cluster together more than ever—mother, wife, daughter: Merytyetes, myself, Meresankh III—yet only feel a void within. Can it be that the gods seize earliest those who weigh the most, as it were starting on them early—getting a good start—whereas the thin ones can be consumed at the last minute? Of course not. Did he ever want to be king? Did he relish being sent out as an envoy? I doubt it, he preferred sitting on a rug and playing with a toy mechanical dog. Something in Ka-wab never grew up and was never made to. He was easy meat, poorly guarded.

46 ▲
MERYTYETES

Hands of a violet hue, don't you remember, though he was supposed to have a poor blood supply. No, I had forgotten that. He had warm hands as a little boy; his stool had an uncommon sweet delicacy to it as if he had been living on sugar. Or syrup. Oh yes, poor preparation for a river journey, my dear.

47 ▲
HETEP-HERES II, MERYTYETES, MERESANKH III

We will have to get on without him. Perhaps he was, secretly, a man of much importance—I mean beyond becoming king one day, as if there could be anything more serious than that. He was bound, as they say, to be *put on,* meaning something more than enthroned. He was a gentle, evasive husband. A child who slept and slept, never squawked when he woke. A tolerant, easy father. What on earth did they do that to him for? He always seemed, without there being any evidence for it, forever at the beginning of a stammer. At summer's height, he loved to bathe his eyes in cold water; he said it helped him see the year complete.

THREE

Afterlife

48 ▲
OSIRIS

There ensues the extraordinary spectacle of priests at their routine work, disemboweling Ka-wab with not the merest attention to his mangled throat. Such wounds are part of the mainstream called insult, and they see much worse all the time, even among the very young. As they carve and heft, they quite naturally (to them) go through motions that others might find off-putting, farting and burping and grunting with the wholly abstracted air of the professionally committed, savants of insouciant gloom. No one watches, of course, though the king might, and there is something deft and tender about their cutting, the gentle release of the organ into the canopic jar (in this case), the pensive peeling-back of the flesh to reveal an empty body cavity that, for all the world, looks ready to receive, and to start business all over again. Poor Ka-wab, slaughtered under an azure sky, unable ever to relish the quiet, commodious, condign growth of his mastaba—no hurry, against that distant day Cheops calls the day of the solar boat (he now attending to his new cause, the design and testing of a model boat, occupied by a miniature Cheops with good eyes).

And then, of course, with his corpse purified and groomed, "fixed up" as some say, Ka-wab looks rather better: rigidified, tautened, sealed up against the intrusions of slapdash air. Presentable. Two types of core-work there in the dank and ghostly gloom; and then two chapels with a special form of niche. As final resting-places go, it is average enough, all of course under the hand of the master-builder Cheops. (Ironically, as if his enemies cannot leave him alone, they have partly destroyed 7110, leaving the monolithic niche.) Ka-wab's splendor is solitary, all right, but he has his Hetep-heres after what one would call a poor trajectory, in the midst of which he was neither "put on" nor given the option to do anything else, nonetheless playing his part in the devilish scheme of the Libyan line, with its signal outbursts of red hair.

49 ▲
PRINCE KA-WAB

Helpless emptiness above me, no roof, all that is lacking is the breeze that tears my linen from me and sends it floating up to nowhere. On such a day, he is glad to be a prince, born to fortune, his destiny assured, his way of living firm. "One must not strain so hard." Now, who told me that when I was a child? Not strain so hard as to make spots come dancing. Well, today is an easy one. For once I am in working order. They all stop and moor while I take care of business. In the blue no it cannot be me, tugged, sliced, losing so fast, so soon—no help, I'm sliding down, all blue.

50 ▲
ERODO

Why do they all come to me as if I am an expert on Egyptian folkways? They must have read me, whatever bogus account I was writing. Because I have a believable face, that must be it, and a plausible demeanor, they count on me to solve the puzzle of who did it and why, while wily old fox Cheops, he knows, he knows—maybe he's behind it—he's behind almost everything, even quite capable of having the wrong son killed to install the right one as the new crown prince except the new one's the wrong one so scotch that theory. He seems to excel at sending people on spurious missions, to get them out of the way, then bringing them back at some disadvantage only he knows about. You'd believe that of a pyramid builder.

All very well, but it creates a problem for me, the local reporter, who must try to probe the mystery without vital information. This happens all the time. Who am *I*, dear Zeus, to figure out the problems that attend a royal line constantly transgressing some as yet unformulated code of consanguinity? My own searches in this area have brought to light the uses of incest for keeping real estate in the family, for guaranteeing a certain bloodline from throne to throne; but also, alas in a father-daughter marriage, the son is the half-brother of his mother, his grandmother's stepson, his mother's brother's half-brother, and so forth. Not bad, but not so good either. I can only conclude that the Egyptian way, the pharaohs' anyway, entails a tolerant blur in matters of breeding, eventually involving (unless I am wholly mistaken) severe thinking about the correct demeanor of a son who is also a half-brother to his mother. I presume this is nothing sinister, although, on recent evidence, I find the behavior of an all-shielding father less than custodial, less than fatherly. Cheops is married to a pyramid. Such is my conclusion. I marvel too at an aging king who, late in life (when he should be settling down and taking care of his lineage), takes risks with the succession, imperiling a son and a daughter (to say the least, as well as a potent agitator-ally); and quite failing to wipe out the one son who will play merry hell, not only with the Cheops building projects but also with the cemetery concept, going his own way at his own expense until his brother princes kill him off. I mean Dedef-ra, of course, the second son in line and heir apparent. For a king to abdicate from interest in people for the sake of a mausoleum with magical properties is certainly un-Greek, yet not inhuman. I do protest, though, it is none of *my* responsibility to guide the monarch into wiser paths. However he has arrived at it, he *has* arrived at it: the throne, I mean, and this applies to all those kings who have preceded him. What right, I exclaim. By what right? If we are not dealing with divine right, then we must be dealing with sheer plunder, outright or subtle seizure, and who am I to demur?

I feel as if I am submitting a progress report to an editor, I a junior scribe. It is none of my affair except as something to report to my betters, in prose as sharp as I can make it. I have traveled in foreign lands and encountered foreign ways, all of which I am content to let be, though Hittites and Ethiopians and the rest of the interfering tribes are not. I can hardly pretend the killings—Chirh, Ka-wab—and the weird behavior—sending Heduanna to Abydos—were staged for my benefit. No, they were the natural contrivings of an old crackpot going blind and losing his grip on everything—wives, sons, finances, scribes, priests—everything but his damnable pyramid. Is he a monster, then? I doubt it. It's just his way of letting his mental grip wobble, when he's not attending: and the fact of a visitor's increasing closeness to him has nothing to do with his methods. Friendship is a factor, not a storm.

51 ▲
PRINCE KA-WAB

More no do can I me engrosses death me shrouds linen washed fresh then if years ten in Two Hetep-heres both us for ready been have would that mastaba rough a for bound failure aged middle a afloat go I home

again live I may

52 ▲
CHEOPS

What began next, although the when of it eludes me, was something I was at once tempted to reveal to Erodo, certainly, convinced he would understand it better than I. Can you tell daughters such things? Wives? I doubt it; I can only call it melody, played on instruments I had never heard before, and music so languid and serene I almost succumbed to it from the first, knowing that nothing else would ever matter again. Who then devised it? Where did it play other than in my head? Had my *ka* gone into some other dimension and seized this glorious work from the exquisite realms of the infinite? Odder than ever, from time to time the music brought me glimpses of another man, aging, somewhat bald, crouched in front of a palatial-looking house: not I, oh no, but just possibly the author of these sounds, brought to me on the wind of his own afflatus—from time yet to come, as Erodo had been, yet perhaps not from Erodo's era. Later no doubt. Nothing fierce or martial in this music, nothing loud or bumptious, but honeyed and swooning—in some ways the kind of music to which our women did their most languorous, inviting dances. It was what Erodo, in his cups, called rhapsodic, as if he knew more than he told, having heard this trance-like sound elsewhere, with many musical instruments fused to create a sublime flow. I stared at the Nile and almost fainted.

"Look," I told him, unable to keep much to myself other than certain royal political maneuverings. "It is like chickens being melted into gold and feathers. Crocodiles rendered down into finest gravy and grease. The pith of palms being oiled for receipt of the naked body. This is music that makes you not wish to resist. In a way, it's the music of a benign death, so is this what we all hear as our time approaches? Is there nothing to fear after all, about being judged in the scales? We hear this gentle harmony, and go where life is good for us?" He stares at me with unfriendly incredulity. "It's not Greek, I'll be bound," he says. "Our music's snappier than that. It sounds to me more like brothel music, hinting at the poisoned faint of some sexual disease contracted among the Ottomans, or the Libyans. and I don't think it comes from Orion either. Surely it isn't the music of Osiris, though he would know that better than anybody. Shut your ears to it if it jars you. Can't you do that? Stuff them with papyrus?"

How little he knows in his clever way, reared in that superstitiously secular society of his. I shake my head at him, then (weakening) tell him about the oldish man who stands in front of a house, clearly the proprietor of the music, no doubt awaiting a cheer. Why does this man seem blind or severely wincing from the sun he faces?

I soon become suspicious of him, cleverdick that he is. He has heard the same music too, whatever he has made of it—no doubt nothing because it won't fit into the arithmetical lattices of the Greek mind. We simpering, toiling, bronzed Egyptians know more than he does. Did he know, as I do, that dancing frees from the loins an aroma not otherwise sensed, but which evokes that of boiled fruit? Always trust your king. Anyway, if he has heard the music, then it cannot be the tunes of death, unless he—no, he is young enough. So perhaps this music is cosmic, addressed to all—of whatever race—who have the wits and tenderness to hear it. Nothing sinister, and so perhaps Orion's or Osiris's after all. Why should it exist unless it be good for us? Or, well yes, it must be the music of the few, the chosen, addressed to them only: a blissful foretaste, my dears, of life beyond the pyramid.

"Never mind, Erodo," I tell him. "It's not for everybody, this music, not even itinerant scribes, unless they happen to be king's daughters. Visitors, no. It says the way you walk is not going to be thorny at all, but soft and mellow, yielding as bosom flesh. We have earned it. It is the sweetest overture in the world."

53 ▲
OSIRIS

Call it if you wish a consolation prize. Perhaps, having so many at my disposal, I was spendthrift with them, not only swapping good for bad, and vice versa, but also swinging deeds and events out of their true time and space, reorganizing history if you will: for a Cheops, a Herodotus, giving them what they have no knowledge of without, however, relinquishing any part of what I know. Behold the know-it-all as time-traveling eclectic. Not at his best for years now, he also receives the gift of music. Herodotus—or Erodo as Cheops calls him—will simply get the gift of knowing Cheops after maligning him in print. There may be little justice in all this, but at least there is action; one does not sit up here in the gods—among them—without accomplishing something, even if it be something on the level of subtle shadow-play, an act more calculated to suit our tastes rather than gratify the wills of humans. In this case, very old ones, though by no means the oldest. The thing is that we tend to ignore the billions of prayers that ascend to us, though we mostly half-listen, and instead impose on human history whatever gives *us* pleasure. This must be hard for them to understand.

See how the photons blur the two of them, composer and betrayed wife, almost as if he were blind already and out of his body. He sees the pair of them standing reluctantly on view right there in the doorway to the paradise garden he called their own, he in drainpipe pants and partly buttoned frock coat, letting his cigarette droop, his eyes aimed downward, a big brow over—depending on that shattered shredded light—his almost simian face. Nattily dainty, he looks lost among those motes, in very much the contrived posture of one who cannot see: a painter's model, perhaps. One step behind her, he stands as if positioned by von Stroheim ("One step backwards, please!" with a flourish of his flyswatter). Our composer, whom Cheops has already seen in his cups, courtesy of you know who.

Did this fellow compose enough? Just about, or so I think. Did he write enough letters to Bartók and Kodaly, say? Almost. Did he write enough to Elgar, that prince of pomp and circumstance and happy wedded bliss? Nowhere near. They ran into each other too late, although having admired each other from a distance for a long time. I find myself overcome, in these middle days of my enterprise, by the usual trite regrets. He did not have the right life, as a colleague of his used to say; yet it would be hard to devise for him, granted his genes, his fads, and his bluff, almost decadent temper, a life different from the one I, mere amateur in music, allotted him. In goes my hand, out from the grab bag he comes, hot and bothered. Had I been better prepared, I would have slid him back into the bag, but he is revelant enough, and mysteriously godlike. I am his echo.

Better that I say it first before some assiduous scribe accuse me of self-importance. I, Osiris, the companion who grew almost into an accompanist over this composer's lifetime. He had, I told myself belatedly, plumbed the exact murmur of godly peace, as we hum to ourselves, whatever is happening elsewhere. I offer accompanist in jest only, of course. I am merely one who murmured along, knowing that a human soul had finally established the gentle importunings of the powerful. So I became the creature who sat by him as his condition evolved, soaking up his table talk and sometimes getting it down, at the same time soldiering with him through the terrible ravages of a disease that softened the bridge of his nose and made him impotent, initiating some kind of brain rot. Often enough I was in the position of someone, a house owner say, confronted by one of those springtime irruptions of moth-flies: tiny black bumbling things that pour out from beneath, behind, a baseboard and swarm across a bathroom floor. Day after day. You mop them up and wait for more. Just so: I mopped up what he offered and awaited his pleasure, growing, if I may say so myself, all the way from overseer, overhearer, into amanuensis, guide, philosopher, and friend to him who, having soared so high, found himself cast down among the infidels: I scurrying about to gather the least crumb, morsel, with which to fill out my account of a life not so much wasted as overspent. I raise a cautionary finger against anyone suspecting me of providing only what the French call *amuse-bouche*, that tickles the mouth and distracts it while it is waiting for something solid to bite on. No, my interstices have significance of some kind because *he* furnished the wherewithal, and whatever he did, granted my interest in him and his melodies could never be trivial—not if you assumed from the first, as I did, his true eventual majesty.

This is why I bequeathe him to Cheops in the hope that the one will chime with the other.

As I say, better to get it off my chest now that I sometimes wax too humorous for him, who was of a more somber disposition, especially as his illness dragged him onward. I discovered that sickness is our way of turning humans into works of art. You give them some rope, then reel them in, happy enough that their screams and winces have a certain style. We carve into you, ladies and gentlemen, and take all pain in our stride. If anyone, in the modest crescendo of increasing friendship, or intensifying acquaintance, waxed the more facetious, it was always I, who felt younger than he and therefore sillier, my excuse being that I had vowed to pledge my life to his (and some others, including the poet Shelley, once forced upon me and gradually enjoyed). I asked little from him beyond an occasional nod at what he thought a comical face leering at him from an upper corner of his music room, and a chance to bask in his all too human glory, with his member dangling out in front of him and the room filling with the cheesy aroma of gangrene.

Let all that keep for a while. Let it be said I tried to cheer him up a little, attempting that so far as to imagine I was always at his side even when I was not—a kind of imaginary sorcerer's apprentice, forever piecing together into the grand swoop of a life the little he told me about—say, letting oranges rot, or ending all his compositions with a quietus appropriate to nature declining, sinking into ooze or magma, slime and slop, yet always with a cheerful benison fitted into his cadences so you knew he was happily surrendering. Surrendering, yes, but happy about it, which we find so rare and at once inscribe in our mortuary tomes. You will see that I, Osiris, the ageless, grew up somewhat while tending (attending) him, not with any hope of becoming like him, but merely in hopes of being a better listener, a more acute sympathizer, which is perhaps what in our more benign moments we would all like to be. He usually heard me out (*Voices Off* he called me, having read a few plays in his time) and nodded while, figuratively speaking, I put pen to papyrus, sometimes changing a word even as I wrote. He spoke as smoothly as he composed, never tense or strict.

During our time together, I must have (with help) messed with the Nile, but I do not exactly recall: I find it easier to stop an inundation than to make someone change his mind. We tend to be that way—rather like celestial sports commentators who, instead of reporting play out there, lapse into private reveries and so produce "dead air." From the end of the nineteenth century I plucked him. We can pluck people from everywhere, bringing them forward, driving them back, even freezing them into their own present for being bores. I told him how old Homer, eminently pluckable, referred to the river in the masculine (*Aigyptos*) and the country in the feminine (*Aigyptae*), but he cared little for such folderol, instead asking me if I knew how much alcohol there was in vanilla extract and if I knew of anyone who loaded up on the stuff. He was funny that way, and often allusive beyond even my bizarre powers of recognition, especially when he spoke of Germany and Scandinavia. He had what I call an "escape complex," forever dreaming about leaving for New York with a virtual stranger, female, aboard an ocean liner, and telling nobody.

So I come to this: What does Cheops now make of him?

And what does Erodo make of what Cheops tells him about the composer in his life?

Already I discern two "betters" dogging me at the beginning of whatever I say. It would be only too easy to begin, ignoring second-guessers even so adroit as Cheops and Erodo (whom I cannot help calling Herodotus, the name I have always known him by). I admit to having, in my evanescent way, tried to instill in Cheops some response to the shift in Egyptian painting—from rather conventional outlines to depth and motion, with more attention to how the painter feels than to what's in front of him; but he fails to respond to this aesthetic overture, being king of course. I go at them all, every second, dead or alive, ancient or future, trying to exact from them a flicker of artistic life, but it is thankless. Either they say a woman is an open door and a man is a battering ram, or they just go blank when I somehow graft into their spent psyches such an idea as, apropos the tango dance, that for some reason in Latin America, in the anterooms of the dance, washbasins and telephones are always side by side, in case someone wanted to phone while shaving, say, or to wash the phone while talking. Gifted with omniscience as they call it, I can produce a dazzling array of effects; I have had a part in all novels, I suppose, feeding bits in here and there, indeed in all political speeches, funeral orations, and elegiac poems. I find it hard to infiltrate the over-occupied skulls of humans. When I turn to Cheops, that local philistine, that architect of blocks, I would like him to tune in to music, and have had some success, but he fails entirely to grasp one of my main points: that music is for the gods only, not for human consumption. In short, we make composers create in order to soothe us for not having full control over our own monstrous performances. He thinks music, which he rather fancies, is for people only—him especially—quite leaving the gods or Osiris out of the equation. I persist nonetheless, trying to humanize him, to offer a Virgil Thomson to his cliffhanger.

I was never the composer, see, never nature's archangel as I once called our composer. It seems only yesterday that we disinterred him (how Cheopsian) from his French grave, reburying him in Limpsfield churchyard to the strains of *On Hearing the First Cuckoo in Spring* and *Summer Night on the River*. Beneath a tree, the grave was illumined by hurricane lamps and lined with laurel. What a day on which to begin to recall, a year after he died, with the taste of triumph poignant on the lips. 1935, when I told myself I was wrong to think I remembered him so well because I had not recovered from his death. It would have been wiser to see that his death had little to do with it. I mean, in no other case had a human's music flowed out into nature and actually become *more of it*, so much so that it sometimes did not even leave him behind—he went with it, out into the mellow plenitude of this planet's life; and his body, carcass, whatever, stayed developed like a cloud-rack neither here nor there but diffused, an account rendered back, a form of imitation without a name (as old Aristotle puts it), the thing made so much itself that it merely drifted back into what it had come from, ravishingly akin. You will see now why I devoted so large a part of my all-encompassing life to his gift. His work as I came to know it was never *about* something, it *was* it.

Here I go, paragraphing as some humans require, merely for the obscure delight of conforming to convention.

Let me be clear: certain music composed by humans had gotten away from us, and surpassed whatever entertainment we fudged up for ourselves. In other words, it was something exqusitely out of our control, executed by humans to please themselves, without their realizing that it in fact pleased *us* more, and perhaps for the same reasons. When the universe outruns or outmaneuvers us, say something in the basic chemistry, we need consolation, which seems, for example, to be what Bach provides.

The bizarre thing is that, if I were to attempt one of those lightning bolts of portraiture (what sort of man was he), just to inspire Cheops, I would disregard for the moment his massive creative energy and his lyrical, ecstatic output, as well as his passion for high altitudes, orange groves, steamy rivers, and Negro spirituals (his distaste for Beethoven quartets too!); and I'd say outright he was also a man of the world, both cocksman and vicar, as I once saw during the night at Grez, when with Jelka bleeding all over their primitive bathroom (in the female way), he fumbled in, scooped up all the miscellaneous mess of towels, kerchiefs, pads, and rags and shoved them into a paper bag he then disposed of at speed, the while reassuring her in the depths of slumber that all was well and natural and that, above her inaudibly, there were nightingales and canaries saluting while envying her for—what did he call it that night—such an estimable bouquet of involuntary nature! All the while daubing his bony face with blood, to join in the rite. He was like that, in tune with some mighty being we could all sense, but in the most intimate, calibrating way. Had he been a true Egyptian, as indeed I hoped one day to make him, he would have invoked the hooded crow, the black kite, the kestrel and lanner falcon, the great egret and the buff-backed heron, the hoopoe. How many times he reassured her in this fashion, I do not recall (I had other scenes to view), but he would accomplish his feat by murmuring *sanies, sanies*, which word he associated always with tipped-out blood, to him a germane part of the music he worked in—I mean he worked in that idiom and also worked music of his own into it. All was music to him, even when gross and maybe foul to others, something that went down really well up here, where only the respectable side of our activity seems to win favor. We try, but often get it wrong. No wonder we need music. Anyway, no shirker he, not squeamish at all.

So he was a man, as we say, enamored of the world, at least of its processes, paddling his hands in it, extending to nature the same kind of obvious indulgence a mother extends to her baby. I think *sanies*, and other such basic words, meant more to him than to anyone else; it must have been a kind of code, an electron brew all his own, so that, you might say, he saw no barrier between what he called *sanies* and the meconium of the newborn infant. He was into all that, oh yes, but in the tenderest way, except that he found it hard to keep his hands to himself with women around him, on ocean liners or at village dances. He got around, at great cost to his marriage and, later, to his well-being (when his hair came off in patches and his skull looked moth-eaten). It is no good impressing the reluctant Cheops with all this, not in one whoosh, but he receives the music, direct from me, and must be dandled with it.

54 ▲ CHEOPS

Something keeps on coming through as if propelled, by which I mean it doesn't seep or trickle; oh it's quiet enough of course, but it seems to have some genuine impetus behind it. Is Osiris, my lord in all things, prompting me from a distance, with noises from unfamiliar-sounding musical instruments? It could be he; but would he want me to succumb so readily to a mode of music that erases your defenses, saps your resistance, and leaves you wide open? Am I such a softie that the merest melody wafts me off? Behind it, too, there's a potent person, though one given to corruption and decay; I hear the music of rot and swill, controlled putrefaction. I am not sure how this squares with the eviscerations practiced by my priests. Music to die by, or telling you to slither away, as I call it. No one will care about your disappearance.

It is not the music of birds by any means, although I detect here and there some kind of birdcall, reiterated; it is more like a waterfall of natural sound—the river splashing, the wind soughing, the rain thrashing down—all fused together not to intimidate but to provide a secure backdrop for one's own impetuous calls. Do you want to delve into me, the music asks. I am fluid, I am syrupy, I am easily manipulated. I am not human, but my cries are genuine. What a morbid wooing crooning music it is. It comes and goes, following laws of its own, followed by my mood—that of a partly blind man anxious to find something to hold on to, never mind how ethereal. Sphinx-like music I find it, merging the strength of the lion with the human head, its unique tone that of the sun rising silently, huge enough to engulf us quite, yet so gently a babe would not resent it. This is the music of the happily returned ibis, arriving at the onset of the Nile's inundation and doing it so often he becomes Thoth the divine scribe. It is the gentle music of rearing, acquired by I know not whom, but as able to win from you a few tears of torpid regret, as to lead you back into the blind peace of the womb. I hear nothing harsh in it, but perhaps all that has been censored out, so it seems there has to be a certain amount of repetition in it, the same thing repeating, as in nature itself. I am tempted to believe that the voice of natural things—from butterfly to cricket—has broken through to me at last, perhaps dissuading me from unorthodox maneuvers, or perhaps egging me on to feats even greater. All I know is that something contemplative and contained has begun to afflict my soul, may Osiris help it. Our land, of rock and desert, treeless but for the riverbank, is a harsh one, not suggested by this borrowed music. Yet perhaps it is seeking to teach me the right gentle way in which to regard all landscape, displaying toward it a tenderness it has not schooled us in. So this could be the music that, after the fashion of our painters, teaches us to see water as from above, with always a fishbone ripple in the pattern. (What can that be an augury of?) Now is the time to change myself into a fallen tree, lying full-length along the surface and supping from the waters of eternity. We hear tales of shepherds up in the delta who, when obliged to journey to lower Egypt to collect purchase-money for their sheep, go almost insane. This music may be the paradise of having no flies to bother you en route. It may be, but I am tempted after a lifetime of stargazing to think that the music of the heavenly spheres has at last reached me, from the newly returned star Sirius—it always comes back in high summer.

If I had to evolve some simile for the experience, not even being an artist except with huge blocks, I would say that hearing such music, imagined or real, would be like managing to fill in the details of drawn birds while setting them against an almost blank background, as if your life had suddenly been rendered in fanatical detail at the last moment, certainly not void.

So, as we draw our goslings and doves, we fill in the tortured life of Cheops, soothed at last because he no longer needs to suppress the truth he knows but dare not blab lest he too be killed. There is the man in life, the man depicted, in his mastaba, the man talked about; they all have to come together. Is this not why Rameses II chiseled away the names of his predecessors from their monuments? Not to have your name inscribed in stone is to hear no music at all, but merely the fitful, untrustworthy desert wind. This must be why his own inscriptions had to be cut very deep into the stone, such as you achieve only after many years of rule. Once I saw a man carving away in honor of some silk herons, a group of which is facing in the same direction while the odd one out looks rearward. The herons of the group are all standing on sturdy well-planted legs, whereas the heron looking the other way has no legs at all. So I feel like a legless heron, amputated for reasons unknown, but left to brood on this uninvited music, no doubt the prelude to something magnificant, which I dearly like to have invade my monotonous days. Am I to receive my legs after all this time?

A moaning comes, a sighing into someone's ear, a parade of breath as of one heavily sleeping, a long labored intake, followed by a high-pitched imprecation known only to certain musicians. Sleepy time, the music announces, in tribute to the milk we use to get us to sleep. Something blissful is happening against a distantly heard concert of birds, but a plash-plash of oars comes too, with a bass tumble of an oar against the sturdy side of the boat; then a sound of plunging, disciplined water. Our composer was a nature-lover, to be sure, whether of sand or something riper, I cannot tell; he did not so much relish, I hazard, the indoors. I wonder only if the combination of flute or nose-flute, hand-drum, tambourine, double-sided drum, castanets—the fusion of which I fancy I can hear quite easily—joined with one-stringed mandolas, seven-stringed hand-harp, and harps with even more strings could yield such music. I rather doubt it. What I hear, or overhear, comes from a more ambitious ensemble—not chamber music at all, not even the aggrandized royal orchestra that sometimes plays when we have gone without a murder for six of our months. If our own music seems improvised, and therefore so much fresher and more adventurous, what I hear seems highly organized even if into a colossal surge of sound, in which all merge while tinily asserting their differences. We have not arrived at such music. As Prince Ka-wab used to say, after the great age of pyramids will come the age of melody and spectral color. Taffeta will begin to sound clunky and brains will foam.

55 ▲
ERODO, TENTH BOOK

Remarkable stories he tells me, most of them about the new onrush of music that fills his head; not music of the kind familiar to him, with or without dancing girls. Where it comes from, I have no idea, but he seems more imaginative these days even though his sight, briefly remedied, is failing again. He tells of long poignant surges played on instruments not even Egyptian, then of their composer, clairvoyantly described as a man from the Low Countries (west of Chios, according to me), but also said to be from Germania or even northern Britain, to whose manners and speech his own conformed. "Born and bred," Cheops tells me, whatever that means to him. It would be just as useful to call this man a native of some tropical region. For his very music, however, he remained a misfit wherever he found himself. Says Cheops: "When he was much younger, before the music that distinguishes and ennobles his prime, they called him Fritz," which Cheops finds hard to say, though names such as Merytyetes and complexer ones such as Ne-shepses-nesuwt trip easily from his tongue.

There must have been sheep around him, he says, because his father was eminent in the wool trade, anxious for a son to follow in his footsteps, instead of wasting time on music. So the boy went self-taught, unable to escape a stern business training, but also able to make music in his head, actually imagining different instruments playing it, and sometimes mangling it too. Above all manufactured sound there rose, in the lad's ears, the natural peal of his voice, even while he was being sent hither and yon, to such countries as existed and had a culture worth inspecting. The young composer soon discovered within himself a mystical never-never land that consoled him when he came to spend hours toiling at one of his father's desks, forever forming golden loops of something deliciously impossible in his rapidly advancing mind. In no time he developed the habit of traveling mentally to all manner of exotic places—islands with jungles only a handsbreadth above the sea—where it was warm, life was primitive and easy, and languor reigned amid a sultry peace. Begging his father to at last allow him to go visit such places, to make their imaginary version real, he pleaded to savor the forbidden fruits of an exotic peninsula and at last prevailed, though not without having to make all kinds of false promises about the wool trade. At this point, his curmudgeonly father did a volte-face and actually bought for him a distant plantation, where oranges grew in abundance, hoping to persuade the precocious boy to recognize the commercial value of the lessons learned among its groves. All he had to do, supposedly, was look after the orange plantation, with the aid of account books, work schedules, and some kind of inspired timetable. It is amusing to imagine the father, far from yielding without a fight, noting the gradations that led from the wool trade, through fruit in boxes, and thence through subtle shifts to the lotus-eating life of an aspirant musician. So the youth ended up amid a community of simple, unschooled singers who sang for the love of it, every bit as unlettered as himself.

At home in the plantation on the St. John River, to him as virgin and unexplored as Thule—the composer-youth gave way to his unruly self, so early in life, freeing the epicurean side that led him ever after into the finest heights of swooning and languishing, belly-licking and cooch-cuddling, to an extent his father would have found monstrous. As natural as breathing was what the young man called this new-found mode of life, even as from 1884 on, he went on a binge of reading and pondering while he canoed with his new black friends (so different from the sallow, uncouth natives of his home region, and the sullen, gruff Huns among whom his father had sought to place him either to do harder and harder sums, or to learn new ways of trading). Dances and choruses took him over. His oranges rotted in or out of sight, creating a delicious stench he could never quite reproduce in later life, and he developed the epic image of himself as the solo white on an alligator hunt, an outsider with deep pockets, sentenced to a lustrous jail he hoped never to quit.

For the first time in his life he was happy, trapped in that timeless continuum of heat and rest, doing what he wanted only when wanted to (which did occasionally include music on the viol he'd brought with him across the tossing seas). Enveloped in this wild and remote world, he felt other cravings, and was soon making the three-day trek to the nearest town in search of musical equipment. There, when he at last arrived, he ran into a certain Ward, a fanatical musician who took him under his wing, regaling him with musical talk aplenty. There he was, dabbling on keys and strings with his accustomed sweet fervor, and there was the illustrious, altruistic Ward (whose ward he was) offering to guide him to this and that off the cuff, as if it were perfectly normal for a musical savant to discover a teachable booby in a seaside music shop. Captivated by the young man's bizarre and sensuous work, Ward interrupted the spell and, waving in half-dimissory fashion at the viols and lutes grouped together in the shiny salon of the store, rattled off a list of his favorite composers, hard to ignore or even comprehend if ever you had been waiting all your life for just such a recital. Who were these music masters? So he and Ward were friends before they even met, of course; the composer had met his first anti-father, with whom to take allusive dinners and, thenceforth, elaborate, compelling lessons in the art that was to obsess him. Seeming never to have any urgent business to attend to, Ward went off with the young man to the near-abandoned plantation, just a little prevailed upon, and stayed there six months, where the two of them designed gorgeous invocations to the local monkeys and crocodiles, the fierce heat shimmer, and the stench of rotting oranges that hung over the constantly shuffling sea, like nasal fire above a skin in motion. He stayed six months, after which the youth was irrevocably converted to art.

Have I said enough in this fairly straitlaced manner, benignly suppressing (as I should) the entire terminal moraine of hindsight? The man's genius twists around to greet the oncoming magic of the youth. Safer, I surmise, to detect the nascent gift rather than insist on its futurity; what he was going to be, young Fritz, was what he was going to be, so it is important to show him dabbling, pounding, fiddling about, jockeying for position in the world of tuneful men. Here was one inspired by his own presence, among those wholly unlike him. His entire life had become rhythmic, even the chewing of a slice of bread.

56 ▲

OSIRIS
Does he look any different, music-swamped as he is?

MERYTYETES
Plotting something new. He should know better at his age

ERODO, TENTH BOOK
What kind of rugged serenity has seized him now? Nothing to do with any of us.

PRINCESS HEDUANNA
More approachable than usual. At least his face is. Then you discover how far away that amenity of his demeanor really is, and recoil.

OSIRIS
They have none of them had much interior delight.

DJEDI THE BLUE HERON CATCHER
Dare I approach him yet again?

PRINCE KA-WAB
Oh to have such peace inflicted on you. Where does he get it from?

HETEP-HERES II
A born survivor. You have to be of royal blood.

CHEOPS
They are all staring at me, especially those with glass in hand in the brief delirium of wine. Little do they know what joy has come upon me, from whence I know not although I have holy suspicions. This must be the onset of the last ascent, known only to kings. The music readies you for the divine climb. Your *ka* is getting ready for the other life. It is time, and I am glad.

MERYTYETES
Less and less knowable. Now, whose fault is that?

CHEOPS
Seen from in front, her nostrils are too big, which is the result of a nose that goes too far forward. You can see too much of what's within. She's lucky. Most of the known adulterers, women, have had their noses snipped off: permanent badge of dishonor, but of course the nose no longer gets in the way of whatever they get up to next.

PRINCE KA-WAB
Were he to come down here into the dank and dark, he would find me waiting, prematurely final, eager to share in what so keenly delights him, as never in his pyramid-building days. Oh, Father.

CHEOPS
I am aware of a vanished soul yearning for me and cursing the abysmal tyranny of time. Plump as he was.

PRINCE KA-WAB
Down among the dead men, a serious song for all those attending me.

PRINCESS HEDUANNA
All those who favored me have been finished off. Perhaps it will soon be time for me.

MERYTYETES
Old fox, tuned in to something hotfoot from Osiris. I have known him and known him and known him. Now this: the aloof rapture.

ERODO, TENTH BOOK
Must get this down, get this down, he's fluctuating so fast I can't even embellish as I go. Just the facts? Not on your life.

HETEP-HERES II
Made you crouch and then peered upward into your folds, hunting—what? The next generation, or checking for the rotten stain of the Libyan line, carelessly sown behind.

PRINCESS HEDUANNA
Would he perhaps send me elsewhere, to meet someone else? I could pose as a scribe again. Steamy boredom here, and they all think I was responsible. Imagine.

OSIRIS
They should all be praying *not* to know. All the leftover stuff, the garbage, goes into my head-set, I the only modern among them.

DJEDI THE BLUE HERON CATCHER
Would he bite my tongue off if I did?

CRF THE FLY WHISK MAN
Your nose, stupid.

DJEDI
I'm not talking about looking for trout in strange rivers.

CRF
Then what, wiseass?

DJEDI
Asking him the time of day.

CRF
Why bother, he wouldn't know anyway, he's miles away.

DJEDI
Then I should remind him.

CRF
If you do, he'll have you crushed with a thousand pebbles.

DJEDI
Well, he didn't last time.

CRF
What did you tell him?

DJEDI
That's between him and me. Honest.

CRF
I'm off. Just remember, herons eat flies.

DJEDI
I'm aware of that. Just think, Crf, they keep building pyramids all the way to the sky, using all those people, and we have to cope with the amount of shit produced daily. The river is full of it, the sands are lousy with it. On the building goes.

CRF
You'd better offer your services to them before it's too late.

DJEDI
No, if I hide my own, that's enough.

CRF
Looking at them, you'd never think they did any such thing. Pure at heart, eh?

DJEDI
Pure somewhere else, you mean. Couldn't our lord and master build a pyramid of *that*, and just leave it to dry in the sun? It might warp and twist, but it would get the stuff out of the way, especially if some poor bastard painted it red.

CRF
I gotta go.

DJEDI
Just what I mean. To hell with architecture.

57 ▲

MERYTYETES

I keep a close eye on workmen wandering in and out of the palace. "Always lurking in dark corners," I say to anyone within earshot. "Plotting revolution, planted by some malcontent."

Overhearing, Heduanna—who has been having a royal doze in a specially adapted carrying-chair, wearing a silken veil, eye mask, soft louvered slippers—manages to murmur, "Just another serf. They don't care. Three square and some kind of bed is all they need. Goodnight. I'm always yawning."

MERYTYETES

There are some people in this world who are frail and timid, whose taste for the waters of life is limited, and they say the minimum—they don't refer to life and living much, or even to the dead, but just tiptoe through, hardly noticing they're alive. You're one of those, my dear—no appetite. No appetites. You take everything for granted. Hardly even visible.

PRINCESS HEDUANNA

You see me enough to see me.

MERYTYETES

Only just. I find you out by smell. I love that smell of oestrus in the morning. You do get around.

58 ▲
OSIRIS

"'*Mother,' please!*" (Merytyetes strolls away, not even aware that Cheops, in his questionnaire for the day, has queried her nostrils, her walk, her high-handed austerity, along with many other features of her being. To him, she is a woman too distributed into life to be seen as a single person: always fighting, scattered, with half a dozen well-tried reserve positions to fall back to in the event of strife. It is not that she shirks anything, but chooses to cut her losses. Yet, elegant, sinuous, bosomy, she has half the men at court gasping after her, even though they sense in her something of the impenitent destroyer of delight. An alpha-matron, you could call her, famous for her discomfiting afternoon walks, during which she contrives to disturb with a look of barbarous aloofness just about anybody taking it easy in the shade, alone, or coupled or multiply engorged. For her, Heduanna, flotsam from an assassination, is easy meat, Djedi the Blue Heron Catcher and Crf the Fly Whisk Man are bits of plaster trampled underfoot.

MERESANKH III
Cow.

HETEP-HERES II
Udder on legs.

She is a golden impetuous edifice, but she knows to whom she does not speak. Bellicose angel.

59 ▲
CHEOPS

I am going to gurgle with it. I cannot help it, it comes through me with its own delicate parlance. How have I ever lived before without being thus thrilled? Slow snail of longing nibbles me. I am going somewhere soft as a satin belly, with goat's milk running through, pus draining from the eye, like lackeys' beloved brew.

What did her mother, Merytyetes's, say about me a long time back? After I became king. "Can't you persuade him to dress properly, in the correct raiment? He'll never get anywhere got up like that."

60 ▲
OSIRIS

Times were when I thought his image preceded him, moving forward with silky speed, almost like the blindness-to-be afflicting Saul on the road to Tarsus, who saw his terrible ailment as a simmering lattice on the very point of descending upon him. This composer preceded himself, much as, I always surmised, he knew beforehand, before actually putting it down, the phrase to come in a moment's time. He leaned forward and I leaned after him. I agree that does not make a very firm basis for matter-of-fact report—just to say you *thought* he did such and such. Although the more you know someone, the better you can sense these slopings-forward into the realm of destined finitude. I am sorry: his music, in which I have been immersing myself so as to regale Cheops with it, so overpowers me that I repeat myself without ever knowing I have done so. I'll say it again. His flow sends you into a gurgling ecstasy. And just look who I am—not exactly a cosmic minnow—virtually surrendering to the millrace of his mind.

Through the music, I back-introduce myself, but he does not hear me, eager as I am to be sucked in, Where the bee sucks, say I, but he's heedless; I am never to be made over into a nobler version of myself.

"Oh," he murmurs to the world at large, without even attending, "in being made over you are to be reborn. I guarantee it. Just give yourselves to the outpouring sound, and you do, as to a slow river, or one flower after another sucked in the right order by bees and wasps, or skylarks and sparrows." Not the birds of my childhood by any means but changelings close to his French heart. You could tell he knelt and pored over the surface of every leaf or petal as if this were his last instant on earth, which his senses wiped out, his mind evaporated, his entire notion of music gone. There was always something desperate even in his most dilatory pieces, and of course you got used to this, remembering from somewhere the man who recommended doing everything slowly, then doing it again even more slowly as practice made you perfect.

I would never forget my initial image of him as the Yorkshire *ingénu* rippling his fingers across the keys of pianos in far-off Florida (far-off to you anyway), elegant orphan of inspiration who, in the August of 1885, took a riverboat up the St. John's River to Jacksonville and opened his career by singing in the choir of a synagogue. With cordial letters of admiration, he next found his way to Danville, Virginia, almost like some young prince reclaiming his inheritance, and became a music teacher at the Old Roanoke Female School—a captivating but somewhat stern dandy, impressing old Mrs. Belle McGhee Phifer as a charmer: "He charmed all of us," she gushed, "this modest young Englishman with such nice manners. My husband was quickly convinced of his virtuosity at the piano, especially the chromatic quality of his extemporizations, which seemed to violate the known rules of harmony. I remember my husband used to sit entranced as the young man played and often remarked, *that man has music in his mind, but when he sets it down it is almost impossible to play it*." So said Mrs. McGhee Phifer in 1942, remembering him shortly before her death, the young man in question having beaten her to it by a dozen years, all his music uttered, all his theories spelled out, all of his pliant finger-probing under girl's frocks over and done with. Flooding Cheops with his delight, I insinuate the cornerstones of his vivid life, thus puzzling him even more than I do with the music, half-convincing him that he, and not Delius, is the lascivious viveur except he just cannot remember having been so sexually busy, what with the need to ensure his line, which was more like deep-river diving than anything pleasurable.

His playing of the Mendelssohn Concerto was what seduced the ladies most. He became a local Florida notable, an alien graft fast absorbed, receiving the aspirant daughters of well-to-do planters for instruction, though not in his own style ever. It was as if a royal sunset had overpowered a tick. After a year of this, he had saved enough to take his leave of them all, dropping behind him shreds of minor praise to keep the daughters musically viable, and left for Leipzig, much commended by Thomas Ward. A conservatory beckoned. Thus extolled by a rabbi, and the Brooklyn organist Ward who seemed to have lost all touch with his native heath, he offered himself for grooming in the summer of 1886, studying with Jadassohn, Reinecke, and Sitt, haunting the conservatory concerts and trekking off to Norway during vacations as if dogging the footsteps of Edward Grieg, who in fact spent the winter of 1887 in Leipzig, forming a good impression of young Delius, who by now had amassed some sketches into a suite he proudly named *Florida*, huge on atmosphere in a Norwegian way.

"Something reclaimed," he said, "and made visionary."

To which Grieg is supposed to have answered, "Something visionary reclaimed, sir. The vision goes with you, wherever, as it should, and you attach it to this or that feature. Blood-idyll I call it." Some of us, seraphically aloof, denied the opportunity to hear the music of Solano until much later, and not so fortunate as Grieg or as influential, have envied the man his abandoned, sumptuous quality, his being able to ferret out from people in all sorts of conditions—not just those lounging in riverboats crooning spirituals—the ancient pastoral yearning that makes just about any human crave a window, a view of grassland or lawn, a waterfall pounding, or a rainbow self-flung through the gossamer of polar ice. He had that. He divined that in people, later on in inanimate-seeming places, and imposed it on his work. Had some of us not occupied ourselves with his every whim, we might have achieved something similar, while spurning music of a dustier, more diagrammatic kind, but we never got around to it, and never would, becoming more and more immersed in his imperious gregariousness. You could see, even in such early works as that Florida suite, an inclination to desert the world and soldier on in visionary privacy, even after having eyed the world and treasured it. He was going to delve inward, even after what some would think the worldly piffle of rabbis, the Phifers, and the daughters of the rich, not to mention the lordly, sagacious Thomas Ward and the great Grieg. Going so far inward might well cripple or mute him, he thought, but go there he would as other creative people have, inwardly fabricating what he hoped was a microcosm of the real, to which I would add something almost cantankerous: Since the macrocosm includes all microcosms or it is not complete, the macrocosm is never enough, and therefore the desire to minify it will always fail. What will emerge will be a pseudo-microcosm only because, even as you minify, or seek to, other micros are being made of just as incomplete macros. It is the sort of hectic rambling I get into when trying to make sense of a genius's plunges, knowing (I) the thing is wrong from the start and therefore predicated on something quite different, say a lyrical surge of the imagination on the occasion of some derivative. Never forget that composers trying to serve themselves are really writing for *us* without knowing it.

61 ▲
PRINCESS HEDUANNA

You don't seem yourself, father, though you don't seem to be anyone else either. Rather than setting around making idle chatter about politics and inundations, I could perhaps be of some use to you, reading for you, advising (if I may), warning you of this or that. When you look at me, it isn't me you see, is it? Do we have to be dead before you take notice of us? I could be your eyes and ears, as I never have. I could report the women to you—Merytyetes especially—and what the palace gossip is. They have begun to nickname you the king who sends people away, to be murdered or saved, I never know quite which. Is that how you want to appear: forever getting rid of us on the pretense of educating us or making us worldly-wise, when all the time you have something else in mind? Poor Ka-wab. Poor Chirh. Am I lucky to be alive? Were you testing my mettle, or what? Perhaps the whole idea of a clever daughter puts you off. If she's that clever, you no doubt tell yourself, she can look after herself anywhere. Well, I can't. Any good luck I happen to have is a fluke. So I ask you, can't you find a use for me, or am I bound to sit around here, gabbing with Erodo and the rest while you sink into one trance after another? They say you are listening to unhearable music, which must be fun if it is true, or that you are planning more edifices for our dead. Some say you have gone away into the anteroom of the gods and take no heed of ordinary people. If so, please come back.

You say nothing. I have not got through to you. There is no talking with you. What they say about you is true, I can tell. I am a plain young woman with simple needs, or so I used to think. Where do you want us to go? Would you rather we were dead? Have you planned something for us too? May the gods help the likes of me, with my small mouth, narrow eyes, nimble hands. I am not myself, not since I came back from Abydos.

62 ▲
MYCERINUS, GRANDSON

He's always like that, Heduanna. They say the only way to get his attention is to threaten him, but as soon as you make any such move you'll get your throat cut. I'm told I am going to be next in line sooner or later, but what chance have *I* got? Who am I to expect such wonders? Who would care to discuss astronomy with a teenager? I am nobody worth knowing, really, but I could whip up a few jokes to stop you from getting bored. I know some bawdy poems as well. My grandfather, he's not the grandfather he used to be. They say it happens to them all after a certain amount of pharaohing. The glazed look. The look-along-the-Nile stare. I even know the word for exposing yourself to a blind person, if you'd care to know it. When he feels his eyesight going, he becomes almost disembodied. I know, I have observed him. And they say observing style is mostly police work. He never sleeps more than six hours and, he once said, he has no need of a lapsing overseer. When he does talk, usually in the evenings, when he's tired, he gets philosophical, going on about language, saying no matter how finicky or fanatical we are about the finer points of word-building—pictorially speaking—the human verbal image remains playful, looser at some times than at others. What you might make of all he says along these lines I leave to you. Dare I believe it? Have I any idea what he means? He talks with such seriousness about such matters and clasps my hands as if to make his points more warmly. Bless him for trying. I'm not a child.

63 ▲
OSIRIS

Noted but disregarded. It is often said that you can get the boy out of Yorkshire, but not Yorkshire out of the boy. One wonders what any composer would be doing in Yorkshire, to begin with. It could have been for the cricket, a game that would have drawn in thousands, if only they had been able to stomach working in wool. Delius himself clung to the old idea that his family were Dutch, but the fourth of twelve children is apt to become blurred, from the sheer noise of breeding, making one wonder about the absence of contraception. What he is likely to have remembered without pause is that his father was a typical Prussian domestic tyrant with, hidden away in or on his being—like an ant on a cuckoo clock—a certain liking for money. Pelf. Which could have been worse for him? The father's ironclad pragmatism, or the only slightly less severe policy of the mother, a woman so uninterested even in music that lifelong she never heard a note of her son's? The astounding thing is that, from time to time, amid that harvest of children (or plague if you wish), genuine artists came to visit the home and play there: Joachim and Piatti, distilling beauty among the crags, and of course infecting the boy, already bemused by traveling circuses, bareback riders and trapeze artists in particular, not to mention more obvious addictions such as walking and riding, to which, in green on white like a fretwork pattern in slow motion, he added the grim, intense local sport of cricket, just mentioned, played up there among the Norse Yorkshiremen with curmudgeonly relentlessness deriving from the Wars of the Roses centuries before, and commemorated in the so-called Roses match played annually between Yorkshire and Lancashire. Bat on ball appealed more to the young composer than the carryover from ancient days of feuding, and he rejoiced in the comparative silence amid which the game at whatever level was played. And he also remembered the social posture of his father, sitting with his forefinger crooked into a claw, the embarrassed aftermath of the nosepicker, converting nosepick into lolling nonchalance as people burst in upon him during his nasal pleasures.

Bradford Grammar School brought Delius out, and the International College at Isleworth near London indoctrinated him with the rudiments of business life over three years of unnecessary tedium, after which, as he recalled with tender affection, he was sent to Chemnitz in Saxony, not that far from Leipzig and Dresden. He had gone through the motions of going home, at least if he thought of home as Germany rather than Holland. Once I had tuned in to him, I thought him as well-prepared for life as a cosmopolitan. Later he would sprinkle his table talk with vignettes not only of Solana, Florida, and New Zealand (these culled from an older brother sent there to investigate sheep-farming), but also, naturally, of Chemnitz and Norway, and also Sweden, St.-Etienne (a wool town), and Monte Carlo, where he gambled his all on the roulette tables and won, thus managing to finance a few weeks on the Riviera: an orgy of recitals and concerts and violin lessons.

Having been to Norway, he developed an interest in plays, actually following them in the original language. His memories, I noticed, had this scenic, commercial flavor, as of places where to send the functioning dead except (in his case) the dead refused to cooperate. Mingled with these were more chromatic recollections of oatmeal and thick molasses, huge enveloping fogs made of vapor from the Pennines, rough-spoken provincials to whom London was the devil's playground, weird smoky brands of toffee, especially the kind cooked in a shallow pan and smashed with a small hammer (and yielding razory edges), housewives whitening their front doorsteps with what they called donkeystone, and rumbling big-bellied men stinking of beer amid that other stink of hops brewed in the neighborhood. Cold wind, thick rain, Yorkshire lasses with wind-stung pink cheeks and Viking hair, half-inviting him with what he came to think of as a nurse's demeanor. More than anything, there was the sound of his own speech, far from the mincing elocution of the private schools, as the conductor Beecham pointed out. So, although he may well have been chatting about the way disdain was based on refined taste, he spoke in the rabid drone of the Yorkshire farmer, patronized and ridiculed in the South, where the regional speech was just as coarse. Larded in among his gab, his French and Norwegian allusions made for an odd mix, revealing him as a man half of the world, but an industrial peasant as well.

A certain fondness for the sounds of local speech, akin perhaps to the comfort squirrels and birds felt on hearing it although without understanding, enabled him to murmur to himself in his cups a few treasured local expressions whose uncouth abruptness made him smile, and brought to mind the prows of Viking ships, the flaxen beards of invaders, the uncraven voices of their beckonings and exclamations. *Eigh-up* was a call to attention, bringing the whole of Yorkshire up short. *Don't thee thou me, thou tharrer* was an instruction not to use intimate forms of speech, or else. And *redlar*, mispronouncing *regular*, had to do with normality and being all right. These rank phonemes tied him to the soil up there, never mind how far off he was in France or Florida: they might sound obtuse to others, but were just as good as any other, and almost the glottal equivalent of the music in a piece he had composed called *The Procession of Protracted Death*, which first endeared him to me, I having heard it long before any other audience. Getting used to his ramblings and his introverted barks, you ended up endorsing Beecham's pithy assessment of his speech as a "polyglot mishmash." His speech through music, however, was a totally different matter, ethereally languageless, culled from nowhere and nobody unless the Farne Islands and the Hebrides (and if so, how and when?). Or he had acquired it from the friezes of the afterlife among which self-delighted gods roam oblivious of worldly concerns. He could never abide the sounds of day and therefore worked at night, smoking and drinking, founding melody on an iceberg of approximate silence marred only by the occasional barking of a dog. Had he worn earplugs, his music might have been quite different. It is interesting to notice how full his music is of sounds overheard, the faint oscillations of eager nature coming to the boil, stuff caught on the wing, or over the egg, the scuffle among dead leaves, the bawling of crows.

I wonder, was Scandinavian culture, to which he always turned, the true ghost of his nature? It is often suggested by learned savants that no composer is more English, but the view from up here, besides his being marvelous, is that there are half a dozen more obvious choices for English composers: Bridge, Howells, Butterworth, Gurney, Stanford, Parry, Vaughan Williams, et cetera. In one sense he is more international than any of them (he knew and liked the French composer Florent Schmitt). I came to call him Pan, though never to his face (I appearing only as a ghost). Or was he Ward the true hymnodist of Brooklyn, N.Y.? Had Thomas F. Ward schooled him in an alien idiom that reciprocated the tunes of Florida plantation workers? He was *spiritual!* It is worth noting his ability to merge into the background, like ink into blotting paper. When his tyrannical father decided to hale him out of Florida, the damage having already been done, so to speak, he had to track his son through a private inquiry agent, a private eye such as only gods can boast.

You see how deeply I have committed to him, actually going so far as to flood good old Cheops with his music. I could have desisted and contented myself with no small thing: I mean our capacity for infinite, instant knowledge—the one and only unmeasurable hodgepodge in the world—thus, for example, contenting myself with some such folderol as John Keats's vision in *Hyperion* is it? (we are sometimes rather woolly on titles) of the old sun-god going down to defeat, raw old Hyperion being forced to yield. I often read it and feel a tear forming, as when I read that cold, cruel poem of P. B. Shelley about Rameses II. To have these wimpy boys fixing on the terrors of our ancienthood, airily dismissing us as old coots, is not the ravishing read it should be, but one is obliged to try to read *something* relevant, just to please the world and come into harmony with it.

64 ▲
ERODO

With that wavering finger of his, he urges me toward him for a presumably wordless exchange. There is no telling with him as he gradually shifts from potentate to introvert, willing to have his crews continue building, just so long as he doesn't have to inspect the results. What intrigues him now is solar boats, huge things for which he has done designs in his wobbly freehand, airily dictating measurements to a small tribe of parasites. These can be found at the base of his pyramid, open to view, and a pretty sight of fresh-air carpentry they provide, a gentle hum of sawing and tapping. Yet I think it is something else that lures him onward, about which he seems on the verge of telling me. He babbles as if speaking with his defective eyes. Now he repeats part of his babble and I begin to glean his drift: some version of the carrying-chair, of the type much used by his mother Hetep-heres, though he seems eager to install controls of some kind, which consorts oddly with the usual passivity of the royal passenger. I can see what he is driving at: some installation previous to the journey along the semi-horizontal shaft that will take him far, far away, among the stars. So, as I try to figure him out, I see him adapting the notion of the comfortable strap-in carrying-chair to his seat in the solar boat, which in turn he downgrades to a mere trolley. Why his mind tracks this way, moving from one false logical step to another, I have no idea, content to accept that his reasoning heeds peripheral things of which I know nothing. Besides, he may be receiving instruction from some outside source, maybe even a whole series of commandments aimed at pharaohs on the wane

He looks different, his mien one of exasperated cheer or weary pleasure. No doubt about it, he has tuned in to some source of power that slackens and saps him while, all the same, compelling him to attend. I ask, but he has nothing to tell. What is private remains so, and whatever topic I bring up in the interest of conversation—his concubines, the Libyan line, the recent murders, the royal succession, his mother's missing body, the plight of Heduanna—he shakes his head and looks away, as if I ought to know what really interests him nowadays; I should be able to come up with it myself after cogitation. It is odd: he seems refueled, yet dilatory and slow. Just the natural course of aging, I tell myself, but if so it's going faster by the day. After thirty, unless they have some uncanny resistance—which a member of the royal family may well have from superior diet and a life devoid of privation—they begin to dwindle. There is then a constant ferment of pretenders to the throne, real and mock princess ready to be put on, angling and jockeying in the hallways of the palace, befriending even the masons, servitors, and flunkeys. Perhaps these same aspirants think of me, the outsider, as a force to be reckoned with, one who has ingratiated himself with a view to—well, you can guess the rest: King Erodo, journalist, who lives in a cave by choice and teaches their monarch Greek. If I do not soon go home, or at least move on from Memphis, I am certain to be suspected of plotting and exerting undue influence on a king not exactly mad, but passing strange, self-involved in a culpable fashion. He who built the pyramid seems quite lost in minor projects. They expect their king to be grandiose.

He keeps licking his lips, smearing some invisible ointment across his eyes, patting his ears as if to rectify them. He stands in a lucrative-seeming dream whose exact yield eludes me, but his posture is that of someone hearing distant music, and wondering why. I envy him as he cocks his head and listens. I hear no such thing myself, and am obliged to hum a little to occupy the vacancy between me and him. Maybe all the prayers he prayed are coming back to him. Maybe he hears the voice of his mother.

Many approach him and try to deflect his attention. Heduanna, morose, yet ebullient, pleads. Mycerinus, brainy grandson, seeks to entertain him with witty stories. Awesome Merytyetes merely stands and observes him as if watching a camel give birth. If, as she might well think, this is just one of his moods, then best leave him alone, but leave with a sedate smile trapped in the corners of that pliable mouth. Prince Ka-wab's daughter, Meresankh III, hangs back, reluctant to accost him, but wanting somehow to express her concern. Son Chefren, husband of Meresankh III, just walks past, firm in his belief that, if you pretend nothing's wrong, then nothing is. Son Dedef-ra claps him on the shoulder and somehow shoves the injunction to buck up into the act, only to have Cheops dip sideways from his clasp. He doesn't try again. Chattering children make a bogeyman of him, as so often before, advancing on Cheops with bird-cries, then "shooing" him before retreating with quite different cries of hide and go seek, come and find us! No use. Their king is being tensely peaceful—perhaps inspired, perhaps demoralized. All along, you achieve a stable demeanor in the face of murder, and then you suddenly crack, at last admitting to yourself the horror of regnant life, eager now to toil on the heavy rocks in the mausoleum outside.

So I ask myself, Erodo, what are you doing here? What keeps you on? Could there still be something to write that would amaze the world and make you a reputation never to be ignored? Among all these retainers and hangers-on, might there still be an untapped story or two? Have you only skimmed the surface of the banker toff who, asked about palace life, said it was like having your privates nibbled by rats; otherwise he loved it? Or the young soldier-doctor ever on hand for fainting spells and hangovers? Or the bossy lady scribe given to flatus? Or the royal dresser who married down (a mere foot soldier) and then succumbed to a throat cancer? Or, Trnd, elegant soldier who was dismissed for having stolen a priceless *dhow* and sailed it downriver? Or the hairdresser who, for getting too experimental and covertly smearing his royals' hair with cow-doo, was flogged by the most abrasive and blunt member of the palace security squad? Use the list, Erodo. Let nothing go to waste, even if you never write it up until you return to Greece. If the royals are dressy, then *these* are their private parts. I resume my time-honored role of becalmed observer. Besides the grandest viziers, it's the senior scribes who run this place and so, when their time comes, get the biggest mastabas.

65 ▲
PRINCESS HEDUANNA

Where is his swagger now? Where is that haughty surge of the chin, not often kissed? Where is that blaze in the face announcing a new onset of decisiveness? What about that regal lift of the hand, sideways expansive, indicating an entire kingdom? Where is his spark? He looks like some perpetual applicant, scribe of the lowest grade, for an always-filled job. Is this even the man who—no doubt inspired by earlier specimens at Abydos—commanded to be built solar boats a hundred and fifty feet long, made of planks mortised together and then set within trenches lined with bricks mortared and whitewashed? He had his boats painted yellow and arranged in parallel like a fleet. Derivative maybe, but revealing his initiative; he had always told me that, in his view, the boat had been undervalued in our culture, not given enough to do, not harnessed to great purposes; and by this he did not mean merely as punts on the canals, leading from the Nile to his pyramid. It was really, he said, a matter of building your boat and then, with both piety and hope, awaiting the divine energy that would lift and speed it to unthinkable destinations. As I told myself at the time, it was no good believing in the sublime afterlife if you expected nothing of it.

So there was bright hope as he was growing up—not just the golden twitter of optimists, though that did figure, but also seen in the indomitable side of him. He knew he could do no wrong, even while, with his habitual onslaught of misdemeanors, doing it all the time. Since then, however, with so many murders, mostly conducted noises off (some on his orders), and the loss of his mother, the near-miss of his daughter (who reluctantly now begins to see the reasoning behind her visit to Abydos), he has slackened, become prey to inward extravagances, as his appearance gets shabbier—his walk twitchier, his eyes poorer, until he arrived, arrives, as now, at a place where he can neither improve nor degenerate, while those around him grow nostalgic for the young Cheops, trying to invent novelties for him to undertake. With pyramid done, boats half-forgotten, certainly marooned in carpentry, he goes about humming, his face contorted into benign puzzlement, no longer a daddy or a poppa, nor a pharaoh either. More like a neglected poet.

"Tell me good morning in the old way, Poppa."

His look circles me, then comes back; has he seen me at all? Is there any way of detecting what he sees?

I greet him formally and receive a nose-tap; I mean he taps his own nose. He could have rubbed mine just as well. So: one nose-tap equals half a dozen words. It is hardly worth figuring out, and I a promising young scribe destined for great things unless he comes to abysmal grief and slowly succumbs to one of his least able sons. In that case, we all move down and bury our heads, unless we have befriended nearly every conceivable ally in the palace, from Dedef-ra down—Dedef-ra the shy, the devious, the premature autocrat whom some of us blame for Ka-wab. The best I can say for Cheops is that he reminds me of the giraffe we use when writing, situating him at the end of a prophetic sentence because he has a long neck and can see what's coming. More properly, however, there is the sharp right angle like a carpenter's set square that we place northeast of any figure in hiding, just to show that he's in abeyance or just "out." It was he, surely, unless I am mistaken, who decided that, gracious as it is to place food and drink for the dead in little external chapels, there might one day be nobody left to feed the fondly remembered, so it was better to have an artist (not so well-paid in our day, alas) paint beer and wine on the inside walls, pleading with the gods to furnish such things for ever.

I have become more and more nervous. My bottom twitches, my wrists ache, I blink nonstop. I spend hours being the luxurious feline that I am, just chewing the end of a rush stalk destined to become my pen—a paintbrush really, yet destined to remain a stalk chewed to death, never inked, never used, all out of uncurbed jitters. I make me nervous. They all make me nervous—none more than that scrofulous, sardonic Greek without whom father Cheops seems unable to get through the day.

I am bad. I have even taken to writing in invisible ink, by which I mean drawing (rather large) glyphs with my tongue, in the hope of some eventual clandestine reader. I have nothing much to say, but I am suspicious. Why was I sent to Abydos, the holy of holies? *Really*. To fall for Chirh? Was he a rebel, or a secret ally of my father destined to arrive at the palace later on to settle the hash of the Dedef-ra gang? Why me? Why then? Was he simply flashing his seed at the man, tempting him with a bawdy daughter? Was I an advertisement and no more? The tale already circulates at court, thanks to Merytyetes, that I was virtually sold into whoredom at my own request, such was my boredom with the palace. And she my mother, or so they tell it; you can never be sure who was mother to whom, or father either. No doubt I should compose the story of my life, once my life is fuller than it is at present. I, who have graduated from scrawling on gesso boards, then broken pottery (the scrap paper of old Egypt), and endured the scalding wit of well-traveled tutors such as Erodo, must one day blow the feathers off this bird, demonstrating who was whose and how the family tree chopped itself up and the pyramids and mastabas slowly filled, my father's main obsession being to have someone's underground cupboard ready, in "working order," there being an absolute guarantee that sooner or later the person would assume his or her place down there and thus become truly needful.

So, I draw him out of love—him who used to be he, beautiful beast doling out his love, but generalizing him of course. I am not the maker of reserve heads:

You do not see the negroid-Mongolian cast of his features thus, but you may glean from it the shadow that slowly shut out the sun.

66 ▲
OSIRIS

On a certain moor in Yorkshire without a hat, irrelevantly runs an old song, all kinds of terrible things can happen to you. You become embroiled in the digestive processes of nature until, in the end, worms take you. This happens to be the Yorkshire version of Shakespeare's proof in *Hamlet*, of how a king may go a-progress through the guts of a beggar. (Gods sometimes are not that well read, or just forgetful, but they know the horrors.) In his early days Delius, or Fritz as he liked to be known at the time, submitting small samples of his music to the little magazines of the period, knew something of this morbid, sordid side of his home county's character, then let it slide away from him, only to find it returning in later years under the impulsion of disease. The mega-beast of his childhood came slavering back to claim him. It may be that he never lost the vision of this monster, but merely tuned himself in to its occasional transits among the best of men. It was the other side of his northern hard-headedness: an assent to fertility, a willing submission to overpowering rot, like being devoured and excreted by a crocodile. Such an assent appears often in his music; he recognizes the malady in human beings, their vulnerability to decay and the putrid; not that it happens to be morbid through and through, but more an acceptance, as Bach had too, that life is not entirely for our pleasure, but serves its own purposes often at huge cost to us all. This is the adult version, I suppose, of greenhorn disgust, in which the bleakness of biological process on the dismal Yorkshire moors meets the magmas of the Florida swamps.

Hence, perhaps, what he allowed to happen to his oranges, rather enjoying their decay because it demonstrated something cardinal. A grove full of rotting blood oranges became for him a mass of nature, in both senses, festering into muck and therefore a memento of what happened to all humans. This flow into rot brought him an inkling of a universal principle that few other composers reckoned with, or even knew how to portray in music, though one should not forget Sibelius, buried beneath an apple tree whose fertility, his widow said, owed much to his presence down below. There are the frequent bright golden certainties, and there are the gruesome disintegrations in which, eventually, all things come together and make—as that Yorkshire song reveals—a kind of compost, without which there could be no continuance in nature, human or otherwise. What composer, one therefore asks, could be more right to take over Cheops of the pyramids, the mastabas, the uncle of all mummies?

This was the man whom Thomas Beecham, his steadfast devotee, described, at least on first impression, as "a cardinal or at least a bishop in mufti. I kept on saying to myself," he goes on, "these same words, for his features had that noble cast of asceticism and shrewdness one mentally associates with high-ranking ecclesiastics." An astute romantic, then? A generous-looking accountant or solicitor? An introverted stamp-collector? He had many more faces than the one he presented to Beecham, one of them being a sobersides look, that of a commonsensical scrutineer far from the swooning romantic or English country gentleman many have thought him. If I am wrong in thinking that, among the millions I have trafficked with, his is hardly a Yorkshire face, I must concede that I also found it the hesitant one of a man ever on the brink of a wave, his gaze penetrating. To change the image, even if only for a moment, I think of him as surfing, riding along the green-water pipe of his own imagination, chancing it amid the roll and wallow of the briny, not to impress anyone in particular but because it was the natural thing to do.

Was the gaunt, withered face of his last years implicit in this judiciously well-tempered mask? I think not, I regarding his emaciation as an external extra, something brought about by circumstance and perhaps the torments of an exile's career. Bony head of a standard *senex* is what I discern in his final face, one that has listened too hard to everything, including the feral whisper of the slow spirochete. Of course, one does not see the face, one hears the music, in which the face is somehow swallowed up, so that listening to it one becomes acquainted with the brain flowing behind the death mask of the living man. Having been invited to compose incidental music for the Norwegian political comedy *Folkeraadet*, Delius was conducting in Oslo when some university student fired a blank at him, upon which Delius fled the pit and the theater for the Grand Hotel, where Ibsen, usefully on the spot, consoled him. When he returned to the podium, the play succeeded and sold out for the next three weeks. Such alarms became predictable, in both Norway and Germany; he was trying to do something different, even if he himself was unsure what it was. Those who heard his music, however, were less unsure and subjected him to hostile displays, no doubt educating him in the use of his favorite finale, the dying fall. He was undertaking something he perhaps wished he had not trained himself to do.

His face, when I first saw it, lacked any hint of the playboy he might have been, not so much of the Western world as of the fjords and the Hebrides. Indeed, something Nordic and unfulfilled kept on coming through, as it does in Bax, say; I might even say faery or elfin, but another side of him kept that under control, more inclined to subdue such fantasy to a warm night on the river, or a sunrise scalding his retinas. It is not easy to formulate, but I think he had a tropical side he underrated, and a Scandinavian side he treasured a little too much, He was several men, of course, and he knew many more composers and musicians than he has received credit for, among the ones I have already mentioned, Christian Sinding. He also knew Ravel, who made a piano score from his third opera, as well as Gauguin and Strindberg. From Gauguin, we must note, for about twenty pounds he bought the painting *Nevermore*.

I babble, airing my knowledge because I think it less likely you will credit me with knowing much, than with imposing my power and personality as I think fit. It is my way, which I sometimes apologetically call "associative meander." It is so nice to have you to talk with. Perhaps he drove or urged me to it, as I struggled to keep pace with his sweeping mind, his tumbling thoughts. Florent Schmitt, in fact, did the piano scores of his first two operas. That is how my mind works—not organizing but assembling, and out of such assembly, creating patterns I never observed during his lifetime. This, I suppose, means that I am getting into his act, now and then anyway, but I justify the tic by telling myself that, when someone you revere is so accomplished, your little wanderings, your impetuous deviancies, are as much his as yours. It is a matter of osmosis, I suppose, with the great god Pan calling the tune, not only giving you back the huge hymn of nature you thought lost, but also inspiring you to novel gestures you would never have dreamed up earlier. Short of doting or fawning, I took him more seriously than his own countrymen did, for much of his life anyway, and that must count for something.

"Osiris," he would say in that Yorkshire-voweled Florida drawl of his, "don't you wish *you* could compose?"

He certainly did not mean compose myself! "Not with the likes of you around," I told him. "One's enough. *Without* you, I perhaps would, but then, would I? With you, there is no need, seeing as how much there is of you to assimilate anyway."

Then it was my turn to go blank; as far as I know I was named Osiris, and I remained quite content with that name, and knowing my write-up by heart:

> Egyptian god who, with his wife and sister Isis, enjoyed in Egypt the most general worship of gods. The main god of fructification. From him comes every blessing and all life, light, and health. He makes the Nile overflow. He seems human. His hue is green; his sacred tree the evergreen tamarisk. To the Greeks he is Dionysus. His brother Set shut him up in a chest and put him to death by pouring in molten lead. The murderer than cast the chest into the Nile, which bore it out to sea; but after a long search, Isis found it on the shore of Phoenicia at Byblus and hid it. But Set found it and sliced the corpse into fourteen pieces,

which he then scattered in all directions. Isis, however, collected them up and buried them at Abydos. Horus, our son, killed Set, and I, though no longer allowed to live on earth was once again regarded as the source of life. I awaken the spirits of the just to a new rich life after death. My hue, in the underworld, is black, my robes are white, my symbol is an open eye.

(He was also the black bull Apis. Plutarch had a book about the two of them: *De Iside et Osiride*. He was blamed for the subsidence of the Nile, the disappearance of the cool north wind, the decay of vegetation, and the shortening of the day.)

All this, time and again, I told Delius, emphasizing how much we had in common, especially the rotting vegetation; but he seemed unimpressed, saying something about demonic possession when, truly, I just wanted us to be friends. We had nature in common, surely. He agreed about that, always insisting, though, that a mere composer should defer to a god. On he went, dreaming and gesturing, at some point shifting from language to music, quite losing me in his melodic transfers. The main question, I suppose, as our friendship began, was: To what extent was I "inspiring" him, making him write music he otherwise would have left undone? We inspired each other, the syphilis chewing on him the same as Set cut up me. We both made noises, obviously, although he was too busy to blend them, and there was no other composer in immediate residence to orchestrate—Debussy or Ravel would have been right, or Fauré. I was fond of the first's *The Martyrdom of Saint Sebastian* as of Webern's *Sommerwind,* but I was in no position to call them up and arrange a brief fellowship just to coordinate the sounds of Osiris and Fritz Delius. All the same, had the blending come about, it would have been molassesy, wouldn't it? Gooey and rich, at least as sweet and agonized as the Delius Violin Concerto. As I said previously, most of us regard human music as music for the gods mainly, as solace for our agony at being cut up or made obsolete, or being reduced to making humans suffer just because we feel so raw. It has often been noticed how, even among people, the healthy, who hate suffering, get to hate the sufferer too.

So, I was able to resist Delius when he accused me of inspiring him with my own stuff. It was always his own. My own rant or melody was a raucous, uncouth, barbaric thing, something that Thomas Ward would have flung with a Brooklyn oath into the Florida swamps. If I had a gift, it was for surviving and helping others do much the same. Look, here I am:

Now, don't you think someone who looks like that could even attempt a piece *On Hearing the First Cuckoo in Spring, Summer Garden, The Walk to the Paradise Garden,* or *Hassan?* Not that he did not suffer, but his suffering came out as defiant compliance—say glycerine for the gonads. Odd how the more he went through—pain in his limbs, blindness, difficulty with speech—the more he turned it into sweetness, like the old lion who lay down and died, and bees built a hive in his belly and, as the legend says, out of the strong came forth sweetness. Once again, you have here an example of a god unable to provide himself with a certain thing, and therefore latching on to a human who provides it. *Usurping* him, if you will, and then pouring him through the ears of helpless old Cheops, in whom, for his almost erotic monomania, his lust for rock, I have taken an inordinate interest, even sending a certain Erodo-Herodotus as a partner in certain ways. I have been active, have I not, and not only metaphorically, with the dead? I'm a jolly, old fellow to rally around.

Perhaps to talk this frankly is to give the game away, and reveal that I miss my ability for godlike interference on the rind of the planet. When you lower the Nile, and halt the northern breeze, let vegetation rot, and make the day shorter than usual, you have begun to lapse, even if you have some heft in the underworld. It's not enough. Only music for some gods, sadism for others, grandiose lying for yet others will save the day. You have to have some kind of compensation. It is no use moaning to Isis, who has peri-menopausal problems of her own, or trying to exceed your own habitual gifts. (In the olden days I used to be able to achieve a darker hue of green when aroused by one thing or another, or a paler one when I wanted to be invisible.)

Do you like me?

Will I do?

Do you mind my having such absolute control of you, if I choose to exert it from my own dismal niche in the parliament of gods? Without his music I would have been reduced to powdered pumice, and I thank Isis, my muse, for finding him.

My head clears at once when I think of him in Paris, as it never did or does when I link him with Norway and Germany. Something in the French air, I mean the atmosphere of Paris, sobers me up, gets me out of *finesse* and into *géométrie*. In Paris he can hardly be said to have been gregarious, apart from his few—Schmitt, Ravel, Gauguin—but he did in the January of 1896 encounter Jelka Rosen, from an old Schleswig-Holstein family, studying painting in Paris, like so many. They fast became attached and he took to visiting her home in Grez, as if he needed a retreat from a retreat. They kept to themselves although frequenting the cafés and *boîtes*, which makes it all the stranger that he allowed me any contact with him; perhaps it was just because, to begin with, I was studying music in my own fashion, though with less than titanic avidity. He doted on her and, having her to sustain him, permitted my intrusions, which initially amounted to no more than contemplating a glass of wine (his treat) and an occasional line of Mallarmé. If I courted him at all—in my metaphysical way—it must have been the mystic in me responding to the romantic in him (and her). She, I guessed, had decided from the first that he was the man for her—drawn to his languorous, cordial precision—whereas he took pleasure in other women, whether she understood this or not. Potential discord always seemed to flutter behind their more conventional niceties, even when in Grez for a while he took lodgings to be near her (they timed their excursions there well, like two coordinated metronomes). She had one big idea and that was him, whereas he, almost always on the erotic *qui vive* like a Nile cat, took an interest as many men do in what is politely called the field, which he played and did not relinquish even after he and Jelka became engaged. Over Christmas, he declared he needed to go back to Solano Grove for several months, and this shocked her, to find him going his own way, heading off to replenish the well and no doubt retool himself in other ways with "the beauties of the forest." She might have been even more shocked had she known that one of his Parisian amours was booked to sail on the same ship to New York, disguised as a young man, and went off with him to Florida. This knack he had for what I came to call *simultaneous intensity* caused him no upset at all, almost as if he were conducting the orchestra of his personality, or changing chord. He returned in June, resumed his lodgings and his affair in Grez, and got on with the third act of *Koanga* and his tone poem *Over the Hills and Far Away,* which is indeed where he had been. And now he was only ten miles from Paris—no disguises—a thoroughly fulfilled swain, all thought of inconstancy boiled away like the froth off milk. He married Jelka Rosen in the summer of 1903, having presumably confronted his demons and settled them. Or not.

Speaking of his women friends, some of them menacingly diseased, he invariably referred to their voices, their timber and tempo, as a musician might, though he got from their speech (those whom he liked) an infallible grandeur, citing one's Dutch composure, which led to her quiet, unemphatic enunciation. She did not disturb or provoke him, he said, but spoke each word with equivalent emphasis, matter-of-factly, so the net effect was one of chiseled calm. I was amazed at how much he got from this aspect of his philandering, almost expecting from him a setting to music or even the orchestration of the voice. He preferred the ebullience of another speaker, however, delighting in her deep earthy delivery, more Italian than German, and the hearty laugh she mingled it with. There balanced, he thought, on her vocal cords metallic resounding globes even after her voice had been resting unused, and this he inexplicably related to the quiescence of her gonads; the quieter she was hormonally, the deeper and more commanding she sounded. I then realized that what he was always after, in this cult of the dark brown voice, *was* something German or perhaps Italian: a voice thickened and corrupted by liquor and smoke, a threnody of the nightclubs, a lazy, sated, page of oestrus, or a bedroom contralto he might fit into whatever was taking shape in his ecclesiastical head. Then I recalled how Cheops had a like fixation on the voices of his women, though he cherished them for somewhat different purposes, desiring, but perhaps never finding, the ideal female bricklayer who spoke through gravel and Nile silt. So, in my parasitical way, I got them together.

With this in mind, indeed safely so, I advanced to another thought in my unending quest to fathom him, having discovered and chosen him. He may have womanized, but he did so not in a spirit of "so many realities" that freed him to treat each woman as a discrete entity, but as if all of them were one, and jointly available. To tup one was to tup all, but why then did he need all? This was true even if his lust extended only so far as dark-haired women, with deep voices and (hitherto) rolling pins smothered in butter. A longing for the maternal, perhaps, another Jelka? I never forgot that he remembered being in his mother's womb and hearing, above, the distorted soothing, mellow melody that soared into the sky, getting ready for him a platform of staves never to be found among the brittle sopranos tweeting and squeaking and warbling the tunes of the empyrean. What he craved was of the earth variety, of the earth earthy, as they say, because it nearly exempted him from music altogether.

This, I told myself, was just another of his Pan thoughts, as I named them, akin to thoughts of God in a thunderstorm tupping the soil, as some renegade author of this same period had already insisted in a book. We who range over the dynasties have little time for decades of difference. If this was pantheism or panentheism, I have no idea. The -isms leave me cold, but the very thought of an escapist *ka* warms me up. He was certainly attuned to the vision of the gods as magical agricultural trolls.

"Hear that voice, that epiglottis?" He often said this, while lounging in a café and absently eyeing the physique that went with it. "Now *there*'s a bedside manner." He was always pursuing an Isis.

So where, you may well ask, did the rather dumpy Jelka fit into his plans? Well, she had a satisfactorily low pagan voice, enough for him certainly—on the dark brown scale of 1 to 10, a raw six. But by no means entitling her to a monopoly. What would you make of her face? That of a proud possessor, one of those over-devoted faces above a brawny Teutonic body, often enough encased entirely in velvet. Seen, at least by me, with the eye of Horus, looking down at him as he sat in wheelchair or lay on bed, she was twice his sprightly size, and no doubt a woman confounded by his saintly cocksmanship. She remained bonny, as they say in Yorkshire, while he got beakier, especially in his last years. No man, though, is privy to the squirmings of another's tool, and still less to the proddings of his libido. No doubt, a good deal of his erotic yearning stayed private, un-acted upon; he thought his lascivious thoughts and turned them into rhapsodies and airs, dances and (after his famous cuckoo piece) what I fondly called his "On Hearing . . ."s. This habit of transformation made him a wizard. I presumed that, had he wanted to, he could have turned all natural phenomena to sex. He was a shape-changer, a man who, unlike many, lived his youth in old age and vice versa, remaining an ageless paragon, a Dorian Gray of dreamland.

Perhaps his illicit demands only made his Cowper's glands flow, and that was the end of it, the thunderball whistling down the viaduct; and the liquidity of his being became music. I could never be sure, but I knew his eternal *leman* (to use an old Anglo-Saxon word for lover; he rather fancied it) was the foison, or plenty, of the planet. In some ways he was like an atomspheric astronomer, but captivated by evolution. I have heard astronomers down below saying how glad they were to have made their living out of what thrilled them as small boys, and I never heard him say anything half so obvious. (Poets and lovers, especially, always hate poetry and girls when they are nose-picking little snits.) It was clear that he always felt something magical going on around him, generating in him an ecstasy, a joy in flow and suppuration. In a sense, this made him less a person than anyone else, for he floated away into the mighty never, leaving only his music behind him, findable on the distant shore only as a hulk or husk saying thank you. Such a man is delighted to have been born, I suppose, and to have happen to him whatever bodily shifts come his way, and even to lapse back into the cosmic slop, for at least having been chosen to do so, submitting to yet another chemical experience.

I go back to what he once told his friend Eric Fenby, stressing the need for soul to speak to soul. "You can't teach a young musician to compose," he said, "any more than you can teach a delicate plant how to grow; but you can guide him a little by putting a stick in here and a stick in there. Composition as taught in our academies is a farce. Where are the composers they produce? Those who do manage to survive this systematic and idiotic teaching either write all alike, so that you can say this lot belongs to this institution, this lot to that, or they give us the flat beer of their teachers, watered down."

I am still uncertain if I understand this, but I do get the drift of his animus. He abominated and despised counterpoint. The tone poem or the rhapsody was what he loved most, what he was most envied for, having dumped all that cerebral baggage behind under the influence of Thomas Ward. In a sense, he gained and never lost the barbaric yawp of his beloved Whitman, whose words he set to music in the *Sea Drift* of 1903. It was enough for him to have written about being alive, although not as heedless of circumstances as some have thought (walks, sails, drifts, hearings, climbs, sits, all figure in the imagery of his titles). I think the subtlest giveaway to his process appears in the instructions to *Song of the High Hills,* a sublime work for orchestra and chorus; he writes that the choir must sing on the open vowel they think best suited to the character of the music—the vocal parts are wordless all through, which means the chorus is an instrument. He does not need them to be articulate, but, in hymning, say, the section headed "The wide, far distance—the great solitude," they need to be awestruck. As he himself said, "the human voices represent Man in Nature—an episode that becomes fainter and then disappears altogether."

One day, out in the desert, he and I were availing ourselves of my shape-changing powers: him I made invisible, as befits a blind man in a wheelchair. Myself I made visible—a kind of short-necked athlete with shaving cuts, almost no neck, and in my hand a hairball from a cow, which is to say a ball of licked and swallowed hair that has built up in the cow's stomachs over the years: a hard, shiny, almost weightless thing. Even I could not see him, and of course he couldn't see me. The game between us was to toss the ball and catch it, or, failing that, to score a hit on the other.

"Here it comes, Fritz," I called as I aimed the ball.

"Aim at the music," he cried.

I missed. Now it was his turn after I retrieved the ball and handed it to him, then regained my stance a dozen yards away. "Aim for the divinity, Fritz!"

He missed of course, perhaps recognizing that the divinity (a poor thing, but mine own) lay all around him. It was quaint, really: my divinity, myself, ordaining and infusing all things, versus his all-encompassing music. We could have played ball for hours, without either making contact with the other: the blind man versus the poor shot. Anyone observing us would have deemed us both fit for the nearby lunatic ansylum—in Memphis if you considered it to be about 2600 B.C., Cairo if you deemed it now. I don't care. I am pretty much always there, helping humanity out, playing a few favorites of course. But this image of a blind man, marooned in his wheelchair in the desert, waiting maybe to be uprooted and laid safely and securely to rest bothered me, upsetting my usual sanguine approach to the ills of humankind. I wheeled him away, detecting what he hummed under his breath (the piece about swallows), and, making him visible again, assimilated his being into mine, retuning him for immediate invasion of the acutely hearing Cheops.

Once a Delius fan, always one.

About this time, I noticed that Cheops—perhaps recalling the carpenters who crafted his huge solar boats with planks and bricks—began to make a much smaller model for the dead Ka-wab, not content merely to whittle it with his fairly blunt knife, but scraping the surface with the blade, until it glowed almost shiny. Blundering about in the model-maker's workshop adjoining the funerary annex, and clad in a muslin smock that actually let dust and liquid through its mesh, he painted the little boat—shuttle-like—with whitewash, which dried in a trice in the afternoon sun, only to be rubbed hard with a handful of sand. When it gleamed a little, he began again: first the whitewash, then the handful of sand, several times an hour, not that the model shone that much, but it was certainly smoother; enough for him to hold it against his cheek as if fondling the boy who had grown up into a portly man. I asked him nothing about this activity, akin as it seemed to such insatiable perfectionism as I had noticed in the blind, the grief-stricken, the numbed, and the insane. He would pass several hours with his white model, hoping perhaps to float away in it, or somehow to rejoin Ka-wab in his mastaba. He too was humming the Delius tunes I myself provided—tunes of Paris, Appalachia, Brigg Fair, *Fennimore and Gerda*—but in an automatic, unexpressive way as if he had heard them all too often already and was humming them to keep intruders at bay—Erodo, the eternal voyeur, the young Mycerinus, his grandson. A huge crowd such as he could easily amass would have deterred him or broken him from his craftsman's scowl and held breath. If it was an act of repetition, as it was, he showed no signs of boredom nor did he make any motion toward water to set the boat in its natural element. Instead, he gouged a trench in the sand with his royal foot, planted the gleaming boat within, and scooped the sand back into place. The next day he repeated this funereal performance with another model, another trench. Day after day he made this offering (as I construed it to be), and I wondered if he had a number in mind, after which he would stop, having done what was necessary to appease the gods. After a week, he stopped, but took to solitary walks on the sand, watched from a discreet distance by security courtiers armed with cudgels.

67 ▲
PRINCESS HEDUANNA

What is it that drags me out of nowhere, into the middle of this inconceivable distance where you know you are not being watched? I am centered on a disc, sometimes called the sun's anvil. Now and then a leafless, thornless tree catches my gaze, which has nothing to live for, much as I have nothing to say to those in the palace. I sneak out here swathed in white linen, virtually invisible, almost a ghost against whose feet the sand drags and drags. If you were lonely here, you would crave in vain for dorcas gazelle or jerboa. A lizard at best or a poisonous snake. You soon become grateful for the merest bit of worn-down shell you can hold to your ear to hear the sea or the river. Only a wild man or a pariah would come out here to be burned, certainly not a well-educated scribe of a girl already skilled in the niceties of society. There is not even a hutch or kennel, no hollow, scooped out of the all-encompassing sand, which has no smell but exudes a paralyzed warmth. We should leave the sand alone to its narrow allegiances and head back to courtyards of cool stone and plashing water.

I come here, I deduce, because some aberrant strain in my blood calls on me to quit the society of men and women, and revert to certain primitive customs of my ancestors in, where was it, Lower Nubia, to which Egyptians made an expedition with a view to trade or the creation of a buffer zone. Who is to know who did not come back with the victorious army? All of them perhaps, because there is no record of any settled population down there at the north end of the Second Cataract. Oh, there was a settlement at Buhen for some two hundred years, but it eventually vanished, the constant presence of our Egypt seeming to have discouraged them and sapped their resources, much as Memphis has exhausted its outlying areas. Might I have an unknown father from there? Is Merytyetes my real mother? Am I mistaken when I feel something Nubian send me off to severe, lonely places where, if I am lucky, I discover men on camels riding in a circle, then setting off in a straight line again, everything they own on their backs or their mounts, foraging with sun-glazed eyes across the never-never, making me oddly homesick?

Or was he some Libyan? Hence all the talk of a lost mother with red hair, whatever that signifies. What is certain is that I am not the daughter of some high priest of Re, unless my longing for desolate places marks me as a true worshipper of the sun-god. I do not have red hair, but that signifies little. I hear rumors about a red-haired Libyan woman with a constantly changing name, but I never get to the bottom of the matter, supposing only that Cheops in his maniacally selfish way became involved with a foreign woman, Nubian or Libyan, or that Merytyetes the enigmatic did something similar, with the whole matter finally hushed up in the interests of family honor. Somehow some exotic strain came in and got itself denounced, even by such as me, who now realize the alien party may be me myself. Factional strife beyond my ken may have fired up once upon a time, possibly when I was a baby, and then extinguished itself. Leave her be. She will never amount to anything. Outsiders never do.

My only pull, which others seem not to have, is the desert—gigantic playground for some whose funerary monuments make the sands seem even desolate and ungiving. He could have sent me off to Libya, I suppose, to whatever fate, but I became part of a different machine I will never know the true nature of. I am lucky not to have been killed along with Chirh; just a few moments made all the difference, and no one could have planned it thus.

No doubt I am being sentimental when I catch myself illicitly longing for the domineering peace of hawk, eagle, or vulture, or the harsh, arid, inhospitable zone that encloses just a few oases, al-Kufrah, say, as if challenging all passers-through to make something elaborate out of nothing—as Cheops does—confronted by the vast nonentity of death. So what is this yearning not to be distracted? A whim? Nothing in my breeding at all? It is hard to tell why I respond to acres of drought, but I do, and this would give me away if known. My name is not Egyptian, nor, quite, is my physique; I lack their sturdy necks, their somewhat flattened noses, their look of invincible haughtiness. Perhaps I am a changeling from the area in which writing began, a throwback, but I am also, as we sometimes say, an up-to-date woman—hardly the narrator of my hosts but sometimes their gossip, witness my chatter with Erodo, who already knows the difference between me and Egyptian girls. This difference I rather cherish, as I think Cheops himself does, and I intend to keep it fresh and fruitful.

Back I go to my uncertain destiny, welcomed home on the city perimeter by a yapping mongrel no doubt a god in disguise.

68 ▲
ERODO

Amazing how gabby she has become toward me. I suppose the trauma at Abydos and the murder of her brother has made something deep within her crack. She has to get it all out into the open, even to a sultry Greek, rather than confide in the marble-faced Cheops, introvert blind man beginning to lose his grasp. Never mind, I came here to get information, and got it I have. There are always limits to prudence and integrity, and I wouldn't be surprised if, under new pressures, all kinds of palace secrets didn't start to emerge into the daylight. The main thing is to get them down for later consumption. Look what they have given me with which to ply my trade: a writing palette—small board with dents made for red and black colored paste, with attached to it a leather pouch for water to moisten the paste with. You close the pouch, water and all, by tugging the cord. And, all hail to the Egyptians; if you feel a bit of an outsider, you need not, because the ideogram for writing is indeed the little palette. So you use it to further depict itself, which you certainly cannot do in Greek. In fact, rather than using this contraption, I use my own implements, but carry the palette around with me as a badge of office, a symbol of who I am. More ambitiously, if I wish, I can carry with me ceramic inkwells shaped like cartouches—or yet another palette, just for colors, with no space provided for reeds. It is all very nifty. A more conscientious scribe than I would dutifully do his work with the traditional materials, thus acquainting himself day after day with implements there seems no need to go beyond.

Well, these are the things that Heduanna carries with *her*, as if to quell suspicion that she is not a scribe at all, but some kind of snoop who gives herself away by drawing a cow shedding a tear while being milked by a kneeling man, whose bent foot resembles a slipper: no toes at all on this generalized foot while the calf tethered to the cow's leg has feet that barely touch the ground (dead giveaway of an amateur at work).

"Enough already of your questions," she says. "The whole palace is mighty secretive. Ask, and you will not be told. Watch hard and certain things will reveal themselves, I mean who is fawning on whom, who's getting the cold look, who is dressing down as a result of a snub, who has decided no longer to sleep with whom, all that stuff they thrive on. Surely that's not the kind of thing you want."

"I'll take anything," I tell her. "All is grist."

"Then your mill is bound to collapse sooner or later."

How crabby she can be, even when, as she no doubt thinks, she is talking with her intellectual equals. This girl has a core of promise, but it has been pulled away from her into bizarre corners and no longer controls her behavior. Here an idealist may lapse into the vicious repartee of the tolerated cynic, an ideal entertainer for a court. Poor girl, everything she's prized or held dear has gone for naught. She has whispered to me about her lost and forgotten mother (I think murdered when she Heduanna was a babe), dumped in the tiniest of mastabas in fractional obedience to some moral code that won't allow her corpse to be left for the fangs of marauding creatures, hyenas and wildcats and jackals. Hence the mystery woman buried under a false name, perhaps that of a stillborn child.

"I feel more welcome than I did," I tell her.

"That," she says, "may be because they want something from you. They have aspirations. They cast an eye toward Greece."

"And Greece to them. We shall be here en masse one day."

"May I be dead." She sighs coarsely.

"They will come anyway. They covet an empire, ma'am." She offers the resigned nod usual with her.

Then she asks if I have wife and children.

"I wander too much," I tell her. "But, on my wanderings, I have no doubt left some seed behind and so populated whole peninsulas with little half-Greek bastards. In fact, if we felt inclined, this very day—"

"All of that burned out of me some time ago."

"Abydos?"

"And other bad events." She quivers with pique.

"My wife is my public," I inform her. "My lovers are my praisers, my encomiasts."

How does she understand Greek? Was she ever Greek? Was her mother Greek? Was her mother, she had to have a mother, one of *us*? She does not know, but it is plain she doesn't quite fit in here. Perhaps that is why he sends her away, to get her out of his sight, and, in regard to Ka-wab, away from his son. He likes to send them all away on various empty missions, just to have heartfelt reunions when they all return. Something strange is going on. Maybe he doesn't want them to see what he's up to, although you can hardly accuse a pyramid-building king of being shy.

She makes as if to write or paint, and I decide to leave her to it, graceful fawn-like creature that she is, her virginity safe inside her as a frozen flower.

Of *course*, he did not, as my old story has it, put her out to prostitution, though he might be accused—of what? Sequestering her. Putting her out to grass. Wasting her mind. Brainwashing her of anything to do with her mother. Confusing her. Making her mourn alone. Had I time, I would write her up as a fondly thought of orphan, or a scribe squandered, with all kinds of court rumors circling her head, and just about nobody taking any responsibility for her. How unfortunate that a girl so bookish, so much a scribe, lives at a time in Egypt when there is so little to read, especially if she has any Sumerian blood in her, for that is where writing began; each day I salute the divinity in that direction, knowing that without writing I would have nothing at all, just the rattle of pebbles in an old earthenware cooking pot. I, Erodo, whom they will not call Herodotus, although, in their mode of speech, *Hrdts* can't be that hard to say. Strange to live among people who mangle their vowels into lazy improvisation. Any kind of burp between consonants will serve, it seems; which makes them concise as scrotums, even when they sound as if their mouths are full of broken pottery. Now, whose is this music our pharaoh keeps dropping hints about, whose marred penis he refers to with grave envy?

69 ▲
FREDERICK DELIUS

I will never get used to this switching about: life after death, then death again after second life, or being transported to and fro across the centuries. There is another effect too, irresistibly daunting, in which the intensity of the listener listening counters the music received, and as it were blows it back. I have never met this phenomenon before, but imagine it has some purpose. Here is Cheops, having my music piped into his skull ad infinitum, mustering such an ear for it that he deters it and almost forces it back to where it came from. This may produce palsy of the composer, to have so ravenous a listener in whom, say, the appetite for the music exceeds that for a particular composer's work. I am unsure how this works, but I find the results uncanny. I am glad I no longer have to write that music, glad I have finished with it, with nothing left over for trial and error conducted in the afterlife. That, I imagine, is what happens to you if you don't manage to get a life's work into your life and so leave posthumous work to be done with no doubt limited resources and perhaps no audience. Whoever is inflicting all this Delius on him is surely going to give him a ton of it, just to make sure. How long, I wonder, does it take to listen to all of Delius (maybe a day), but you have to listen to it interminably if you want to figure out either him or me.

So be it, I have no control over anything, am myself as passive an observer as could be. I am called upon and harnessed, yes, but no longer able to seize on the exact degree of finitude life allows and so pin it down, expressing all the shades of waning and diminution, as the human soul gradually goes home to sleep the sleep of resentful permanence. No more lovebirds on the seashore, stolen from Whitman; no more summer gardens, cuckoos, swallows; no more Fennimore and his Gerda; no more Irmelin, no Paris, no songs of summer and no more sunrises. The paradise garden, never mind which couple might be sauntering into and through it, is brutally locked—like that little park I once saw in New York, with babies being wheeled by nurses all of whom possessed the key. I dump on death with its charcoal pageantry. I would give anything for just one more sunrise, the rays gently tickling my eyelids as I give the star the Delius stare.

No use. I am left to wonder if, when your music fills the airwaves, the effect is partly to make you yourself fade, as if the net effect of achievement were to diminish the achiever, seeing as how the work is now outside him, disseminated, stock, with no chance to make it better.

One is left to wonder if the music brings with it any of the compositional details. On hand in Grez I had an opus of Richard Strauss—half of all the scores I owned were of his music. He taught me how to orchestrate and develop themes along an extended timescale. *Paris: the Song of a Great City*, for example, I intended as a nocturne of both night and early dawn, with which the piece begins and ends. The music includes all sorts of peculiar street cries too. You might call it a tone poem of a typical man-about-town at last becoming the recluse he really was, or, if you must, a cocksman's delirium, a *viveur's* trance. *Paris* is not about isolation, oh no, or the joys of a cosmopolitan life, but attempts to convey in myriad colors and hues the adventures of a soul in a great city.

I wonder if my overhearers have got that from it. Or if, turning to *Brigg Fair: An English Rhapsody*, they have gleaned even a whisper of such a Delius mood as shows in these lines from an old country song:

> It was the fift' of August
> The weather fine and fair.
> Unto Brigg Fair I did repair
> For love I was inclined.
> I rose up with the lark in the morning
> With my heart so full of glee,
> Of thinking there to meet my dear
> Long time I wished to see.

The song has a stertorous, disjointed quality absent from the music, so I might be said to have smoothed it out. It is hardly more coherent in French but its very incoherency may be regarded as reflecting my own emotion regarding songs at country fairs. Witness the country fair to which Sali and Vreli go to get away from their troubles in *The Walk to the Paradise Garden*, only to be recognized and pointed at as the two children of feuding farmers. Shamed and denounced, the young lovers elbow their way through the crowd and out of the fairground. Hand in hand, and lingering to kiss, they stroll to the very strip of land that has put their parents at loggerheads. They will be unknown here, Sali thinks, amid this pastoral of weeds where there remains a run-down inn, with lighted lanterns dangling from the verandah in the early twilight. At the river's edge they find a barge full of hay, moored without purpose: the lovers' bed. Behind this simple tale filched from Gottfried Keller, there lurks my own feeling that love has to make its way in a harsh and fateful world. Whatever begins, good or ill, has to end, which is devastating for Sali and Vreli, who having at last found fulfillment, have yet to discover that although love may endure it has its terminus, rudely and crudely inflicted by an uncaring universe. They seek their bliss without realizing what a killer it is. If this be sentimental, well then the whole world is sentimental—as it is for the solitary lovelorn male bird left abandoned on the seashore, stared at by the boy who has watched them mating every day, cautiously peering, absorbing, translating. All summer and all night, the little voyeur watches the remaining one, the solitary guest from Alabama that cries out to the ocean wind and the stars to bring the other back.

The crucial emotion there, sung by baritone and chorus, evokes the sea's cadences, the swollen universe of human pain brought about by love and death: the mystery of apartness; the irreconcilable opposites of the human journey. So too with my childhood sweethearts Sali and Vreli, forbidden to meet but swayed by love, determined after a brutal separation to have one day of love together. They go to that bed of hay near the dilapidated country house become an inn, aware in the landscape of a bygone beauty: the garden overlooking a long valley through which the river winds its way. In the distance are snowy mountains. It sounds propitious, but the Dark Fiddler, the evil genius of Keller's drama, impedes their lovemaking. They cast themselves adrift on the barge and scuttle it. It sinks and they are both drowned. The walk to paradise has become a walk to death.

70 ▲
OSIRIS

It is easier to recall him at Grez, standing with hands clasped behind him, one step behind the tubby Jelka, whose paintings of their tiny French hamlet grace the walls alongside work by Gauguin and Munch. The garden outside is her true masterpiece, though, and perhaps the ramshackle, uncoordinated house is his, with its windows flung stagily wide, espaliers growing all the way up to the roof, the front courtyard's garden crammed with vegetation, so much so that both merely edge their way inside to be enjoyed and photographed. The house stands, an L-plan, on the village street between the old church and a ruined keep, its lofty stone walls slanting down past an orchard to the river Loing. At home he keeps a handful of scores, half of them Strauss, as already said (but the point needs to be made again and again). He is no longer Delius the importuner and voyeur, the expatriate picaro, but Delius the mystic and recluse. He is harvesting not so much isolation or rootlessness, however, as the vision of consummate Pan. It is as if the composer, brought here from abroad—lifts from Florida to Norway and Paris, then disappears into himself, coming out again "pastoralized," laid to rest in a bower of his own fecundity—a scene not far from that of October 1929, when, blind and paralyzed, he attends the week-long festival organized in London by his old friend and admirer Beecham. Carried in his invalid chair, propped up on cushions, he goes down the ship's gangway to a waiting ambulance. Silver haired, he has a gray felt hat, heavy overcoat, tortoiseshell glasses, a pale wrinkled ascetic face, as his sister notes at the time. There are to be six concerts, at which Delius, no longer the impassioned composer, wriggles around in an armchair, bathed in sweat. He lies on a litter throughout, swathed in flowers, perched on a balcony, in the end managing to rid himself of a few syllables: "This festival has been the time of my life." No more than that.

Like one of his own human voices among the high hills, he dwindles and soars in a delirium of pain and morphine, spasms and violent twists as Eric Fenby reads to him from a favorite novel. First buried, as he wishes, near a church "where the winds are warm and the sun friendly," in June of 1934, he's resurrected, brought from the south of France to Limpsfield churchyard, where the winds are keener, the sun sterner, to the tunes of his cuckoo and, on a summer night on the river, his punt.

Those who judged him a creator of formless rhapsodies had got him back. Those who believe all tone poems end in mystery reclaim him from the aether, perhaps committing themselves to the words heading the score of *In A Summer Garden* (1908): "Roses, lilies, and a thousand scented flowers. Bright butterflies flitting from petal to petal and gold-brown bees humming in the warm, quivering summer air. Beneath the shade of ancient trees, a quiet river with water lilies. In a boat, almost hidden, two people. A thrush is singing in the distance." For him, this is only medium lush, but prose is not his idiom after all. The rest and best of him is tonal. He was a hummingbird.

So it is to have known him as I do, plucking him from the air and directing him at Cheops: ritualistic blind man to ritualistic blind man, far apart in time, but spiritually, having something in common. If only we cared as much for all humans and furnished them the music that might see them through. I berate and pester myself with such a notion, wondering why, picking out someone else of severe disquiet, I do not accord him similar privileges. Are the gods lazy, crazy, or red in tooth and claw? Have they suffered too much and can manage only spasmodic gestures toward the sub-species in extremis? It would be worthwhile to know, but some overbearing cosmic agency keeps us from it, and you end with merely whimsical offers: millions of people praying for succor but the gods dishing out precious little, or as they say in the English-speaking countries, bupkiss. The test is to sustain one's interest in someone; having rendered unto Cheops my Delius, after long cogitation, I think it would be better to move on, leaving the gift behind, only to ferret out something else even more appropriate; but we do not work like that. I wish we were as worldly as this forthright poem of Cheops's people, bequeathed upward to show us how:

> The servants of yours
> have come with their provisions,
> beer and loaves of bread,
> herbs and bouquets from yesterday and today,
> all kinds of pleasing fruits.
> Come, spend the day in happiness,
> day after day, three days perhaps
> sitting in my shade with your friend on your right.
> She lets him get drunk and does whatever he says.
> The beer cellar becomes more and more drunk,
> but she stays behind with her brother.
> Her garment is below me,
> the sister is moving about.
> But I keep silent and shall not reveal what I see,
> nor what their lips speak.

It all depends on what kind of view you have of us, we who read *The Book of the Dead* as if imbibing a warm milky drink to get to sleep on. We do not wear, as the British say, "flash clobber," but function mainly as a shower of antiseptic capable of unwonted kindness from time to time, but also given to outbursts of gratuitous petulance; or even, while dreaming Promethean dreams, doing real damage without meaning to, like someone kicking out in the middle of a deep slumber. We cannot help it, perhaps because we know that there is too much sadness in living for us to do much about it. Here and there a gesture, a trick, a benison, and then the big black tarpaulin comes down again, dank and shiny, not from us, but from wherever.

Cheops, we hope, will carry the sounds of Delius with him to the end of his days, foisted upon him from who knows where, but he might do better merely to contemplate his pyramids, as less giving, making him less vulnerable. Who is to know whether his pyramid delights him more than any Delius music? Those of us deemed omnipotent are merely overseers, superintendents, a superior version of the ground staff who suction waste from the toilets in the bellies of wide-bodied jets parked for the night (if such analogies help you at all). We checker all careers, do we not?

71 ▲
CHEOPS

Here comes the king. I am strolling on fluid. My ears purge a golden wax. My brain has become a gilded honeycomb. My voice is a series of mellow chimes. The sand underfoot is soft as gold-dust. My eyes, heaven help my eyes, they run with palest blood-fluid. I am not better, but I am different. I do declare I have been in touch with the god Osiris, who has changed my being, made me less of a king, more of a magician. It is time to go. So say the people, watching my every move, although I am so swathed in magnificent robes it is hard to see the true me. Boyish physique; I am not a heavy man, though my head is big. I often walk abroad in this fashion, even soliciting the comments of the populace, or rather I should say the questions of Djedi the blue heron catcher, who asked something the last time I was out. Now he sees me in all my glory and asks "Is your reign over, Cheops? Will it soon be someone else?" Already they have a whiff of what is going to happen. Perhaps Osiris tells them.

"Can I be king now?" This is the infamous Djedi, insolent as ever, although he looks older. Can it have been so long since I last encountered him? What can I have been doing in the interim? Lost time? Lost face.

I am beyond answering him, but I wish him a decent burial

and pass on, catching in my hand a tiny winged creature that just alighted, presumably a messenger. If this were a less generous society than it is, they would be telling me it was time to step down, yield to Chefren or Mycerinus, the one noble, the other too devoted. Thank goodness I have the good will of all my rock collectors, and an endless supply of red paint for pyramids, yellow for boats. I return the bows of the women, stalking forward into the sun's full blast. We never have a cold day and I find it hard to imagine any such thing. They think I am being readied for my pyramid and its long shafts, but I am only mounting my carrying-chair in order to visit a few sites. This is when I step out of my palace and tread infinity, a body borne by others, slowly flying, I suppose, cruising over the land at the speed of an unmilked cow. For this "carry," as we call it, you need the right demeanor, which my mother had; the posture, the exact type of thought to busy yourself with while riding in state.

We set out full of glory.

We return just as full of glory, but the bearers weaker.

Why must it be the same team on the return? Tradition.

I have inspected. It is all ready. My brain shoots forward to when robbers will smash my own tomb and *I* shall be stolen, behind me a mess of rubble and rejected reserve heads lolling in the middle of nowhere. Then, since you have been "dismantled," as I call it, you know it is over, once you are missing. Strictly speaking, you should remain in the same place, the place you were put into, in order to please the gods, who have a strong sense of propriety in these matters. Move on, and you are lost. Yet, even if you were cemented up, they would batter their way in and remove you, no doubt to work some evil changes on your exquisitely prepared body.

As I understand the plans for me, at their most recent, I am to be buried with music as well as food and furnishings; that must be to placate Osiris, the plan entailing, I suspect, the live burial with me of those very musicians I have grown accustomed to. Until they perish for lack of air, and all music with them. The world will halt for all of us in there, until—well, perhaps we will wake together like all-night carousers demanding a second breakfast.

Could Djeda and Crf possibly be foot soldiers of the Libyan line? Sent to plague me at the last?

Where is my mother and what devilish sorcery is being worked on her remains at this very moment?

Reunion with Osiris will assume the form of a kiss, the sweet and tender rubbing together of noses during an exchange of breath symbolizing the breath of life, except he will be an erect phallus, the head having an inbuilt nuzzling snout, and this will be the god-head conveying his breath to the little, baby-like pharaoh. His head is a glans, which does not at first seem likely, until you think hard, for this is the head of heads. A pharaoh might just as plausibly have blown life's breath into a child, indeed into every child in his domain. Now it comes again, as if ignited, that tender bleating sound of the music, peopled by a chorus not using words but a mellifluous hum, and heeling, or wheeling, over to slow, introverted fiddling that seeks no end, not even as breath-blown instruments have to cease. It is the old music, the old theme, sent out as if to restore me to myself, to him, to remind me of what is important in this world of wasted opportunities. Yea, he tells me through his breath, seize the arrow's barb before the tense string quivers.

72 ▲
MERYTYETES

"Soft soap" I tell him after he says to me, "You are looking younger every day," to be followed surely by his scaly hand raising my linen and clutching home. He used to have these outbursts in the old days and I often let him get away with them; it seemed, as almost nothing else with him, a natural thing to do. He had suddenly, after nightmares full of bricks and rocks—sketched-out designs for greatness—remembered he was human, whereas I was not, not much anyway. Now, however, he does not bluster and get away with it, his hand left hanging, as if it were a brand. He flinches, withdraws, as if he has been caught stealing, and I resume my chaste ways, unhappy to deflect him thus but, after so long, somewhat weary of his miscellaneous preludes and overtures: the hand gallop, and the lovemaking that's done with the face (two faces, rather) and the pent-up recitation of unrespectable words. After all, he has a brothel in the palace in which to squander what remains of his seed, and, I gather, a matching set of statues depicting each and every concubine, off which, some anyway, he has had the hands removed, sawn off with carpenter's tools. No one knows why, but it counts as a decisive gesture, I am sure; I just hope he doesn't extend the trick to the real live girls. Is that what he has in mind for me, or will he wait until I am dead?

"You should hear this music," he says, quivering.

"Which? I hear no music."

"In the head, woman. It comes and goes, from, presumably, very far away, I have no idea whose."

"This conversation," I answer, "threatens to be one of those whose meaning remains undisclosed. If talk we must, how about something audible, tangible? Then I'd be happy to keep you company."

No good. He's determined to keep it secret, although to pay homage to it in his obtuse fashion while the rest of us stand around amazed but unamused, because he's king. It is not even pyramid music, I bet.

"Intermittent concert," he says. "My whole day is attuned to it. I half suspect Osiris has some hand in it."

He half-suspects Osiris in the same way as you half-suspect a star. There is no curbing him, what with his red pyramid, his yellow solar boats, his perpetual hankering for transcendence. Here comes Heduanna, the astute changeling with Berber blood to keep her wild. He tells her much the same, but all she can find to say is something about how she would dearly like to get rid of the sounds *she* already has. "Anything to blot out certain overheard cries." I know what she's getting at. What does he have in mind for her next? He treats her as experimental offspring, just to see what she'll do next. And that will be to go away again, if anything, to avoid his conversation, his roaming hand. Hands.

Rumors have it that he is going to invite us all to some kind of showdown in his pyramid, which he will enter in a carrying cart, alive, and not leave. How can this be so? What has he planned? Can it have to do with the solar boats, in which I'd heard he's lost interest anyway? Or is there something more far-fetched, such as being entombed alive?

I suspect what happened to his mother, stolen and most certainly dismembered, is working on him again. I imagine his addiction to Osiris has something to do with Osiris's being cut up into fourteen pieces, and scalded to death with molten lead. He has to find her and put her back together again, so as to—well, what? To re-bury her, I suppose, though the poor old lady isn't going to look so pretty after all she's been through. It would not be fair to call him a mamma's boy, but it wouldn't be fair not to either. Merely to think of her disparate parts flung to all corners of the earth puts him in a swivet. If he ever finds her, and he's sure not to, he wants her properly entombed at Giza, not Dahshur, in a workmanlike pyramid. Has he found her? Surely not. Not even his incorrigible bodyguards are that good. He should make offerings of food to her, but he can't. So perhaps he's found a way to find her, using music as a guide.

He almost gets my sympathy when, motioning me aside away from courtiers and other prancing posturers, as if to reveal some shard of pornography, he instead lifts his middle finger and scoops tenderly at the little fleshy bleb in the noseward corner of his eye. What marvel will this produce? Gold-dust? There, tiniest island of smut on the pad of his finger, lies a dot which, he tells me, is the blood from within his eyeball turned to crystal by natural healing. As if he knew. "It's coming out bit by bit," he says, "even if it is going to take years. It feels like grit, but it has a bloody tinge. I should collect them up, Merytyetes, until I have a sizeable crystal which, dropped in water, will return to its natural state—the same amount of blood reconstituted as was in the eye beforehand."

There is a certain charm in this telling; a child has sprung from within himself and is reassuring me that he is going to last. Odd, if you look right at him, you see nothing at all: no blood in the white of the eye, since it is all contained. I have seen him bloodshot, but never so alabaster white as this. You'd think he had found the cure instead of deludedly mistaking, as *I* think, the ordinary fleck of sand for something momentous. If he were in the desert more, he might discover that what he so proudly hoicks out from the corner of his eye is nothing to do with blood at all. All the same, it is with a certain pity that I look upon him, eagerly holding his hand out for me to admire. He's a deferential old scoundrel, to say the least, but otherwise a pain, too mastaba-minded for the likes of me.

"I'll recover," he says, squinting.

I say nothing, knowing better than to argue with him.

"I'm beshitten with it," he adds, resorting as so often to language unworthy of a pharaoh.

"I can see," I tell him.

"Well, I can't," he answers, and begins to rub both eyes, pushing his finger tip at them, then smoothing tip over eyelid to clear something.

"One day, in the future," he predicts, "this will be as nothing. They'll stop it before it starts."

"I don't doubt it, Cheops. And how do you know?"

"Straight from Osiris, woman. From whom else? He and I have an improving relationship these days. Quite the prelude I'd say. Imagine being sliced up like that, and then put together again. He understands what ails us."

I leave him to his divine maunderings, and try to find his colloquial daughter Heduanna, whom he trifles with.

73 ▲
DJEDI THE BLUE HERON CATCHER
CRF THE FLY WHISK MAN

Their conversation usually takes the form of tried and true one-liners offered in a spirit of confirmation: old saws about women, the Nile, the behavior of cows, the presence of the pyramids. You answered with yes; anything else would have led to a long evaluation of the topic, leading nowhere. It was better to agree and let the day go forward based on solid unanimity. A few times a year, though, they broach new conversational terrain, mostly in the form of response to something new in their lives at home: a broken adze or a wounded bird. Today, however, Djedi has found the time to ask Crf if he has heard the news.

"What is it?"

"We're going to get a day off."

"Don't put me on, please, life is hard enough. If I get a day off, the shock will no doubt kill me, and where will my family be then?"

"It's true," Djedi persists. "I listen everywhere, and the story's the same. A day off. A whole day."

"No more hauling blocks of stone?"

"No more anything. You can put your legs up, friend, and have a doze."

"Well, snip it off and boil it, I like that, I really do." Crf begins to smile; his leathery face relents as if covering more area.

"There's only one snag."

"I thought so."

"Well," says Djedi the blue heron catcher, "we have to do one thing. There's a chore."

"The story of my life," Crf sighs gamely. "What exactly is it? How long will it take?"

"I don't know. They haven't said. But everyone is off although commanded to be in a certain place by midday."

"What for?"

"No idea," Djedi says, beginning to lose faith in his own idea and the brief eminence it has brought him.

"Not lifting and hauling? Not even trimming?"

"No idea. We get the rest of the day off, so it won't take long. Crf. All these years and the day of plenty is at hand. Osiris be praised."

"Maybe," Crf says, "they are going to kill us and replace us with—"

"Nubians? Could be. No, silly: it won't be that."

"Always trouble where there's Noobs," Crf says sagely. "I *know*."

Now they move on, Djedi to consult other blue heron catchers, Crf to other toilers with rock, both eager to find out more, but not that anxious to discover what the payoff is going to be. Cheops's daydream of having workmen buried with him isn't that far from the workmen's expectations. In its individual way, their first conversation lingers in their minds as something that didn't ring quite true; yet it proves haunting.

"What," Crf asks Djedi, "do you do with the herons once you've caught them?"

"Try to make them stand still in gardens." Is Djedi kidding?

"Honest?"

"Sometimes we feed them wine or beer to get the same effect. They either stand still or they fall over. Either way, though, they're better like that than when flapping all over the place."

Crf is shocked, his view being that hewers of rock are real men and don't mess with herons in that girlish way. But Djedi has persuaded him that heron catching is quite a demanding chore, demanding muscle and brains.

"Could *I* be one?" Crf has ambition still, but none of the training. Could, he wonders, I graduate from rocks to blue heron grabbing?

The fact is that what Cheops has in mind has never been done before, so there is no problem to keeping it secret. There are so many other possibilities for people to tantalize themselves with, not all of them pleasant by any means. Torture, beheading, disemboweling (not for funeral purposes), and the famous Osiris punishment of hot lead being poured into the box that traps you—all these come to mind and cannot be dismissed. He isn't even dead, people said. He hasn't even been prepared by the high priests. Indeed he has not, and of what he proposed the priestly caste knew nothing and would have damned him for blasphemy if they had. Cheops goes his own way, half-blind, music-enthralled, graced and goosed by the sensual music of Frederick Delius—at one with Osiris, but at odds with his family: ungrateful son he is (as he thinks) to his mother, careless father to Ka-wab and Heduanna, curmudgeon to his wife Merytyetes and Dedef-ra the son next in line, though fond encomiast of the brilliant young grandson Mycerinus—He interrupts this captious review, wondering what he's left out, and whom, increasingly unsure these days of anyone's exact genealogy, but certain he could shed all attachments in the interests of Osiris if only he can pull off this final, or penultimate feat. Now he remembers his father Sneferu, teaching him not to peel an apple but to summon someone to do it for him. Luxury.

He has begun to realize life is much untidier than he ever thought it, and how his old assumption that, in order to depart it in seemly fashion, you had to bring everything to a neat end, was groundless. You went hence in full untidiness, and were received by understanding hosts who did not chide you for loose ends. There would always be somebody else left behind to take care of such things. You did not have to depart trim and tight, but merely open-minded—mouth agape if need be, all bodily orifices ready to receive. Had he realized the worry he caused Djedi and Crf, he would have been unmoved, having recruited the entire population to his cause, at least after they finished harvesting. He does not hear Djedi's "Damn me if I know" or Crf's darker "It'll come to a bad end, mark my words." He has few presuppositions, least of all those purveyed by priests. He dispenses with miscellaneous gods by the dozen, intent on Osiris only—with whom, he thinks, he ranks high, high enough to be allowed something beyond measure. No lead in a box for him, nor dismemberment into fourteen pieces, but something gentler, inspired by music, and touted by Osiris himself. Osiris awaits him. Cheops knows what to do next.

74 ▲
OSIRIS

Having spent much of his life in planning and calculating (no pyramids without math), he still has a fair grasp of numbers and ratios, but the fruit of all that skill is embodied out there in scarlet rock. What remains is a geometry regarded as music, into which he has now learned to plunge. He imagined himself inquiring of all those corpses, Are you doted on? Have you regrets? Are you mourned? Were you ever beloved? Did you ever panic? Did you breathe your last breath knowing that it was? Am I your confidant and helpmate? Will I ever pass muster for you? Will you rise from the dead and befriend me?

What intrigues him now, however, is how such records as there are—papyrus, chisel work—emphasize the lives of the living and those who survive. There is no record of those who perished—they were born, lived anonymously, and then died, with no record of their doings, however humble: bait salesmen, blue heron catchers, garbage shovelers. Nor is there any sign of those in higher station, what they studied and grew up to do with finesse and love. They too have vanished, more so than if they had never been. The paradox interests him: the dead are deader than the unborn. And it is not Osiris's fault; he may be able to mend himself, after scalding and dismembering, but he has not the power to complete the records of scribes, priests, that nobody remembers, not even those grand viziers, of such short tenure. Death, he understands, sweeps many away with a careless arm, indeed even those who would otherwise have made a record of those others (how they smiled, signed, cried). Cheops does not know what literature is, and his vision of art is that of a hoopoe being awakened by the blood-red salmon spill of tropical sunrise. He has a sense of life wasted, of gifts deployed then thrown out of the unglassed window.

In a way, such thoughts reflect his own life. He has always worried that his powers of concentration were insufficient, and that, if he is not careful, he will never accomplish anything. This is why he builds pyramid and, for the rest, as second king of the fourth dynasty, takes a lively interest in the religious sciences of his day. Solar barks came and went, and then music seized his soul (thanks to someone held in awe). Not bothered by his tendency to use forced labor for his gigantic enterprises, or his occasional indifference to human dignity, he keeps his mind on the job—which makes of him a miscreant monomaniac, kingly yet narrow. Going about his business, musing that off Merytyetes has always come a fume of fermenting berries, and off his mother an aroma of wet sawdust, he finds himself appalled by the vast numbers that death allows to be born, raised, trained, only to let them after a taste of life fall and rot, with no chance of a repeat. In this way, he dimly recognizes, the great charts and histories get written, but regarding only the figure against that forgotten ground. This includes himself too. I myself refer to this as the "Ozymandias complex," courtesy of one Diodorus Siculus, Greek historian of the 1st Century and patent successor to Herodotus. Ozymandias is the Greek name for Rameses II, of the 13th Century B.C., over whom I have some sway. Just think how much later than Cheops the complex goes on.

So be it. I have my preferences as I am allowed to time-travel, backward, forward, even up and down. I have my favorites, and these far from the most favored of kings. If they can stomach the music of the gods, the music we console ourselves with, then they belong in my good books and I try to grant some congruous fate. Back to Cheops, then, whose aberrant soul I have been dipping in music. Actually, I regard my own tastes as rather obvious and backward—too oceanic and sentimental for the modern mode, though Mr. Schnittke has come to my attention, and Messrs. Finzi, Mahler, Ravel, Debussy, Fauré, you know the rest. Were there time for Cheops to inspect and relish the entire treasury (including Isis's favorites and those of other gods), I would be able to sit back and enjoy the spectacle, but Cheops is failing, perhaps because he wants to fail, has said his fill in Egypt. In *my* time I have supplanted such a god as Sokaris at Memphis, and an ancient god of the dead at Abydos. Some gods rise and some fall, almost as if complying with the laws of drowning. I am content to seem to die with nature, and come back to life. In history, as I no longer have to remind anyone,

I was a good and wise king whom his brother killed—you know the story. This is how venerable history becomes a myth, and how you manage to achieve personality long after your reign is done.

Cheops's application may be said to be in, and more or less rubber-stamped. He will be allowed to leave, which is approximately equal to voluntary retirement with benefits and an annuity. Is he then to be deemed emeritus? Only if he passes certain tests, such as accepting his future role without demur. In the hands of an Erodo, he will have to fight to salvage his good name, especially as Dedef-ra is going to make gestures that virtually disown him. He will receive all the aid I have to give, but let it be understood that these days my gifts are mostly musical from some cosmic shifting of the muses. It is like having to whistle to yourself in the dark when you have been accustomed to judging the hearts of the dead when placed in the scales. No doubt some feel I have been trivialized, handed over to music and literature after a lifetime of Houdini-like escape and physical flight from the Jack the Rippers of my day. Yet look what I am told: You have the privilege of anachronism, and the gift of time travel, o Osiris. Rest content. I try, but I am an interfering old so-and-so. I think at times I really belong to the Greeks, and Herodotus (Erodo) is the undertaker arrived to take me off with him, a potent trophy to be renamed Busiris. I too am obliged to suffer change and demotion, and to have the illusion of power without quite being my own lord and master.

Cheops, then: almost a goner.

A landed migrant, as some countries say.

At a solemn music.

75 ▲
CHEOPS

What do they care if I am sitting here like a man with broken legs? Sooner or later a king has to admit to some kind of weakness. The orchestra, so-called, playing in front of me is loud, but it is really several small groups of players favoring us with contrary melodies. The resulting discordance fits my mood. I am being tugged this way and that: anxious to please others; feeling no such thing; eager to please myself; feeling no such thing; hoping to be worthy of my mother; feeling no such thing. Above all, hoping to please Osiris. There is muttering that only a dead man is capable of—a king certainly; but this is only a rehearsal, and who knows what may intervene between this dry run and the actual event, by which time I might even be dead? True, I am faltering, beginning to wheeze; my eyes do me poor justice; my heart flutters with anxiety. Daily my record becomes poorer, meriting an assassin's knife or the pelting stones of a carefully recruited mob. Those near and dear eye me and walk the other way lest an old coot of a king accost them for tedious conversation about religious philosophy. There remains a spark in the old man yet, but it gutters, oh yes, it draws whatever power it has from some buried sun. I put familiar questions to myself: Were you loved? Or just admired? Were you worthy of Sneferu your father? Have you been faithful to your wives? Did your children adore you? Have you left them a suitable heritage? Have you put right any of the ills you visited upon them? Did you accomplish anything of unquestionable valor? Will you be remembered for your mind? Did you save anyone who had been condemned? Did you promote to high office anyone who was unworthy, merely for effect or to repay a shabby debt? Did you find your mother after all? Was there something within you without which you could not have survived as king?

Around and around goes the whirligig. The answers fly and twist. I am not the man for self-interrogation. I am aware of having built and built, as if that were enough. If only I had wept on bended knee, or set an arm around some vilified colleague. Here I am in the carrying-chair, perched on the brink, deafened by music not of my own choosing, eyed suspiciously by priests and scribes alike, unapproached by those who ought to prize my doings.

What is he going to do? Where will he await his death? Will they then disembowel him? Has he asked for his body parts to be set within a canopic jar? Has he mentioned the succession to anyone at all? What has he given away? How much of his chambers' furniture will he require? How many serious illnesses now afflict him? If only their questions signified worry and concern, rather than a gossipy interest in the outcome. As it is, they comment that I have certainly taken care of myself, quite ignoring my cemetery plans for everyone of notable rank, their mastabas judiciously arranged as if an audience had sagely arranged itself to hear a pharaoh speak. I am not the man primly playing the nose-flute—not played by mouth—yet with the blowing hole at the side. If only it were I playing the tambourine, the hand-drum, and the double-sided drum, just to make the racket worse. I would love to be playing the castanet-like wooden clappers, or be plucking the strings of a mandola, with its elongated sound-body, no more than an oval of wood and skin. Or with a plectrum. I would only too gladly play the hand-harp to myself, caressing its long bird-like neck. Anything to prove myself socially useful, even the systrum or hand-rattle, making a tinkle smaller than you might expect from tiny metal discs attached to several rods. I have seen the body of the harpist fuse with the shape of the upright harp, the player's smile one of tranquil sobriety. Ah, the long fragile neck, the ample curve of the body within the cotton robe, the swerve of the buttock behind the intucked knee. Dancing girls have volunteered by the score to perform naked, but can you trust their motives? I am reminded how many of our own women have a feline face, stout neck, a haughty, post-marital look. *My* dancers, as I think of them, usually sport short skirts tied with a rear ribbon, with extra ribbons crisscrossed over the chest; but not today. They keep their distance, though, the naked ones, no doubt dreading the swollen onset of an aging king. A singer begins, his face all dutiful release, and the flute player near him twists his neck the better to check the sequence of notes from the singer's lips. The singer leads, of course, as ever. Lined up like soldiers, the mandola players play the same phrase, as if in some slow-moving tableau. I watch them spellbound, wondering if there is anyone here willing to match my own motions, and come with me to my final reward.

No volunteers They want their lives, they will go away from

this ceremony, at the mouth of the pyramid's main shaft, to their lovers—to a well-earned dish of fruit, a slice of roasted beef. Which is to say they assist at ceremonies, reserving the right to walk away to something less grand, but to them overpowering in its ordinariness. How I admire the musicians' muscular thighs within their transparent cape-like wraps. The dancers wear neck-scarves and nothing else. Hair tied in long strands that have pompoms at the end. Oh for another year of *that*. I would give a thousand turquoise hawks for five minutes with any one of them. Oh to have ruled with such appalling success, leaving behind me a shoal of such hussies all dancing to the same clappers.

Well, this is rehearsal only. I will be going back, for whatever antics I can muster, but not the next time. Having proposed and attended the ceremony in full regalia (wearing nothing transparent, exposing the muscular calf), I can hardly be said to have changed my tune. Speaking of which, I hear only our national music, not the slinking ovations of sound that invaded my soul. Next time, for certain, that Osiris music will reappear to get me through the ritual and its sequel. Such faith. Perhaps, when I appear, I look too fancy for a merely rehearsing pharaoh, what with cut pieces of glass pasted in my bracelets, my collar of faience beads, glazed and tubular, with imitation carnelians made by putting red earth in the gaps, and inlaying rounded crystal above. The sun beats harshly through the collar and punishes my skin. I have made the best of myself.

76 ▲
DJEDI THE BLUE HERON CATCHER
CRF THE FLY WHISK MAN

Everlastingly the man of no account who had bandied words with the great Cheops, Djedi continues to live in an aura of unearned fame. Trading on his reputation, we might say. He toils all day, his curses subdued below the sound of his heavy breathing, but usually manages to work alongside Crf, a man just as militant but not one to tackle the pharaoh in a confrontation. Their chatter goes on, although impeded, and they try to find out what is afoot, much as some people navigating an event seek to triangulate it, drawing lines that narrow down the zone of the happening.

"*We* weren't invited, of course." Djedi doesn't really care, but he says this for effect and hopes to stir the other into some kindred complaint. "I do declare there's something going on. The pharaoh was seen at a special ceremony. I've heard that much, but nobody seems to know what it was all for, especially as he's not dead, though ailing a bit. Now, what do you think they're up to?"

"Polishing their knobs." Crf is in a bad mood today, unlikely to respond with even his own version of logic.

"Be serious, man."

"Knackering their missuses, like all royals then."

"I mean," Djedi insists, "what do you *think* they were planning, getting up to?"

"Oh the usual. Shafting the workers and feathering their nests. That Cheops is a real slave driver, mark my word"

Djedi, whose mind is that way, wants more detail. He, much more than Crf, has the right mental set to be a spy, and would like to practice his trade on the royal family, at almost any risk. But there is no way out from the virtual slave labor imposed on him. The single-mindedness of Cheops has always stopped him cold, but he fantasizes arcane plots and bloody reprisals. All his fantasies need is fleshing out.

"Listen, Crf, if he's not dead, then how can they bury him? Is he planning to die? If so, when? Is he just showing off for the sake of show, or is there something else involved that will change our lives for ever? Imagine if Cheops had finally decided to build no more pyramid and stopped the quarrying, trimming, lugging about, the positioning of huge stones? How'd we feel then, hey?"

"We'd feel like pharaohs," Crf tells him. "We bloody would."

"Then," Djedi says, "don't you think that some kind of enormous change is going to happen? We've waited long enough in our hovels. They do say that Greek fellow lives in a cave out of sympathy with us workers. Imagine that."

"And his head," adds Crf, "is still on the bastard's shoulders. He must be well in."

"Tell you what," Djedi says. "I think the old kingdom is coming to an end and things will improve. We'll have time to spare for getting into trouble. They'll treat us like half-gentlemen."

"Dreamer."

"Better than being a cynic."

"Well," Crf says, "if you want to think that way. You're looking at power, my lad, and power never gives up until the head drops off the body. It's too late for us already. I might have become a scribe in a different country."

"And I," Djedi says with combustible venom, "might have been a grand vizier with a mastaba as big as Egypt. It makes sense. Somewhere else, we wouldn't be nobodies after all, would we?"

"Oh yes we would. That's what they mostly need, nobodies. They're hardly worth burying."

"Oh, I'd have aimed higher," Djedi tells him.

"Only to fall down again."

"Never mind." Djedi abandons that line of thought for a riper speculation: "Mister Cheops is attracting attention to himself. He wants to be seen while living, he doesn't care what will happen afterwards."

Then an appalling thought recurs. What if he and all his fellow workers were to be executed, perhaps during an orgy of death lasting days? Instead of being gathered together to hump rock, they would receive the tribute of cold steel from Cheops's little-seen security legion, and that would be the end of the Memphitian laboring class. A ridiculous idea, Djedi tells himself, but a plausible figure to stalk through his daydreams. And was it any weirder than the stories that circulated about their ruler: that he cached little messages inscribed on strips of papyrus in the openings of his body and urged the children of courtiers to pluck them out, unroll them, and read them if they could—rumors of impending death for some, promises of impending promotion for others? Djedi is not after a raise or a new assignment, he would merely like to live out his short Egyptian span; but what are the chances of surviving when you are virtually anonymous among many? Perhaps, however, since on that famous occasion he is supposed to have rebuked the pharaoh, who might remember him, his chances of both death and promotion are good. A suasive loudmouth, he has a put-upon wife and two girls to support. He can hardly please himself, and at all costs should button his lip. Otherwise, even the role of blue heron catcher demoted to that of rock-roller will not be his. He will have to *want* to be degraded; that much is clear. What puzzles him—because above all he is a rational person although quite without education (one of nature's instinctive reasoners)—is that his own *ka* is much the same as Cheops's. In the realm of soul-making, the formula for soul is familiar, and the *ka* that singles someone out as pharaoh is little different from the *ka* that animates a heron catcher or a fly whisk man. All men are spiritual, he thinks, and all should, once reaching the barrier, be much the same.

Clearly he has not reached the point in politics at which historical incongruity confronts philosophic awareness, and he never will. Choice meat to become a rebel, he lacks the support of the downtrodden multitude, but he can dimly see how a leader could enlist the vast legions of the poor, in order to demolish a dynasty that thinks itself invulnerable. He will not live long enough to develop that degree of vigor, nor will his workmates; and it will be centuries before the penny at last drops, under Greek, Roman, or Turkish influence. For now, he is a fascinated spectator, eager to go back to herons, but locked in, while wiseacres go about proclaiming that Cheops enslaves no one at all. In fact, he is the monarch of an enlightened pressgang, whose badge is those huge triangular domes at Giza in which Cheops, now, has almost lost interest. Such overload as Djedi's spirit has will transfer itself down through the centuries like a balance unspent, but visibly there, to someone's credit.

Someone observing these toilers, their lives predicated on serving the pharaoh and his elite, has cause for wonder, as centuries of dull servitude gradually give birth to a golden age of the arts, in light of which such pioneers of arrogance as Cheops seem no more than opinionated rednecks. Millions of mastabas enclose these laborers, whose lives are as blocked as certain pyramidal shafts promising outlet but culminating in a dead end with portcullis. Visitors such as the out-of-time Erodo—Herodotus only to his own people—find themselves ill-prepared for this seminar in social justice offered by the likes of Djedi and Crf. Yet, this is the way the world runs, exercising the force and power of divine right, as well as the privilege of murder. Their deaths, like their daily heaves and lurches, go unnoticed; but this would be true even if it were an age of records flagrant for the *scratch-scratch* of scribes' pens. The vision of men as conned over-obliging dogs does not escape our notice, prompting perhaps the thought that one day the world will be so choked with corpses accumulated over centuries—in the quest for self-aggrandizement on the part of a pelfy few—that civilization will choke itself to a halt. Proud thought unavailable to Djedi and company.

77 ▲
ERODO

Although he may not have taken me into his complete confidence, he's told me enough to give the contours of his ambition, if I can call it that. I know about the lyrical music he hears, and the occasional glimpses he gets of a bald man standing in front of a cottage, with a portly matron to whom he obviously owes a good deal. After a while, you can fill in the gaps for yourself. I'm sure he's wandered from the perfect path of reincarnation and intends something less orthodox. All the details of his performance I have noted down: including his voice a bit higher, his rump a-twitch, his eyes now beginning to glaze over into what I have heard called the thousand-league stare (from gazing up and down the Nile), and his complexion paler (with small white discs forming on his cheekbones and nose). Not that he is unfriendly; far from it, he encourages me in a host of ways, preferring the exotic, I suppose, and constantly urging me to move into the palace so as to give us a better chance to confer informally. He wants company, I know, as most tyrants do. If they cannot chain a meteorite to their desk, they have to take it out in talk and executions. The final truth about him seems to be that the vastness which initially inspired him (revealed by his pyramid-building), has given way to this music thing, overwhelming him as nothing before. Not that it has made him milder or more genial; it has merely made him more introverted. He cares just as much but no longer insists on keeping his pyramids red. His solar boats' yellow faded long ago, but he has something in his skull I have been unable to tease into the open. All he does is promise me that, "when the time is ripe," he will involve me in his enterprise, making of me a stand-by, a scrutineer, indeed a spy.

And that is where I pause, having no idea what he plans, I recognizing that with the paraphernalia he has on hand there are only so many things he can do. Perhaps the most original thing ever attempted vis-à-vis the tombs was the plundering of them (something wholly unsuspected, and piously abominated). To tell the truth were they to do to the mastabas any such thing, that would be original, but of course they do not. Instead of giving me clues, he recounts the gold process: bars melted in the horn-shaped crucible; the fire kept hot by blowing hard through tubes; the air that streams out from the lower end; the engraving of a dwarf. I forget the rest, but the process is fabulous and dainty. These people love and wear gold as if it has come abundantly from the very sun. Cheops points out palace girls wearing cones of myrrh and diffusing behind them in the inside heat a fume of squashed strawberries (which tickles the men no end and sends them stalking). Some of the girls wear their hair loose, but not many; the vogue has not yet caught on. Everywhere, by the way, the Eye of Horus, ceramic glass, opaque, dark carnelian, beads; amulets engraved with baboons, dwarves; and bronze rings bearing marguerites, lotus blooms, uraei crowned with the sun's disc, and horned hawks of Horus, their hairs twisted together to make a tie. I could easily have been seduced here and begged to stay. The astounding thing about their jewels and finery is that, refined as it looks, it still retains what I would have to call a primitive patina, so much so that I envision the craftsmen looking both back and forward, losing naught of their ancestral cleverness while evolving subtler and subtler ways of shaping bones, feathers, claws, teeth, shells, and splinters of crystal. In my own possession, a gift from the pharaoh, I have a flint knife coated with gold leaf and decorated with lively cameos. If one day I have to leave, it will not be for lack of my love.

78 ▲
PRINCE KA-WAB

Muttering through, this thing so far short of language yet still radiant energy of sorts tunes in to him at the last and asks what do will; he, what will he do, can he do; nothing expiated oh no, not that ambitious, but what is left according to settled life style . . . I get all stuttery when even think about it

again start, render point if possible, so much of me turning to dust and fiber, just the dried mud left behind after river passed and dried

care still even if only one left; schooled in how to get up out there and do it, be it, have being for never so long, be a big man behind a big band

"Multiply bread you give to mother, carry her as she carried you." Have quail in hand. Give basket of figs . . . Laxative . . . Midwives' screams. Last fruit from tree in noble bowl. Hair on doll loosely plaited flax. Bits of my throat joining together for pliancy with the good old dear old language. Tug of war without rope. Feet together at line. Feather and handstaff for runners. A living roundabout of girls. Hathor dance with mirrors and wooden clappers hand-shaped

Thorn   foot   knife   late

79 ▲
HEDUANNA/MYCERINUS

Even now, after so many changes in his life, some of which we will never know about, he keeps some of his old habits, perhaps so that—as he walks through the lion's den he claims to inhabit—we can still recognize him—as if anyone might forget. Yet no doubt he is addressing the future, most of all someone like his son Dedef-ra, the likeliest to forget him and set him at naught. Still, thank goodness, when he has said or done something unusual (rare enough in these days of introversion), he goes into stunned immobility, almost as if struck dumb by his own virtuosity. Amazed by himself. Unable to acknowledge praise or thanks. It is as if he has all of sudden discovered his own sweetness. We are not going to forget him, oh no, but what are we to make of such a rehearsal as his recent one at the entrance to his pyramid? And why have certain skilled workmen been hammering away within, when we all thought the construction was finished? Clearly he intends drastic changes he refuses to discuss. He hears music and voices: that much he admits, but he hears or intuits other things as well. Mycerinus, bright boy, says his grandfather has discovered the meaning of death and burial and will make these matters public.

Sometimes after maundering like this, and persuading herself she can hear the timbre of Ka-wab's baritone in the arid wind off the desert from as far afield as Libya, she thinks she can see daylight amid the machinations, the palavers, the lies: Cheops, she realizes, is worried about Mycerinus, and how to save him from the inevitable evil reign of Dedef-ra. It is not aloofness then, but far-sighted worry that hounds her father and turns him into a political deviser. Perhaps he calls for elaborate, preparatory-seeming ceremonies only to distract, to keep them guessing, as when, in one of their few recent candid exchanges she asked:

"Is everything all right?"

To which he responded: "With eyes such as these I see perfectly. They look at this world, and they also do not."

"Are you praying?"

"Constantly."

"To Osiris?"

"Him and others. In our Egypt you can't afford to be selective, but you can play favorites."

"Will you tell some of us at any rate if anything serious comes up?"

"Probably not. Let me be aloof."

This unrewarding stuff can go on for hours, so she ends it, telling herself to grow up, be less of a doormat. He may be right, and one day Mycerinus will be king with a fuller stock of knowledge than any preceding pharaoh. The puzzle remains: why has this enlightenment, if that's what it is, sapped and withered my weak-eyed father, rather than inciting him to reassurance and splendid proclamation? Why so silent, Cheops, you who used to stroll the halls of the palace with a bright, considerate word for everyone? Will you ever come back to us? What has Osiris done to you, who seem so loving of him, and so awed?

She pauses to recollect this ghost of who he used to be, trying to relate the wasted patriarch of now to the glamorous potentate of yesterday, splendid but always approachable. The only misgiving she has is that she has idealized him, and he was never the paragon of pageantry she thought he was. I imagined him, she says, and I should get credit for that. I still cannot fathom Abydos. Was he trying to palm me off on Chirh, or did he want to immerse me in the mysteries of that sacred town? His sympathy with people has always fallen short of explanation, and now is not the time to hound him for reasons.

She remembers the melancholy gist of talks she has had with Mycerinus the golden boy, waiting in the wings for the wings of some—clearly Dedef-ra among them—to come apart and flutter down.

Is he less genial to you, Mice?

Not often; but now his face stiffens when I speak and his eyes glaze over, as if he is no longer with me.

What do you say then?

I try to quote something I have read. It goes like this, but obviously he does not know it, and then I wish I had got by heart some sacred writing he prefers:

O come to your sister quickly,
like a royal envoy
whose lord impatiently awaits his message . . .

How precocious of you, she says. Who's in charge of your reading?

Oh, Hed, I go from one to the next so fast I can't remember who, half the time anyway.

Heavens, she thinks, the boy is on the brink of pornography already. But then he would be. Puberty has come and gone. He *shaves.* Owns a copper razor, a royal one. It is I who dawdle in his foamy wake. He is advanced in ideas but slow in the uptake, yet still nice.

Mice, she asks, am *I* nice?

Sometimes, he says, you are a funeral parlor. Other times you're as fun as a fishing expedition to Abydos. Nice? Of course.

Her mind rebounds from the savvy filial, to the banal (a scene of hairdressing: in her mind she sees the dresser's coiffure more elaborate than the customer's, the mascara of both as thick as laid-on tape). Where this image came from, she does not know, but other images follow in quick succession, led in by drawings of monkeys, who always have a sexual aura. She recoils, from puzzlement into the salacious: a man, with long organ inserted into a pleat that runs from the woman's loins up to her armpit; now the wooden votive phallus from Deir-el-Bahari; then, a team, troupe, a trio, of one woman between two erect men, the front man waving his erection to the wind, nowhere to put it. Is this, she wonders, the true yield and booty of her Chirh fixation at Abydos, or is it something subtler? In her mind because mostly taboo, the sheer natural force of an erotic picture leaps from the surface and becomes dangerous. One is allowed to dream it up, she decides, but not to adorn one's mastaba with it, certainly not with vervet monkeys, or people coupling with beasts of the field, about which she has heard.

Mycerinus, she murmurs, is already ahead of me. Him next?

80 ▲
OSIRIS

Poor Heduanna, worrying herself silly about matters Cheops is never going to explain. What she does not know is something I, with all my wisdom concerning variants of human whimsicality, do not quite fathom. An acute, alert girl, she has the mental equipment but, because of gruesome events during her trip south, lacks the effrontery to use it. Before she left, Cheops gave her, in a copper box wrapped in linen, a small statue of himself, for safe transmission, he said, to a retired scribe in Abydos, the sacred city. What she is not to know is that no other statue of the king existed—for good reasons, at least according to him. Morose about the removal of his mother's body, he felt the same way about himself, half-knowing that, after the mother, they—whoever they are—would steal the son. Yet, even as his body went wherever it would, his statue would survive (and, as I Osiris can attest, it ended up in a Berlin museum). And it would be unique and authoritative. Secreted safely in Abydos, it awaited its next handler even as Heduanna got the eye from Chirh and witnessed his death. Yet, with so much going on around her, she quite forgot the little statue and brought it back.

Now, you may well wonder why a king with a pyramid celebrating him, the seventh wonder of the world if you care to think in such terms, would make such a fuss about a statue, and restrict himself to only one. Apart from one or two monofilamental outlines etched on a stela, this was the one and only image. One can only say that, to a mind habituated to balance, the complementary opposite of a huge pyramid was a tiny figurine. It stood to sense, and it would survive, it would not vanish, rot, blow to powder. After all, this is the pharaoh in whose burial chamber his cartouche, bearing his name, figured on the wall, high up, alongside another inscription done by the gang of workmen appointed to the building of the chamber. In red, the gang said who they were and what they had done. Graverobbers find it too much trouble to steal such graffiti, the proud emblem of a working class, of interest only to a future sociologist. An actor called Omar Sharif would be the last person to see it and have it read aloud to him on camera.

There is another point, for recognizing which Cheops should receive full credit. With Ka-wab gone, Dedef-ra was the next in line, and he something of a renegade: self-willed, antipaternal, and obtuse. He refused to be buried at Giza, cut off all money for building there, and must be held responsible for numerous thefts, defacements, and demolitions. Cheops anticipated this, divining from Dedef-ra's behavior in the present his depredations to come, and so took steps, knowing that, even if Dedef-ra mangled his pyramid and removed his body—if indeed someone did not beat him to the punch—the figurine would be safe in Abydos for future relish.

Cheops being such a giant of anticipation, he no doubt deserves credit for an act of sheer clairvoyance, unless he and the next son had made an arrangement. It would be Chefren who, after the eight destructive years of Dedef-ra's reign, put things to right again, financing chapels left unfinished when their owners ran out of money, and reactivating Giza as a burial site. Chefren cleaned up, in other words, although he was not actually a son of the chief queen Merytyetes. The pyramid of Dedef-ra, never completed, Chefren reduced to virtual ruin in order to avenge the shabby treatment of the Cheops family and the presumed murder of some. Helped in this family cleansing exercise by the only other surviving son, Min-Khaf, a prince, Ankh-haf, and Nefermat, a grandson like Mycerinus, Chefren also played a major role in the formation of a cult devoted to the wise man and soothsayer Dedef-hor, whose aphorisms and saws Dedef-ra had had erased. I languish in these labyrinths of forgotten feuds, but I love them, as I do all that happens.

Such were the inroads into the royal line made by the misdeeds of one forgotten, unnamed wife, even amid the tempest of nepotistic incest homogeneously engaged in by the royals. Dedef-hor, an early thinker, survives in his writings, restored by the noble Chefren, but *Hr-dd-f* is long forgotten—like your guide, philosopher, friend, cicerone, and overseer, Osiris himself.

I was explaining Cheops's weird behavior, his fiercely attuned sense of anticipation, his ultimate faith in the deadness of the dead and their almost orchestral spacing around him, and his catafalque of Aswan red granite. He also—and this proves to me his agility, rather than his duplicity—dreamed up an alternative exit that might fail, yet failing might nonetheless inspire. Hence his rehearsals, and his selection of a special team which, with wooden mallets and phallic hammers, he appointed to clear certain passages on the pyramid's third level. This was no doubt to make the final procession easier (the third or top level having been the last built and so more cluttered with rubble, tools, and lamps). All this, he said, had to go. The question, which he made no attempt to answer, was would he be dead on his arrival there, or not? And then, if alive, what would his priests do? And what then of him? The pyramid has resounded for weeks with the thud of copper-bound wood on rock, but the only ones to hear are the outside workmen, such as the blue heron catcher and the fly whisk man.

"Are we getting nearer?" Crf.

"To get nearer, old bugger," says Djedi, "you have to know what it is you're near. What are we doing?"

"Mainly waiting, and honestly, Djedi, I don't mind the rest."

"He'll start with a star. We're waiting for that." In his wasted, but nimble head, Djedi has done some sums, reckoning there are twice as many of them as weeks ago; but still he's unbriefed, presently at a minor standstill, cracking bits of rock to little purpose, what he calls "shit-wipe scree."

Little do they know they are to play a major role.

"Dead or alive then?" Crf tells him dead.

"I bet not," says Djedi. "Not him."

81 ▲
OSIRIS

Now he turns into a night owl, both haunting his pyramid, as if in search of his mother still, and making a serious expedition of it, with flares and musicians. The boatmen even begin to speak of the king's parading and vie with one another to be chosen to row him. It is as if he wants to know the building in detail, omitting nothing—not even the skulls held in bone-rooms, or the corpses of those lost on ventures of their own flung unceremoniously into the pyramid. He has never seen so many niches, crevices, crawl spaces, attics, hiding places, or offertories, and he begins wondering how many of them he himself devised, never mind how absently. He tours the shafts with a jubilant murmur which those accompanying him strive to echo, though their main effort is to cluster around him. Beneath his robes, they wonder, is he wearing whatever that leather and stone body-brace is. No, they decide, he hasn't gone that far yet. Of course, the long, faltering echoes unnerve the party each night, except for those repeating the excursion. He says little, motions them along, points to flares beginning to gutter, and makes an occasional royal bow as if his mother has just passed by in her carrying-chair. All this he tells himself again and again is his; it is what he has sacrificed his nation to provide, although what they do not understand is that his life is already forfeit to Osiris and may therefore be dealt with as a finished entity. Any further debts to the gods he will pay later, as befitting a man whose head has been flooded with Delius, gift of a god who himself needs solace from music. As a music-lover he offers himself to Osiris as a going concern. After several hours in that dank, smoky interior, they file out, not far from the entrance to *H-d-t*'s cave, where he is busily at work on Book Ten of his exploits, unaware of the retinue outside, as of the king's presence among them. When he concentrates, his senses close down, his loins grow numb and he automatically eases them, rocking back and forth on his tilted Egyptian bed. A little discomfort, he contends, sharpens the imagination and the mind, whereas luxury among harems and Turkish baths, odalisques and plashing fountains blunts them quite. He writes on, imagining what his mind has found.

This time, however, he hears them and, stuck for a moment by an uncooperative *mot juste* in Greek, he slinks to the mouth of his cave only to witness the disappearance of the disheveled, drooping team into the gloom, the king in front, all of them dry-mouthed and hungry. Cheops has been at it again, roaming through his handiwork before putting it to final use (and no doubt evicting *H-d-t* into the palace, only to be thrown to the wolves by Dedef-ra).

He has already gleaned a little of this, knows it is time to hurry up and take his leave; but he wants to see the ritual Cheops has planned. So he joins his royal friend when Cheops, having reconnoitered the pyramid to his heart's content, turns to wandering also at night through the dim-lit palace, with fewer retainers and flares, and making less rattle. Is this to be a farewell? A last benison? An apology, even? The king, having laid his nation waste, moves through them—the elite at least—perhaps to say how sorry he is; his purpose has just been too grand for human scale. Can this be it? The scribbling, abbreviation-making *H-d-t* wonders. Is this restitution? If so, it should be addressed to the laborers who worked on his scarlet honeycomb, whose lives have taken a back seat to his hubris. The Greek writes busily in the rush light, watched ironically by the squinting, blurred Cheops, who will miss his companion.

Now at the open door of Heduanna's bedchamber, Cheops pauses at the dangling beads that obscure the interior and motions *H-d-t* inside with him, He descends upon the sleeping girl and drags her to him, shushing her while he applies to her the part of his body she has never known, Erodo catches a glimpse of leather, a harness, and an obelisk of white stone with which he seeks to grace her. But the maneuver is no sooner begun than it ends. Cheops has rumpled her in sleep, touched her for a last time presumably, and now wrapping his ornate linens about him hastens away, his Greek in tow. The night is over, his bond with Heduanna still obscure although sturdy, his retinue dispersed long ago like a flock of vivid crows. Behind him, Erodo yawns and stretches.

"Are you stretching? Or retching?" Cheops is not often this witty after midnight, more habituated to a beery plunge into monsyllables, which is to say utterance almost unvoweled: just a splurge of verbs made in the mud of his lower jaw.

Not answering, Erodo (as we up here sometimes prefer to call him without in any way slurring his status as an honorary Egyptian) yawns. Cheops by night will make a dramatic interlude in Book Ten, although Erodo wishes he'd been invited along on those visits to the pyramid at Giza. A *long* walk, he thinks. Why should a king extend himself so, without good reason? Or, and here he quickens to imaginative life: perhaps the muffled figure on the Giza outings was not Cheops at all, but a double, while he of the palace was the real king. Sure he is right, Erodo hastens away to write it up, fixing his mind on the newly-made fact that the waft left behind was that of a sootier, more carnal being, aerophagous and salty, while the Cheops he's known has always been marmoreal, caustic, and altogether heavier in build (an older Ka-wab). Forming sentences even while falling asleep, Erodo vows to write them down next morning, knowing the world is his to adorn.

With cleared mind and stifled voice he wakes after too short a slumber and decides to head back to the palace, aware that, when he is close to Cheops, the pharaoh ignores him, but welcomes him in when he's walked all the way just for a chat. It makes a curious kind of sense. Walking to and fro thus he has become thinner, and now he wonders why he resisted Cheops's invitation to live in the palace at Memphis. What had he said?

"A feel for the country, your highness."

"As distinct from a feel for the palace?"

"Apparently, sir."

"It does not appear to me."

I want to be my own man, sir, he'd said, not a lackey-in-waiting.

"Then you'll be all right, won't you," the king said, "so long as we don't cut your balls off in the night. Walk and be healthy, sir. I hope that, having come here, you won't ignore us."

"No," Erodo says, capturing a hint from well-versed Osiris, "my vocation is looking."

"Then look. You may witness wonders yet."

Now, later, *H-d-t* is convinced he was right and that witness wonders he will.

82 ▲
PRINCESS HEDUANNA

In one kind of sleep you rest like stone. Whatever comes near you has no purchase, unless in the form of an etching. The other night, slumbering after a remarkably poignant day, I felt this current pass through me, right from the sun, as if I had been instructed years ago to wait for it. I did not know I was that desirable, but someone made me tingle; and in my dream I cried out, Don't you think I am your friend, can't I prove I am your friend? I was merely addressing myself however, but how can I say there was an affectionate presence without saying who? If this is what it's like for the rest of my life, I will give it up: sly, potent shade cutting into me like a razor, to no purpose. I will go to Abydos again and remain there until it becomes a mere village and the Osirian sanctuary—where the head of Osiris was kept—has turned to dust. I will be one of the last pilgrims to visit there, one of the last to see the drawings of ritual navigation as mummies from all over the kingdom arrive in the sacred necropolis. It will be a career of sorts until I become a mere water-carrier for lack of vocation. Tell me, Osiris, did I have to go through all that—the murder of Chirh, the beguiling and infatuation—just to be readied for searing intuition? It has been no life at all with an otherworldly father and a brother-spouse killed. If there is some supervening force that will eventually make a poet of me, I relish its advent and bare my palms for it to show me how. I am yours, I tell it. To consume, to devour. Do anything to me that is not vicious. Or am I to become a priestess of the storms and elements, having been *touched*, as they say of madmen?

Heduanna pulses with new life, joining herself with the Nile which, for all its floodings, its catastrophes and plagues of locusts, remains useful for navigation—not only for the ferrying of mummies, but beans, lentils, chickpeas, fruit, wine, and the rest. Something has made her flow uphill.

FOUR

Next World

83 ▲
CHEOPS

Gold leaf on the septum tickles, but not as much as on the rim of the nostril, the *caruncle* of the eye—in the funerary workshops you pick up all kinds of shadowy words. First, you begin to feel muddy, as if some crud-caked hippopotamus had moved through your heavenly essence, blurring and impeding. When the leaf takes hold, the sensation is not unpleasant: astringent, making your skin taut, your breath less measured. Then you start to feel starched, tightened up, a monster of wrinkles, and that feeling does not go away. No aroma of gold that I can discern, but, as one might expect, a flash patina from the light of day, making you an altogether shinier specimen—more a salamander than a Re. It all comes down to waiting things out. With so much to be done, you'd think they would wait, but they set about you at once, harboring, I suspect, some desire to see the pharaoh sheathed in the sun's color—one chance only, if the entire operation works and all the additions do their job. This is the first time any of them have watched the king go live to his reward, and, though the traditionalists (all of them) scowl at the brash innovation, they put up with it, no doubt thinking it will never happen again, not even with such a rebellious dolt as Dedef-ra, when *his* time comes. If there were room in my ritual for him, I would gladly take him along to whatever fate the gods can spare. A certain mutinous pique has shown in him since he was a youth, and ever will, the net effect of his demeanor being that of someone chomping on a big fruit around which his entire face is clenched, which gives him that affronted, envious look. But no, no company in this; I invented it, blueprinted it, designed much of it, making explanatory votive offerings to my dead—Sneferu, Hetep-heres, Ka-wab, Chirh, and others—in case I had never made my originality clear to them before.

I, only I. This is what I said to them, ignoring all the consort queens and pseudo-princes. You can have too much of a good thing in the palace, and the last fling should be your handiwork, no one else's. Where did the ideas come from? Probably from Osiris, who has experienced everything. You, who have had to endure the constant motion around you of courtiers, now have to branch out on your own, leaving behind a pattern for your successors perhaps, but taking whatever risk you think wise. I have discovered the limitless prowess of mind: how much you can *be*, without ever being in the least deflected from your primary goal.

I am a boy slinging stones at a date palm, leaning as far back as possible to gain the full slingshot effect. I am pulling a girl's hair, both of us seen in "pure" profile. Or I am caressing a duckling while the wind tousles my hair. Between the sturdy legs of Sneferu I am assuming the position of prayer while the breeze ruffles the duckling's down. Depicted by an unconventional artist, my wife's arm passes behind my back and poses a hand lightly on my shoulder. Women in chronic mourning lean toward one another. Just think how many ills we die from, not long after growing up. A foot-rest resembles a cage always empty. Beds rest on high lion's legs. The mattress, even of the carrying-chair, is woven from fine flax cord. The administrator of the king's wardrobe has a deformed body, an ironic contrast: a sport of nature among the ceaseless perfections. Why are we always depicted as children holding quails? Do we need, eat, so many figs? Isis (I call her *is-is*!) nurses Horus on amulets of motherhood: wooden or of bone, or glazed faience, or mass-produced in bronze. Dolls are flat with token arms and legs, the head hardly a head, the hair made of clay beads or rumpled flax. Boy stands on another's shoulders. There is tug of war without a rope, feet together at the center on the line. Raucous boys holding a feather each play a running-guessing game known as "pressing grapes," while among them girls play a Hathor dance-game in which they make passes with mirrors and wooden clappers. Not such a bad world to leave when you come right down to it, but well left all the same. I have wasted my best time.

Am I to have decorations then? Will I get what is already prepared: an idyllic plowman whose wife sows in the next world? I made no provision for any such thing, knowing full well my needs would be quite different. A poignant portrait of a blind surveyor, his hand on the head of the boy who leads him through the corn, would be poetic, but only for whoever was there to see it. For purposes of the water tax, he measures fields so as to gauge later the height of the crop. He measures with a long coiled cord. In the next world, where labor is unlaborious, corn grows unassisted to three times its usual size. All you need is a sickle and a big basket. These things could tempt me, but they will not, although scenes from country life make the heart pause, especially when you see sheaves being gathered and bound together by placing the ears at alternate ends, thus locking them together. We are not slow. We thresh corn by driving wild asses in a circle enclosed by a wall. A model of a state granary to accompany me? Someone asked the question ages ago, hoping to fit me out with farm idylls galore—with roof-holes, scoops, chaff scooped into the wind by girls wearing head-scarves to keep it out of their hair and eyes. No, I am not going there, I never did, but the sweet mummery of it all lingers on. A loincloth parts and I see a perfect snipped penis tamed.

Suddenly, out of the sky that in this land yields no rain, there appears like a sandstorm a man named Kush, with whom I have had no dealings before. He never stops laughing, an odd thing in a funerary inspector who specializes in teeth in the perfunctory fashion of our culture, more accustomed to knocking them out than to tending them, and only rarely to scraping and bleeding them. With almost courtesy, of course, he has me yawn and expose my teeth, but with what you would expect of him: the fatalistic nod of the final inspector. It is not that he smiles at me; millions have and do. He laughs out loud at some private joke that never ceases to please him, not that he ever tells it. He must have discovered the basic absurdity of life, the way it lives up to all our expectations of it, always getting worse while for the gullible getting better. Perhaps this Kush, an auburn-haired man from an almost extinct tribe that wears linen kilts and carries stout canes, must have long ago given away all his worldly goods, just to be rid of clutter and stuff, and then tried to rid himself of his own body while retaining awareness of it: the blank relishing the cadaver of yesteryear. Tumultuously he inhales the rank stench of his own breath only to puff it into the mouths of the dead and disemboweled. Some such fearsome collision of flesh and idea must have assailed him, some impossible paradox of being alive.

He cackles, gibbers, roars, giggles, shouts an old desert obscenity about the lips of a whore's pleat, then yields to gently purring laughter. Into none of this risible display are you invited to enter, as if your experience of life has been wholly different from his, and unworthy. He is the kind of man you see slinking along the meaner streets in Memphis, looking for a handout or a glass of salted water. He talks to himself the whole time, letting out shrieks and gurgles, all of which render his aim erratic even when dabbling with the teeth, the eyes, the loins and toes of the dead. So here am I, alive, his first sentient specimen, smothered in gold leaf at great expense. Here I am, momentarily dreaming about the copper mixed with gold and thus hardened, after repeated smelting and beating: gold from the mountain ranges of Wawuat and Wadi Hammamat, and river gold from Upper Nubia. There are indeed papyrus plans of gold mines done in color, revealing the names of all the galleries in certain regions.

You would think what would appeal to him in all this is the aspect of contagion: gold poisoning the body it encloses, which it would if the body lived on. No, it must be the entire human spectacle that exultantly agonizes him, all the running about and planning, the getting and spending and taxing and promoting/demoting, the killing and saving, birthing and dying, all to no purpose save—what? The helpless promotion of the whole antic that cannot be an end in itself. We are born merely to push a process, even we pharaohs who can help ourselves to the lives of everyone without, however, cheating them of death. Your king dies aflame with unused opportunities. An Osiris might clarify such gibberish for us, but he is too busy. Besides, he has known death already and is therefore not allowed to come up from the underworld.

This Kush numbs me with his controlled hysteria, laughing at my golden getup, my career, my desires, my pyramid, my home-made religion. Or is it that he has never cackled in the face of a living king? He chuckles to think what I am going to, of the tomb that will one day (he thinks) contain me, as some pit will contain him. He laughs at the abundant presence in life of mauling death, and the serene standing of Osiris vis-à-vis the last gasp. It slays him to minister to the dead's teeth, perhaps making them neater than in life. He is—as has been said of him locally—pathologically cheerful, overcompensating with good hearty cheer because death demands enormous resistance, though it's useless at that. He knows all this, and his laughter is the last laugh deriding itself as the most vacant human gesture of all, unless we read it as some numinous symbol. Death, he shouts, well I'll be fucked, what has it ever done to you that it left you the worse for wear?

Now I am wondering if this cantankerous Kush is not the palace Fool unappointed by me. He's certainly not one of those wizards we sometimes invite in to startle our darkness. Why this aroma of ginger off him? Why the weird hint of simoon that blows off him whenever he approaches? What is this clammy, yet stinging touch of his, his preposterous gift of earwax cached in his palm? Does he etch his name on the unresisting teeth of the dead? Does he bite their lips in a paroxysmic farewell of sympathy, ever awaiting a shriek from one not quite dead in spite of the eviscerated body and the carpentered lungs? Who *is* he? Whence and why? I ask *H-r-d*, my constant companion *in extremis*, but he shrugs, and quietly assigns Mister Kush to the lowest orders of Memphis society, maybe a rank above Djedi the Blue Heron Catcher, whom I once encountered (the one citizen I know).

I have come to the conclusion that Kush does not exist. He is Laughter, not of anyone in particular, but amalgamated laughter, awaiting us all as we slump into the teeth of the furies, at the last cooking up some holy fantasy to get through into the next mess. He is the mirage of the extravagant sadness we have nowhere to put: no owner, no tenant, no broker, no home.

84 ▲
PRINCESS HEDUANNA

Here I am, summoned at his request, adorned in gold leaf, at his command, merely to put questions to him about plans. Who have you been then, are you satisfied with that? What have you done? Whom have you loved, apart from consort queens? Where did you go? With whom? To fight or to love? Whom have you known, killed, adored? Whom have you hated? Have you known enough people, or are you mortified (careful choice of word, Father) not to have known millions? Were those you did know enough? Is there anything you and someone else might have done together? Have you known and relished being you? If there is good left in you, where did it come from? If evil, whence that as well? Did you ever ask for what you never got? Or get what you never asked for? Have you a sufficiency of sisters and brothers and children, by-blows, changelings? Will it matter? Are you going to end all of this now? Is this a responsible ending for you, well-deserved? Is there a future for you? Are you not already divine, to begin with?

He says nothing, mumbling in a broken breath the words taught him by a visiting wizard, for when he went out on Majesty rounds: *approaching cadavers,* as foul a bit of gibberish as he could ever want, and worthy of inspection.

"Whose have we been, father?"

He is saying nothing, but a renegade foam, brackish, concentrated, breaks loose from his lower lip as if the right opening word has tried to emerge and been rebuffed.

"*Who* have we been then? Ignored, squandered, exploited, defrauded, fobbed off, rejected, disguised, turned loose, shipped away, parked, lost, Left To Our Own Devices? Don't you recognize any of the words, old gold leaf?"

"We have been Osiris's," he whispers.

And she knows that sums it up. To him, then, there was never anything higher, and certainly not now as he begins footling on the brink of the divine precipice; but she smells something inadequate in his absolute. She agrees that, beginning and end, we belong to

Osiris or whomever, but not in between. Surely life has to be something more than abject passivity in the paws of a god.

"You got it, daughter," he croaks.

"Got what?"

"Why, the in-between, girl. It isn't ours. We think it is, but it's only loaned, like Libyan blood."

"Who have we been then? Just a royal family belonging to somebody else, some other order of being?"

85 ▲
PRINCE KA-WAB

lots of old, lots of bold, but so far here no old bold souls they have not come they go otherwhere no good reason so cold so dismembering you start wretched and get wretcheder a waft of air sunders your spine floats your kneecap free can't eat the raw meat in the niches the milk off the bread green I myself raw off green broken for keeps until Osiris come help me out of this constant shiver shudder it's no love tryst this tell my father so

86 ▲
DJEDI THE BLUE HERON CATCHER

Cut the balls off a baby bluebird if I can figure out what's going on; he's in there somewhere all gussied up in gold leaf, the solar boats are unmanned and have nothing to do with what's going on, whatever that is. The shafts and passageways are full of water, his pyramid is going to float away down the Nile. That's it, I've figured the damned thing out, the whole of weepy Memphis is going to float away after him, whose heart has always been so full of love for us.

He always wanted to be good to us without being king. So he's assembled a crowd of watermen and stonemasons, those with big shoulders; puts them to work, breaking a thousand backs for one last bow, and here we are, liddies and gennermen, being screwed all over again up his royal ass. It takes days to get these guys off their chairs and into action, sod their rotten mothers, and their fucking fathers and their children. Please, Osiris, get him to get a move on, all Memphis is at attention for a command performance I bet is going to be one big fraud. He'll just come back to the job as per usual, refreshed by all that golden leaf.

87 ▲
CHEOPS

She reminds me of someone who used to find her way unobstructed, but now discovers obstructing her a gate installed overnight. Her hand reaches for the top of it, cagily feeling at something where there used to be nothing, and settles there, anxious and rebuffed. Is she always like that when she's rejected? She has been a difficult girl to rear, the most dominant among her range of facial expressions being the one that says "I almost . . .", when she means she almost committed a gaffe, which could be serious in a court as finicky as Memphis. I should have found such an acute sense of misgiving charming, but I did not. Even if it amounted to her saying "there but for the grace of the gods I almost . . ." (cleared my throat and spat). I have noticed a similar expression on people's faces when whispering about me which seems to say: if he were less of a dictator and more humane, he . . . You can't afford to overhear, but you can't afford not to either. Who'd be a king? Only someone who in a moment or two won't be a king anymore, I promise you, I promise them, his aims having shifted from secular to godly. It doesn't matter now. If only my shift or robe did not itch me so much, the worst part a patch right over the collarbone, where the robe catches, activating the skin. It is one thing or another, the hair shirt or the abraded skin, working against one another, bound sooner or later to drive you into the ultimate frenzy of the itch. How I wish I could slide a finger in between shin and body sheath, just to let it squirm around a little and save me from trembling.

How I miss the musical cocoon once foisted upon me by Osiris, in which I could swoon away almost to the point of delicate abeyance. The musicians I commanded to be here have run out of steam already. Imagine them asleep in the corridors and shafts, the echo having long since died out. Osiris has the gift of permanence, in every way; once he regales you with music, it is yours, you are its. I sense that is my ideal relationship: I am just as much a thing's as it is mine. As it is, and I should know, people are fizzling out all over Egypt; you do not have to make the full gamut of Majesty rounds to become aware of that. Watch the street, as I used to from one of those open-air windows in the palace—and you see people walking around who will be dead tomorrow. The walking dead, I call them, whose hand should be held, whose gait should be reinforced; but they perish anyway, as if part of a divine plan; yet they die in comfort, knowing what they are going to. I can't imagine why they don't all die at once, out of sheer gladness. If I were a commoner, I would, blissful about my destination. In a sense, I am nobody already, I have virtually abdicated. The suspect Dedef-ra may as well take over, with his measly plans and hypocritical stance. It is too late to care, even if only about the grand ovation I've planned for my stepping-down—for when I've grown too old to dream. Too late for that kind of misgiving, that kind of lapse. As for the holy enjambements of *The Book of the Dead*, with our legs all twined together while the meaning hangs fire, I do not any more have the patience to mimic it. None of this relay race, passing on the baton to the runner standing next in line. I am against that kind of cooperation, always have been, but securer in harnessing thousands for a worthwhile work of masonry.

It occurs to me as I stand here swathed in finery and unnecessary polish, that I have been deprived of music because the gods need it more than I. Such a thing has only just come to me, but it makes perfect sense: I was vouchsafed a glimpse, a snatch, of what the gods enjoy, and without which they could not perform half as well as they do. Odd, to have gods born with a weakness such as that. You would think they sprang flawless from wherever gods spring from, having no needs except to have us learn that fact. Instead, it is as if they enter this world bleeding from the hip or the throat, already in need of emergency care. First they need surgery, then they need music. What next? All this while we, the walking wounded, in hovels or on thrones, yearn for all kinds of things we will never have. *There but for the grace of the gods* saves you from doing something atrocious, the cocoon of music is a bubble only too easily pricked, and we all keep on dying. The Majestic rounds visitor is dying even as he makes his tour, murmuring that wizard's phrase, *approaching cadavers,* suspected of being an ancient Hittite curse handed down in a fit of political jealousy, and spawned in some mountain cave. To utter this over one dead is to say it to yourself of course, which is why I gave up on visiting corpses.

Outside the horde awaits. I am standing on the brink like a diver. Water is pouring out from every aperture in the pyramid, but they do not understand my reasoning about this. It will all work well when the time comes. No formal goodbyes. No official handing over of authority. Dedef-ra will already have signed his first execution order (sword or bludgeon for most, though the copper garotte works well for those who need it). The important point remains: you cannot control everything for ever. You will be replaced by those you despise unless you slaughter them first, and even then . . . There is always someone else, waiting to drop the hammer on your throne.

What are they saying then? Nobody apart from the endlessly quizzical Heduanna is saying much at all, and Merytyetes has that stricken, partly envious look again. I have not seen it in years. What would they be saying if they said anything then? They would be saying how much they were going to miss my inspired kingship. They would be remembering the time I said of Merytyetes that anyone who shows that much leg cannot expect divine guidance of any sort. They would be missing me. What they would never say, because they cannot imagine the situation from *my* point of view, is how much am I going to miss myself, whatever the orthodox religion says. You cannot go into the underworld without at least a pang for a sunbeam. I will miss myself: that is the thought that shocks me, whatever else I believe, and I see no way around it unless Osiris has special plans, is going to make an exception for his favorite pyramid-builder. It could happen. Dafter things have happened beyond the frontier. I do not want to go. I do not want to stay. I do not want, not really. I wish to become music, after having been architecture, and who would not, if he had heard the suave melodies that filled my ears not so long ago? Go to hell, I would say to all comers, I am in heaven already.

Miss? Miss what?
That itch.
These pesky eyes.
Hoopoes circling.
Severed heads in the gallery.
The Greek, all things considered.
Heduanna, the loyal.
Merytyetes the multiple woman.
The Book of the Dead of course.
Interpreters.
Gondoliers.
My mother's whereabouts.
Pyramid.
Pyramid, of course.
Those blue heron catchers, nuisances.
Hewers of stone.
Sailing the Nile en route to Giza.
Papyrus.
A certain ivory statue.
Being called by my name.
Granaries.
Stars?
Rustling bead-curtain to certain rooms.

88 ▲
OSIRIS

Mêlée of superlatives, the show ensues among shabby brickwork, the splendid inviteds paddling around in run-off water, cool for their feet. Cheops is at the far end of the passageway, a ghost, aloof, awaiting, someone present at his own absence while they all, milling around in the half-sunlight, occupy themselves with thoughts not altogether of him. Merytyetes, the one practitioner of the scooped-out lemon to stave off pregnancy, what with family members both formally and informally squirting their best into her when the occasion arrived, thinks of the passageway: no one shall pass, unless allowed. Someone flooded the pyramid with thousands of gallons from the Nile, but who knows for what? This is more like an investiture than a funeral and the live guest of honor has not announced his program. Perhaps he will make it up, thinks Hemiunu's daughter, Kha-merer-nebty, who will one day marry Chefren, the sage, the replenisher. Impromptu. It is hardly a send-off, but it cannot be much else, can it? The main thing, Hetep-heres II is thinking, is to marry whom you have to, but make sure your daughter by the dead Ka-wab marries into the direct line. How they maneuver while supervising the arrival of preserves in plain jars, ox-heads, haunches of beef, neatly-sliced livers, eyeballs, ox-tails for diligently watched soups, breads the size of infants, fresh-brewed beers and fruity wines. It all goes into whatever niches have been provided. It is what he is going to need on the journey and while he is there, which is going to be forever (if you believe the rumors).

In other words, a command performance for the family, convincing enough for them to be in attendance, but their minds are on the chaos to follow as the so-called succession begins and the great pax of the pyramid-builders begins to crumble. The squabble for power begins, with ever in the background under or on the bed-sheets the unbridled tumult of erections butting their way into futurity, spawning princelings and consort sisters in a spray of royal potency. What a mess Cheops is going to leave behind him, no doubt with relief, but what is all this water for; what is the mob of stonemasons outside going to do, other than merely watch? Anachronism, thinks *H-r-d*, the most privileged among the invited, is the opium of the time-traveler. Let him make the most of it, he Cheops, the master of his own ceremonies. *H-r-d* has almost mastered the names of the women, the men were easier; but he feels—apart from enjoying his made-over name—ill at ease among these fertile aspirants to power. No one is coveting his body for diplomatic privilege, though flirty Heduanna seems to be available.

"You can detect *his* hand in all this," says Merytyetes, blasé as ever. "He was always the one for unannounced surprises." "He isn't gone yet," counters Heduanna, "have some respect for the old boy. He's doing his best to be innovative. Organization was never his strong point, but abstruse fabrication always was, and this, my ladies, is abstruse fabrication. He is going to show us how he does it, still standing at the far end of the hallway like a frozen butterfly making up its mind. This is *him,* and may the gods love him for it." She cannot escape the feeling that they have turned up merely to be surprised, not to say good-bye, although a good-bye it is bound to be, whatever else has been cooked up. As for the least maneuvering of his progeny, along with Mycerinus the clever grandson, she has no expectations. She is hardly one of the family anyway and therefore bound to be snubbed once he has gone. He does intend to go, doesn't he? Still, she wonders about her father. Did he really not know, all this time, where his mother's body had been removed to from its tomb? Had he really swallowed all that Hemiunu, the vizier, told him just to keep him calm? Later she may find out, but no one will say, and by then the whole matter will have been forgotten.

Chatter surrounds her. He was always a chewer, every last morsel ground to bits with his pristine teeth. And a fidget; never a chatterbox or a clown, but distant, with a mind forever lost in the clouds of beyond. Not an ideal king at all. Did you ever know a man who, even in the throes of love, would forget to come, and then stroll back later to finish off, just in case an heir was there in the offing? Never hot to trot, you could be sure of that, ladies, but with huge balls, full of what ails you. Tickle those and he would stay put, no more dashing off to check on the position of a star. Mycerinus, the boy wonder, shrinks from such venereal talk, murmuring something about women invented work, men invented love, which he has invented himself, not garnering it from anywhere.

Osiris is watching it all, opinionless as a crag. When the talk is of how Cheops often appeared naked at social gatherings and fully clad in bed, there is the usual amount of oohing and aahing, but not from the attendant god, one of whose mysteries is being enacted today, though never before with Cheops's touch of unbridled originality. Osiris is willing to see and savor, Cheops can hardly see what is going on. The talk is of a solar boat hidden away until the last moment, and a cape of gold leaf—the actual flesh of the sun—he's wrapped his body in.

And the dead, as befits an Egyptian cocktail party, have their importunate say as well: his mother Hetep-heres I saying, "He never came and got me, he left me in the lurch. Now I'm not there, and he felt so comfy about it all." Poor murdered Ka-wab, to whom grammar is rotting glue, can only muster a butchered phrase or two: "Mud mouth and dust come get me when it rains Poppa." Even Chirh, Heduanna's possible intended, manages a creak with his mouth: "Got me without even trying, they did. Watch out." The dead have little say in all this, though one would think they knew more about it than anyone living. Their access to speech has been botched, and the most they can come up with is a quiver in the ribcage, a few rotten syllables like a gnawing on nettle.

The hubbub is frightening. The music comes and goes, and there's milling around within the pyramid, with few of them daring to march down the passageway to confront the frozen-looking Cheops. He is thinking of the little ivory statue he sent to Abydos and wondering where it will end up, no doubt in Greece or Libya, he no longer cares, knowing the final events of his reign will outweigh anything else. For biography they will point to the sky, in what he supposes will be the heyday of Mycerinus, who already separates the ascetics from the bullies, the mystics from the climbers.

89 ▲
HEDUANNA
MERYTYETES

"So what did he smell of?"

"Easy. Thyme and hyssop."

"Did he apply it to himself?"

"No it just came out of him, it was his natural smell."

"Then that must be the natural smell of the spaces between the stars."

"No, of the man who doesn't come enough."

"Oh, you mean a spermy smell, Merytyetes."

"None of your nevermind. Take it from me, I know the stink of men. And women."

"Let me get this straight. He didn't have a male smell, but thyme and hyssop."

"Whatever you say, inquisitive cow. Ask of those who have been there, and take their word for it."

"Cow yourself, 'Mother.' Some men do not smell at all. But some men, even their blood has a distinctive odor."

"It takes one to know one."

"Ah, so it does," groans Heduanna, "I never had the time to find out much, but I was all ready to go, to find out, and then that was the end of it."

If only, as with the dead, she thinks, one could read the life in the hand, the remaining days congealed like honey in a baby's fist.

90 ▲
H-R-D, TENTH BOOK

Needless to say, I take notes all the time, I wonder which audience I am aiming for when I write up my Egyption observations later. His face, sheathed in coppery gold, resembles an egg, from within which, now and then, his tongue like a chick's beak will protrude to say something concise. In his high, almost toppling headdress, he looks almost inhuman, which in a sense he has been all along. He gives no sign that he knows or sees me, or indeed that he is performing for me, which he might just be doing: *cursor mundi,* he must be thinking, or hypocrite of the future. Whatever he plans, he is well equipped, with resplendently garbed attendants scurrying around him to get him ready. The floor is aswill—no doubt part of the exercise—though I cannot see what for. I catch myself in the act of writing, within the ampler confines of my papyrus pad, some narrower paragraphs, more pungent and more concise—the true journalist's contribution:

> The smell coming off him has rotten
> eggs in it, mingled with silky asafetida,
> only part manly an aroma, while his hands
> make constant jerky motions as if freed
> from month-long bonds, and his feeble
> eyes look dimmer and more silvery than ever.
> In truth, Cheops agonistes.

This is not the Cheops of old, when I first arrived, with the clean-cut shoulders, the erect head on the slender neck, the trim military face, the bearing strict and schooled. Only the ears, huge and promising a long, resilient life, have not changed, although he seems about to change that. Within the nest of gold leaf, his features have fattened up into an almost Mongolian pudginess; he looks a little squashed, too much face accommodated into the old outline, and convexity everywhere. In truth he used to look very much like Cheops the army's commander, with that hint of a mustache and a narrowly folded robe slung over one shoulder, the whole appearance of him suggesting, Don't take me on, I fight back. Well, he doesn't look like that any more. He's thickened, swollen, bulged, perhaps become even more imposing, not so much the young commander going to war, as a comfortable conservative going to hell. He used to answer, but not with the long delay you expect from him now, his mind on some disappearing act only he could have dreamed up. I am here by his grace, I know that, and am grateful, but in spite of the gold leaf and his other accoutrements methodically added, he is not the spectacle he once was. It's a pity really, in that. If you mean to exit with a bang, you should look in tune with it beforehand.

Sorry: yours truly has not weathered the storm all that well either, what with constantly scratching at his scalp to remove small scabs (we Greeks keep our abundant hair curly wherever we end up, whereas your Egyptian clips it short for the heat), removing the offending scab (it could be a mite, I suppose), rolling it between finger and thumb, and spinning it far away to start a new colony in the sand. I have begun to lisp, a result no doubt of some slackening in the jaw and the facial muscles, or the grinding-away of the front teeth's tips. Because I have developed an itch in the ear, I tend to send my little finger, either side, to burrow in after the cause, as it were plunging the cavity until the air pressure changes and I can hear properly again—this the result of constant heat and humidity. My left arm is not quite what it once was, at least until I stretch it out and produce an elbow click that seems to right the muscles and straighten the whole limb. All this must come from living in a cave when a palace was offered, but *H-r-d* has to keep his independence even in the act of allowing his name to mutate in accordance with local custom: Herodotus—Erodo—*H-r-d*. Quite a sea change, you might say, indicative of the respect I feel for Egyptian ways. It's quite a feat, is it not, to thus permit a free hand to concerned Egyptians, who keep modifying the name to keep it right and congruous? I do not mind. I remain the same old wag, mind on the future and all those lectures on the doings of these people. I only wish he would have more to say as he approaches the self-imposed climax of his reign: no reminiscences, no album thoughts, no aphorisms intended to encapsulate a long career, even if it amounted to only one huge block after another, perhaps best remembered as a series of aristocratic grunts. *He* didn't do any of the lifting after all, and it remains to be seen what of his latest feat he will himself take on. I feel somewhat disappointed by this theatrical show, maybe because he remains alive, and they don't have his corpse to empty out and otherwise fiddle with. Such is his wish, however, and I can at least console myself with his departure's being unique. I mean, who else has ever witnessed such a thing? If this is not "hot" news, what is? It still astonishes me how, after all I wrote about him, he has forgiven me and taken me more or less into his confidence, as if I were one of his advisers. "Come, Erodo." He does not say that any more, but has resorted to hand signals and cants of his head. Indeed, he has become so still that I half-suspect him of having some invisible sculptor forever in attendance, sculpting him anew for generations to come. Yet is that any different from his own *H-r-d,* after many a long thought getting to grip with his Tenth Book, ever perfecting a series of utterances for the delectation of readers to come? We are alike in this, each smoothing the image, settling the reputation, pushing the dominant images into view like figures against a receding ground, so that future appraisers will sift the gold from the dross and, for instance, just exclaim with delight that the old Greek was actually there and beheld all this at arm's length! I get quite excited just thinking about the prospect. They won't be saying He's the father of history, but: He's the king of anecdote. Look how he changed his tune about Cheops. Had he never gone there in the first place, and then yet again, little of his conversion would have come to light. Cheops is no one to slander, but to admire from a huge distance, in both time and space. Herodotus is the father of all that, not what's-his-face? Lucian. I am delighted to anticipate this prospect: Erodo the onlooker, Erodo the scribe, *H-r-d* the included outsider crowning his own king for posterity. Say what you like, I *have* been here.

Behold my sketch, copied from stele, of the man as he used to be. Surely he was away on military expeditions most of the time, his nimble athletic body directing all manner of onslaughts on the Nubians and Libyans. You can just see the potential for it in his clean-cut limbs, the no-nonsense straight glance here marred by the huge eye-patch created by the stele-wrecker. I have to confess I copied this as best I could from an unidentified carved mural perhaps abandoned as too martial, but left out there for all the world to see. It's

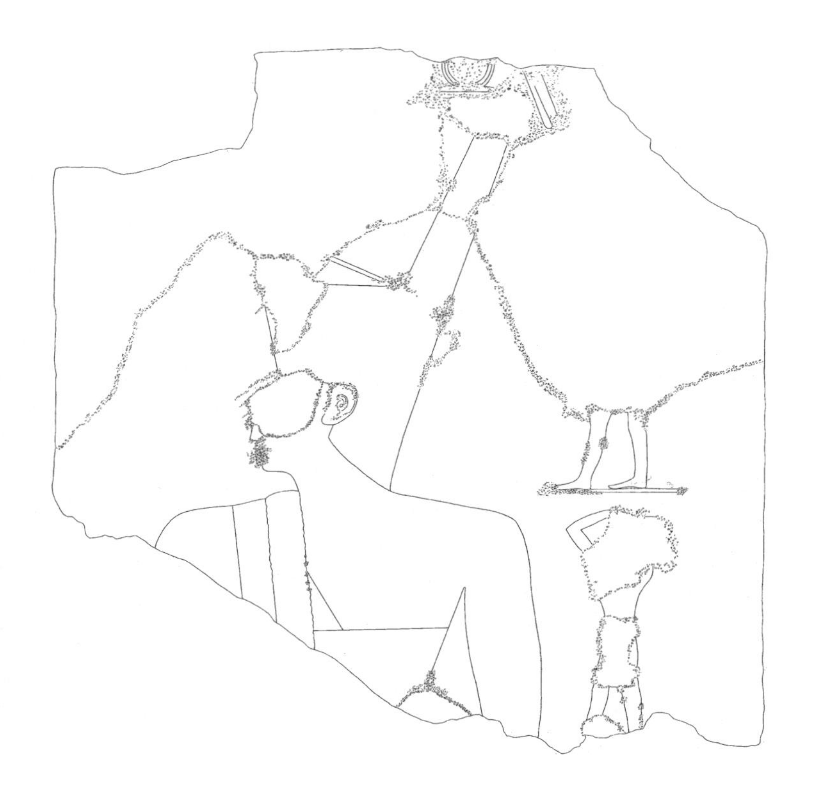

the sort of thing you find only after the subject is dead and gone, although I personally see nothing wrong in recording his early demeanor for the likes of me, scuttling around the cliffs and plateaus in search of memorabilia. How easy to forget that, in a time-twist, you have privileges that would otherwise be denied you; so I have treasured this line-drawing (to remind me of the original) by folding it tight into a small square held against my body with a tight thong whose impress has scarred my midriff for life. I did it just to keep the outline for later. Now that I have it safe; with Cheops beginning to perform last acts, I feel vindicated. Funny: no one else seems to care, I have seen nobody carrying such a thing around, in awe or envy. When in a distant life (you never know what's next), I am asked for my papers, I will produce this drawing and proudly declare "Cheops the Great." That should gain me admission to just about anywhere at all.

91 ▲
ERODO

Over sherbert and limes, Heduanna confides to me that just before taking off Cheops drank from a golden chalice, possibly a suicide potion, although she had no idea of what. It was not like him to double-deal in that way, though perhaps he wanted to make sure and not leave everything to Osiris, that connoisseur of boiling and dismemberment. She and I will soon be off.

"Would he really?" She has doubts. He blew on hot drinks.

"Wouldn't *you*?" she asks, frowning.

There were Greeks who had, I knew that, but Cheops was different, wasn't he? Was that why he vanished so fast, caught up in a cloud of his own making? Perhaps he drank for us as well, wiping us out in a single gulp—we too were dead, ready for the high priests and their probes, their knives. This was Egypt after all.

Then I came to my senses. To be speaking Greek after his death was ridiculous, and ludicrously unliterary. We, Heduanna and I, were the soft registers of her society, were we not—putting it together in the teeth of seething opposition? I had managed to get to know her well enough, whereas with just about everyone else I had come to know them without befriending them. I, the original coiner of the yarn that claimed he'd sold her into prostitution, had surely made amends by now; we were not going to tattle about her father's suicide *during* his suicide. The main thing was to leave Memphis as soon as possible, but what held us back was something gleaned from his own delay as he fidgeted and changed stance. Hang on, he seemed to be saying, I haven't quite done yet, but then he would say no further good-byes, do absolutely nothing; he was playing for time, perhaps tuning in to the erratic Osiris, renowned for always being late himself.

I had begun to wonder about maltreated Osiris, less a god than he was an impresario—like a cuckoo devoted to invading other men's nests. Perhaps he had talked Cheops into this felo de se stuff, depriving him of his pyramid as some parents deprive a child of a model boat. You know the type. Now and then Cheops had let it slip that Osiris rather fancied the pyramid; he had heard so, Zeus knew from whom, and it made palatable sense, as did the famous notion that the gods needed as much in their afterlife as Egyptians did (things of comfort, say), whereas the Greek gods just went on narrating and interfering. I gave up on such airy speculation, just about convinced that Cheops had done away with himself to look *thorough* and so lay claim to a double reward when he passed over. In this, I was wrong; it had been a harmless refreshment, a sweet soother to water the crop of himself for his journey.

92 ▲

Not to keep him waiting, after so much endeavor, we station him in the seat, the spare pilot, who has asked if he might fly the Boeing during the climb-out while the captain visits the bathroom (though why he couldn't wait we do not know; he could surely have gone before takeoff). In a burst of enthusiasm, Cheops begins to transmit a holy formula, in many cases uttered as a matter of course as a semi-pious nonce-word, but gets into a riff with it, saying it fourteen times, which alarms all who are listening. The plane dives. The captain returns, expresses dismay, ordering Cheops to pull back with him, but Cheops forces the aircraft into a dive, deeper and steeper and faster until the planeload of helpless, cooperative souls jets into the ocean far from land, and at lethal speed. The window closes on EgyptAir 990. Quits. Quietus. Quick.